THE VARIATIONS

Patrick Langley's first novel, *Arkady*, was longlisted for the RSL Ondaatje Prize and the Deborah Rogers Writers Prize. *The Variations* is his second novel.

Praise for *Arkady*

'A gorgeous novel... A livid and visionary brotherly love story set among our ruins. I loved it.'
—— Max Porter, author of *Lanny*

'Thick with smoky atmosphere and beautifully controlled – this is a vivid and very fine debut.'
—— Kevin Barry, author of *Nightboat to Tangier*

'I haven't been able to stop thinking about [*Arkady*] – such a tender, hopeful tale of brotherhood and belonging, set against vividly imagined urban topographies. I haven't read anything like it in ages.'
—— Sophie Mackintosh, author of the *The Water Cure*

'*Arkady* raises questions about what happens after capitalism finally collapses. ... The prose crackles with energy as the narrative follows the constant movement by placing the reader on a well-oiled tracking dolly, often zooming out to remind us of the bigger picture. Langley is a highly visual writer and *Arkady* an assured allegorical debut about a near-future Britain that is potentially only a recession or two away.'
—— Ben Myers, *New Statesman*

'Langley's invented metropolis was a joy to spend time in. In my visual imagination, it looked as if it had been half-painted by L. S. Lowry and finished off by H. R. Giger. And the ambience was a little bit *Stalker*, and a little bit *Tekkonkinkreet*. But then at the heart of it all was this complex, tender relationship between brothers, and Langley's writing – which somehow managed to be both unembellished and evocative.'
—— Sara Baume, author of *A Line Made by Walking*

'Patrick Langley's *Arkady* is a strange trip – luminescent, jagged and beautiful. A debut novel that twists, compels, descends and soars. I highly recommend it.'
— Jenni Fagan, author of *Luckenbooth*

'*Arkady* is a utopian project: not the top-down kind that never works, but the bottom-up kind that (in this case anyway) works so well it reclaims something of the world. It's hand-built, beautifully, from loose memories, salvaged people, and wild blooms of the psychogeographical sublime. Tense, vivid and humane, this novel gives us not only a dark future but also – over the horizon, past the next riverbend, through that hole in the fence – a chance of saving ourselves from it.'
— Ned Beauman, author of *Venemous Lumpsucker*

'A distinctly post-Brexit novel, *Arkady* is set in an unnamed city that both is and isn't London, thick with the atmosphere of the riots of 2011, and the stricken, devastated aura of the days after the Grenfell fire. ... *Arkady* suggests that we'll build our own arcadias out of the dreams that haunt us, both threatening and protective.'
— Lauren Elkin, *Guardian*

'The Romulus and Remus of a refugee nation embark upon a drift across livid cities, liberatory canals and compromised occupations in a parallel present mere millimetres from our own. Langley gives to the reader the taste of the Molotov fumes and the bloody heft of the personal-political in this propulsive, acid fable, a dérive for the age of urbex. How can the orphaned subject escape the surveillance state? Read on to find out. We, also, are in Arcadia.'
— Mark Blacklock, author of *I'm Jack*

'[A] haunting and brilliant debut.'
— Luke Brown, author of *Theft*

Fitzcarraldo Editions

THE VARIATIONS

PATRICK LANGLEY

CONTENTS

'Variation is among the oldest and most basic devices in music. It originates in an inherent tendency to modify identical recurrence.'
—— Leon Stein

'You are Irish you say lightly, and allocated to you are the tendencies to be wild, wanton, drunk, superstitious, unreliable, backward, toadying and prone to fits, whereas you know that in fact a whole entourage of ghosts resides in you, ghosts with whom the inner rapport is as frequent, as perplexing, as defiant as with any of the living.'
—— Edna O'Brien

I. ELLEN

On a winter morning in 1518, in the Holy Roman city of Strasbourg, Frau Trauffea started to sing. This was not unusual in itself. But she was in public, in the middle of the street, wearing a gown but no hat in the windblown sleet. A young woman with a round face and long, red hair, she was neither a professional singer nor a beggar. Nor was she singing to any accompaniment – not that anyone else could hear, at least. Passers-by paused and gawped as her gestures grew savage and emphatic. Some, both concerned and confused, dropped offerings at her feet or crossed themselves in prayer. Those who stopped to watch and listen asked Frau Trauffea what she was doing. Others laughed at her, declared her mad, bewitched, possessed – predictable accusations directed now at her clothing, now at her voice.

Noon came and went. Frau Trauffea did not eat, drink, rest, or relieve herself. Her song grew expressive of a soaring anguish, by turns delicate and desperate, emphasized by her upturned gaze and outstretched arms. No soothing word or gentle touch could persuade her to cease her wailing song, which rose and fell and rose again, two low notes followed by two long, high ones, before the melody repeated. Her exertions were brought to a halt when she collapsed in the street, from apparent exhaustion, several hours after she'd begun.

That might have been the end of it: a minor aberration in the city's psychic life, an outbreak of religious-seeming ecstasy in a century marked by countless similar occasions. After Frau Trauffea had been carried home, where she was fed and watered, rested and recovered, and where, in her first speech since she began, she babbled incoherently about not seeing but *being* her grandfather's ghost, her first action, upon waking again, was to get out of bed, wander into the street, and sing, in a manner that suggested no force could prevent her from returning to that precise position in the busy street leading past the bishop's palace and the bridge to St Magdalena, in the shadow of the intricately pinnacled and ballustraded bell-tower, where she continued to perform as if no time had elapsed since she'd stopped.

She continued in this manner for days, repeating the same compulsion. Rumours flew around the city. Small crowds gathered to watch. Coins, flowers, dried fruit and other offerings would litter the rimed, snow-dusted cobbles upon which she moved. She left them to wither and rot in the sleet that blew in at intervals. The city's beggar children were delighted to collect the coins and baked goods Frau Trauffea didn't seem to know, let alone care, had been dropped at her feet.

Who was her husband? Did she *have* one? Her father, then – where was he? The sight of an unchaperoned woman was, for some, enough.

One day, a young man joined her. He had straw-coloured hair, watery eyes, and wore a long, fashionable navy-blue coat suggestive of modest wealth. Was this her belated husband, returned from the periphery, here to save his wife and in so doing extinguish the spectacle?

He stepped towards her and reached out a hand. Rather than calm her with a rational word, he began humming along, the notes moving in and out of step with hers. The transformation seemed perverse; an aberration which, for several among the crowd, could only be expelled through laughter. Soon he had become like her, singing and moving in the same unpractised and passionate way.

Next morning, this same young man – he had never met Frau Trauffea before the previous day, was no relation or acquaintance – joined her again. And so it followed for a couple of hours, the two of them singing ridiculously, but also, it had to be said, movingly. That afternoon, to the alarmed hilarity of the crowd, a middle-aged woman joined the pair, to form a trio. They sang and moved with no shared music to guide their unpredictable steps and wild gesticulations, despite the bitter winds and biting snows which had begun to whirl around them, obscuring their faces, stinging their eyes, blending their voices into a dissonant drone out of which ugly discords would clang and clash before resolving, unexpectedly, in harmony.

Within a week, some thirty people had joined Frau Trauffea. They were a mixture of men and women, young and old, firm and infirm, but possessed by the same impulse: to sing. None could be persuaded to explain why they were doing it. The sound was atonal, and therefore uncivilized. These deranged figures blocked the street from horses pulling coaches and carts, drawing the attention of the feather-capped guardsmen thumbing the pommels of their swords as they watched and listened to the voices by turns erratic and monotonous, bleating, shouting, nasalizing, howling, sometimes clapping their hands or rattling jewellery. If the singers' exertions caused injury – a sprained ankle, say, or exhausted vocal chords croaking to silence – it did not slow them down. They were oblivious. If they felt the snow on their hair and shoulders, it made no difference to them: it melted into the sweat of their foreheads and trickled down their straining necks.

Rather than instruct the dancers to stop, the city's leaders made a decision which, from our twenty-first-century retrospect, might seem surprising. They believed that *more* singing, not less, was the way to get rid of the problem. Perhaps they believed that this collective possession – if that was the word – would burn itself out eventually, and that the best solution was to throw gasoline on the

16

fire. To exorcize it, in a manner of speaking. Or perhaps, just maybe, they felt that what these people wanted was to be understood – which understanding may have required that they be touched by the mania, however gently, themselves.

Musicians were assembled to accompany the singers in the city's guildhall. They improvised musical structures – simple rhythms from a marching drum, lute-strings plucked in modal drones – that underpinned the singers' collective, unpredictable music, lent it shape and rhythm, a sense of *purpose*. Framed in this way, as music or theatre, passers-by found it easier, if not to understand, then to begin to accept what these afflicted souls were expressing. The rhythms in their bodies, the pulses in their tongues and minds, were continuous with a shared, acoustic environment, which moved according to known laws of time, and of which more rational – as they saw themselves – souls could partake. Professional dancers, meanwhile, were hired to help the afflicted move in ways that conformed to the fashions and techniques of the day. As such, their movements and song became more legible, at points even civilized-seeming, if no less peculiar. Rather than quash the contagion, these civic accommodations only helped it to spread. People flocked to the guildhall. Having done so, many felt compelled to join in, no matter their age or status: indeed, beggar boys, prelates, accountants, minor nobility are reported among the crowds, who sang in that guildhall for days and weeks.

I sometimes wonder what the atmosphere would have been like in that hall, what it might have sounded and felt like, in the heart and sternum. Perhaps it would not have seemed so extreme at all, but rather like a mega-church or rave. Such ecstasies are commonplace now, and I dare say that society needs them – to release some

17

psychic pressure, to remind us of who we are. That said, a few participants in Strasbourg did exert themselves so strenuously that, if one believes the records, they died, two by dehydration and one of heart failure. As days went by, the mania did not abate. The city's civic authorities wondered what to do. Keep the guildhall open, and they risked supporting the spread of this bizarre contagion. Shut it down, and the behaviour would only spill back to the streets, which originated it in the first place, and from where it could infect the whole of the city, the empire – Christendom itself.

The city authorities, embarrassed and desperate, drafted a letter to the Holy See. Before it was dispatched, the song plague, as it is now known, ended as abruptly as it had begun. Ecstasies ended, the lost souls returned to their lives. Some had no recollection of where they had 'been'. Others, mortified, denied having sung at all: it must have been someone else, they claimed, a case of mistaken identity... For a few, life from then on was unremittingly boring, and they longed above else to return to that heightened state. They claimed they could remember only the sensation, overwhelming but not unpleasant, of being surrounded by other people; not just the dozens in the guildhall, but thousands upon thousands of singers, making earth and heaven shake with their collective song, which, despite its volume and its magnitude, had a whisper-quiet quality to it, like the faintest rustle from a million distant wings.

Why do I begin with this anecdote?

I myself am not entirely sure what bearing it has on my account of an incident which occurred late in my life, and which concerns the fate of a person who, before he appeared before me, I would not have recognized in the street. And yet I feel compelled to begin here, casting the arrow, as it were, far back to see where it will land, knowing that it is destined to fall precisely there, on the snowbound streets of Strasbourg, a city I've yet to visit, in a century that I can only access, most of the time, through printed words and coloured pixels.

To begin with the simplest answer, though, and if you'll forgive an older woman her meandering ways... but according to my gift – according to my dead – I am descended from Frau Trauffea.

I am the dean of a hospice and a master of bells. I am neither a geneticist nor a genealogist. The connection I claim, furthermore, is not exceptional. Thousands of people now living could trace their line back to the Frau, should the records allow them do so (though it is highly doubtful that they could, in my case or anyone else's – the documents long since crumbled to dust, rotted in middens, burnt in grates, if they were ever written in the first place). The same is true, as is sometimes noted, of Charlemagne and Genghis Khan. If my beliefs are anything to go by, however, my connection to the Frau – so tenuous as to be effectively non-existent, yet as irrefutable as my very flesh – may explain why, several centuries later, I felt as I did on that night when a lost young man knocked at the hospice's door, in the same singing state as my ancestor had been, claiming to be – to be *from* – an old friend.

The harsh clang of the telephone woke me. I swore at it, but it kept on ringing. So I pushed back the duvet, put my hearing aids in, and staggered down the corridor. As I lifted the receiver and held it against my ear, I avoided eye-contact with the withered ghoul in the mirror.

19

'Ellen,' said Katherine Ash, 'he wants a lobotomy.'

'Who does?'

'You didn't see my message?'

Of course I hadn't. 'I was asleep.'

She explained the situation. A man had turned up at the hospice. He was singing loudly, sometimes shouting. Katherine believed he was gifted.

'Where did he get that idea from?'

As I stood in the chill of my corridor, my nightie hanging loose round my ankles, I heard echoes of Trauffea's song. In the late forties, during a dark period in our history, lobotomies were performed on the gifted in this hospice, almost always against their will. Doctors would push an orbitoclast – not dissimilar to a pick-axe – between the eyelid and the eye-socket in order to sever the connections to the prefrontal cortex, the inventor of which procedure was awarded the Nobel Prize in Medicine. A grim business. It stunned me that a person so young should know the word, let alone desire what it referred to. Then again, if he really *was* gifted...

'You need to listen to him, Ellen.'

I already was, in fact, faintly and on the line. Yet the rules are clear on this point. However distraught the stranger, they must be told: our beds are full, our remit narrow, please be on your way. 'We have been here before, Katherine. This happened last month. The poor man needed a *hostel*. Not a hospice. You understand the difference.' I rubbed my aching temples, and my vision came to rest on the window. Raindrops refracted the amber from the street lamps below. 'What about the message isn't getting through?'

I don't recall precisely what Katherine said at this point, only that she was making excuses again, and in a whiny, nasal tone I find insufferable. Sleep, from whose oblivion I'd been so violently removed, was infinitely preferable to this: to light-waves, odours, textures, textiles – consciousness was vulgar and affronting to me, a swarming mass of needless details. My brain felt swollen, or my skull felt shrunken, I couldn't tell which, and did it matter? Katherine was talking about a person, a stranger, a young man, our doorstep... he was in trouble... his skull was cut open? – Fragments.

'Ellen, listen, please–'

'I *am* listening.'

'You're not.'

'Does he have a name?'

'Presumably, yes – I did ask, but–'

'Wallet, bag? Nothing?'

What irritated me further was the telephone on which we were bickering, the bell of which had woken me only moments ago. This magnificent object once belonged to my father, who was the first in our village to subscribe to a GPO line. He was a doctor. Privately first, of course, before the war and the NHS, when he drove from house to house in his stately Singer Roadster with his Gladstone bag on the passenger seat (as I well knew, having sat on the seat beside it several times). Yet I sometimes wondered if he would have been better suited to some other industry related to communication, one whose networks consisted of copper wires and transmitters, not irreparable veins and nerve cells. I have had countless long conversations on this telephone over the years, and much prefer it to so-called smartphones with their fiddly piggames and face-mashing apps, their addictive irritations, which never fail to bamboozle and bore me, and not just because I am old and don't understand them... Recently, the Bakelite phone had begun to decay, the tarnished wires crackling as I spoke, sometimes dropping out for moments at a time. Voices sounded grey and faded through it, as though speaking through fog.

'I wouldn't have bothered you unless I was certain.'

Before I could tell my colleague to turn the young man away, the aid in my right ear squealed with feedback. It was so sudden and loud it felt as if my ear drum was being needled. I switched off the aid and swapped the telephone receiver to my left ear.

And that's when Katherine mentioned a name I had not been expecting. Selda Heddle.

Beside the telephone is an antique chair, which I rarely sit in. Carved from applewood, it is upholstered in densely woven canvas decorated with songbirds amid branches and lyres, which hang amid the sage-pale leaves, their brown bellies swollen with the promise of song. I sat down – practically collapsed – onto the chair, and asked Katherine to repeat herself.

'Selda Heddle.'

So. I had heard her correctly.

It was the second time I'd heard that name in recent months. Earlier that winter, a former ward had sent me an email containing a link to an online article. An obituary of sorts. Her body had been found near her remote Cornish home in circumstances that unnerved me, not least because they evoked the bleak scenery of her operas, with their austere librettos and haunting arias. She had died during the recent snowstorm that had brought the country to a standstill. (To say it was unusual would be to understate the meteorological case. Briefer but colder than the 'Big Freeze' of '63, it was all the more surreal given the forest fires raging on the other side of the planet.) As the snows fell, and continued to fall, burying the city, wards ran outside and larked in the street, in contravention of the hospice's rules, livestreaming

22

pranks by the wrought-iron railings. Snowstorms, perhaps more than any other extreme weather event, have a
deranging effect on one's experience of time. The flash of
the wards' mobile phones, the electricity in the lamps, and
the branded clothing they wore were the only indications
that the scene was taking place in our century. Enrico
had covered for me weeks later when, after a sleepless
night, I'd driven to Heaven's Knell for the service. When
I arrived, however, I found myself unable to get out of
the taxi. I had arrived at a time in my life when, among
the people I had known, the dead outnumber the living.
Selda was not the first friend that I had lost. Neither of
my parents were still alive. And yet my mind refused to
accept that she of all people was gone. The depth and
force of my emotions confused me. They seemed entirely
out of proportion. I had not been close to Selda for a lifetime. Only when I heard the chanting was I able to get out
of the cab, yet even then, I remained unable to step foot
inside the building.

Katherine was telling me something, but my mind
had drifted so far from her words that I had taken none
of them in. Rather than admit that I hadn't been paying
attention – not a comfortable fact for the head of an institution ostensibly dedicated to the art of listening – I
asked, for the third time, if the young man had really been
singing a piece by...

I couldn't get the syllables out...

'Ss. Sel.. da. He. Head. Excuse me. Selda Heddle?'

'Listen for yourself,' she replied.

I pressed the receiver against my left ear. There was a
scuffle of feet, a muffled movement – and then a voice...

What struck me was not the content of the words, for
I couldn't make them out, nor the faded sound they made
through the phone's decaying veins. It was the melody,

which I recognized instantly, two short high notes followed by a long, low one, the four-bar sequence repeating and changing as he sang. An aria from Heddle's *Snow Trio*.

The claim was generous. He was imbuing each note with a throttled, tormented quality only barely approximating the tune. It was closer to screaming than singing – though one is able to blur the distinction, and some of our wards will exorcize their rage by growling like the frontmen in death-metal bands, dredging up, from the very depths of their viscera, all manner of animal howls.

'So, what do you think?' Katherine asked, her tone abrupt and sprightly (a sign of her anxious frustration).

Although I was struck by the sound, it did not alter my position. The timing would not do. The day's schedule was already crammed. In the afternoon, I was due to give a public lecture on musical phantoms: Echo condemned to her cave; Paul Wittgenstein's right arm, amputated in a POW camp after he was shot in the elbow during the Battle of Galicia; Clara Schumann's account of her composer husband, Robert, driven mad by shape-shifting spirits and dictating his last piece of music. I had an outline in my head but had yet to write a word of it. In the evening, a long-deferred dinner with Gerald, the thought of whose company inspired a desire to drink whisky in bed. And in between these events, tiring enough in themselves, was the usual business of running this place: the daily upkeep of this variously demonized, patronized, scorned, venerated, vilified, and today largely ignored and near-bankrupted institution. I say this by way of explanation. My answer to Katherine was and had always been no, before I'd picked up the receiver, been woken from the silence of sleep. The young man could not be helped. Later, perhaps. But not out of the blue, at whatever-o'clock in the morning. We might invite him to apply as a ward, I offered, administer the tests. No special treatment. Yes, we studied ancestry, but no, we did not pander to dynasties, if anything we disdained them. To my annoyance if not astonishment, she pressed me a final time.

'He asked for you by name.'

Well, this *did* surprise me. Just a little. Until I remembered something obvious: my name is visible on our homepage, where I am listed as the dean. Anyone could have looked that detail up on their fiddly phone.

Was my language polite? Perhaps not. I hung up.

Rather than go back to bed, I stayed on the chair and looked through the window. My top-floor flat gives me vantage of the hospice as it currently stands, as well as the numerous plots and parcels which we have been forced to sell off over the decades. (To give some sense of our former glory: at the turn of the nineteenth century, our hospice owned an acre of London land.) My gaze roamed the slate roofs, turrets, sandstone walls and arched windows, the main hall pocked by shrapnel and blackened in places by soot, the taller, redbrick blocks towards the rear in which our lectures take place, and tacky boxy structures reminiscent of the polytechnics that sprang up in the seventies, all yellowed panels and aluminium brackets, home to hot-desking office spaces now. I wanted nothing more than to return to bed. Instead, I waited. City traffic, the creak of my hall clock's turning hands... what else was I listening out for?

When gifted people age, one of three changes takes place: they die; they learn to live with the psychic intrusion; or they make peace with the gift, such that it no longer infiltrates conscious thought but rather runs

25

beneath its surface like a subterranean river, shaping its energies, piercing its roots.

The last was true in my case. Historically, it has been considered a form of 'mastery' to have passed through the various stages of training, relaxing if not dissolving the borders of being – artificial to begin with – to allow other voices and memories to occupy mine.

This is what I once believed, at any rate. In recent months, I had arrived at a conflict; you could even call it a crisis. The achievement of integration, of which I had once been so proud, now seemed the product of decades of dullness and sacrifice. What was the difference, after all, between this so-called 'mastery' and sublimation? Had I absorbed ancestral memory into every fibre of my being, as the texts and my teachers had promised I could, or had I censored it and in doing so both flattered and diminished myself?

Such thoughts led to a fundamental question, which has haunted me throughout my career. What *is* the gift?

I of all people should know, or at least have a plausible, well-rehearsed answer. I don't. Or I have too many. Depending on when you ask me, they are prone to change.

Ask me as a girl confined to bed by her doctor father and her stenographer mother, whilst her siblings disport themselves upon the sunlit lawn, I will tell you that the gift is the radio on a rainy day: an audible connection to places and moments beyond these walls, by turns exciting and ridiculous, tedious and confounding. Because I contracted polio when I was a toddler, I have no memory of the disease which altered my body and thus my life. Indeed, there exists around the virus a strange, almost prenatal amnesia: sometimes, I tricked myself into believing that polio, a common enough infection before the vaccine, was the result of an event that took place before my birth and for which I was being punished. I did not die, of course, but the virus affected my development in two related ways. The neurological damage left me with unreliable hearing in my left ear, a mild but constant pain in my left arm, and a weakness in both legs which renders walking tiring, if not always difficult. The second lifelong effect of the virus was that my father, a doctor, never forgave himself.

Ask me as a young woman after I have studied at Agnes's, and I will tell you that the gift is a waking dream, in which the great past – inaccessible to living memory and beyond the purview of historical texts – is endlessly reconfigured.

Ask me twenty years ago, and I will tell you that the gift is an epigenetic response to inherited trauma.

Ten years ago, I would have told you that the gift is a burden from which I am seeking to rid myself. That if I could pay a surgeon to conduct a hypothetical giftectomy, if not a lobotomy, I would give it serious thought.

Today, I would struggle to answer, except perhaps to note that, as anyone who has read a fairy tale knows, gifts are rarely what they seem at first glance. The challenge in finding an accurate analogy for it is this: the gift is as familiar as the voice in your head (who alive doesn't have at least one, whether they like the damn thing or not?). It revises and contradicts itself. It tells lies and tall tales. It hectors, hypnotizes, supports and cajoles. Such voices both are and are not ours, echoes of countless strangers to whom we owe our lives.

Whatever the case, as I sat on the chair, I could not remember the last time I had heard the gift; not directly at least, not with *words*, rather shadows moving at the very limit of conscious perception. And, whilst I was certain that these were the product of the gift, of the collective memories which passed like weather systems in my head, there was no longer any speech or song, no whispered asides or unwelcome jokes.

What snapped me out of it? The lamp – it flicked on in a dorm window. Then another, and another. Soon five or more windows were lit.

Their glows confirmed what I already suspected: news was spreading, wards were waking – and all because some wretched young man thought hospice meant hospital. I filled the kettle, prepared some coffee, and returned to the window, rubbing a knot in my neck with one hand and holding coffee with the other. A few moments later, the telephone rang a second time. I knew who it was, of course. 'Yes yes I'm on my way,' I said. 'Tell Enrico to meet us in the sunken room.'

I have been dressing near-identically for twenty years. My limited wardrobe saves me the daily dilemma of having to choose what to wear: white shirt, black patent-leather court shoes, one of three mohair suits, and a short bellringing cape that hangs about my shoulders. For years this outfit has lent my presence a gravitas and status that befits my role, as it did many deans before me; now, people tend to think it looks archaic and stuffy. And yet I persist in wearing it, if only because its weight is reassuring.

Before I put the jacket and cape on, I fitted my sash, another traditional garment worn by the master of bells. Sourced from a tannery near the Bridge of Awe, it is a supple, sturdy item, not much thicker than a belt, its full-grain calfskin treated with aniline dyes and liquored with emulsified oils. Along its length are four hoops, to which bells can be attached, though most days I wear only one: a thimble-sized ceremonial bell which, as with much of my outfit, and perhaps my personality, people think of as somewhat antiquated. I spent a moment in front of my cabinet, consulting the half-dozen bells that I retain in my apartment rather than in my office. Each is chosen according to the day's needs or whims, some for music, alarm, or ceremony, and others – so people claim; I don't believe it – to ward off demons.

The medicine bell felt right that morning. About four inches in height and one inch in diameter, it dates from tenth-century Bath and was commissioned by an apothecary who plied his trade beside the thermal spas. Its copper surface is coated with a patina of verdigris, the chalky, greenish hues of which, rough beneath the thumb, evoke the antacid peppermints my father fetched from his own, much smaller cabinet whenever I was nauseous.

As I crossed the black and rain-wet courtyard I took pleasure, as I always do, in a decisive sound: my cane's taps doubled, tripled by the hard walls. I can't have been much older than ten when my father announced that, from that day forward, I had to take one with me wherever I walked, along with my bottled pills, plasters, bandages, leg-braces, and all the other paraphernalia and prostheses that my condition, to his mind, required if I was to have any hope of, as my mother once put it, 'being taken off the shelf'. Overnight, as if by a curse, I transformed into a crone. Dashing men offered me seats on the bus. Children snickered when the cane slipped from my grasp and kicked it across the schoolyard. Strangers offered to carry my schoolbag or help me cross the road, their faces wincing with excessive concern. In revolt, I refused to use it... but that was many years ago, and I have since become fond of the thing. The smoothness of the wood, the smartness of the polish, the crisp, percussive sounds it makes as I walk – not to mention the fear it can summon in wayward wards when pointed with vigour, at the appropriate angle. It's an elegant object: a stem of scorched maple topped with a polished brass handle shaped into a hare's head, with wide wise eyes and slipper-soft ears pressed smooth against its cranium, capped at base by a brass ferrule. Yet the hard echoes caused my aid to squeal, a second time, with feedback. Pausing to turn it off – I would deal with the dratted thing later – I looked up at the dorm. Even more windows were lit than before. Instead of calling Katherine, who I knew would ring me if the situation got worse, I pressed on, into the entrance hall.

First: darkness, comforting aromas of wood and stone. Then, as my eyes adjusted, the grand, panelled hall – the oldest part of the building, its most arcane and costly to preserve.

I crossed the worn tiles, heading towards the desk behind which, I noticed with dismay, Leon was asleep. Oil portraits of former deans hung in the dimness, each depicted with their principal instrument, lamps glowing in recessed alcoves between each frame. I glanced up at my predecessors as I walked. Anthony Wight and his lyre, J. T. Pendle propped against his harpsichord, Leroy Loudermilk – the dean when Selda and I were wards – and his electric guitar, slender Helen Setzen clasping her flute. I paused by the portrait of Stith Simms who, uniquely amongst the paintings, does not have an instrument. Next to her was Bartholomew Ware, blessed with natural aptitude for a much-mocked instrument. A silver triangle hung from his raised right hand, and I imagined the prim little yelps the instrument must have made, as if startled by the orchestra's bluster and force. He was our briefest master, in post for a mere six days. One night in Oxford, walking home from a pub, he slipped in a rainstorm and drowned in a weir. It would not be long before

I joined that half-forgotten pantheon, fixed in dusky oils with a bell in my hands or on my sash. The thought made me weary; I decided not to dwell on it. Yet everywhere I looked, there were signs of decay. The paintings' varnishes, cracked and stained; the grilles near the ceiling, bearded with dust; the skirting's varnish, scaling away. All the more reason to preserve it. Behind the reception desk was the largest and gaudiest painting of them all: Agnes on a windswept heath, ringing a bell, her ear turned to a clear night sky scattered with stars across which comets trace golden arcs.

The creased bulk of Leon's head, adorned with those wonderfully ample and pendulous ears, was tilted far back on the headrest, feet raised on the desk, his fat hands lightly clasped on the heap of his paunch. Everyone knows that he sleeps on the job – mostly on the grave-yard shift, understandable enough, but sometimes during the day, when his sonorous snores resound in the hall as wards snigger past him, to lunch. Perhaps I should have fired him, but he's our longest-serving employee – I hired him thirty years ago, the week I was promoted to dean – and he has always stood his ground, risking his safety on more than one occasion.

Having reached the desk at last, I cleared my throat, and stared into his open nostrils, in which curls of tangled hair grew like wild shrubbery. They were whistling faintly, but it might have been my aid. I raised my cane over my head, then brought it down on the desk with an almighty whack. Leon woke so violently he almost fell off his chair. He righted himself, smoothed his tie, his blood-shot eyes rheumy and blinking.

As I berated him for sleeping on the job, my voice re-sounded off the walls and the masters' portraits. Was he oblivious to the situation we were in? Had he forgotten his job? I gestured at his walkie-talkie with my cane.

'For heaven's sake, Leon.'

Standing now, patting his tie to flatten it, I thought he was about to salute. 'I must have–'

'Forget it, no time to waste, just come with me.'

The usual route to reach the dormitories is out the back entrance, past the recording studio, across the square, and via the fire exit, but I prefer to take the auditorium. I opened the doors and halted in the aisle, waiting for Leon to follow. Selda and I first performed together here, she on the piano and I on the accordion – this was before I had discovered the foundry. The lights came on with heavy clunks, audible reminders of how desperate our building was for repairs and modernizations it could scarce afford. As we moved down the aisle, emerging from the shadow of the upper circle, the proscenium announced itself in a crescendo of crimson and gold, heavy curtains, carved cherubs aloft on scalloped wood. I reached the stage steps and turned, as I often did, to survey the vacant hall. The seats had an expectant look, as though awaiting people to sit in them. The raddled ostentation of the fresco struck me afresh, a midnight-blue backdrop fretted with stars and divided, as the painting outside had been, by golden arcs. But the paint had paled, in places flaked away to reveal patches of blank plaster. At a fundraising performance the previous week, during the third movement of Beethoven's fifteenth string quartet, the fresco began to moult. Cracks appeared; snowy flakes began to fall, sifting through the hall to whiten audience members' hair. The audience erupted in gasps and screams and scattered laughter, plaster falling all around them.

'Ellen?' Leon asked, holding out his hand as a husband might: we climbed the steps together. The skin on his truncated ring finger was smooth, its removal the result of an ugly incident many years ago when a ward, who had lost his way, stormed into the entrance hall flailing a machete in one hand and a long plastic tube in the other, which, as he spun it round his head, emitted a haunting, breathy wail. We crossed the stage, past the shrouded piano and a stack of plastic chairs, from where we slipped between the curtains.

In contrast to the (faintly ruinous) opulence of the space we had just left, the backstage was stark and unadorned, raw breezeblock hung with ropes, pulleys, speakers, drapes and weights, metal fixtures gleaming. Through a fire exit we reached the railings at the edge of the hospice's grounds. Only then did I try my hearing aid again. Another squall of feedback, and then the city's soundscape came into focus: a moped's nasal whine, the deeper chug of a street-cleaning machine, both rendered dry and a little tinny.

'They're awake,' said Leon, glancing up at the dorms, and less ominously than wearily – both of us would rather have been asleep.

The dorms were built at the turn of the century. Housed over three floors, and embellished with narrow windows and iron balconies, it has the imposing, exclusive air of a Mayfair hotel. Its design and construction almost bankrupted the hospice, yet its apparent grandeur was part of a concerted drive to impress the city, architecture mobilized to defend the institution against accusations of quackery and iniquity. This latter accusation derived from how often the wards indulged in music in private, late-night ceremonies deemed by some to be satanic in nature. From the street or nearby park, the city's nosy residents would glimpse distorted shadows on the walls, or hear cavorting noises through open windows: feet thundering on floorboards, orgiastic howls, and angelic, high-pitched chanting. This tension – civilized society, unknowable interior – was reflected in the building itself. Its solid, legible façade conceals eccentric and dysfunctional floorplans marked by crazed corridors and irregular rooms, like a building from a dream. It took Selda and I a full year to work out how to navigate it without getting lost.

'Shall I follow you in, or...?'

'Leon, my dear, this is your *job*.'

I opened the side door leading into the dorms. Immediately, I saw a pair of young wards in tracksuit bottoms, creased T-shirts, and headbands – they ducked to avoid my gaze, leaving a wake of hissy giggles as they disappeared through a door labelled with health and safety stickers. As I moved in the opposite direction, the door closing behind us, a gust caught my gown and made it flare, the fabric catching the corridor's too-narrow walls and hissing as I warmed to my disciplinarian role. My cane a cattle prod, or perhaps a sceptre, I arrived at the hall with my face fixed in a thunderous glower. My blue-grey eyes had grown colder and more pitiless with age, and at times such as these a kind of fury would still my veins, a hellfire righteousness that brought my task into focus.

The lobby resembled a slovenly common room. A chandelier hung crookedly over our heads, several bulbs broken, casting blocks of light and spindly shadows across the double-height space, with its cream walls, scalloped plaster, and overgrown cheese plants flanking the door through which the young man, still nowhere to be seen, had allegedly entered. Dozens of pyjama-clad wards were lounging on the stairs, sitting on the floor, chatting and signing in excitable huddles beside the door (closed, at least), thumbing their screens with those empty,

34

anxious eyes, the air ashiver with gossip and speculation. I raised my cane, cleared my throat – and to my dismay, not one ward appeared to have noticed me. The noises in that space were disjointed, rising to a pitch of such agitation that I wondered what had taken place between my leaving the flat and arriving here. An orgy? Drugs? Was everyone here off their head? I should have paid more attention, should have listened better to their needs, should have known what to expect; I scolded myself for not having been more *prepared* – I, their invisible dean, had failed them.

It was not the first time, in recent months, that my concentration had slipped. Then again, I was not the only staff member on duty. Katherine was on the night shift. I looked around. Where was she? Did Leon know? He stood at my side and I sensed, or perhaps imagined, that he was puzzled by my actions.

My skill set may be limited, but it has stood me in good stead: I brought my cane down hard. The ferrule met stone like a gunshot, and brought the room to abrupt attention. Wards *shhhhhed* each other or halted mid-conversation, comically frozen and open-mouthed. In the held-breath quiet that followed, confusion sizzled audibly over their heads. That's when I realized: I was concealed by the unlit corridor, veiled in my shadowy gown – invisible, after all.

'Well!' I said. 'I must say, it's a lovely surprise to see you all awake, so bright and early.'

Some of the wards, I could tell, were not yet certain that it was really me. My routines were infamous, at the best of times, so predictable – so went the predictable joke – that one could have set one's watch by my comings and goings. In recent months, however, my schedules had diminished further. I had confined myself to my office, sending out for lunch, instructing staff to leave me alone, barely exiting except when nature or essential meetings called. My daily timetables – which I observed with a kind of passion, which gave my life the structure the world, unwieldy, noisy, lacked – had been fixed for years. I was not the ghost of Hamlet's father, nor the stone guest at Don Giovanni's door, yet judging from my wards' expressions, I might as well have been. With theatrical flourish, I stepped from the shadows and into the glare, my face fixed in a scowl only halfway faked.

'Now, each of you will be *acutely* aware,' I said, 'that congregating in this manner, in the middle of the night, is explicitly against the rules of this hospice, correct? You will be equally aware, I have no doubt, that such behaviour will forfeit you the right to live here, in the dormitories, yes?' An empty threat – I wouldn't have followed through with it, was overstressing the villainy, perhaps, as I prowled amongst the wards, a head or more shorter than most of them, yet undaunted by their stature, their youth, jabbing the tip of my cane at their faces. A ward at the back spoke up. Darcie Allen, thirteen, Sheffield-born, a prodigiously accurate drummer in the metrical, marching-band mould. Her long hair was gathered in a ponytail atop her head in the 'pineapple' style that has been in and out of fashion several times over the decades, and whose emergence never fails to dismay me. 'But—!' she began.

'But nothing.'

'I was going to say—'

'What? That it's not your fault? That you've come here out of *charity*?' At which point I slipped into matron mode, summoning the spirit of my battle-axe grandmother: 'Come off it. Go on. All of you. *Shoo!*' The ceiling was painted a deep blue, as was my office, to imitate the night sky. Above the window of the reception, in faded gold paint, was a quote from Johannes Kepler: *The heavenly motions are a continuous song for several voices, per-ceived not by the ear but by the intellect; a figured music, which sets landmarks in the immeasurable flow of time.* A Christian as well as an astronomer, Kepler believed that we are born with an ability to appreciate harmonious proportion; in the context of music, this manifests in the perception of euphony. That some part of us is divine was proven, he believed, by our innate appreciation of the divinely or-dered universe – a root and its fifth, its seventh, its octave. The gulf between his exalted rhetoric and the situation laid before me might have made me laugh, were it not a feature of the hospice's day-to-day life.

'What are you waiting for?' I demanded.

The wards exchanged glances, some chastened, others tickled, and shuffled off on stockinged feet. Soupy mur-murs burbled through the emptying room. That sound – which conveyed the sense of many mouths moving, many minds thinking; which retained the rhythms and syntactical structures of speech yet hovered under the threshold of language – resembled, in some ways, the gift.

'Miss Ash,' I said, at last remembering a question I should have asked right away. 'Where is she?'

Darcie, in her pink pyjama top and yoga leggings, stepped forward. 'I don't know.'

'But she was just here, she called me from that phone in the corner.'

'Miss Ash told us to wait here,' Darcie shot back. 'We're here because she said so. You can't punish us for doing what she asked.'

I wondered if she was telling the truth. Darcie grew up with her aunty, uncle, and cousins. Her elder siblings would assault her when she sang in her sleep, which she did most nights; the adults turned a blind eye – until they made her sleep outside, on the floor of the shed. She had been at the hospice since the previous December, after being referred by her school. It took her a while to fit in. The same is true with most of our wards, but Darcie's early months here were perhaps more chaotic than most. She fell into frequent trances, was caught smoking in her room, verbally abused staff, and stole minor things – pencil cases, hoodies, lighters – from the other wards. She ran away twice. The first time she was gone for twenty-three hours, at which point she called us from a service station outside Birmingham. The second time, she made it only as far as Leicester Square. Tourists who mistook her for a street performer, or driven by a crueller interest in mental distress, took videos of her on their phones. Volatile, aggressive, disruptive – she could do all of those. But she was more or less incapable of dissembling. If she was angry, she screamed her head off. Sad, and her lower lip jutted out like an awning. She could not have masqueraded for all the money in the world.

'I see,' I responded, sure that she wasn't lying. 'Why?'

'Safety,' said another ward, hair in braids. 'He looked, like, ill.'

Another: 'But not dangerous.'

'No.'

'I swear Miss Ash said we should stay.'

That's when I heard it – an anguished, bestial cry. Halfway between a scream and a song, it traced the rough shape of a melody.

'Fine – but go back to bed.'

With that, Leon and I followed the sound through the side door.

Katherine, at last. She was standing in the yard between the dorms and the conservatory, where our recycling bins were kept, arms tightly folded at her chest, watching the

38

iron door and its luminous, clouded panes. Dressed in a long, grey coat, black jeans and heels emphasizing her stalky legs, she reminded me of a heron at the edge of a lake. Years ago she arrived at our doors aged twelve, in rather less dramatic a fashion than the stranger had. Her desperate but sceptical parents – wearing, as I remember, matching jackets and hand-knitted scarves – had driven from the Paris suburb they'd moved to when she was seven. She'd had a similar look about her, then. Her sharp-featured face was hectic with freckles, the eyes alive with tension and intelligence. She scrutinized the world as though it were a fascinating animal she wished to pet but feared would bite if she got too close. Older now, and tenured, she had a few grey hairs, crow's feet, but the expression was just the same.

'Stop that,' I said, gripping the wrist of her hand, the nails of which she had been biting. She jumped, turned to face me: 'Ellen – oh.' Her hand in mine, I examined the taut olive skin of her fingers, the frayed cuticles.

'You'll only ruin your nails. You had the monkey off your back, didn't you, for months – months! And now –'

'Ellen, please,' and she yanked her hand away.

A sniping, mother-daughter style had set in between us over the years, our semi-professional lingua franca – at least when we believed that no one could hear us. They could that night, of course. Leon looked so cold in his shirtsleeves, standing by the dorm door, veiled by mizzling rain, that I almost dismissed him. Katherine and I discussed the question at hand: whether the stranger needed tests (my view), or treatment (hers), first.

'Knowing if he's gifted – *how* he's gifted – will guide the course of treatment.'

'Yes but, I keep saying this, but it's *urgent*. You can hear him, yes? *See* him, too, if you squint...'

The conservatory, lit from within by strip lights, was an architectural eccentricity with which myself and the board felt unable to part (any sane or financially prudent person would have sold the land long ago; and yet, given the passive dark magic of capital, not-selling was increasing its value almost by the hour). That night, it seemed both living and unreal, a crystal carapace suffused with a greenish glow. Each pane of glass was obscured by impenetrable condensation; only vague, irradiated shapes could be seen within, their tufted, bladed, blooming forms reminiscent of specimens in murky jars. Was the young man alone? It seemed disturbing to pen him in this way, as if he were a wild thing, a creature of dark plants, an alien himself, though Katherine had rightly judged it better for his safety – contained from the wards, hypothetically visible.

'He isn't a threat,' she said.

I didn't ask what she meant by that, what her definition of 'threat' was. Instead, I remembered something I had forgotten, which was the importance of hospitality – of welcoming the ghost, as Agnes had when it appeared at her door.

We approached the greenhouse, and I heard it again; that low, lamenting howl was in the truest sense pathetic. It emanated from the other side of the clouded glass, and like the light spilling out of the windows and onto the glistening ground at our feet, the sound – and the pity that it aroused in me – did not seem continuous with the sonic texture of the night but transmitted into it, piercing it, zapped in from another place and time. The condensation formed into droplets which, sliding down the glass, created limpid strips in which the interior was visible. The yellowish stone paths, lined by chunky iron grilles. Overgrown, dozy greenery, their vast leaves spread like parasols, framed the view of the circular clearing at the heart of the greenhouse, with a few benches – more chunky, blackish iron – for guests to sit on.

It was then that I saw him at last. For a moment I thought he *was* some kind of alien, or chimera. Down on all fours, head hung low, so that I could not see his face, his back was arched. He rocked gently from side to side, shaking his head. He could have been examining the stone, attempting to read a language into its particulate surface, though I doubted it. I turned to Katherine.

'I see now. A bad case.'

'Shall I come in with you?'

'I think better alone, we mustn't crowd him. Leon? I'm sure he's no threat, but all the same...'

He nodded briskly.

'You made the right call,' I told Katherine, as I opened the greenhouse door. 'Have your phone at the ready, all the same. We might need Nasser. Or, heaven forbid, an ambulance.'

The damp air, heavy as breath, carried a peaty smell of vegetal putrefaction, of the cycles of death and fecundity by which dead plants' minerals are absorbed by their living counterparts. (Certain Agnesian practices involving the consumption of loved ones' ashes – perfectly safe and hygienic, yet for obvious reasons frowned upon by the population more broadly – for a time earned us an insalubrious reputation.) I adjusted my sash and stepped forward, balking slightly at the sudden heat, sweat already leaking from my brow. Perhaps the young man had heard me enter: he howled again, half-musically.

And yes, there was an aspect of comedy to it, as there might have been for a friend who had overindulged at the bar. Katherine however was quite right. I understood that plainly now. Left much longer, and he could slip into a malady or even a coma, perhaps was already heading that way... and in that moment I knew where he'd been, even if I had no idea, as it were, where he'd come from. His hoarse voice cracked and withered as its melody rose, his vocal chords giving out as Frau Trauffea's reportedly had. I had a better view of him now. In a raincoat and black jeans, which were muddy and wet at the ankles, was a skinny young man, his face obscured by trails of inky hair, his fingers – crescents of dirt under the nails – splayed across the flagstones as though afraid they would fly off.

I approached him slowly, careful with my cane; I lowered it gently, gently. Banana trees and fan palms rasped against my shoulder as I moved. As I sometimes did in these situations, I felt like a priest attending an exorcism – except in one crucial respect. I did not believe that the young man was 'possessed' by anything outside of himself. Unlike those who pathologize the gift, I have never believed it to be 'external' in that sense, something that invades or infects a pure mind. That which we would banish is native to our being. We absorb the dead, drink their minerals; we must offer them sanctuary. I do not believe – I am stridently opposed to the idea – that the gifted must be 'purged' of something grotesque, as was widely believed in the nineteenth century, when the hospice acquired its most recent name. Instead, I have fostered openness: welcoming the gift, letting it roam, not attempting to 'tame' it – for in the taming is the most severe violence.

Still, it is a question of balance. The many moving parts of which a self is composed, the interlinked and co-dependent processes encompassed by consciousness, can fall out of synchronization. A cog jams, a fuse blows ... but mechanical metaphors won't do. Better to imagine celestial geometries, arcs, parabolas, orbits, and the harmonies produced by the planets' grave rotation, falling out of place and creating dissonance in the mind, a jagged, frenetic noise, as of stars colliding and imploding. Disorder reigns. The gift dominates. When that happens, the dead must be returned to correct proportion; sometimes, in fact, they need to be forgotten. This requires delicacy.

The centre of the greenhouse has the feel of a forest clearing, hemmed in by dense greenery. The only sound in that space was the buzz of the bulbs and the jets hissing vapour into the silken air. And the high, tinny whine of my hearing aid, that harsh distracting metallic sound – I turned it off. One ear would have to do.

Adjusting my sash, I removed the medicine bell, approached the young man, and introduced myself. He did not respond or look up. He burbled and murmured and sang, his head lolling towards the floor; but I no longer felt any pity for him, only an inexplicable fear. A hypnotic worry, which narrowed my attention and drew me into it, the way illustrations of monsters, werewolves, and vampires used to in the books that I read as a child. I could not have turned away from them. I didn't want to. I was thrilled by my proximity to danger. Yet in the same moment I knew that he posed no serious threat, except perhaps to himself. Call it instinct. Or recognition: I had been there before.

I rested my cane against the wrought-iron bench. It was a risk, but I needed both hands.

Explaining what I was about to do, I approached the stranger slowly, step by step, until I was standing over him. He sang another run of music – yes, I thought then: *Snow Trio*. That jolt of recognition almost knocked me off course. I cleared my mind, lifted the medicine bell by its loop. It was hanging over his head, now, chalky green metal against wet, black hair. I waited. His breathing slowed. I struck the medicine bell with the tine.

That sound – it is remarkable. At once piercingly clear and relaxing. If I could compare it to anything, it would be a short shock of a drink; cold vodka, say, knocked back neat. The effect in the greenhouse was almost immediate. The young man sighed deeply, his whole body relaxed.

Play a note on almost any musical instrument, a piano, say, or your own voice, and it will carry a range of frequencies that correspond to the central pitch. Those that form a regular arrangement – whole multiples of the base frequency – are called harmonic. Frequencies in bells, on the other hand, are *not* harmonic. A curious fact emerges. Put simply, the pitch we hear when a bell is played, in contrast to those in pianos, voices, stringed instruments, and so on, does not always correspond to any actual frequency present in its sound. If you hear a middle C in the sound of a bell, say, there is no guarantee that a frequency matching that note is in fact being transmitted through the air. Rather, the *experience* of hearing a middle C is an epiphenomena, a kind of ghost: it is the mind's attempt to make sense of the richly dissonant vibrations produced by the instrument. The analogy doesn't quite fit, but it would be a bit like looking at a painting and seeing a vivid blue, where no blue paint has been used. The pitch heard in bells is virtual. It is generated inside the listener's head, an impression of something which is not there, frequencies surrounding an absence. This purely subjective quality offers one explanation as to why, in my experience, bells are so effective in the treatment of psychic distress. For whatever reason, they correspond more closely to the paradoxical experience of the gift than language ever could.

I waited until the trail of sound faded, then struck the

44

bell again. This time, he breathed in sharply and assumed a new posture, kneeling, as if he was about to pray. I struck the bell a third time. As the strike faded, it left behind a clean, empty feeling in its wake.

I asked if he could hear me. His face was downturned, I could not see his features, just the straight line of his nose. He had forgotten about me already. The medicine bell has that effect. Its healing powers are often paired with, perhaps partly comprise, amnesia. Snapping the listener out of their trance or torment causes them to forget the more recent event of the healing itself. Often, the listener will look at me with a bewildered expression, wondering who I am, or why I am standing so close to them, despite moments ago having begged me to heal them. The young man muttered something I couldn't quite hear – I remembered my faulty, turned-off aid. I explained where he was, what treatment I had administered, how we would take care of him. He was in the right place, there was nothing to fear. At which point the stranger looked up, and for the first time, I saw what he looked like.

I had seen his face before, and it belonged to someone else. As I realized this, its features seemed to shift and change before my eyes. He was a fine-boned, sallow man with lank blackish hair and a distant, dulled expression. At the same moment, he was Selda as she had been when I knew her, with ratty brown locks and mismatched eyes. He had a sharp jaw and broad lips; he had Selda's chin and sticky-out ears. Both faces were alive in the same face.

'Wolf,' I said. 'Is that you?'

The sunken room, two floors below street level, was built during the Cold War and at a time when the basements of the Jensen Centre doubled as bomb shelters. The room was designed to deaden vibrations as completely as possible, an effect achieved by cocooning the structure in layers of reinforced concrete. Each is several metres thick and separated by airless cavities that muffle the thunder of passing tube trains, the floors cushioned by iron springs which absorb the impact of external noise. It is amongst the most acoustically 'dead' rooms in the country. Click your fingers, and it sounds like a dry twig snapping in a matchbox. The walls are hung with foam spikes that further absorb and isolate sound waves. Scientists occasionally use this space to measure vibrations and to monitor the effects of pulsations on fragile materials. In the sixties and seventies, MI5 and MI6 agents were known to recruit wards on the understanding that they were, to put it one way, exceptional eavesdroppers. Adopting covers as musicians or conductors, they muscled suspects underground and interrogated them in absolute silence. I dare say that, for some, it was a form of torture. These days, the sunken room is rarely used, except by wards who wish to isolate a particular sound; the sizzle of burning candles, say, or the muffled roar of the vascular system. Some people claim, as John Cage did when he entered an anechoic chamber such as this, at Harvard, in the fifties, that if they spend long enough in this room, they can hear not only their axons and ganglia singing, but atoms teeming and colliding in the air: Brownian motion, named after the scientist who observed pollen grains dancing under a microscope. It is a lonely room. Doubly sunken: secreted underground and removed from the sonic commons of the city above, the untamed clamour that reminds me, sometimes gratingly, of life. In the sunken room's pristine, lifeless air, sounds are artificially severed from that residue of chaos – of noise – that confirms that every effect has its cause; that no object, no thought, is separable from the universe out

46

of which it emerged and to which it will return. I have spent my life seeking to tear down such walls, building bridges to such islands. That is why the room unnerved me. It spoke of loneliness. I fear it more than death.

Enrico appeared at the corridor's end, stooped in the sunken room's doorframe. He had made an effort, by his standards, at professional attire. His shirt had been white in a previous life; now, it was greyish and lavishly spattered with yellow turmeric and darker marks that I hoped were wine. He'd oiled or pomaded his hair to an old-time lustre, combed back from his high forehead, his sombre eyes enormous behind his wireframe glasses.

'I'm sorry about this,' I said, 'another midnight walk-in.'

'Last month,' he whispered, his voice hoarse from all the joints I turned a blind eye to, 'at the meeting–'

'I know, yes, it might look like I'm contradicting myself, but the new policy still stands. Enrico – this is *different*. A very serious case.'

He stood there for a moment, silent as a sphinx, as if considering whether or not to slam the door.

Whenever people see Enrico and I at public events or travelling on the tube, they are keen to note the physical differences between us, as if we hadn't noticed ourselves. He is roughly twice my height. He has to stoop when he walks through doors, as he did that night in our basement corridor. He is thin as a sapling, with narrow hips and shoulders, yet his boyish proportions conceal a formidable, dextrous strength: I have seen him bend dinner spoons between fingers and thumb as if they were made of warm wax. He lives two floors below me, but my picture-frames rattle when he does his morning star-jumps. When he was a young man he boxed bare-knuckle, grim stories he'll only tell when sufficiently drunk, pointing out raised scars, the gold teeth, the kinked rib that never set right. When he arrived here, his gift was a curse from which he wanted to escape – a common view, here at the hospice. I am not quite so imposing, at first glance at least. Nor am I some soothsaying hag or dithering dispenser of caramels. When I strike metal instruments, I make them clang – carillons of awe and alarm. I heal people, yes, but I wake them up too. I raise hell.

'Okay,' Enrico said, stepping aside to let me pass.

We followed him into the sunken room, with its foam spike-covered walls and taut mesh floor, not dissimilar to trampoline fabric. He introduced himself to the former stranger, who had confirmed that his name was Wolf, and asked him to sit on the chair provided, opposite which he had arrayed two cymbal stands: one of these was empty. Enrico removed a bronze cymbal from its padded carrying case and fitted it on the stand to the right. Even bent at the waist, he is enormous, yet he handled his instrument with a watchful devotion. I found, as I always did, his tender concentration rather moving to behold. He applied wax to his bow. As he did so, he explained the procedure to Wolf. The poor young man's head was rolling this way and that, and I wondered how much of my colleague's words he was taking in.

'It's a very simple exercise. You might find it relaxing. If you fall asleep, hey, no problem. No right or wrong answers here. I will play, then stop, and I will ask you a few questions... I would like you to tell me what these sounds bring to mind. What they help you remember. Should take around twenty minutes. Ready?'

He rested the bow against the side of the cymbal and began to play...

This is not a tribunal, I do not wish to sound defensive. All the same, and for the record: had I known the severity of Wolf's condition at that time, then I would, of course, have acted differently. As it was, we set about conducting a series of routine examinations in order to test his sensitivity to the gift. An early warning sign, which I should have caught: a few minutes in, his head began to droop, he gestured at his throat. I brought him water. He sipped, barely able to hold the glass, squinting as though a bright light was beaming at him – back in the Cold War, perhaps, with MI5 instead of faculty – though the room was softly lit.

'We ought to postpone,' I said.

That instinct was correct. Instead, in desperation, I played the medicine bell again.

Rather than wake Wolf up, as it had a minute ago, it subdued him, and quickly – he slumped. I tried to reverse the effects, but too late. Like a marionette dropped by its puppeteer, he slid off his chair in a heap of limbs.

Enrico glared at me, his bow quivering in his hand like a fencer's foil. 'What did you do that for?'

'It worked the first time.'

'But surely–'

'Enough,' I snapped as I knelt beside Wolf, and gently shook his shoulder.

The damage was done. I have witnessed the gifted fall into such states, the symptoms by turns reminiscent of fugue states, catatonia, or somnambulism, and suggesting both dissociation from one's immediate surroundings and absorption in a daydream. It had been years since I had been called upon to treat such a case, and rarely in my life had I witnessed one so severe. Perhaps Wolf *was* ill or injured, as I had suspected, or 'on something', in a state that exceeded our ability to treat him. A delay of a few minutes could mean the difference, if not between life and death, then catatonia and wakefulness.

'What now?' I asked, my voice thinner and drier than paper in that acoustically arid room.

At one point, Agnes's halls, including its current entrance hall, were lined with beds. For years, they were single four-posters made from wood, with red curtains on either side through which Agnes's staff could administer to the gifted, and which doubled as listening booths. These were cleared away, replaced by fewer, less protected iron bedsteads interspersed with all manner of contraptions, bizarre assemblages of wood and metal, glass domes and keys. Some resembled the electro-acoustic instruments of the twenties and thirties (theremins, cathodic harmoniums, ondes martenots); all were designed to 'fix' the gifted. At that point in our history, we had only two beds left, one of them groaning under a mountain of storage boxes. As soon as Wolf collapsed, we brought him to our sick bay immediately – we wasted no time, not one second. Should we have called an ambulance at that point, too, having thus far neglected to do so? The answer may have been yes. As he lay there, in that whitewashed room, which smelled, more than anything, of lavender and ash, I pictured the days unfolding... and yet my own reputation was uppermost in my mind. The stranger would languish. His parents would sue. Agnes's would become the focus of a scandal, there would be online mobs, bricks through the window, a criminal case. The details of my crime escaped these panicked prognostications, but negligence would surely rank among the charges. Had I forgotten who he was, the connection to my friend?

Nasser Shah is among the most outwardly successful of my former wards, a fact that his immaculate shirts and shiny shoes, his twinkling rings and Swiss watches, always impressed upon me whenever I saw him. He arrived at our doors at eleven years of age. Timid, daunted, he was practically mute. He wore enormous polo shirts and had buck teeth. A small, sallow boy with no social wiles to speak of, he was crippled by shyness and melancholy. I came to think of him as one might an injured bird that one finds in the garden, nurses to health, and keeps as a pet, knowing – or fearing, as my father had with me – that exposure to the outside world will kill it. Other wards bullied him with vile racist terms, or with repulsive acts of self-debasement disguised as ritual humiliations (one ward defecated in a shoe box and left it under Nasser's bed). I expelled three or four wards on his behalf. His bullying had brought to mind my own cruel treatment here, on quite different but no less idiotic grounds, so I had some understanding of the damage such thoughtlessness can cause. His favourite place was a particular carrel in the Jensen, isolated from the bulk of the desks, at which he would read for hours.

Until, out of nowhere: the change. Was it really all down to puberty? He shot up like a rocket. A beard sprung from his suddenly bulky jaw. His squeaky voice dropped two octaves, acquiring a depth and gravitas that a news announcer would have coveted. In a few weeks (so it seemed), he was on his way to becoming the renowned – the lavishly remunerated – paediatrician he is today. Two months prior to our reunion, I later learned, his fifth child had been born prematurely, her first three weeks spent in an incubator. Had I known this at the time, I might not have presumed upon him so readily, to tend someone else's child. Yet he was nothing if not professional. He appeared before me, his clothes immaculate, his teeth porcelain-white. Yet there was a harrowed quality to his face, the ashen eyes of abiding exhaustion.

And yet, that sprung tone: 'Ellen. Delightful to see you.' That was Nasser. 'What seems to be the issue?'

Never mind his qualifications, intelligence, and sensitivity: his handshake was medicine. I wondered then, as I sometimes did, if I had guided him, however unconsciously, into his profession. He reminded me of my father in a few respects. The Gladstone bag. That handshake. The ambassadorial courtesy. I showed Nasser into our little sick bay, thanking him profusely for having come, at such short notice and at that hour.

'He's taken a turn,' I said. 'Katherine filled you in?'

He set his bag on the side table, removing tools with a practiced ease. Stethoscope on Wolf's chest: 'How long has he been unconscious?'

'He's been in and out since he arrived around, oh, an hour ago. The state he's in currently, twenty minutes.'

He examined the young man thoroughly, checking his pulse and blood pressure, shining a light into his eyes, lifting the arms, letting them fall, speaking to him and taking note of the answers, which, when they came – I was surprised they came at all – were half-formed at best. Wolf appeared to be in good physical health, said Nasser, but urgent tests were needed to rule out encephalitis and alcohol poisoning. No sign of injury to the head, however, or anywhere else. Heartrate normal, meaning drugs weren't the likely cause. He inserted a needle into Wolf's arm and filled two vials. The colour of blood, released in this manner, never fails to astonish me: it makes complete sense that this fluid, impossibly red, sustains life. Nasser prescribed some intravenous medicines and I handed the slip to Darcie – she was hovering in the corridor, thinking I hadn't noticed her, her trainers squeaking on the lino.

'Fetch these, will you? Take a friend. The pharmacy down the road should be open.'

She took the slip, nodded, and was gone.

As Nasser and I spoke, the hospice was warming audibly to life, alarms going off, shouting down the corridor. He spoke briskly, quietly. So entrancing was his steady, soothing speech that, whilst I was certainly attentive to the sound his voice made, I failed utterly to absorb the linguistic content of whole passages, urgent and clear though they were, basking instead in those eloquent rhythms as a cat might in its own purr.

My mind drifted to Selda. My tall and mercurial friend from Coventry, with her awkward body language and skilful hands, her messy hair and piercing eyes, her fondness for screwball comedies and ham-and-apple sandwiches. Her haughty disdain, her vulnerability. I saw it all. The public seriousness was matched, in private, by a silliness no less passionate; few people have ever made me laugh with such wheezing helplessness as Selda could with her impressions of other wards and staff, performing jester-like in the kitchen. At times, she would appear to fall into the alarming, in-between state that her grandson was now in, too (the propensity was of course genetic). These maladies have been with us for as long as the gift itself, which is to say many thousands of years. The gifted who succumb to them are rarely able to remember any details of where they have 'been', yet many recall being surrounded and saturated by music, which paralyses them as an opiate would; others, by contrast, recall grinding discord and roaring noise. It happened so often with her that I used to wonder if it was a reckless technique. If she was submitting to an inner disarray out of, or in reaction to which her most pristine and regulated music emerged.

Yes, I remembered: her trances could infuriate me, because they seemed so faked, so performed – lazy attempts to cement her reputation as a 'genius', in the crazy and tempestuous man-made mould. I hated, as I saw it, her fakery. (I may also have felt she was abandoning me, in some way.) Unlike Darcie, whose abrasive moods were so legible as to be almost relaxing to witness, Selda was a mystery, a blizzard of codes in which one could get lost, too, and forget oneself. But, I wondered then, her 'disappearances' may have been genuine. In attempting to describe 'where she went', whilst she was lying right there, on a bed or the floor, she used imagery pulled from a dream: endless systems of underground caves, blue deserts, skies that dripped white fire – and music, total and enveloping, somehow amniotic, which in its density and speed resembled swirling liquid or white noise. These were analogies, at best. Description obscured what it sought to illuminate. At the time, I was less generous even than that. I thought she was making it up for attention.

Nasser said something which snapped me back to the room: '— that we will lose him.'

I blinked. My cane wobbled. I gripped it firm and asked a superfluous question: 'What do you mean?'

'The longer he remains in the malady, the less likely it becomes that we can get him out of it.'

'So you do think it is one,' I said, using the antiquated-sounding phrase, 'a *malady du mort*?'

'I'll refer him for an MRI scan as soon as possible, to rule out any underlying causes. And I'll have his blood looked at right away. They should give a clearer picture.'

'And how long has he been in it?'

'Judging from his response times, I would hazard, well, perhaps as long as a week.'

Nasser did something unexpected. He guided my hand to Wolf's forehead. It was unnaturally cold. When I ventured that this may have been on account of his long journey, Nasser shook his head. I asked how long we had to treat him, and how best to go about it, and he thought for a moment. 'The next few days,' he said, 'are crucial.' Bed rest, hydration, nutrition, and whatever acoustical remedies we could administer. If he didn't come out of it soon, said Nasser, he would spend the rest of his life in and out of it, neither awake nor asleep.

—

I do not wish to sound defensive. It's quite true that my choices were not so urgent as they might have been, had I been quicker to grasp the facts. But consider the following context: Nasser had himself once fallen into one of these states, and the person who had pulled him out of that state, using those same bells, was me. As it was, only at this juncture did I make any attempt to contact Wolf's next of kin. After the greenhouse, Katherine had been hard at work in the office downstairs, tracking them down online, but for whatever reason had been unable to locate them. I remembered the email that reached me earlier that year, inviting me to the funeral. After I arrived at Heaven's Knell, I was unable to meet with Selda's child and grandchild — I'd met them so many years ago I doubted they would recognize me — and kept my distance... In truth, I skulked, and to such an extent that I don't think they noticed me. I replied to the email with my phone number, then googled the daughter's name: Anya. I stared at photographs of her, yet was unable to find the resemblance. She was the director of an educational consultancy firm, and in a generic portrait photograph on its page, set against a neutral blue curtain, she wore her hair tied back in a ponytail. Just as I was about to try another means of contact, my phone rang. It was her.

How would I have acted in her situation? A woman I had not seen in fifteen or twenty years paced – ran, almost – across the entrance hall, handbag clamped close to her side like an American football. The circumstances could hardly have been more grave, yet I was overjoyed to see her looking 'so grown up' (as the cliché goes, so hated by those to whom it applies). There was a directness about her clipped, quick gait, her severe expression with its tense mouth and livid eyes, the dark hair cinched in a ponytail (a few stray strands awry like corn silk). Even the power-casual clothes she wore, dark shirt, black slacks and tasteful trainers, impressed and in doing so moved me. It was her manner, and not her appearance, that reminded me of her mother during her late night writing sessions, when I would descend into the Jensen Centre at what I thought of as a penitent hour — ten o'clock on a Tuesday night, say, when other wards were sneaking to jazz clubs or strangers' beds — only to find her in a carrel haloed by a banker's lamp. I tensed before Anya reached me, because she did not seem to be slowing down: I half expected her to tackle me to the floor. A few young wards were idling near the stairs with music folders as props, holding them open but staring at us.

'Where is he?'

'In our sick bay. Come, I'll take you right away. A doctor has seen him, he's quite safe.'

'A GP?'

'A paediatrician,' I said. 'He's extremely reliable. World class, I assure you, he—'

'Take me to my son.'

The lift was a cramped creaky box at the back of the hall. Similar in size to a phone booth, it pressed us awkwardly close. I had explained the basics on the phone, yet as the lift rose, swaying and jerking, I reiterated my account. Wolf had arrived in the early hours. Naturally, we had let him in immediately and without fuss. I had seen to it personally, in fact, insisting that he be given a bed right then, on the spot. I called a specialist doctor immediately and administered several effective therapies, drawing on many years of extensive experience of such – she snapped.

'Treatments? Why didn't you call an ambulance?'

Perhaps it was unconventional from her perspective, but as I told her, as our airless box winched higher up the building, these acoustical therapies have precedent. We do not frame harmonic philosophy in terms of micro- and macrocosm, subjective and cosmic order, but interpersonal tension and its corollary, release. Harmonic intervals exist not only between ourselves and our living family, friends, and tribe, but between the living and the dead. This is one further reason why music is so central to our system of thought – it helps us identify points of disharmony, and restore balance. Clinical trials? Few and far between. Rather, the usefulness of our treatments had been proven, not by multinational companies, but by century upon century of use by parents such as she. Indeed, they had helped her son.

As I delivered this little disquisition, her expression grew only more twisted and grave, until she was glaring at me with open disgust.

'He is in a safe place,' I said, but my voice was frail and I hardly believed it. She had seen right through me. I was a fraud.

Wolf, on the bed beside the window, was hooked up to a drip. Darcie had fetched the prescription already: it was in a paper bag on the side table. Anya's composure, so tightly controlled, cracked. She cooed and cried and kissed his forehead, kissed his head, told him she was there, could he hear her? 'I'm here now,' she said, 'I'm here.' And hearing her repeat these words — a faint echo of one of Selda's pieces, I couldn't remember which — almost brought tears to my eyes. The gift, which had been restless all morning, but had yet to speak, surged and roared with such intensity the room began to spin. I was still unable to decipher what it was telling me. Anya checked her son's pulse and touched his skin, kissed his forehead, kissed his hand. Enrico, who had been holding vigil in the corner, on a flimsy plastic exam-chair, slipped silently outside. I felt quite confident that, now we were here, all the misunderstandings would be cleared up. When I turned back, however, Anya was holding her phone to her ear. 'I need an ambulance please. As soon as possible. My son is unconscious. I don't know for how long. A few hours. No, no injury, I don't think,' and so on.

Once she had hung up, I attempted to reassure her that there *really* was no need to involve the emergency services. Not because I feared reputational damage on my part, I hasten to add, but because I knew — I was certain — that the best course of action was for Wolf to stay here, with us. Anya demanded that I leave the room, and made an accusation which, I must confess, astonished me. 'Help me make sense of your behaviour. Are you a sadist or a fool? I don't know if you're deliberately jeopardizing my son's recovery, or if you sincerely believe that your ridiculous bells and whistles are going to help him. I don't know which is worse. But I *do* know something. You do not, under any circumstances, take chances. Not with anyone. Not with my son. Is this policy in this hospice? To take vulnerable young people away from their parents' protection, waft some bits of metal over them, and send them on their way? Not when they arrive at your doorstep in grave

58

distress, no, you don't. Not when he could be having a seizure or a brain haemorrhage or God forbid what else. Do you understand me? What if *your* child was lying there?'

For several seconds, I looked into her eyes. I had first done so within days of her birth. She was my beloved friend's only child, a girl I had spoon-fed, cleaned up after, read books to, and taken to the park – if only when she was a little girl, and at a time when my friendship with Selda was already a pale shadow of what it had been. Memory's ways, one hardly needs reminding, can be ironical and cruel. I doubted Anya remembered much, perhaps any, of the events that in my mind at least had cemented our sacred bond. Nor can she have known how, on a rainy, dreadful evening from which our friendship never really recovered, I made a promise to Selda to help her daughter if she ever came into distress. Indeed I would have flattered myself to call Anya a kind of daughter. How deluded I had been. I felt terribly ashamed to have indulged, for so many years, that baseless affinity. I wanted to close the distance between us, to relate the volumes of knowledge, the decades of experience that explained my decisions that morning, to convey the depth of feeling that her presence and her son's, her mother's life and death, had instilled in me. It would have taken days to relate, even if I could have found the words. I wanted to tell her everything I knew about Selda before she met Garth, Anya's father – it was I who had introduced them. *Me*, without whom Anya and Wolf might never have been born (did either of them realize?). We were bound together, not by blood, but Selda.

I didn't tell her any of that, though. 'I'll wait outside,' I said.

—

Days went by. I heard nothing from Anya. I wanted to check on his progress but I held back, restricting my contact to an email to her, in which I offered my services and the hospice's facilities, should she ever wish to call me. She didn't respond. Her silence confirmed that she held me at least partly responsible and I wondered if that blame had ancestral precedent, related, in however unconscious a way, to Selda having studied here.

In the evenings I kept myself busy, working late in my office. I ordered food in and ate at my desk, sometimes nothing at all; most evenings, I filled a glass halfway with whiskey and topped it up with ginger ale. I had an idea of what would help. But no, I didn't want to reach into that dusty underworld under my bed, to retrieve the suitcase I hadn't opened in years, the one containing the memory bells I had almost thrown in the bin.

It was during one such late night that the phone rang. It was Anya. 'Hi,' she said stiffly, 'I didn't think you'd pick up.' Wolf was in a stable condition, but the doctors remained unsure what had caused his coma, if it even *was* a coma: his brain was active and he could, with effort, be woken up. It was a curious conversation. Clipped, short. It contained no new information and had a monotonous, time-filling quality, a kind of verbal muzak. I listened, as carefully as I could, to the gaps between Anya's words, to the silence in which the call's true intent was encrypted. Had she remembered who I was? Was she calling to check I was still alive?

Two days later, around lunchtime, she emailed. *The good news is that Wolf's condition hasn't changed. That's the bad news, too.* He was in and out of consciousness, though; twice, he had mentioned my name. *Anyway... I am at my wit's end, and I wondered if you would mind visiting during hours?* She listed the slots. If I left within the hour, I'd be able to see them that very day.

At the hospital I was directed down a corridor of purgatorial length, along which a few empty beds were placed, its lino bathed in bars of yellowish light from the tinted windows. Wolf was on a ward with a few others, as my mother had been in her final illness, before, in her last days, they moved her to a private room. I had wanted nothing more for her wellbeing than to be beside her until the very end, to stroke her hand and say soothing words (hearing and touch are the last of our senses to go) as her body went through the stages of dying; a gradual diminishing and withdrawing inwards over several days, then hours, then minutes, as her laborious breathing slowed, and slowed, and quickened, and stopped at last; and she was gone. It was hard to enter that medicalized environment without hearing a historical rhyme, or thinking of my mother and Wolf as experiencing two versions of the same ineluctable, endlessly repeating event. Of course, they *were* in fact very different: my mother had been at the natural end of her life. Wolf, a young man, lay in a medical bed with an adjustable back, chrome railings along both sides, dressed in a whitish gown. Anya was at his bedside. She said something to me – in my excitement, I had left my aids at home, and could only hear muffled, underwater vowels. I squinted instead at her lips, understanding her at last.

Thank you for coming.

Having made eye contact, she broke it again.

A blondish, broad-shouldered man in jeans and a blazer sat on a chair in the corner, beside the narrow window, flicking through the *Economist*. I guessed he was Wolf's father; he flashed back a grimace of greeting, the muscles of his blandly handsome, boyish face – it was easy to imagine what he looked like as a child – flexing expertly under the skin. I was familiar with the belittling move, which typically came from men: to politely neutralise my presence in the shortest possible time, to limit the chore of having to talk. Yet whenever Anya spoke, he dropped his page and followed her speech, uxorious and alert.

'You must be worried sick,' I said to Anya, 'absolutely sick.'

She spoke, but since her face was turned away, I had to ask her to repeat herself, so that I could lip-read. *I've barely slept since you called. I lie in that chair and hope they won't throw me out. Has this happened to wards before?*

I nodded. I almost told her that it had happened to her mother, but something held my tongue.

I sometimes wonder what went through Anya's mind in those next few moments. I felt the twitchiness, the dreaminess leave her. She took me to one side, out of hearing range of her son (and the man I later learned was not Wolf's father after all, but a second husband, called Todd). In the corridor, tucked away from the bustle of the ward between a toilet and an office, she asked when Wolf had arrived and in what state he had been. She requested that I run through the treatments I administered. Which bells, and why did I play them, and how often? I was in the dock, defending not just myself but the hospice, even Agnesianism itself.

I answered her questions. Then she told me the story.

After her mother's death, Wolf had begun to hear voices and music, as her mother had before him. He attempted to conceal it from her, but she knew him too well, and it came to a head on their trip to Bell Hall. *That*, she had thought, was the end of it – she was wrong. They'd sell the house and its contents, pay off all debts, and move on.

A few weeks later, someone called her. An old friend of her mother's, a cellist. He was worried about Wolf's behaviour – he was back at Bell Hall, alone. Anya had no idea. She tried calling, texting, asking friends. She drove straight down. But the house was empty.

That was two weeks ago. Her son had been missing since then.

Countless times, I have found myself in a similar position: managing the expectations of a parent who believes my attempts to heal their child are what 'sickened' them in the first place. Added to the bargain, they will ask about my own children, and, learning that I have none, use it as further evidence of my inadequacy and ignorance, at times even outright villainy.

And so, ordinarily, this exchange would not have affected me so strongly as it did. Since she was Selda's daughter and, I could not help but feel, in some tangential, adoptive sense my daughter too, I became defensive.

We returned to Wolf's bedside. Anya kept close the whole time, as if to ensure I wouldn't 'do anything' to her son, such as poison him (possibly for the second time, she may have thought), or drip sleeping potion into his ears. Instead, I cleared my throat and sang a song of healing and purification. Anya's husband (Todd is a ludicrous name for an adult, a syllable short of a baby) physically rolled his eyes and closed his money magazine, as though I had dashed his entire week against the rocks. It's true, people hate spontaneous song. It is often the very last thing they want to hear, particularly if they are English. But as I kept it up, that repeated lullaby, the high notes and the low, the words' repeated patterns caused one of Wolf's eyelids to twitch. I removed from my sash another medicine bell, different from the one I had used upon

63

Wolf's arrival, this one blown from frosted glass. Anya did not speak. I felt her anxious doubt like a kind of heat and saw myself as she must have done: a charlatan.

I struck the bell and heard the phantom D-sharp strike tone, its densely woven partials; heard them clearly, even without my aids.

To her surprise, if not mine, it worked. Briefly, at least, he woke. Blinking, he glanced around, as though awaking from a dream.

Later that evening, I spoke to Selda. I took a seat in one of the old listening stations, those wooden booths so reminiscent of confessionals, and settled into that primal silence, that inner quiet in which, if one is lucky, one meets oneself. Lacking practice, it took a long time to return. Worries and commitments, irrelevant memories and sense-impressions sparked and jangled in my mind. I waited for the gift to speak. Rather pathetically, I listened for that low and steady voice of Selda's, her over-solemn tone by turns amused, impressed, and irritated: I had internalized it, it was part of me. Why didn't she speak to me, then? I listened. Creaking pipes. Distant music. Perhaps it took an hour; at last, I sank into the quiet.

What emerged from that inner dark was the closest thing to an apparition: a voice. My own, at first. I spoke her name, an act of summoning. A memory from when I first knew her, long repressed, appeared before me.

More of an image, perhaps, than a moment. There she was as she'd been in our childhoods, long before we stopped talking. She was a haughty teen in corduroys and a cotton top, with strappy sandals on her feet. Bob-cut: her new style. Her coral lips were chapped, her knuckles parched. Her mismatched eyes held the candlelight — there were candles now, in my memory, lighting up the wooden walls of the booth. Selda was standing right in front of me, in the past, she was with me and she was not here.

'Selda,' I said, 'it's been too long.'

The excitement I felt to see her again was shot through with fear and shame.

'I saw your grandson again. He's in trouble.'

Selda stood there, aged perhaps fourteen, listening impassively as I told her about the son of a daughter who'd not yet been born.

When was the last time we'd met?

I lost the image. Waited. Another returned.

Selda and I: she was older, a few grey hairs, no longer with Garth, Anya at school, there was rain at the window, two memory bells on the table beside us, the roar so loud I could barely hear her, let alone the gift, dull thunder to the north. She sat across from me, in the booth and in her front doorway, now and then, here and nowhere, anguished, making me make a promise: to look after her descendants, but why? What did she imagine? I can't remember what I said, just that I agreed without question. Raindrops hit the image, my vision liquified...

When I came to, I was not in the booth but in my flat, with a bell in my lap and a bottle of vodka on the side table. I had spoken to Selda at last. She had not spoken back

Anya wrote again. Her tone was no less brisk. I had the impression that she did not understand what my role in her, Wolf's, or indeed her mother's life had been or could be, whether I was friend or foe. She resolved this ambivalence by summoning me to the hospital, but keeping me at bay behind a wall of ice.

One visit happened to coincide with the birthday of

another patient. Her age emblazoned on a helium balloon, cards and books and stuffed toys propped on the side table. Anya and I went downstairs to the cafe, where, one way or another, the subject of husbands came up. Wolf's biological father – a scientist of some description, if not distinction – had all but vanished when he was five, taking up a research post in a snowbound radar station near Yellowknife, north-west Canada. He ran some kind of fiddly software that analysed data from giant radar dishes pointed at outer space.

'He listens for messages,' she said. 'From aliens, in theory. He hasn't found any little green men yet. At least as far as I know.'

What if silence itself was a message, I wondered, one we could not decipher without destroying? Anya didn't respond to the question (which may have been the answer it deserved).

Having been married to Gerald for some twenty-two childless years, I had some experience to offer. I was not entirely free of my husband, and nor did I want to be. I kept his surname, Montague, because I liked the star-crossed structure of its sound. 'I am, as they say, née Paine,' I said, amusing myself if not Anya. 'My father was a doctor, you see. Some of his patients found it very amusing, but others feared him. They thought that Doctor Paine would deliver on, not from, the threat determined by an accident of birth.'

Just then, Anya's phone rang. It was the registrar. Wolf, apparently, was wide awake and perfectly lucid – I wondered if the family across from his bed had sung 'Happy Birthday', and if the familiar song had brought him back. We rushed upstairs, the journey can't have taken more than five minutes, but Wolf was as he had been when we arrived. It was typical of the cruel and exhausting rhythm of those days: a sudden hope, a false alarm.

Five days passed. Wolf showed no sign of change. As Nasser had explained, the longer he stayed in that state, buried, in a sense, on a plane of existence between life and death, the less likely he was to claw his way back to the surface. The only thing Wolf responded to – I felt exonerated by this – were the medicine bells I brought, which roused him from his trance for long enough that he could open his eyes and gesture at us. Sometimes he even managed to speak or write, to rest his head in Anya's arms. Twice, he pushed himself out of bed to take halting, geriatric steps around the room. On these tours, he asked strange questions – was it now or the future, was he dead or alive – or described some fantastical dream-vision or other: riding a boat between shores, say, or walking through a labyrinth in an ocean of fog. I had to be precise about my instruments. We heard reports of patients in nearby rooms waking startled in the night, or wandering down the corridors, wide-eyed and elated, in pursuit of that beguiling sound. At a certain point, brash with my apparent success, I told Anya that her son might be better returned to us, at Agnes's. Her tone was as frosty as ever.

It may have been the alcohol that did it (its freezing point, after all, is lower than water or blood). Arriving at the ward for a by-now traditional visit, I arrived to find Anya flustered, coat on and her bag on her shoulder, preparing to leave. At a pub nearby, she ordered something to eat, and I got us a bottle of atrocious house red.

'Agnes's *Hospice*,' she emphasized, because the latter word carried morbid associations. One reason she'd been so quick to remove her son, besides that she did not trust me, was her feeling that to allow him to stay would be to condemn him to palliative care – to death. 'This won't surprise you,' I said, 'but you're not the first to think that. I've often wondered if we should change the name, but what to call ourselves? We're not a hospital, not quite a school either, though we *do* teach, of course...'

I had the sense that Anya, whether due to exhaustion, wine, or the stodgy pub meal she'd just eaten, did not want to talk. Sensing a chance to explain our institutional history, and in so doing to defend myself, I continued.

'Agnes', I told her, does not refer to the Catholic saint, the virgin martyr, or the civil parish, but the lesser-known Agnes of Dartmoor. Born in around 900 CE on the edge of the Somerset tin mines, her early years were spent assisting her father in his blacksmithing work. She grew attuned to the Pythagorean music that his hammer-struck anvils made, to the gossip and strife of the miners who returned, or did not, from their work, often singing whilst they did so, and to the women who cooked, cleaned, wove, raised children, and sang. Little is known about Agnes's childhood. Yet there are many stories, not all of which I credit, that she apprenticed herself to her father in her early years, and was making her first instruments — bells and lyres — by the age of ten, and that her earliest music emerged from this time in her life.

'We can change the subject, if you like.'

'I'd rather you spoke,' she said, sinking lower into her seat.

One night around 920 CE, I continued, and not long after her father died, Agnes left home. She later claimed her departure was prompted by 'a ghost at the door', if not the feast: a term once taken literally (a visible spectre came knocking), now commonly interpreted as a reference to the gift. For several years she wandered across these islands. Guided by the dead, she sought the place where the voices were clearest, moving from kingdom to kingdom, settlement to settlement, across a battle-torn Mercia and the Five Boroughs of the Danelaw. Several times, as recorded in numerous plaintive paintings of her gazing out to sea, the gift led her to the limit of the land, beaches and cliffs. We know that she sailed to Wexford, from where she travelled by foot to Connacht. To Agnes's wanderings we attribute the idea that our lives begin with a kind of loss, with lostness. She believed that we are born into a state of incompleteness, desiring to know where we came from, yet lacking means to find out. She attempted to heal this perceived lack with silence and asceticism. She sought counsel in learned academies. None of these approaches worked. I have always imagined Agnes less as a charismatic leader (she is often caricatured that way) than a wandering scholar, driven as much by curiosity as conviction. As had happened with Frau Trauffea, people began to join her. Few textual records remain. Rather songs, stories, and oral histories attesting to the ad-hoc and itinerant spaces she established, and in which they would sing and celebrate, heal and mourn.

'I'm sure *you* know all about this,' I said to Anya, coming back to myself.

She shook her head. She had never been a student, she told me, of Agnes, despite her mother's efforts and references. If anything she made a point of blocking it out, or ridiculing it to belittle its power.

'Agnes,' I said, 'was a historical personage. There was only one of her, as there is only one of any person. Yet she herself claimed that she was not the first and nor would she be the last. She came from somewhere – some-*one* – and would be reborn in other bodies and times, just as melodies recur in certain musical forms. It's from her that we derive our understanding of the harmonic correspondence between the world of the living and that of the dead.'

'Hmmm,' said Anya, pinching the stem of her wine glass.

'Hence the centrality of music to Agnesian rituals, and the formal traditions which Selda herself was inspired by: melodic phrases that repeat and in doing so change, tones that reach towards the perfection of a ghost-note that does not exist.'

'It was also what was happening musically at that time, no? The whole post-war repetition thing... I always thought it had something to do with the internet.'

'The internet didn't exist yet.'

'I know. But I think the minimalists anticipated it. Sometimes their pieces sound like trains or assembly lines or whatever, but what they sound like most of all, to me at least, are algorithms. Well, if we could hear algorithms... Ways of making sense of information, of predicting an uncertain future.'

'Hmmm,' I said, echoing Anya. 'I'm not sure I see it that way myself.'

Erik Satie, I noted, was no stranger to repetition: his aptly named 1893 piece *Vexations* repeats two lines of notes eight hundred and forty times. He referred to it as *musique d'ameublement*, or furniture music, used to cover up awkward silences at the dinner table; a forebear of muzak or 'music for airports'. For Selda, repetition served a deeper purpose. It brought us closer to hearing the world as the dead might: submerged beneath or outside time, and yet vividly present. For some, that aspect of her sound was transcendent. Others just didn't get it. (That is the risk one must take: in reaching for profundity, one may grasp bathos instead.) I was in the former camp, needless to say. Indeed, it was partly by my encouragement that her music took this course...

'What happened to her?'

I gulped. Had she not read the obituaries? Then I realized my mistake – she didn't mean Selda at all.

'Well, I've given you the, ah, the whistlestop biopic, but if we skip ahead, let's see, yes, to 950 CE, give or take, we find Agnes in prison. Since there is no record of her death, however, some have argued that she escaped before the sword fell or the wood was lit, disappearing into rumour, hearsay, music — into conversations, such as the one we're having now, I suppose. Two texts record that her body was burnt on a funeral pyre before the ashes were scattered, but that's all we can say for certain. Well, not certain-certain...'

'Do people... speak? is that the word? with her?'

'Some claim to, yes. The county-fair circuit. Agnes has hundreds of direct descendants, if you take their word for it.'

'Do *you*?'

I glanced at the pub's dull carpet and high, shiny tables, wondering how to reply. 'No. But I think it's fair to say we, the gifted, suffer from a credibility problem. That's been the case throughout history. There are hundreds, thousands of examples of the gifted performing what look, from the outside, like impossible feats of recall and retrospection, but is it ever enough? You must think I'm closer to a duck than a doctor.'

'I'm not sure I follow.'

'A quack.'

Anya raised her eyebrows but did not laugh. She had been temperate with her wine. I, as if to compensate, was rather more Falstaffian, heat rising to my apple-red cheeks as I knocked back another large glass. Perhaps a few dry-roasted peanuts would sober me up.

When I returned to the table, a change had come over her. She seemed almost feral. I wondered what she'd been thinking about in the brief time I'd been at the bar.

'I haven't asked you yet,' she said, 'what you think is the matter with him. Your diagnosis. Do you have one?'

I weighed my options for a moment, but Anya spoke before I did.

'The thing is, Ellen, I've begun to realize something, however belatedly, that I should have known all along. I've been doing with Wolf what I did with my mother. We have our indirect way of talking about the gift but I've not accepted that he has it. Not deep down. I didn't want to lose him, you see, the way I did my mother. And now look.'

'You mustn't feel any blame,' I said. 'It may take time, but he will come back. I promise.'

It was a reckless remark – some wards never return – but I was desperate to comfort her. She seemed about to cry. Instead she turned away and inhaled sharply through her nose, and in that small, self-disciplining gesture I remembered how she'd been as a young child. 'Oh Anya,' I said, 'you poor thing.'

'He's gone somewhere where I can't reach him. And in order to bring him back, if what you're telling me is true, I must accept that he and I are not the same. That he is closer to my mother than I was.'

'Well, I wouldn't put it quite like that...'

I wanted to reach out and hug her, but she would have rebuffed the attempt. In its place I offered a meandering, inadequate account of what I thought might be the problem: that it may have been better to ask *where* and not *what* was at issue because, in my opinion, her son was here and elsewhere. I was seeking, so far as I could, to reassure a mother – yet in doing so I withheld a part of the truth.

72

Had I felt the phrase would not alarm her, the simplest way to put it may have been this: Wolf was in the land of the dead.

Arriving at the hospice later that evening, I reasoned that, since a hangover was already guaranteed, I might as well make the most of it. Instead of heading home, however, I went to my office. After gulping down a whisky soda in double-quick time I poured another, opened the window a crack, lit a few candles and a panatela, and put some music on. I stood for a while on my carpet, swaying like a riverweed, smug with inebriation, and admired my cabinet. It's the only one of its kind in Britain (the 'ringing isle,' as it once was known). I've no idea what it's worth. From end to end and floor to ceiling it stretched, a grid of cushioned shelves and felt-lined alcoves, each one padded to dampen impact and prevent unintentional ringing. The bells themselves ranged in size from thimble to cowbell to saucepan, in colour from smudgy black to burnished bronze, tallow-white to candy apple. Many came from the Agnes foundry: iron bells rung from towers at midnight, bells in whose strange alloys memories were stored, bells of brittle glass hung tinkling from the windows of the mentally infirm, bells of copper, ash, and ice, bells struck on walks through the city's streets and squares to mark invisible boundaries, silverish bells hung from lampposts to remind the living of the hospice's presence... There were dozens, hundreds, some so small a cat could wear them, others big enough to boil said animal alive in, if you turned them upside-down. I thought about playing them all, letting their competing musics clash mid-air. But that would not have gone down well with Enrico, the wards, or the city itself...

I could not settle. When the dorms were dark, I headed

through the hospice's empty corridors and stairwells until I reached the listening booth where, a few nights prior, I had summoned a version of Selda.

What more could I have done to reach her? I removed my hearing aids and ran through the usual listening exercises. I even rang various bells, including some memory bells of my own design. *Come back*, I begged, *speak* – not Selda, this time, but my dead. They muttered and ruffled and turned their capes. They did not heed my call.

I had a theory about what had happened to Wolf and wanted to talk it through with Selda, like we did when we lay on the floor and stared at the ceiling, long into the night. My mind, at least in theory, reverberated with the voices of ghosts. And yet this conversation – with a particular person, recently deceased – was impossible. It has always been this way, a merciless irony.

If I could not discuss the case with them, I could at least with Nasser: we arranged to meet. I dined on cold ham and crackers in front of the television — some mindless wedding-themed reality show — my mind drifting from screen to memory and back again, but more often lost to dullness. At nine, I called a cab. The car app said two minutes. I waited curb-side, in the rain. Five minutes passed. The on-screen car had yet to move. Rainfall drowned out my tinnitus. Not long before, we'd had the snowstorm; that day, the city was drenched by fat drops of rain like warm oil. I cursed my absent mind: my brolly was in the corridor. At last the car arrived. Moisture crawling down the windows. The radio was blaring, I told the driver to turn it off. Spring was a season of increase and renewal. Yet I felt half-dead, a denizen of the shadowlands whose outer reaches Wolf was roaming through. Under the tarmac, decay. Maggots, worms were seething in the lightless place for which my flesh was destined. Those strata of rot and loss were more real, in that moment, than the city we drove through: a dreadlocked courier braving the downpour in cycling shorts, wet leaves catching the stop-lights' glare. Yet I was not dead. Not yet. I wanted desperately to talk with Selda, to tell how it felt to be alive in that moment. So I did. I told her everything. I ranted and praised and complained. Rumbling on the car roof, the wipers squeaking left and right. I know, I know — my promise. I hadn't forgotten. She sat at my side and listened, city lights reflected in her eyes. I looked away from her at last, and for the briefest instant mistook the driver for my father.

Nasser's security guard led me through to the spotless hallway (I had some trouble on the drive, which the rain had transformed into gravel soup). A vast mirror on one side doubled an abstract canvas on the other. Overhead, a chandelier cast warm light on the Edwardian stone of the floor, which was uncluttered except for a red toy truck. A spindly, kohl-eyed teenager clad in black leggings and floaty rags flickered into being at the basement door, a nocturnal creature startled in its lair; she vanished just as rapidly. From the upper floors, a toddler's cry.

Nasser appeared at the top of the stairs, in a cashmere jumper and tracksuit bottoms. Wordlessly he led me through the grand kitchen, which smelled of grilled fish and roasted potatoes, to the dining room in the back, the vast garden visible through French doors. He breathed deeply and often, as though pumping a bellows. Something was off with him. I wondered how his baby was. The house felt unnaturally quiet, as though his loud family were pressing their ears against the door.

'Drink?'

'Brandy, if you have it.'

I wasn't sure whether to feel offended or flattered that he set the whole bottle in front of my glass. He did so clumsily, or pointedly: a hard clunk on wood.

Once we were settled, I told him all I knew. After buying her dinner and wine, I had convinced Anya to send me copies of Wolf's most recent MRI scans, which Nasser examined. His child cried out, and my hearing aid squalled. As a consequence, the only word I heard him say was:

'— done.'

'Pardon? My aid...'

'I don't know what else can be done. Judging from these charts, and what you've told me, they've tried everything I would have suggested.'

'Not *everything*.'

He seemed to think I meant surgery; I assured him that I did not, but that the stranger's last request, before he'd gone under, was precisely that. Nasser sipped his chamomile tea, blinking forcefully, as though the act would banish the sleep deprivation.

'Where did he get that idea from, I wonder?'

'We used to do them at the hospice,' I said. 'I say *we...*'

'But not for half a century or more?'

'Exactly. I've no idea – unless the gift itself.'

Nasser had discussed Wolf's case with a colleague of his, a neurosurgeon based at a university hospital. He related what he'd learned, but the words sounded made up. Serotonin, dopamine: I don't doubt these substances exist, nor that they facilitate the powers of thought that allow doubt to exist in the first place. Yet they sound to me like pure abstractions, verbal mirages, and I've never been able to trust them. 'I'm sorry,' I said, interrupting Nasser. I took another sip of brandy as he looked at the slices of Wolf's brain, coloured clouds moving over its grey landscape. We had competing theories. To my mind, Wolf was with the dead. The gift, in other words, had consumed his mind entire. To Nasser, he was in a state somewhat closer to dreaming: body paralysed, mind alive – but with what?

'Electrical signals,' he said.

He asked about the treatments I had administered, and the atmosphere shifted in the room. I became sharply aware of the smell of brandy, it must have carried on my breath. I mentioned the songs, a botanical tea I had brewed, the several bells I had rung at his bedside – the medicine bell most of all.

'Do you have it with you?'

Before I could say that I didn't, I saw him glance at my sash, where the apothecary's bell was still attached. I explained its provenance to Nasser: the apothecary who made it was an ancestor of mine, he was part of my gift. When Nasser asked to see it, I bristled. I did not think this was a wise idea, its effects could be potent; surely he knew this himself, had attended my lectures and demonstrations? Had a conversation taken place of which I was not aware? I unlatched the bell and handed it to him, watched him examine its chalky-green surface in the light, observe its hollow interior, then hand it back to me.

'Are you sure this isn't the thing that sent him under?'

This, from Nasser, was a shock. 'Of course not.'

'And yet you played it just before he went, as you say, into it. I'm just trying to establish the timeline.'

'I visit him almost daily, Nasser. I stand at his bedside. Those bells are the only thing that bring him back.'

'*Different* bells, though, as I understand.'

How did he understand? Were there spies at the hospital? 'Listen, Nasser... I know we're all stressed, and you've been extraordinarily kind already, so I won't take up more of your time. But this really won't do. If you have something to say, say it. Perhaps the simplest thing is a demonstration. You can hear for yourself.'

I held the bell between us, slowly turning on its short loop of string. I fancied I could already hear it ringing. I tapped it with the metal tine kept for that purpose in the breast pocket of my shirt. Nasser watched the bell's edges blur as the sound rang out and faded to silence. He sat back, frowning.

'There, that's all it is.'

And with that, I stood up to leave.

There was no getting around the ugliness of Nasser's accusation. As I saw it, he had meant to imply that Wolf's trance was my own deliberate doing, enacted through the very object with which I had attempted to heal him. I could only presume that Nasser blamed me for his own, historic trance, which had lasted several months; that he had confused his painful past with Wolf's present, and decided I was responsible for both. In one sense, he may not have been wrong. Then again, something else might have been the cause of his mood. It occurred to me that I hadn't once thought to ask about *his* child. I emailed him. An out-of-office bounced back. Meanwhile, I tried everything to speak with the gift, but I might as well have had the same reply. Had I been deluded to think I could ever hear them? The attunement tests had concluded, had they not, that I was indeed gifted, and only a few weeks before Selda arrived... all the same, I began to mistrust my own past. I fell into a crisis, and I sought solace in reminding myself how we got here.

Millenia ago my ancestors, who were migrants to these isles, lived in clans. In these social formations, they assumed responsibility for the sick, injured, and infirm in a system that we would recognize today as mutual aid. Music was integral to their rituals and entertainments, not only to mark but to solemnize calendrical time.

Between the ninth and eleventh centuries, during which span Agnes was born (reborn, some would argue) and died, social, religious, and mercantile guilds offered security to their members. They did so in a more formalized, and in theory more democratic, manner than clans, since membership depended on application, not bloodline or place of birth. For a time, Agnesianism operated in this way: by application and initiation into a community of knowledge. Security took the form, for some, of employment as musicians and minstrels; for others, it meant the treatment of sickness and injury. All were taught, all passed some knowledge down. When suspicion grew that some among our number were faking it, the attunement tests were devised: a legacy of mistrust, but a useful tool.

After the Norman invasion, guilds retreated into boundaried boroughs; into manors, defined not by clan affiliation but property. In the new, more bureaucratic society established after Domesday, Agnes's followers built the first Agnesian 'chapels', adopting and subverting a dominant terminology: boundaried properties in which to listen and to heal, to encourage interaction between members of a given group, many of them itinerant. Bells, already in use in our attunement tests, grew in popularity during this period. Resonant symbols of change and containment, they functioned as technologies, too – summoning, remembrance, severance, song. Agnes's followers, hitherto a wandering, voluntary bunch, here committed what some purists (I am not one) consider the movement's original sin. They settled. The movement solidified, seeking property and power. Some would argue that, in doing so, they lost sight of – could no longer listen to – Agnes's deepest teachings.

I felt compelled to explain all this to Anya on my subsequent meeting. Perhaps the impulse was defensive: an attempt to convince her of our institutional legitimacy. The weather was fine; we met outside for a walk, ambling close to a duck pond.

'After the Reformation,' I said, drawing my potted history to a close, 'the guilds' wealth transferred to the Crown. Royal hospitals were fashionable under the Tudors – Agnes's Hospital, as it was then known, was patronized by Edward VI. In the fullness of time, specialized hospitals became more common. Agnes's Hospice for Acoustically Gifted Children was born. We've changed considerably, but we're yet to shake the name.'

'Surely you can change it. You run the place. Why don't you?'

I shrugged and said something facetious, but not untrue. 'It's carved in stone above the door.'

An outside consultant visited Wolf and considered him a hopeless case (that judgement, I suspected, was designed to preserve him from an embarrassing fact: that he was out of his depth). Anya took this personally. To her, it was an insult. She was considering other options – those she could afford. They didn't amount to many. I offered to conduct one last attempt to revive Wolf. An Agnesian ceremony, involving a range of acoustical remedies. Not just one bell, but several; not just me, but our community. When they were wary of moving Wolf in his condition (we would have to conduct the ceremony in a suitably resonant space, the one which sprang to mind was Agnes's auditorium). I didn't know how to persuade them, until a question sprang to mind. Had they heard stories of comatose patients who, after however long in their paralysis, could be revived by a familiar song? Something in the structure of music, its pattern, corresponds to how memory is stored in the brain. In certain instances, music can return us to the present (just as it can plunge us into the past). They said they would consider it.

Two days passed. I heard nothing. Then everything came to a head quite swiftly.

The consultant with which they'd been quarrelling misadministered a drip, prompting a harmless but frightening seizure. They would be moving Wolf home.

'Why not come to Agnes's first,' I said, 'and we will attempt one last treatment?'

This time, they said yes.

We set aside an evening the following week, when the auditorium would be empty. I informed Katherine, Enrico, and Leon about the plan, and we set about preparing. Alongside the logistics, however, some introspective work was needed. If I was to be able to fulfil the ceremony to the best of my abilities – if I could not, there was no point in trying – I had to ensure I was properly attuned. I had to dust off the memory bells which I had kept in a suitcase under my bed for years, decades, without using.

—

Dusk was falling by the time I arrived at the off-site chapel, the pavements thick with crowds, gaudy rickshaws lining up along the curb. Theatre lights twinkled and pulsed. Tourist shops glared: Big Ben keyrings, paper masks of royals with cut-out eyes. A small wooden plaque was affixed beside an unassuming wooden door. 'Agnesian Chapel' was etched into the polished oak panel, serif letters picked out in peeling gold. Louder signs advertised yoga, foreign languages, coding classes, kick-boxing. I pushed open the door, which no one on the pavement appeared to have noticed was there.

Coloured tiles and dark wood, a low table crowded with leaflets and flyers. I took the stairs up one floor, finding myself in a crowded alcove lined with books, and a desk with a computer, a cash box, but no one at the chair. Above the shelves, laminated posters had been designed to propagate feelings of safety and calm. The gift was a source of reassurance and protection. One depicted a smiling woman enveloped by benevolent-looking spirits. Another placed a hip young man grinning in a cloud of floating text.

I parted a set of curtains, of a musty, once-purple fabric, to reveal a kind of antechamber, the walls lined with house shrines, those sacred alcoves home to bouquets of herbs and flowers, marbles, wrapped sweets, toffees, toys, old coins, choice pebbles, dried seaweed and theatre tickets. Fairy lights glowed here and there. Despite its air of dereliction, this chapel was still well used. The ones with names attached were sponsored. Agnes had once run a similar wheeze, counting nobility amongst the more lavish sponsors of its shelf-sized, ancestral shrines, in front of which choristers chanted daily.

There was movement behind the next curtain. Behind it stood Howard Kassick.

It took a moment for him to recognize me, at which point he shuffled over, twinkly, crinkled, and professorial, with socks and sandals on his feet. We exchanged the usual pleasantries – I saw him once a year at most – and he asked what had prompted my visit. We communicated mostly via sign.

I see. Would you like me to listen for you?
No, thank you. I just wanted to sit.

Away from the hospice?

Yes.

I pictured him then, as I often did, moving from shrine to shrine and from shelf to shelf on his creaky knees, blowing the dust off fairground mementos, plastic necklaces, books no one would ever read. At Agnes's, he'd been a regular sight in the Jensen Centre, pushing a tank-like trolley around the endless stacks, though his hair, back then, was curly and voluminous. In our last year, he was rumoured to have ingested so many magic mushrooms at a festival near Long Meg and her Daughters that he went missing for forty-eight hours, when he was located by a wandering horticulturalist on the edge of a nearby village, having stripped naked, daubed himself with mud, and climbed a tree.

Can I ring a few memory bells?

Trouble?

Yes. It's sleeping. I think it's gone for good.

It will come back. I didn't hear it for almost a year.

I didn't tell him that it had been more than a decade for me.

The chapel is basic. With its office chairs and strip lights, it hardly looks like one at all. Then again, Agnes herself promoted the idea that a chapel could exist wherever her followers did. The floor was dotted with chairs, dried violets in each corner.

I wanted to ask about our friend.

Friend?

He mouthed it: 'Selda.'

Sad. That limp word was the best I could muster.

I remember her.

So do I.

Younger than Selda and I by close to a decade, Howard had joined Agnes's at a similar time, in the late fifties.

Selda and I had known him well. He met his partner, Daniel, an engineer, after a hospice concert. I sat in a booth to one side of the chapel.

The first memory bell was cast from bronze. It was heavy and domed, shaped somewhat like a bullet. It had been a long time since I'd dared to use a memory bell, let alone several. Since then, they had been gathering dust in a box under my bed, each one padded with rags. I took a deep breath. I exhaled into the metal. And then I struck it with my tine.

My father spoke quietly. He had a warm, slightly plummy voice. Privately educated, an anxious child, he had briefly considered the priesthood; when his sister fell ill with tuberculosis, he settled on a medical profession. He was not always well himself. A skin condition – his 'sin condition', he called it, amusing no one but his Christian self – had blighted his childhood. Even as an adult, it would flare up from time to time, blotches blooming on his scalp, forehead, hands and neck. Their angry antacid pink was rimmed with drier skin that moulted off his hands as he worked (work was a cure for uncertainty). I once stepped onto the landing to see his bedroom door open. He was topless in front of my mother's make-up desk, his braces limp loops at his waist, and he was smearing a thick, opaque ointment resembling petroleum jelly onto his chest, across which an atlas of sore red patches had spread. I never saw him suffer. That seemed to be the rule: to admit to no pain. It was a shock to see him this way, half-naked, vulnerable, doctor to himself. I sat in the chapel and stood beside him, the tones of the memory bell blending this moment and that. And I heard it, as clearly as if he was right there, in front of me, not dead all these years: his subdued speech, his mellifluous manner, his quiet tone calibrated to reassure me — and in doing so belittle, however unintentionally — the man who loved me with such intensity he could not let me live. *Hen... Bed... Now...* And as the tones and their overtones faded, they formed a new arrangement. Now I was on the back seat of his car... we were driving home from one of his patients (sometimes, if my mother was away or unwell, he took me along), the Gladstone bag beside me, the headlamps of his car probing the dark, bringing the smoke-grey road to the surface... until it faded. I returned to the room.

The second bell was again cast from bronze. Yet it was an older and far more delicate model, its surface dinked and scuffed, coloured pollen-orange with mustard blooms like a kind of metallic lichen: I had not seen the effect on any other bell. The sound it made, when struck, was so vivid I felt it flash across my mind, cardinal-red and startling.

You're not his prisoner! Braces! Pills!
This was Selda speaking. The year: 1958 or thereabouts. She was walking down the corridor in Agnes's. My father visited once a week, at the start it had been thrice, to place a wooden spoon on my tongue, stethoscope to my chest; to top up my smoked-glass vials of vitamins. 'You're an adult now, Ellen, you don't need all that fuss and bother. Not until you get married. *If* you get married. I don't think you will. You've got things to get on with.'

It was in the air. I might have absorbed the possibility some other way, by cultural osmosis, despite my sheltered childhood. But how many lives just trundle on, never noticing the things that might transform them, never tuning into that obvious sound which, once attended to, can never be ignored? I did get married eventually, a little impulsively. But the shape of my life, for good and bad, was set in course by a throwaway comment on our way to a lecture on Kepler and cosmic harmony.

The bell's tones shifted, and the memory evolved...

'Ellen, this has gone on too long. I can't stand you being here all the time, hovering – it's too much. All this phoning and letter-writing, all these endless late nights, your negativity! I don't have time for it.'

It was periodic, cyclical. Selda would deny any closeness between us, recast our bond as a suffocating dependency, as though I was the child and she the adult, whereas, from my perspective, the opposite was true. She didn't know her own needs. She'd go days without food, let her hair run wild and greasy. And who would be the one to help her? Did she ever acknowledge my influence? Or did she turn her back on me the moment success came knocking?

The chapel was filled with half-light. People came and went. A visitor broke into song. I felt compelled to join in. Unlike Todd, I did not mind such spontaneous eruptions. They brought me comfort by belittling my pain, making it part of something larger.

We made each other who we became. That, I suppose, is the root of it. We hadn't spoken in years... Our friendship, which had once felt like a kind of emergency, relentlessly in the foreground, had faded and receded. But if you trace it back, to when we were young and unformed... it would not be an exaggeration to claim that we were more important to one another than family, and that the course of Selda's life – certainly mine – were influenced by our friendship in such a small but definitive way that, as our lives went on, it shaped them profoundly. When we met, we were putty and clay; tender, pliable, susceptible to pressure. We taught each other how a person could shape another, and how the aim of that mutual influence, the ideal to which our shaping would tend, was a better version of ourselves. Until we drove each other mad, that is; until we pushed pins, screws, broken glass and bits of manky sawdust deep into each other's putty, deforming its shape. But that was a lesson, too.

I struck another memory bell, this one made from iron. Its deep and doomy resonance was a shadow descending from above, plunging me in darkness.

My life before Agnes's was mostly spent indoors. My psychic environment was structured by taboos and routines. I was endlessly washing my hands. I screamed at sudden noises, slept with a lamp on, took cod liver oil several times a day (that foul taste remains obscurely reassuring), stood mute when strangers spoke to me, crossed myself before leaving the house. I prayed to the gods of my compass, the god of lawn, the god of water, the paper-white god of the mail. Without these prayers, I feared, reality would crumble. Innocuous objects such as wardrobes, wooden spoons, milk bottles, possessed a hidden terror. Stairs were death traps. Sockets crackled with malevolence. The very air was a conspiracy of codes, radiation and transmission. Even window panes seemed to me a species of grenade: a sudden gust could blow them to smithereens, unleashing their latent energy. That not one of these imagined accidents came to pass did not assuage my original fear. Since it was independent of reality, my anxiety could not be calmed by the evidence surrounding me, medicines, bedding, a family. In retrospect my father's kindly but excessive attempts to 'cure' my various ailments, many nervous, only reinforced my intuition that there was, after all, something to worry about. That something was at once acute (specific to me, Ellen Montague) and cosmic (the howling storm of the human predicament). It was heavy stuff, for a young girl.

Selda shifted my thinking. Opened it up.

I never stayed in touch with my brothers. They showed little interest in me, and the feeling was reciprocated. When I tell people I have three brothers with whom I do not speak, they are often surprised, assume that something terrible or scandalous must have happened; that I was ostracized. Only people who have experienced similar estrangements, come from similar homes, understand how effortlessly it can happen. More often than not, we are born into the wrong family. That dissonance is a blessing and a curse, for it drives us to seek new ones, to build homes in other people. Without Selda's influence, I would never have apprenticed at the foundry, developed the memory bells I was using to reach her, met Gerald, joined Agnes's faculty... And without me, she might never have taken her composition seriously in the first place and gone to those early auditions. Or to Muswell Hill, where she met Garth Martin, whom she married in Brighton a few years later: the man with whom she had a daughter, who had a son, Wolf, who showed up at the same doorstep Selda herself had darkened in a different century...

The next memory bell was not much larger than a thimble, yet the sound it produced filled my head with a melodious roar. As the shock of its strike tone faded, it brought trees in close around me and speckled the ceiling with stars.

How many times, at Agnes's, had we kept each other company in the dorms and the Jensen? In the wooden seclusion on the listening booths?

Not that anything 'happened' between us. But it felt different then, not only on account of the whisky or the remoteness, the sense that our gifts were matched, somehow harmonious: we thought of ourselves as distant sisters, blood relatives.

We'd gone on an adventure, after the atom bomb but before the moon landing, the last thing we did together before leaving Agnes's, camping in the woods. A downpour, a deluged tent. I rested my hand on her hip. Between jumper and jeans was a crescent of skin. The bridge of her nose was freckled like the shell of an egg. 'Sing to me.' So I did. I can't remember what song, some kind of lullaby or show-tune; Selda offered a song in return. Three high notes followed by low ones. I was sure I remembered the melody, from the radio, a dance, or somewhere further back. Perhaps my own mother had sung it.

Where's that from?
Don't know.
You do.
Promise.
You made it up?

What I said next, the bell did not know. Something to do with her music, or that remote heroic place in Greenland, the School of Silence, to which she eventually applied in the eighties, and where she began work on *Snow Trio*. In return, she told me to apply to the apprenticeship in the foundry. What's remarkable to me now is that each of us stuck to it, even if, as I'm certain Selda would have agreed, our lives didn't turn out how either of us might have expected. But what lives they were, the direction they took owed everything to that moment, although I hardly understood it at the time, as a stray hair had wound itself around my tongue. Pausing to pull it out, I took the soft lobe of her ear in my mouth. I don't know where this behaviour came from, it wasn't much. It was erotic, more so, I dare admit, than losing my virginity had been, but it was far from sex (which would have been illegal at that time). Indeed by the standards of the sixties, with its breathlessly mythologized but unevenly distributed sexual licence, to hold a close friend's earlobe in my mouth, a coin of flesh whose value was life itself, was a laughably quaint transgression; childish, in fact. But its effects were more dramatic than an outside observer might have guessed. An insignificant moment can have significant ramifications, like the apocryphal butterfly whose wingbeats trigger a tropical storm, or the sound of a shout on a mountainside which, by the time it reaches a listener far down the valley, has acquired the cumulative force of thunder.

Selda and I were not close, properly close, for all that long. Such, however, is the power of influence – the right kind, at a formative time in one's life. Not the dark persuasive influence of those who police social laws, who school you in wearing the acceptable footwear and smoking the correct brand of cigarettes at the right times and places. Or a husband – let's call him Gerald, let's say he was mine – who claims to have seen the very core of your being, a shameful essence, and who presses this knowledge upon you daily, in countless inferences and disappointed looks; who holds that grim mirror in front of your face and says, *don't believe me? here you are, look at yourself!*, a mirror in which your features are grossly distorted yet which you mistake for a terrible clarity, one that strips away the comforts of denial to reveal the pith of misery. It is a mirror of self-destruction. It is a mirror of shit. It is, of course, an illusion. A bad husband can hold it in front of a wife, and if she looks into it long enough, she will forget how to hope. For a while after leaving Agnes, I relapsed into a self-annihilating belief: that I was defective and therefore unworthy of love. A reject, nothing – the mirror of shit. My infantile paralysis was partly to blame. From the start I had believed that, whilst a man might wish to protect me, he would never want me, and that without a man's desire to validate my existence – to stamp a strong form upon my yielding wax; to trap me, as my father's best intentions had, in a paralysis of dependency as insidious as polio – I might as well not exist.

But that came later. That I was able to escape at all owed itself to the moment when I took Selda's earlobe between my lips and gently bit it, as if I could internalize her, make her a part of my body and the life it sustained...

The sound of the bell began to fade, the memory it conjured becoming less distinct. Returning to that moment between an old friend and I had redeemed my sense of history, or what it purports to salvage. As the memory bell rang out in the chapel, I had a vision of the past in its totality. As a kind of monument, inconceivably vast, composed of every brief moment and fleeting sensation. Not a series of partial texts chucked each second and by the skipload onto a pyre of collective amnesia, but a transcendent record in which everything changes and nothing is lost. (The same eternalist concept would appal those who would sooner forget their bad dates and browser histories, or the horrors that history records and conceals.) Yet that moment – once lost, retrieved by the sound of that bell – had sealed a pact between Selda and I, one that seemed to say: remember this moment forever, cling to it forever, hold on, hold on... Estrangement had diminished its urgency, forgetfulness had obscured it from view, but I had not allowed death to break it.

Howard put a hand on my shoulder. How much time had passed? I wondered if I'd drifted off. The chapel was empty. Its half-light had given way to a gloom alleviated only by a few tea lights on a side table. I gazed upon his creased familiar face with love and confusion, unable to speak or think, my head still ringing with the sound of the bells. There was one more in my bag, rough-textured and dark, but I would not ring it yet. He asked if I was alright; I managed to sign *peace* and *empty*. He smiled and nodded; he knew both me and the bell's effects well enough to let me go without further enquiry.

I remember little of my journey back to Agnes's. The hours after the chapel were marked by that sense of unreality that always follows immersion in memory bells. By the time I made it back to the flat, my coat wet with rain, it was past midnight, and I was utterly exhausted. The bells were ringing in my mind, with that distinctive, warping sound that makes one question whether the world one is in, at that very moment, is in fact a memory, too.

In my living room, window ajar, I poured myself a large whisky and lit a panatella. I could not then intuit the significance of the change that had taken place within me, but it felt decisive; as meaningful, in its way, as the remembered moment had been. At Heaven's Knell, when I found myself unable to leave the cab, my paralysis puzzled me. It had continued to do so ever since. Until the memory bells, that is, when I heard the whole thing afresh. I could not face the sight of Selda's body. It all seemed too tragic and horrible. That may have had less to do with her life, however, than mine. Or rather, a life we had shared, and which, in some parallel dimension, we might have shared for longer; a wished-for future which had never come to pass.

There was only one thing for it. I had to say goodbye. And so, when the city felt still, I brought Selda as I had known her to the forefront of my mind. She stood before me, with that fierce, enquiring look, with her kindness and her humour, as she had been here, with me, at Agnes, when we came to know ourselves. I spoke to her firmly, but tenderly too. I told her that I had to let her go. Of course I told her that I loved her; that the end of friendship had not been the end of love. Tears were streaming down my cheeks. My voice began to crack. I looked at her, in her big woolen jumper, her hair awry, her gaze as intense as ever. And then I broke our pact. She looked hurt. But she did not protest, she did not scowl. After a moment, she smiled, returning the silence out of which I had summoned her. At which moment I knew, or at last accepted, that I would never see Selda again.

—

I spent the morning in a daze, neglecting duties, forgetting where my sentences were leading before they had ended, leaving wards and colleagues bamboozled. Yet somehow I managed the wherewithal to summon Katherine and Enrico to my office for an unscheduled lunchtime meeting. Enrico sat at a rakish angle near the window, his arms folded over a white shirt and black jeans. Katherine, seated in front of me, was perched on her chair and tense with apparent concern. Nothing new, for her. Though this time it was directed at me and not a ward. Twice, she asked me if I was alright.

'Quite alright. Why? What's the matter? You're looking at me like I'm wearing a harlequin outfit and spinning noise makers over my head.'

'Well it's just... I don't know. You just seem...'

'A little manic? Well, perhaps. But I'm very much in my right mind. In fact I haven't felt this lucid in years.'

I told my colleagues of my plan. Before the next academic year was out, I would step down as the Agnes dean. They looked at each other. Shared a glance. Then back to me. Enrico objected. Katherine voiced concern. But my mind was made up; I had felt a great weight lifted when, upon waking this morning, I saw my future laid out in front of me. I asked Katherine if she would be my replacement, with Enrico as her deputy. Again they looked at each other, and back to me. 'See,' I told them, 'you're already behaving as one.'

'Has something happened?' Enrico asked, sitting upright. His chair creaked, and I fancied that a bell in my cabinet let out a brief and muffled chime.

'No, nothing,' I said. Which was true; and yet, in the same breath, everything had.

'I'll need to think it over,' Katherine said. 'I'll need to talk with Enrico about it, too.'

'Fine,' I said, 'fine. But my mind's made up. Now, about this evening...'

All I could think about, for the rest of that day, was the ceremony, which was due at seven that evening, and the procedures for which I had consulted several books in the Jensen Centre, under the banker's lamps Selda basked under when sketching music. Once the day was over, I went straight to the auditorium. With Enrico's help, we readied the stage, playing tuning forks, waiting, listening... had any one seen us, they would have thought us deluded, or perhaps just the very most avant of the garde.

When Wolf at last arrived, delayed by city traffic, we transferred him from the wheelchair and onto a camp bed in the middle of the stage and clipped a heart-rate monitor to his finger. I waited, thumbing my hare's head cane. On the floor of the stage were a few scattered lamps, rather than the unforgiving rigs we employed for concerts. Anya and Todd stood at his bedside. Darcie was in charge of a group of wards who had volunteered to help, if only because of the spectacle, trailing extension cables across the flagstones, plugging in lamps and microphones. Enrico set up two cymbals at the head of the gurney; they brought to mind the Catholic practice of placing candles at the head of a corpse. I set up a station at his feet, a stool and a table on which I had a brace of bells. The auditorium to my left, with its rows of velvet seating, resembled a vast dark cave: it brought a half-formed memory to mind, though I could not place it. We gathered around the bed, framed by the crimson curtains and the proscenium's faded gold. City noise filtered in through an open fire door: I instructed Darcie to close it. Eyes were on me. I thought of Selda and felt like a fraud, a wicked old bitch whose deceptive sin had been to convince the world, if not herself, that she was making things better. Well, at least I knew where I stood. Lamps were glowing on the boards, which were in need of fresh varnish. I felt the moment between my teeth.

'Everyone ready?' I snapped my cane on the boards of the stage. The clap rang out in that still air. 'Then let's begin.'

The ceremony called for a piece of music which held a particular connection to the gift. It had been Anya's idea to play parts of *Snow Trio*, and the moment she had suggested it, I knew that she was right. There was a longish pause during which nothing happened. I stared at the pages on the stand. Enrico's bow rested against the cymbal, his head bent forward, his enormous eyes closed, the lenses catching the glow of the lamps... Then he began to play, the bow's vibrations moving through the metal and making it blur, as my medicine bell had at Nasser's. A sense of calm pervaded my body. At that point, Katherine, who was standing beside me, and in front of a group of wards, breathed into her clarinet and held a note. The sounds blended in the air, and as they did I felt the atmosphere thicken, brighten – and all at once, the gift returned. It spoke and sang around us. My cane fell to the floor: I needed both hands. I played a once-broken bell I had fixed with Selda's guidance, its onyx panels fused in place by molten gold. I played a tin bell forged near Ypres. Two glass bells from Zambia.

Last of all, I played a very particular memory bell. It was one of an identical pair I had forged here at Agnes's, perhaps the dearest of all my instruments. It was fairly small, about the size of a mug, with figures embossed round its rim, and cast from a rough, blackish alloy. Selda had the other. I had not played it in the chapel because I feared its effect on me.

And perhaps with good reason. For that moment, something changed. Whether anyone but me witnessed this, I do not know, but it seemed that others were on the stage with us, more than seemed likely or even possible. I smelled burnt pine and bay, hot metal and glacial water. I remembered things I had not lived through: heady vistas, bloody battlefields, wooded villages, dark valleys. For the briefest moment, the auditorium opened on a vision of itself: a mirror in which the moment we were living through was doubled and redoubled, containing all the rooms it had ever been or would be, past and future merged, strike tones and overtones blending mid-air. I lost any sense of proportion, and must have blacked out.

I came to a moment later. Darcie, leaning over me, held

water to my lips. *Snow Trio* had not stopped. Far from it: all the wards were singing now, every voice raised, and it no longer felt like a concert hall but a moor upon which we had gathered with Agnes, with all the world's shades, to sing. I struck the memory bell again, heard it resonate with the other musics in the room, reaching a new pitch of dissonance.

Just then, there was a creaking sound. My memory bell rolled off the table, hit the floor, and split in two. An ugly crash, then silence – and Wolf sat up.

II. WOLF

I. THE WILL

When my mother tells me that her mother's body has been found, not long after the snowstorm, I quit my matinee shift at the Everyman, pack my bags, and cross town. By the time I arrive, it is sunset. Bottles of champagne and water crowd the kitchen table with jugged roses and candles. My mother is beside the open window in a white shirt and dark jeans, her hair loose around her shoulders, looking more stunned than upset. I hug her tight. We'll talk properly later. Todd, sturdy and blond as a labrador, decants champagne into an assortment of incongruous drinking vessels, humming as he does so. I take a drink and we hug for a while. My mother's friends arrive one by one until, around ten, we're throwing a small party. More fizz and flowers. More laughter-and-tears-and-laughter-and-tears in kaleidoscopic cycles. We tell stories we've been telling forever and which we enjoy because we know how they end. How Selda was born in the Coventry Blitz. How her father and mother met. Great uncle Charles who died in the war. My mother's birth during a power cut, candles illuminating the ward. The premiere of *Snow Trio*, how the audience got lost on the way to the venue and almost missed the show. Her cigarettes. Her laughter. Her drinking. I've never seen my mother smoke before, but there she is, lighting a snout off a candle, exhaling smoke through her teeth. Peculiar sensations pass through my body. They aren't unpleasant exactly, just strange, like gravitational fields or low-frequency noise: they warp my sense of space and time. At midnight, at my mother's suggestion, all the guests stand in the kitchen, lights low, where we join in an Agnesian chant. I haven't sung in this way for years. The practice has always seemed utterly stupid and mortifying to me.

Our voices rise and blend in the air between us, over the empty bottles and hardened wax and scraps of tinfoil. In doing so, we attune to one another. At which point, something shifts – though it might just be the shock, the wine, the smoke in my eyes.

Shortly afterwards, my mother and I are alone in the front room. My mother squeezes my hand.

'Will you promise me something, Wolf?'

'Anything.'

And I will. If she asks me to do something extreme, murder my father, tear my spleen out, sew my mouth shut with twine, I will commit to it without so much as a blink. All she asks for, in the end, is secretarial assistance. Arranging the funeral, talking to the solicitor.

Of course, I tell her. Anything. I offer to move in, take my old bedroom, deal with the calls, the forms, the bookings, the lawyers. She rests her head on my shoulder.

'And you,' she says, 'you're alright? No migraines?'

I straighten my spine. 'No,' I say. 'Why?'

'No reason,' she says, and she lifts her head. 'I just thought...'

'I should be asking if *you're* alright.'

'It is the right order of things,' my mother says, squeezing my hand. 'It's not a child death. It's the right way round.'

The next day, I pack a suitcase and move in. It doesn't feel like a regression. If anything, our roles have reversed. I shop in the mornings and cook in the evenings, cleaning up as I go along. When the phone rings, I answer. Colleagues, friends and lovers offer their condolences, fond memories: that time Selda started 'raving' to techno in public, or bursting into song, her random good deeds, her Muttley laugh. A few voices bawl like the divas they are. Almost everyone uses the phrase *a great composer*.

Others remember Selda as being *wonderful*, which genericism betrays that, whilst many admired her, few were close to her.

Condolences first. Then questions.

Yes, I am her grandson.

No, we don't know what she was doing alone in the snow or why she had a bell in her hands. I hadn't spoken to her in months, hadn't seen her in over a year – I don't tell the callers these details. Rather I construct, by omission not direct lie, the impression that we were close 'til the end and that I was devoted.

I respond to questions with my own.

When was the last time you spoke to her? Do you know what she was doing in her final months, weeks, days? Who was she with, where was she going? Did she ever talk about my mother and I? Did she seem *okay*? Healthy, happy, sane? Had she begun to forget things, dates, names, places? I am concerned for her in a way I would be for someone alive, someone lost.

Or: I am absolving myself of guilt.

What do I want them to tell me? *There was nothing you could have done.* Would I believe them?

Oriana Armstrong, a mezzo-soprano, speaks in a dusky, melodious growl. Her speech is punctuated by frequent pauses for breath, and muffled trumpet-honks as she blows her nose into a napkin. She has an idea what Selda was up to ('Something important, oh. MAGNIFICENT.') but insists she must relate it to me in person, as if the information is too explosive for the line. I arrange to visit her Wiltshire manor in the coming days.

Blanks and contradictions. Selda was in high spirits, say some, her headstrong and hilarious self. To others, she was catatonically depressed. She'd given up writing music, and she was working on her magnum opus

– her most ambitious piece yet. What do these vignettes, rumours, anecdotes, prejudices, misapprehensions, and half-truths amount to?

A dancer she once worked with asks: Did she leave any work behind?

I don't know the answer. She may have.

Someone asks if the gift will pass to me.

The question makes me tense. Never mind that the gift is with a person from the start, that it waxes and wanes, good months and bad, that some never notice it and others can't think without crutches, blister packs of prescription pills. I try not to think about it too much, but the attempt at suppression is ironic at best. Try not to imagine a polar bear, said Dostoevsky, and the cursed thing comes to mind every minute.

Selda always insisted the answer was yes, *you have it too, Wolf. Once I'm gone, you'll hear them like never before.* Was that the missing part of the statement, *when I'm dead?* She was just being Selda, wasn't she? Archetypical eccentric. Old woman alone in the middle of nowhere drinking wild nettle tea, writing music for ghosts.

I did and I did not believe her. Her delusions were true.

According to family legend, Selda christened me on the maternity ward, before I'd even opened my eyes. She took me mewling in her arms and spoke the name of a creature which, if this was a fairy tale, would have swallowed her whole, worn her bonnet to bed. There's a different name on my passport, but everyone calls me Wolf now. So when my mother calls my 'real' name one morning, I sense that something's wrong. On the kitchen table is an envelope, plump, official-looking. 'I don't know how I could have missed it,' she says. 'It was mixed up with a couple of cards. I couldn't sleep, so I came down to tidy. I just found it.'

'What is it?'

'It's from her solicitor. Look, the address on the back.'

I spoke to him two days ago. A steady, patrician voice. Reassuring, almost diffident, about the legal procedures of death.

My mother slits it open, the knife greasy with butter from the toast she just made. I watch her from the kitchen for a moment, reading, biting her nail. She beckons. I follow her into the winter sun.

Selda's will and testament has the feel of her late-career music, precise and enigmatic. She has requested an Agnesian funeral and left instructions on where to scatter her ashes. This latter part reads most like a score, with its list of locations, durations, song choices and so on, planned to the minute. It begins at midday in Bell Hall, heads through the forest towards a beach, and ends in her favourite local, a low-ceilinged place called The Boatman's Rest. Her final request is that we stage a performance there.

'See, she's controlling us even now, from beyond the grave!' my mother says, pacing around back and forth across the lawn. I laugh and she does too, a buried pressure finding release.

'I can't remember how we're meant to do it,' she says. 'We'll have to look up the rules.'

'Nor can I.'

'So we're off to a good start, then.'

Christian and Jewish funerals, the only other kind I've been to, have involved speeches and eulogies and hymn-sheets and prayers, followed by the parts I liked best: in pubs, under white marquees, the buffets were often sadder than the mourners – dry sandwiches, toy-size pork pies, and pickled fish, tables tacky with spilled champagne, the mirrors draped with sheets. Old friends, subdued rivalries. Heavy boozing. The only other Agnesian funeral I attended – I can't have been older than seven – seemed anarchic by comparison.

It was in Budapest, I think. I recall an enormous river, steely turquoise, down which freezing winds blew, and squat reddish buildings topped with turrets and copper domes studded with stained glass, and narrow alleys, and squares around which pigeons swirled and settled, and doors leading into restaurants pungent with duck and spiced cabbage. Selda – it must have been her – led us into a chapel on the edge of a public park. It was a small and unimpressive building, grey, sparsely furnished, a kind of cave. People gathered for what felt like hours. In the centre of the space was an open casket raised on trestles, its lower half draped in embroidered cloth. The top of the coffin was open. Inside, the walls were lined with spotless white satin; its sheen resembled mother-of-pearl. The fabric, faintly iridescent, lent a clean look to the corpse, as though it had been dropped off by the tailor who'd made the suit. It, or he, was both object and man: the eye-sockets deep, his cheeks concave, the coral lips so stiffly pursed I wondered if they'd been glued. Before we got there, I had feared seeing a body, but needn't have. The most unsettling aspect was how still he was. I kept expecting the eyelids to twitch, his chest to rise or fall. I knew that he was dead. Here was the supreme evidence of the fact. The waxen flesh was categorically distinct from a living person's despite my never having seen a dead person before. Wasn't some part of him still alive? His voice – it was meant to be with us, floating unseen in the air. In my child mind, death was not an end but a stepping behind a curtain, and a kind of ventriloquism.

Without warning, a person began to hum. It may even have been Selda (I remember her fake-fur coat). And for an instant, the myth was alive: the voice in the air was the dead man's, trembling like a cello note. Then other people started joining in, as they had in my mother's kitchen. The room filled with living voices. And, perhaps, those of the dead.

A month ago the country was snowbound. Icicles clung to windowsills. Stretches of the Thames became Victorian postcards, children trailing scarves as they glided and collided across the blue-white ice. Now it's so warm that daffodils pierce the dry dirt. The branches above our heads are dotted with black, plasticky buds. Hip-hop thumps from a car parked two streets over as I read Selda's will. She has donated half her money, whatever is left of it, to Agnes's Hospice for Acoustically Gifted Children. I recognize the name but can't place it. An orphanage? A hospital?

'Not exactly,' says my mother. 'A music school, but for people like her.'

'What's her connection?'

'She was there for a few years. She was young. It had a different name back then.'

'It was an insult, though. *Gifted*.'

'When she was little.'

Selda has left Bell Hall, its contents, and what remain of her savings, to my mother, as well as any further royalties (they won't amount to much).

She has left me three items: her upright piano, her Fiat Punto, and her papers. Her car, nearly thirty years old, is testament both to her atrocious driving and her supernatural resilience, though it might have been luck: a patchwork of dents, scratches, and repairs which, by some miracle, she never wrote off. She kept her piano for sentimental reasons. Some connection to her father, I don't remember what. But she rarely played it, at least to my knowledge. It makes a honky-tonk sound that no amount of tuning can repair. Papers, though. That's a mystery.

'Your guess is as good as mine,' my mother says. 'Maybe she wrote a memoir?'

We burst out laughing. I don't know why. Growing up, I was vaguely aware that Selda was famous. Or as famous as an experimental composer, who happens to be a woman, is ever likely to get (barely, in other words). But I never knew about her life in any detail, her early life hardly at all. Though she was full of anecdotes about her working life, salacious gossip delivered in gleeful whispers, she dismissed her own childhood as *nothing special*, and changed the subject whenever I asked. I knew that something was being hidden from me, even if, a child myself, I could not understand its true nature. Yet her evasiveness on the subject only heightened my curiosity. I compensated for lack of knowledge by imagining what it might have been like for her in Coventry under (as I pictured it) the coal-smog hanging low over bombed-out buildings, the streets dazzled by theatre marquees, that janky old piano and her mind alive with music.

'I have a favour to ask,' my mother says. 'It's about the house. Bell Hall.'

That sound, the doubled Ls – a fiction. The building didn't have a name when she bought it. It was a tumble-down farmhouse surrounded by fog, a granite heap that hadn't been occupied, except by spiders and mice, in months. But to her it looked perfect: pine forest, fields, the wind carrying rumours of saltwater and storm, a decent pub to be walked to and staggered back from on foot. Not a real big house, but an image of one.

'I'll have to go back. That might sound obvious to you. But would you join me? I don't think I can manage it alone. All those boxes and things. Todd would come, but he's tied up with work.'

'Of course.'

Selda's parents were lower-middle class, I'm pretty sure. Her father was a clerk at a clothes factory, or a rubber factory, I forget. Her mother worked for a time as a nurse. Her career, in any case, complicated her class identity: rough diction, big house; dragging her no-degree self to Royal Opera House soirees. Music had been a way out, or up. As much had been true, in theory at least, since the eighteenth century. (She would at times compare herself to Leonard Bast in *Howards End*, predicting that her cultural ascent would meet its abrupt, inevitable demise at the hand of an irate aristocrat.) Why Bell? An ancient Agnesian symbol: birth and death, work and renewal, and so on. Hall sounded grand. And if you were drunk, muddled the syllables, it conjured a sulphurous mirror-image: demons cavorting in Regency garb, shadows flung by candles up the walls – the Hell Ball.

'It'll be a lot of work, that's the thing,' says my mother.

I want to know what precious heirlooms we will find, but under my greed lurks fear. When I was little, the gift was always strongest down there. I put it down to being near Selda.

'Just tell me when.'

'After, I think.'

There's a beat before I grasp what she means. 'Of course. We'll do that first. Do it properly.' Why can't we say *funeral*? The thought makes images, memories, see-saw. I see a house on fire, a boat floating under the moon.

'Of course. Yes. Everything.'

That's that, then. Settled. 'Does Garth know about it,

by the way?' A measure of how distant he feels from my life, compared to Selda, is that it's only just occurred to me that someone ought to tell him. But my mother has, he's ill again, she doubts he'll make the flight.

I've not been to Bell Hall since – I can't remember. I was fourteen, I think.

What *do* I remember?

Forest paths, spiderwebs, wet socks, evil hum in the basement, wanking at night hoping no one will hear, Mozart's *Requiem*, burnt sausages, the purr of rain, city riots on the nightly news, transferware plates, lightning slicing the night in half, an oilskin coat hanging up in the hall, fury in a hot red room, wanking again, plate exploding like a shot clay pigeon on the dining room wall...

Why did she walk into a snowstorm like that?

To answer that question, I'll have to put my deerstalker on, and follow her. Find out where she died and go there, see what I can see, work out where she might have been aiming for. It feels important. Don't know why. Evidence, clues. More than that: so that I can be beside her.

TOO LATE

done now, finished now, all gone

he knows what happened, dead

said she'd never return

didn't think that she meant it

o it's late but at least it's not never

I push a pill out of the blister pack and swallow it down.

what'll he find?

bones gold clothes mould

'What will we do with it?'
'Sell it.'

so much for the generations

'I had an idea. We could turn it into something. A school, maybe. Or a museum.'
'A museum?! For what? *Her*?'
'It was just an idea.'
'We can't afford to keep it going. You know what we'll find, don't you? It'll be like one big junk shop.'

The garage in her childhood home was stuffed with instruments, with trumpets, trombones, lutes, gongs, cor anglais, cigar-box guitars, tablas, and soon her parents were forced to park the car on the street, grumpy Garth plucking tickets and dead leaves off the windshield every morning before driving to the lab. In 1977, outside the premiere of William Walton's *Prelude for Orchestra*, which Selda was professionally obliged to attend despite loathing the composer's music, he collapsed, was rushed to hospital, and fell into a coma. Diabetes ran in his family – two of his relatives had died from the same condition – which fact emerged only after he'd recovered. (Selda joked that what made him sick was Walton's 'atrocious melodies'.) That he did nothing about the condition, until at last it did something about him, was testament to my grandfather's powers of denial. So too, I suspect, did whatever behaviours drove Selda, a few months later, and for reasons which have never been completely clear to me, to leave him with my mother in tow. The space my grandfather occupied was given over to instruments, the box room that might have been his study piled high with guitars, tape decks and synthesizers, his favourite armchair now home to a fatherly double bass. My mother shared a bedroom with a Rhodes piano, a drum kit, a bass oboe, a fleet of banjos. A cello stood mute in the downstairs loo, rendering it near-inaccessible. According to her, these instruments had lives of their own, violas and radios, synthesizers and cymbals blarting crashing jangling on their own accord, or discord, as Selda moved around the house.

'Alright,' I say, 'we won't know what state it's in until we get there, anyway...'

We plan out the next few days. Selda has left instructions for the funeral. A modest ceremony, which she would like to involve laughter and drinking. *No sombre clothing or facial expressions.* People will gather and sing and be merry. She has requested a chapel with a ludicrous name, Heaven's Knell, an hour or so's drive from her home. In a few days' time, we will drive to Bell Hall and perform the formalities. I will visit the coroner, collect Selda's last effects from the morgue. The rituals will follow. Honour the life, burn the body, empty the house, scatter the ashes, sing the songs. And in between, some drinking.

Once it's over, once we're back, the gift will fade.

Days from now, this will all be over.

'One last thing,' my mother says. 'This piece she wants us to play at her funeral, we'll have to get someone to sing it. She didn't really expect *us* to, did she? Perhaps we can ask people who rang...'

'I'll do it,' I say, without thinking. I can think of few things more embarrassing. Until, absurdly, I get to my feet and start nodding. 'Absolutely. Yes. I'll do it.'

Dash, a friend from the antediluvian schooldays when we cracked these jokes dozens of times per day, texts to point out that I *literally live in [my] mum's house* now. A vintage playground cuss. It might normally elicit a snort of laughter, and bring me into contact with something beyond these walls, the rituals they contain. But the world that I usually inhabit feels distant and muted now, if not totally irrelevant. Life is no longer located where it used to be. It now exists in the shadowlands between Selda and I, an agile thing, flickering just out of reach.

Later that night, when the house is empty, and my mother and Todd are at a dinner party, I go in search of it. In the empty living room, surrounded by flowers in vases of greenish water, I scour the internet for news and reaction. Someone, I've no idea who, transposed Selda's Wikipedia entry into the past tense within an hour of me hearing the news (I joined the site so I could edit the page, would check it once a month or so: I never told Selda about it). A music magazine has run an obituary-listicle of her top-five compositions, the 'Black Glass Aria' from *Snow Trio* is at number one.

Hyperlink by hyperlink, click by click, I approach a subject I've been deliberately avoiding for years.

Speculation as to what the gift might be, where these ghosts 'live', is rife. An old theory held that we, the gifted, knew the dead the way prophets knew God. If it could be explained or rendered audible to others, then it wouldn't be authentic: evidence would have refuted the claim. During the Renaissance, surgeons would examine our corpses, seeking out the crevices in the sinews, hidden places in vein and bone in which these voices spoke. Finding no obvious home, they declared the gift 'swam in the bile'. Selda herself contended there was nothing different about 'us'. Everyone had the gift, she argued, to greater and lesser degrees. Everyone's ancestors ring in their head.

Growing up, *migraines* was the euphemistic name my mother and I gave the episodes I could fall into, if only for a minute or two at a time, and which the literature knows, for whatever reason, as *maladies du mort*. In a few Agnesian sects, these dangerous states were deliberately cultivated, in pursuit of forbidden knowledge, as if the mental weather wasn't stormy already.

I pace the room and rub my eyes. Since I heard the news, waves of strange feeling pass through me. I picture them warping space-time, dark heavy rains that fall from a great height, or walls of sonic pressure. I put a CD on – the shiny discs feel almost as antiquated now as wax cylinders – lie down on the carpet, watch the white ceiling as *Snow Trio* plays.

Opening notes cascading coldly through the air. Glockenspiel, marimba...

But it's not the right piece. I play something earlier instead, a motet from 1981.

Selda first wrote for voices in the late seventies, when her early, procedure-driven music had begun to loosen up, allowing room for improvisation and chance.

Technology had something to do with it. She expanded her exploration of canonical forms and approaches – counterpoint, madrigal, fugue – to tape decks, synthesizers, samplers, and even (to the horror of some) drum machines. But it was thanks to that ancient and relatable technology, the human voice, an instrument older than flutes carved from bone, that attention came her way.

There were recitals, recordings, commissions – thanks in no small part to a Faustian pact with her agent, Kristian Rose, a svelte Swede who she assumed on account of his name was a Rosicrucian. He was more closely connected

with ad execs and film producers than alchemical broth-
erhoods. In the eighties, Selda's music, which had hitherto
played in dingy basements, car parks, and stages built
from packing crates, if at all, began lending gravitas to arthouse soundtracks, TV spots: something of its
urgency and mystery seemed eloquent of the moment,
or a balm to its speed and excess. Two years after *Snow
Trio*'s premiere, at the turn of the Millennium, she won
the Varèse. My mother and I flew to Cologne for the
ceremony. An orchestra performed a new work of hers
in a theatre built from gigantic pillars of what my child's
eyes saw as solid, burnished gold, impossibly upheld by
ribs of polished wood and ebony, the chandelier glinting
overhead.

Everyone's account stops there, at the recognized
zenith: resplendent ceremony, trophy hefty enough to
function as a murder weapon – as indeed it had in the
case of Prosper Rossi, whose lover stoved his head in with
one during a row. No one ever mentions Selda's decline
when, for reasons she never explained, she announced
she would stop writing music.

Nor do they acknowledge the cruel and lurid rumours
that began to circulate around this time, about how she
was blind, demented, and drank her own urine, how she
guzzled drugs washed down with moonshine in a house
overrun by wild cats, how she worshipped bundled twigs
and called them pagan deities, how, in a fit of madness
one tempestuous afternoon, she cleared out her savings,
in cash, and burnt it all in an Agnesian ritual, or how she
drifted along the shoreline in a damp black veil, her long
hair lank as bladderwrack, mermaid purses trailed in her
dress, wailing of sailors cremated at sea, sundered lovers
and plague-ravaged towns, fathers drawn and quartered
fighting the English invaders. That these stories reflected

114

their tellers' prejudice, more than truth about her, escaped me when I was little.

She was *tired of music*.

I think she meant the business, the starched shirts and crappy contracts, but not the form and the feeling it brought.

In her twenties – influenced by Stockhausen, the Vedas, her peers' performance art, Agnesian rituals, the gift – she decided she would create 'acoustic situations' rather than symphonies, songs, and so on. Listeners created meaning as they moved through her pieces, she reasoned. They were environments to explore, not paintings on the wall of time.

Such generosity, if that's what it was, did not extend to explanation. Her public remarks were gnomic and far between.

No beauty but in sounds was one.

Did she care to elaborate? Selda did not.

Nor did she wax on about her influences. Consciously or otherwise, she was echoing Cage's *Silence*: 'No purposes. Sounds.' And her approach to form if not harmony belied the influence of Schoenberg, for whom art should not adorn, but instead be truthful. I remember her quoting Byron: *There is music in all things, if men had ears; / their earth is but an echo of the spheres.*

How to square this with her love of doo-wop and barbershop? Did it need squaring at all?

There was a streak of the fifties tearaway in her, a rebellious immaturity. Spite, sometimes, and a prideful insecurity. In the long shadow cast by the Bomb, she followed quantum theory with interest. To conceive of the universe as a jangle of subatomic tensions, infinitesimal orchestras performing reality's discord, made instinctive sense to her. That a particle could exist in two places at

115

once, by contrast, seemed to her a far stranger and less intuitive phenomenon than the ability to speak with the dead.

She held formal musical theory in disdain, perhaps because she'd never received much herself. (She'd received it later, whether she wanted it or not, from the critics.)

I'll give you a music degree in two words, she offered in a speech to a music college after it awarded her an honorary degree, *and save you the bother and the boredom, not to mention the fees. Tension and release.*

These were the primordial forces out of which music was born. Jackpot and liquidation, the green shoot and the canker, sex and death. Tension could arise and be resolved in a blink or a thousand lifetimes, in a scratched itch or the fall of Rome. These were her materials. Push, pull. Not binaries, exactly, but inextricable energies: space-time and life-death. I knew from her library how much she loved Blake: without contraries, no progression.

A better term for music may have been *noise*. The audible trace of chaos that reminds us that we are mortal, powerless, and alive. (She had a weakness, as quoting Byron suggests, for grandiosity.)

Noise was the excitation of otherwise smooth transitions, the buzz of random events disturbing illusions of order, the grinding of broken spheres and fallen orbits, where cosmic order formerly obtained. A discomposed or decomposing universe. Its harmonies marred by bombs and death-camps. Smokestacks, cocaine, credit cards, pornography, wanting to fuck Ronald Reagan.

She was less interested in dissonance resolving in harmony than pattern emerging from disorder. And its mirror-image, entropy. She was sometimes labelled a post-minimalist for her emphasis on rhythmic repetition which, paired to melodic shifts, resulted in her mesmerizing *situations*. She herself was wary of pattern.

Or a certain type of pattern. She disliked genres of art – minimalism, optical art – she deemed anaesthetic, too clean.

Grids kill the mind.

That was another of her utterances. I guess she felt that music you could control to that degree was untrue to life. (This was her later position: her earliest works were all pattern, stiff grids.)

The bars on prison cells were a kind of pattern. Fascism was all pattern, arbitrary and inflexible. An intolerance of tension – *disgust* of tension – manifested in certain minds as a will to subjugate others, to obliterate noise. That brittle will was enforceable only by marshalling negative energies. Hatred, denial.

Squashed sounds had a habit of bouncing back in other forms, a tremble in the air, a high whine in the ionosphere. The gift knew this.

All of which skirts the question of what her music *sounded* like. Repetitive and hypnotic, intimate and grand, moving in and out of western and twelve-tone scales to create all manner of unusual harmonic effects. I admired her music more than I really enjoyed it. Growing up I wanted songs that moved me physically, that made me rock my head and move my feet, slow techno, American hardcore, industrial noise and jangle pop, I didn't care about the genre, all I asked from music was that it broke a frozen lake or lit a fire. Growing up, it seemed to me that her music was secondary to, or illustrative of, something more complex and self-involved, a grand scheme of dark immensity, the complexity of which exceeded her being and mine, but which connected us somehow.

She wanted to know where she came from. Where she ended and others began.

Family was a kind of music, inheritance a kind of pattern. Parents, who were children themselves, having children, passing it down, again, again, tinkering, mutating, a fluke, a shift, a defect, something new. Life was noise. But *a* life – that was melody. It conformed to a musical shape. We don't know the song but we know how it starts and ends. Out of and back to silence.

I turn off the music. The house is quiet.

Lying in the dark, I try to still my mind.

There is a jerky, creaking feeling in my chest, as of a rusty cog being turned, a tightness in my temples and a dryness in my throat. In the end, the shift isn't much of a shift at all. The gift is right there, under my tongue. It never left.

Should I be worried?

about...?

swinging axes plucking pheasants pouring poison down your well

Talking with you.

ha!

how could we hurt you, boy?
can you see touch feel us?

Sometimes. Active in my knuckles, knees and guts, staining my vision with rage, making me hard for no good reason. Like a form of possession.

always a reason

> *you're the last singer*

> *if you go silent*

> *so does the song*

Parasites?

> *so is everything that lives*

But you aren't alive. Don't you know your Parmenides?
Being is and not being is not.

> *why professor, you humble us*

> *ever cut off a leg with a hacksaw in a field tent, boy?*
> *now THAT'S knowledge*

So what are you, then? Spectres, figments, proof of my
insanity?

> *you've asked us this a million times*

> *truth be told we ah, um, we don't know*

You don't stop talking. Ever. You're there when I wake,
you murmur to me in my dreams.

Who did Selda say we were descended from, where we
came from, who we *are*? I've forgotten. We're Irish and
we're English: we colonized ourselves?

All the eccentric advice you gave me growing up, it
hardly amounted to applicable wisdom. Never trust a
Smith with a shilling. If a Jones crosses your path, cut
him down. Shelter any red-headed bairn by the name

of Denning. Stories hard to stomach and impossible to verify because these unrecorded events took place before Domesday, before the invention of writing let alone the discovery of bronze. What about the silences? The things not said, ugly stories you'd rather stay buried. Give me your guilt, your unfinished business, make me mop up the spilt guts and bad blood? I refuse. I owe you nothing. The crack of the whip, the flutter of merchant sails, dogs on the hunt – who *are* you?

family

Don't buy it. How far back is it meant to go? Do I follow the lines to the Ice Age, the savannah, bacteria that colonized cells in the backward of time, ocean, stars, the early universe? Specifics, please. Name, birthday, address, income: material facts. Selda told me some, but, okay, so I've forgotten. In any case, that was her gift, not mine. I've never thought to ask you before. I've never liked you, actually.

we've noticed

But it's us, now, trapped.

where?

Here.

Mercia?

Me. So we might as well get acquainted.
Tell me. When did you live?

mnrnph... cccan't rumememburrrrr

What *do* you remember, then?

They wash over me. Voices. Each anecdote, detail, and cry a drop in a wave crashing in through the windows, collapsing the ceiling and the walls, washing the furniture into the garden, a howl so loud it sounds like nothing, the dull thunder of blood in your ears as you sink below the surf.

II. ORIANA

The coroner fogs the lenses of his glasses with his breath, then rubs them with a napkin. Heat shimmers off multiple radiators. There's a faintly rancid, waxy smell from all the polished dark-wood furniture.

'She was an impressive woman,' he says. 'I particularly enjoyed her soundtrack to... oh, I've forgotten it. That film about the dancer, the one set in Berlin?' He replaces his glasses, which catch the light of the window behind him, picking out a fingerprint smudge in the lefthand lens. 'Very moving piece.' He notices the smudge, repeats the procedure.

'Zagreb,' I say.

One of only two films that my grandmother soundtracked, it was part of her late choral phase: several years after *Snow Trio*, before she became a recluse. I remember the city it was set in, the grey, planar sets that adorned the stark stage, but the title escapes me.

'Quite right. Fascinating woman.' When I first glimpsed the coroner a moment ago, through the reinforced glass in his office door, I mistook him for a child. In his chair, which is directly opposite a tall window irradiated by the grey glare of the afternoon, he sits trim in a tweed jacket and striped shirt, his rigid, centre-parted hair the shade of balsa wood. His eyes are hard and black behind his oval lenses. 'I hope you don't mind me saying this,' he says, in a tone that suggests me minding or not makes no difference, 'but the first time I heard her music, I had the strangest feeling. I was convinced that I had heard it years ago. During my childhood, in fact.'

think he's onto you, think he knows

122

knows what?

he killed her

'Convinced. The recognition was instant. It had a certain sound to it.'

get out, him? *pr'post'rous*

not as in directly, no, not with his bare
hands perhaps, but all the same

'I believe she drew on motifs from folk music, correct? A bit like Janáček, but more, well, *Irish* in flavour? That piece of hers – I forget the name now – it reminded me of songs my grandfather used to sing to me. He was from Tirana, though. Not a Celtic bone in his body.'

Selda was up the pole, man

no way to live, that, postal at home

'Listen, I have an appointment after this, if we could...'

traitorous ingrate

ancestor detestor

'It wasn't the melody or the cadence, though. I couldn't tell you what it was, but I was mesmerized by it. *Transfixed*. I even wept, right there by the radio! When I told my wife this, in quite some agitation – my grandfather raised me you see, he and I were extremely close – when I told my wife, she laughed. Can you believe it? *Laughed*! She told me that your grandmother's piece had premiered the previous month. And lo, she was right. I began to wonder if I was losing my mind.'

♪*they sing in your head*
the merry old dead♪

He erupts into laughter and claps his hands.
Anything but the singing. Not now.

♪*what a palaver!*
sang the dancing cadaver♪

People often talk about this quality of Selda's music: its mirage of familiarity. It comforts some, unsettles others. That she never disguised her interest in folk traditions, as the coroner points out, or choral monophony, a tradition traceable back through Agnesianism at least to the Byzantine church, and whose roots without question go further back still, to the echoing caves and the open plains, may have had something to do with it. Twice, she was publicly accused of plagiarism by a fellow composer, both of them older, more established, and male, but the controversies collapsed when her accusers failed to locate the originals she supposedly plundered. Her contemporaries cut up the work of dead composers, with their frothy collars and talced wigs, to form new postmodern songs, borderline pop. But her sources were elusive.

'Forgive me,' the coroner says, typing something onto his laptop.

'It's fine,' I say, 'but I–'

'My wife and I still chuckle about it from time to time. She likes to put the piece on after dinner, to wind me up.'

buttercup

I could walk out now, or cause a scene. But something fixes me to my chair and holds my tongue. 'I really need to be going soon.'

'Of course.'

> *what good's all this bollocks, what good is anything*
> *he'll be dead soon enough too, and then*

The coroner peers at his screen, and reads me his report.

> *same old story, I see*

After the snowstorm a fortnight ago, a lone hiker, thrilled by a chance to use his rarely worn snow-shoes, went for a journey near the cliffs, where he saw an odd shape in the snow. Brushing away the upmost layer revealed the toe of a woman's boot. She was lying on her back in a field not far from the edge of her land. The police who arrived at the scene were unfamiliar with the area, which was remote and wild, the land so densely wooded they failed to notice that Bell Hall was right there, hidden from view by a hedgerow. This error may have had something to do with the conditions on the morning in question. The wind blew from Siberia, gathered force over Scandinavia, crossed an ocean that was formerly Doggerland, and hit the coast only two days before. Roads became impassable. Power lines were downed. Although the worst was over, mist thickened the air like cornflour slurry and rendered visibility close to zero. It took the police forty-eight hours to identify Selda's body. She had nothing on her, no purse, credit card, or phone.

They checked against the register of missing persons, but she lived alone and kept few appointments: nobody knew she was out in that weather, including my mother and I. The only clue the police had to go on was a dry-cleaning receipt scrunched up in an inside coat pocket. That, it seems, is the extent of the report. Nothing we didn't already know.

'I know you're short on time,' he says. 'But since you're here, I wondered if it would help to ask some questions. I wouldn't normally, you understand. And I'd rather you kept it between us... but I'm well into my third decade here, and I may be able to shed some light on the circumstances.'

I want to run out of this stifling room, with its low light and seventies furniture, its brown-and-orange carpet, the coroner perched on his chair with his hard black eyes, the window behind him blank with glare. I want to leave, but I can't. Something prevents me, keeps me here, and docile. It's not just the fact that I want to know more, that the mystery of her death still gnaws at me. It's something else, which I can't yet perceive.

'Certain details seem just a touch puzzling. I do find it's better to nip those puzzles in the bud, if you'll pardon the metaphor. It does help to have *clarity*, as far as possible. Firstly, I believe I am correct in assuming that your grandmother suffered from what some would call mental ill-health.'

I tell him she did not, which is a partial truth. 'She claimed that she could speak with our ancestors. Not everyone believed her.'

'Did you?'

forget bad apple he's a whole rotten orchard

I tilt my head.

sick of the idle crick, this kid

and the belly-work in the head

'It has been a belief far longer than it hasn't, if you see what I mean. In many countries it remains a widespread practice. In Britain, of course – different story. The Enlightenment put paid to that. Not to mention all those trials-by-fire and so on. Gruesome stuff.'

That my grandmother will soon be cremated hangs in the air, a crass joke that Selda herself might have cackled at.

'Barbaric,' says the coroner. 'A stain on our past. Now, I might not be able to hear the dead myself, but only a fool would deny their persistence, wouldn't you say? My brother-in-law is gifted too, you see. That's what I'm really getting at. I used to think he was making it up for attention, but then I got to know him, really *listened* to him, and I realized how closed-minded I'd been. Just down the road here is an Agnesian chapel.'

'We're holding the ceremony there in a few days.'

♫*on the shoooore of the sky*
stood the queen of the night
and her silvery tears
were shiiining brrrriiiiiight♫

'She didn't indicate anything untoward, anything unusual? She wasn't behaving *strangely*?'

I blink at the coroner's face and consider how best to respond. She didn't, she wasn't. Or behaving in ways that other people thought strange was, for her, normal. In any case, the question is a sensitive one. We weren't in touch. Is the motive for his questions to uncover how unfaithful I was, to expose a betrayal?

> ♪*and she sang to her love*
> *who was deep in the sea*
> *and he opened his arms*
> *to her rapturously*♪

Another possibility presents itself: that he suspects me, not only of negligence, but of active ill deeds. No one here has been accused of foul play. He himself ruled it out, in fact. Selda's GP identified her body. As with any death outside a hospital or home, the police arranged an autopsy without first seeking permission from the survivors of the deceased. And its conclusion, the coroner says, was definitive.

'Heart failure.'

> *she was half-cut, bunged up on black strap, no?*

I blink. 'Has there, uh, has there been a mistake?'

> *we'd been led to believe something else*

I think back to the night when I first heard the news. On top of the shock and the tiredness, I had drunk too much whiskey and wine, and it took a moment for the sound to make sense. You know her. Euphonia. Pneumonia. Since then, I've believed that cold was the cause of Selda's death. Never have I questioned why my mother said pneumonia, not hypothermia, whether she spoke the wrong word or whether I heard the right one incorrectly. She may have said something totally different, or nothing at all.

'The evidence is irrefutable,' the coroner says. 'No one would have survived it. Not even someone so young as yourself.'

I find my mother and Todd in their crooked bedroom, under the chalky plaster and liquorice-black beams. My mother looks as though she's been crying. Todd holds her in his arms, he kisses and strokes her head. The man is emotionally stable to an uncommon degree. This is true even in the midst of a bereavement, during which his unfaltering calm is at once reassuring and eerie. When I was younger, and felt more unresolved towards him, I would watch him spill coffee over his laptop, get involved in traffic jams, lose money down drains, sustaining that upbeat emotional monotone in the face of all calamity, and think: *nothing excites him, nothing depresses him, he'd probably be the same if I lamped him.* Which gave rise to his superhero nickname – Mr Exister, whose special power is simply *to be.* I tend to forget that his own parents died quite suddenly when he was seven, and thereafter he was raised by his uncle and aunt. If these losses have damaged him psychologically, he doesn't show it, although the not-showing, the mister-existing, may be a smiling epitaph for lost innocence. My mother dries her face and sits up. She's better now: sometimes, it comes and goes as quickly as that. Todd bounces to his feet. In the en suite, he changes into lycra shorts and slips outside for his weekly 10k. I watch him through the window, sinewy untanned calves flashing down the street until they blur behind curtains of misty rain.

My mother and I order room service lunch. It brings to mind the time we went to Portugal to see the premiere of *Snow Trio*, arriving at midnight in a remote hotel, snacking in front of the television until we both fell asleep. A subject we haven't yet broached, except in passing, hangs between us as we eat sandwiches and chips off our laps. Selda might still be alive if we'd kept in touch. If we'd visited more often, known more about her life, if we'd refused her the isolation she seemed to crave.

Once we've eaten and made instant coffee, my mother puts the box of grey, unlabelled cardboard on the bed beside her.

'You're sure about this?'

severed head

boobytrap

BOOM

I hold it firm whilst she prises the lid.

it's diamonds I'm tellin you, wads of cash

Inside are Selda's clothes, neatly folded. Black trousers, red shirt, wool jumper. To one side is a dark-metal object about the size of a mug. The surface is charred-looking, almost porous, reminiscent of volcanic stone. Rough figures are embossed around its rim, pipers, dancers, winged figures, their features eroded and vague. I know my mother wants to touch it, too. But neither of us reach out. I don't know why, it isn't a body, but since it was the last thing Selda held, it carries a certain charge. 'Do you know where it came from?' I ask. My mother shakes her head. 'Shall we play it?'

'I don't know.'

'I think we should,' I say.

'Maybe later.'

Some degree of superstition is understandable. 'I doubt it will ring,' I say, 'with all those clothes to, like, absorb it.'

'I know, it's just... oh, maybe I don't know actually.'

She laughs. I lift the bell in my hands a moment, feel its texture and weight. Why this one, and not another? It can't have been the easiest thing to carry. Can I hear it ringing, however quietly, or is that my imagination? I pack it up and put it away. Then we lie in front of the television, a Regency drama neither of us watch since we're both on our phones.

Just before Todd comes back, reddened and sweating and hale, I mention something I forgot to, about the true cause of Selda's death. The *official* cause, rather. Delivered to me by a coroner who, the longer I spend outside his overheated office, the more I suspect of being wildly unprofessional; since he's the first I've encountered, I can't tell.

'But we knew that at the start,' my mother says.

'We did?'

'Of course.'

She says this so flatly, not looking up from her phone, and I begin to question my sanity: even allowing for memory's games, distorting what it records, embellishing what it retrieves, etc., that seems a notable omission. I check my phone. Time to leave. Later, once the funeral's done, I'll walk in Selda's footsteps, to the place where her body was found. Was she having an episode, a malady? Was someone with her? The gift was, of course – but that's different. I say goodbye to my mother. We agree to meet at breakfast tomorrow morning.

I have someone to meet. She has news, she says. Something important.

I take my mother's car keys and put the address into my phone. Craggy fields, open mines, trees leaning twisted and moss-clad over the bends of the winding roads, the atmosphere churning overhead, a Turner of pastel-tinted, turbulent clouds. The sky grows darker as I drive.

A tune comes on the radio. An R&B track I remember from school.

Most of the time, I wished I didn't have the gift. The other kids were merciless, sniffing out difference like sharks do with traces of blood in the water. I learned to hide it. But it wasn't always that way.

I met Dash in my third year. He heard me blabber-mouthing in an empty corridor, talking with the gift, and he mistook my rhythmic back-and-forth for a garbled attempt at rapping, avant-garde white-boy bars. I thought he was taking the piss. Back then, the gift had a hold on me. Had my tongue. I couldn't keep it under control. This was before I discovered the relief of repression and pills. When the gift possessed my tongue, teachers assumed I was impishly seeking attention, needed tough love and/or sedatives; that I had 'a condition', and maybe I did. Dash, a skinny black poet and former skateboarding head, was the first person I'd met besides Selda who'd thought of that language in musical terms. We discovered a shared love of comics and music so obscure as to feel arcane. We swapped mixtapes, blending beats with a bunch of high-brow, abstract stuff, and twilight audio we found online: interviews with psychopaths, unusual laugh compilations, number stations, field recordings, documentary segments on the sex lives of slugs, the deep cuts and oddities that made us go, *no fucking way, what IS that?* We wanted to freak each other out. On the bus home, sharing earbuds.

During one of those trips, Dash played a piece by

132

Selda. I knew the name but had never listened to it before: a dissonant work for piano and voice, beautiful and harrowing.

'You know that's my grandma.'

'Shut up.'

'It is!'

The look on Dash's face. 'Shut up, man. You're messing.'

'I'm not messing.'

'Pfffff. Don't buy it. You would have said.'

It took a while to persuade him I wasn't making it up, that Selda was who I said she was. I showed him a backstage pass dating from years ago which I kept in my wallet like a talisman, *look*.

Then the question: 'What's she like?'

'She's alright, man. She's pretty scary. But cool. We're really close. We talk all the time.' Lies. I hadn't spoken to her in weeks. But the question had wrong-footed me. What *was* Selda like? How could I answer that question?

'You never said. I kind of don't believe you still, you know.' He fell into one of his thoughtful pauses. I knew something was coming. 'I've actually been sampling this tune a bit. Your granny's banger.'

He was laughing. Beneath the laughter, he was apprehensive. I'd hated him seeing me speak in the corridor, and there was an edge of that here too.

'You put my grandma in a *track*? This means war!'

'Pfffffff. Nothing is sacred when it comes to my beats.'

'Play it man, let me hear!'

'Nah.' He was timid again. 'It's a work-in-progress thing.'

A month or so later, he invited me back to his place. We perched on his single mattress, and he showed me an EP. He'd produced it on a cracked copy of Fruity Loops installed on his dad's prehistoric desktop. He sampled loads of stuff. Bits ripped from games and films, field recordings, people speaking and singing to him down the phone. And a couple of pieces by Selda. He set the clips to bass-lines that warmed the bottom-end like embers, and broken, shuffling beats enveloped by a sonic fog of crackles and drones. There were enough eccentric tricks – blasts of saxophone, dissonant chords, sampled yelps and gasps – that I laughed. Dash thought I was taking the piss, as I had assumed about him: he thought that I thought his production was shit. But he was a genius. That he sampled Selda's music excited me. It scrambled the edifice, broke it down into samples, chopped and screwed, fed through all manner of effects. It put into musical form something I'd felt about her music, which was its eeriness, its undeadness, because, at that stage in my life, the broad genre in which she operated, western classical, seemed at once dominant, irrelevant, immortal, and dead, a cultural juggernaut-zombie. Dash, in destroying her music, revived it. He passed me a flimsy plastic microphone plugged into the desktop jack.

'What's this?'

'Lay down a few bars.'

He was joking. Wasn't he? 'No way, man.'

'Do what you were doing in school. I've heard you! Do that. Doesn't have to *be* good, I'll make it *sound* good. Come on.'

'Fuck you. That wasn't rapping.'

'What was it then?'

'I – I don't even know.'

'I just think it would sound kinda vibes.'

'It would sound shit! What do you think I am?' And I launched into an impassioned rant about the ethics of the scenario. He just started a track again, nodding, grinning, eyes lit up with inverted reflections of his screen, 'Just see what comes out, make it up on the spot, whatever man, just say whatever. Doesn't have to be good.' I listened again to his beats. He'd hung a bedsheet over the window. Incense was lit. His room felt like that, the world shut out and muted, time slowed if not frozen. His mother was cooking chicken soup downstairs, his sisters were watching TV, some American thing. I thought about it. Then I refused. 'No way, no way. *Never.*'

In the end, Dash persuaded me. It took another week, another track. This time on a Sunday, when he'd faked a stomach bug to duck out of church, and the house was empty. We smoked a joint, turned off the lights. Nothing ever happened, but there was always a tension between us, a closeness that could go either way. I let my mind go as calm as I was able to, overtaken by the voices, flowing from one to the next. It was a jumble. Babble from a dream. I was embarrassed. It sounded as ludicrous as I'd expected, giving myself to the gift, letting it say what it wanted to say, stories that made no sense. I wanted to impress Dash, freak him out. Whatever psychic muscles I'd been tensing all through school, I let them go – and nonsense flowed forth. And the more it did, the further I felt from the room. Until the world went blank.

What happens? Where do I go? These migraines, blips, episodes – how to account for them?

I came to an hour later, somewhere near the common. It was dusk. Amber light in the trees. Dash was gripping me by the arm, saying, 'Man, what's the matter man, you're freaking me out for real now Wolf, can you hear me man? Stop messing, man, stop messing. What's going on?'

I'd been singing, he said, at the top of my lungs.

Brenda Jones grew up in the Valleys. She later moved to Bristol and changed her name. Oriana Armstrong was born. A mayoral assortment of necklaces, with their dark-gold links and heavy gemstones, is arrayed on her décolletage. Her midnight-blue trouser-suit is embroidered with paisleys of metallic blue thread. Diamonds splinter light at her ears, hanging glam from the pendulous lobes, and the rings on her fingers emit soft, comforting clacks when she moves them. She sits in a rattan throne in the conservatory. Her cheeks are powdered and rouged, peacock shadow in the eyes, vermillion lipstick smudgy round the mouth, the pigment bleeding down the fine creases, diluted by water or wine. Behind her, the dark garden is visible through the liquid mirror of the lamplit glass. Tucked in the shadow beside her chair is an oxygen tank, a fine plastic tube tucked behind her back and emerging again at the neck, where it loops under and into her nostrils.

'I've seen your willy. Wolf. You probably. Don't. Remember.'

'I'm, uh. Not sure I do, actually.'

'No need to be. Embarrassed. None at all. I've seen so many. In my time. I've lost count.'

'This was at Bell Hall?'

'Running around like. A savage. Willy flapping. Everywhere.'

'I had a few questions about your time there, as it happens.'

'Did you know that. When we sang *Così fan tutte* together. At La Fenice. I saw Luciano Contaldo's. Every night? And did it bother me? Not a jot. Neither here nor there. Whether the finest tenor of his generation. Has a distaste for attire. It might bother. Some people. These days everyone is. So easily. *Offended*. But not me. He had a

taste for. Cognac. Wanted persuading to put. His costume
on. At the curtain call. I was the only one with the power
to. Command him. Not the director. Not the producer.
No... He had *respect* for me. You see. *Look, Luciano*. I'd say.
It won't do. Brandishing a pair of trousers from. The prop
department. You know. He listened to no one else. We
had enormous respect. For each other.'

When we spoke on the phone a few days ago, Oriana
warned me, several times, about the effects of her medica-
tion. Her ankles are swollen over her velvet ballet shoes,
the sequin trim of which glimmers, like every other inch
of her outfit, in the glow of the lamps. The house, which
fell to Oriana when her husband died fifteen years ago, is
a museum to her other life, both ephemeral and immortal, the one she lived on the stage. Its walls are adorned
with framed photos of her as Carmen, Isolde, Griselda,
the Queen of the Night, the titles and venues embossed
on the cardboard mounts around each image. Her elaborate costumes, flounced and yoked, with floating sleeves
and crinolines, look cut from old curtains. Wigs waterfall
down her shoulders and chest. Her forehead glares with
sweat. Her eyes and mouth are invariably blown wide
open by terror and excess, black maws whose volume, as
I glance at them, I can almost hear from across the room.

'When was this? I've forgotten.'

'I expect you have. You were knee-high to a grasshop-
per. And stark naked. Apart from your slippers. Running
around like. A pint-sized Contaldo.'

'I see. I don't remember it.'

'Selda was a genius, of course. Marvellous composer.
Marvellous. I would say. As radical as Berg. But as stirring as Beethoven. And as clever. As Cage. Other people
thought she was awful. Too clever by half. Couldn't get
around her being. A woman. We played bridge. That was

137

our thing. Bridge and gin. She wrote *Snow Trio*. For me, you know. Would you like some Tokaji? No?'

She has her own glass. She thumbs the stem, then takes a sip.

'When we spoke on the phone,' I say, 'you said that Selda was working on a piece in her final months.'

'Mmm. This wine is. Rather lovely. Are you sure. You won't have. A very small glass?'

'I'm driving.'

'Sweet. But not too sweet. Just right.'

'It's strange. I'd always understood that she'd retired. She made a point of it at the time, during an interview for a television show. It was quite definitive. I was too young to remember any of this, but my mother does. It seems strange to me. A puzzle.'

'It's from Hungary. You know. One doesn't associate. the country with. Wine somehow. One expects big. Hats and brawny. Sausage. Bath soap. Fur. But it rivals the finest sauvignons. Got hooked. On the stuff in '95.'

'Oriana, I hate to press, but I do have to get going soon.'

'I have admirers, you see. Even now, I have them. And they send me offerings. They beg me, *how can we lavish you. How can we please you.* Invariably I tell them Tokaji. *Send me Tokaji.*'

Oriana invited me here. She claimed she was unable to speak about Selda on the phone, though the reasons for this were obscure. Now that I am here, her evasiveness is grating. A while later, after more talk about wine, I tell her that I have to get going. The threat of departure sharpens her at last.

'She *did* retire,' she says. 'She'd had enough. But she started on other work, too. More local. A singing group of some kind. Working on. It was. I don't know. Important.'

'I see.'

'A painful subject.'

'How so?'

Five years ago, Oriana and Selda fell out. She won't tell me why, but it had something to do with her singing. Reading between the lines, Selda snubbed her for a role in preference for someone local, an *amateur*. To Oriana's mind, this was a violation of trust, decency, decorum, but above all art. Not only was she justifiably praised as among the finest voices of her generation, she counted herself as Selda's friend. They met and worked together. Oriana's role in our family lore is fixed: she's the one who drove Selda to the hospital the night my mother was born, a week or so premature, during a country-wide power outage precipitated by the oil crisis and which, in variously dramatic retellings, extended to the hospital itself, with the result that my mother – who tends to relate the story at candlelit dinners with friends – was delivered by candlelight. After Selda left Garth, Oriana loaned her clothes and money and babysat my mother from time to time. Out of that period emerged one of Selda's most famous pieces, *Limit*, the score of which instructs singers to hold a note for as long as their breath will allow, to push and push the notes until it breaks, fades, dies out: repeat. Singers hated it, claimed it ruined their vocal chords. Oriana sang in it. It made no sense for Selda to choose some ginsoaked bint from the pub over her, did it? Oriana tells me this information 'not to settle scores, of course', but by way of explanation. If they hadn't had that little falling out, she would have more details to offer.

'She fell out with a few people,' I say. 'It's part of the puzzle. She was more and more isolated.'

'And she wanted it. That way.'

'She did?'

'Of course.'

It had a lot to do, Oriana thinks, with 'those ideas of hers'. Selda's priorities changed. At the start of her career, her music was all about numbers and patterns. Precisions. 'One had the image of her in a lab coat, selecting each note with tweezers.' Towards the end, she was interested in something else. Something looser, simpler, more direct. Oriana didn't know what the music sounded like, but she had an idea of its form.

'Selda was. Writing a. Motet. She said. A song. For more voices. Than ever. Before. But I don't know. More than that. You need to find. Someone who played it.'

III. THE CHAPEL

The first choral piece that Selda wrote was called *Counting*. She submitted it, in 1959, as her final thesis in composition at Agnes's Hospice for Acoustically Gifted Children. Written for a choir of seven singers, from bass to soprano, the rhythmical complexity of the piece – she wrote it with the help of a computer – belies the severity of its form. As its title more than implies, its structure derives from an act that would be familiar to any pre-school child aspiring to their carers' praise: counting from one to one hundred. (Selda's early pieces are over-serious, their titles so poker-faced they become unintentionally funny: *Short Composition 5*, *Fast Piano Piece 3*, and so on.) The repetitive patterns the singers made corresponded to a set of predetermined mathematical rules deriving from an algorithm – for a time, Selda was impressed by Fibonacci – which, when played together, produced complex, shifting effects.

Here are eight beats of the opening bars.

one	one	one	one	one	one	one
two	one	one	one	one	one	one
three	two	one	one	one	one	one
four	two	two	one	one	one	one
one	three	two	two	one	one	one
two	three	two	two	two	one	one
three	four	three	two	two	two	one
four	four	three	two	two	two	two

The piece is metronomic, hypnotic. Each number is divided into its constituent syllables and assigned a shifting series of notes based on the cycle of fifths.

In some of her lesser-known pieces, of which *Counting*

is one, Selda paired simple melodies with cryptic texts which, written out, resembled concrete poems: short, simple phrases alternating between a handful of singers. They were sketches for larger works. Ideas explored here, in miniature, would reappear later in more fully realized form. Intricate patterns emerge as *Counting* unfolds, chords forming and breaking apart, cadences rising, descending, reversing, inverting. The tensions in the piece – between stasis and change, the elementary libretto and its richly estranging effects – was central to its point. *Counting* was written, Selda said, to induce hypnosis, a kind of trance.

♫*o can you wash a sailor's shirt*♫

I play the only known recording of the piece off my phone, a crackly bootleg uploaded to YouTube six years ago (127 views). It loops as I brush my teeth, tie my laces, button my shirt, notes and numbers in dizzying sequence, until at last the piece fizzles out in its final accounting: one hundred, one hundred, one... I check myself in the mirror, the halogen light picking out the scar on my chin, just below my lip, a place where my beard never grows, which I have variously attributed to a plane crash, a bareknuckle brawl with a rabid tiger, a plummet from a mountain cliff, a glancing shot from a sniper's rifle.

injury, minor defilement

tripped on flagstone and SPLAT

One hundred, one hundred. That scar was from a bike accident, though. Was it not? What year was this? Why did I trip?

*face-first on the gravel, broken glass in his
chin on a trip to see Selda*

blood everywhere, and mud and tears and snot

Heavy rain, gravel, crushed pine, tonguing the cut in
my chin. Primitive taste to it, iron and salt. And Selda –
I see her now, swimming out of the downpour, her hair
jewelled with rain. The rough authority of her touch, taking my chin in her hand.

*a jumper wrapped round her waist, she wetted an
edge with saliva and used it to wipe you down,
kneeling, dabbing, painful, wait –*

cry or be brave, which is it?

My mother and Todd are at a corner table in the hotel
restaurant, halfway through coffee and toast. My mother waves me over. Will the buffet be ready, will the white
wine be chilled, will there be enough parking. 'I'll call
and check,' I say. Having no appetite, I head outside and
cadge a snout from a kitchen porter. Seagulls whirl and
caw above the houses as I smoke. I never do this, usually. But self-ruination feels right for the day, in all its dire
glamour.

tight little bastards

Palm trees lend the sturdy grey streets the incongruous
air of the tropics, their silhouettes framing the tarnished
silver of the sky.

a big day for you, o son of sons, don't fluff it

we reckon he will, we reckon he'll choke,
he'll open his mouth and –

peh!

nothing, just a dry tiny –

peh!

like a kitten, pathetic

Briefly panicked, I pat myself down, reassured by the tinfoil *click* of the blister pack in my breast pocket.

I run through today's performance again in my head, the notes in sequence, the interlocking harmonies: a duet in three acts. Not that I need to learn it. I got that from Selda. Having heard it once, I know it by heart. Same goes for everything, even the tunes I don't *want* to remember, the crooner's lament, the jingle for frozen yoghurt, all stored in the musical library.

It's my voice that I'm worried about, not the notes. Strange fear that I'll open my mouth and no song will emerge, that water will pour out instead.

Not strange, really: it happened once already. Up until the evening in question, I was a creature of the limelight. I photosynthesized attention, fed on it to survive. Until at school one Christmas, starring as a go-getting urchin in *Coal*, with my smudged cheeks and my oversized baker-boy hat, I stepped into the spotlight, right on cue, opened my mouth, and – nothing. No sound. Dignity throttled by unseen forces, live on stage. Even now the memory prickles at the back of my neck. I was the scion

144

of a musical dynasty, so Selda liked to tell me. We were descended from singers, composers, balladeers, and our illustrious lineage culminated here, in me: a young boy in costume held together by baste-stitches and glue, trembling, blind with stage-light – then running off stage, out the back door and into the car park. I haven't sung in public since. Instead I stand in the dark of a theatre, ripping tickets, working shifts, nowhere near the stage.

The seagulls caw. My throat is dry. Should never have smoked that snout. Without the nerves, I'd never have asked for it.

The chapel is one town over. Todd offers to drive. This is welcome news. It means I can take another pill.

The murk of the morning has cleared, and now the day feels bright and open. Selda would have praised the breeze, the wildflowers alert in the fields, blooming a season too early. Cow parsley: her favourite plant. She requested that we use as many of them as we could in the funeral service. I spoke to the florist, who was only too keen. Should have instructed them to use more of it, to mob the chapel with the shivering things. We crest a hill. The sky is a bedsheet hung out on a line. Sun graces everything it touches with freshness and definition, the paleness of tarmac, the fields stippled with incipient daffodils, the leathery wads of wet dirt at the sides of the roads.

Now that I'm back in a landscape I've not returned to in years, memories return in vivid flashes.

According to Selda, a branch of our family were wedded to the innards of these lands, to the tin and the coal we pick-axed, hauled to the surface, and were crushed by. But even more branches could be traced to lakes and villages many miles from here, beyond the borders of parish and county. Country, too. We were always moving, restless, Selda said, driven north by war, south by famine, west by exile, east by love. A story she told about an ancestor comes to mind, a rope-maker's son who, sometime in the fifteenth century, migrated from Bath to Devon for no other reason than a smell on the wind, a meadowy sweetness one morning. He survived by thieving bread, sharpening knives, selling eel traps he wove from willow, and lying through his teeth to everyone he met. He seduced, swindled, then scarpered, and his voice was as rich as wine. This man was all charm and no conscience, and we are his (distant) blood relatives. If it wasn't for his aimless and degenerate sowing, Selda wouldn't exist, nor would Anya, nor would I. A lot of her stories ended that way, in ambivalent affirmation of the randomness of lineage. It contradicted her other statements about our past. The vivid tales she spun about who we were descended from, and about how those predecessors, our ancestors, had shaped who we were. Another complicating factor: from conversations with Garth, a geneticist – who like my father walked off the family stage, starting a new family in another country, rarely seen from again – Selda had come to understand that ancestry has a horizon. Go back two generations, and the ancestral correspondence is strong. But ten generations? *Twenty*? No genetic data survives that migration. They might as well be strangers.

We wander up through the town. There is something faintly obscene about the sight of people drinking hot chocolate, or buying cheese, or waiting for the bus on this, the day of my grandmother's funeral. Shouldn't they all be dressed in black, saluting as we pass?

Todd's suit is too small. It makes him look like a schoolboy, with his striped tie and side-parted hair, trousers stopping short of the ankle. Given the solemnity of the day, he has adopted his serious expression. A stiff pout, a furrowed brow.

'Did you decide yet,' he asks my mother, 'about a eulogy?'

'Not sure. I haven't got notes or an outline or anything. Don't know if I want to, really. Is that bad?'

'I don't think so. Good of you to sing though, anyway,' he says, nodding at me.

I catch my mother's gaze: 'You can give one, if you want to. But no one's going to judge you if you don't. And if they do, they can fuck off.'

'I don't care about that.'

'Stage fright?' asks Todd.

'Not even.'

'What then?'

I can't read my mother's expression behind her enormous bug-eye shades.

'Superstition,' she says. 'Selda took me to those chapels quite often, growing up. We'd go and sit for hours. All those people singing. Hard to shake it. Not that I really believe in it... not that I'm one of them... But the sound of voices ringing off stone walls, the ceremony of it... it gets inside you, in your bones, you don't shed something like that easily.'

We drift further up the hill. The sounds of the town are muffled, as if heard through glass. This frightens me until I remember how high I am.

'I feel unsettled about the whole thing,' she continues. 'I know you do too, Wolf. That bell. It's such an odd thing for her to have taken out into a blizzard. Did you have a chance to ask around?'

'No one has any idea. They mentioned a friend of hers, something Montague. We invited her, didn't we?'

147

'It reminds me of something, I can't think what, and it's driving me bonkers.'

'They use bells in rituals, no?' says Todd. 'To wake the dead.'

'No, actually,' I begin. But I can't remember what they were used for, if not that.'

'I suppose there'll be uh, *singing* later?' he asks, a slight twitch in his left eye.

'You know very well there is,' says my mother.

'And how long is the service?'

Heaven's Knell isn't much to look at. No stained glass, no spire. But approaching it from below, taking in the gorse and the trees that surround it, their outlines engraved on the stone-grey sky, it has solid Gothic heft. Out front is an ancient ash. The tree is symbolic to Agnesians. This specimen's trunk, buffeted by the ocean wind, is leaning at an angle of forty-five degrees, its branches tangled like hair. Grand and strange, severe and inscrutable – you could have described Selda that way. How far is Bell Hall from here? Was she trying to reach it the night she died?

A funeral has just ended. We wait for a few minutes whilst the mourners depart. Richard Hernandez, who runs the chapel, told us we had to be prompt; another family is booked in after. When the doors open, we head inside. The building is like a cave, cool and still, the light dim. Chairs are arranged in concentric, overlapping circles, like interference patterns on the surface of a pond. At the centre, the coffin is raised on a trellis. Dozens of pillar candles burn on the floor. A cry rises and flies round the ceiling, filled with light from circular windows built high in the stone. A sense-memory comes to mind: a church or chapel someplace hot, icons glimmering high on stone walls. I spot Hernandez across the way. With his skinny hips, drainpipe legs, and high-domed forehead, he looks less like an officiator than a lecherous intellectual. The short mauve-velvet cape at his shoulders has something to do with his role: the closest thing Agnesians have to a cassock. He shakes our hands one by one, and offers his condolences.

'A person's death can be a gift to the living,' he says. 'It teaches us how it all works.'

Todd says something I'll puzzle over later. 'There's a moment of high drama and then there's a shift. Everything's repeated with different people.'

Hernandez nods. 'I'll wait outside. Come out when you're ready.'

When I video-called him to book the chapel, I saw tarpaulins on the parquet floor. Paint-daubed children ran amok with cardboard sabres and plastic brushes, knocking over chairs, declaring war and demanding juice. He only had one slot available for the service. This surprised me. No one uses Agnesian chapels any more, or so I thought. It was important to find one in this particular style, though, a high, hollow structure of sculpted limestone, the curved ceiling of which funnels sound upwards, where it reverberates in the heaven above our heads, and where our imperfections, our dissonances, form something larger and more complete than separate individuals ever could.

The room clears. We approach the casket. How sunken her eyes, how motionless her throat, how white her hair, how smooth her skin. She lies in the simple wooden box, in a clean linen shirt, a blue blanket pulled up to her throat. My breath is so shallow I have to make a conscious effort to breathe. A roar fills the room. I place my hand on the cover and tell her I love her and wonder whether she can hear me. The roar crescendos and abruptly cuts out, leaving silence. Out of which questions arise. What was your childhood like? Talk to me about Garth. My mother's childhood, where our family come from, the dead you spoke with, who walked at your side. Were they there at the end, holding your hand? Tell me everything, spare no detail, every second, every wish. Pour your life into me so I can keep it. Selda, what happened? So you died, huh? What was *that* like? My mother weeps and so do I. For the first time since I've known him, so does Todd. Then I head out the door and into the car park and stare at the trembling line where the sea meets the sky.

Speak.

> *bout what?*

Her life.

> *what does he want? why? the unexpurgated*
> *warts-and-all litany of every last glancing detail?*

If you don't know the end then you can refresh the middle. You know things. You were there with her. She told me.

> *and he believed her? he listened?*

I did.

> *but he stopped... maybe he doesn't want to any more*
>
> *maybe he can't...*

Her fingers on piano keys, playing a chord. Her hands beside mine, playing Chopsticks. The texture of the skin on her fingers, complexly creased and liver-spotted, with a slight iridescent sheen. Clutching a glass of wine, sitting in the living room of Bell Hall as a sound rang out, a struck bell, spilling into the hallway, the kitchen, the South Wing, the evening, the orchard, the fields, quarry, forest, farms, hedgerows, roads, bays, valleys, sky.

Dozens of people arrive. They stand out front and take in the sunlit scene. They shake hands and smile and filter into the chapel. I stand at the doorway and hand out hymn sheets. I smile at faces I must have spoken to on the phone. Thank you, thank you, yes, thank you, yes, take a seat wherever. Flora Hartmann appears, to my relief and dismay. Half of me was worried she'd miss the ceremony and Selda's wish would remain unfulfilled, the other hoped she'd miss it and save me the mortification of having to sing. She grins at me and takes my hand in hers. Her sons and husband skulk into the chapel without a word. In contrast to their graphite-grey suits and black shoes, she is dressed head to toe in fuchsia and azure.

'Are you ready?'

'As I'll ever be.'

'Should be fine. It's an easy piece. Well, compared to *some* of her stuff. The early ones were torture.'

'I'm nervous.'

'Oh, don't be. No one will judge.'

'It's not that. But anyway. Shall I give you the cue or...?'

'You do it. How long 'til we start?'

'Ten minutes?'

'I'll find my place.'

The chapel is filling up. More people filtering through.

cow parsley, heal-all, thrift

I'd take another pill but it might make things worse, and there's a dry, constricted feeling in my throat already. My mother is sitting perfectly still, her face unreadable, but she isn't bawling her eyes out or throwing herself at the casket.

meadow fescue, Yorkshire fog

I think she wants to be left alone. I can't tell. She isn't looking in my direction, she doesn't seem to be looking at anything now. Perhaps her eyes are closed, so that she can listen, like she did with Selda when she was young.

I close my eyes and hear breath through the nose, a stage-whisper, fidgety fingers, cracked knuckles, shuffling shoes, a plucked string. I see a rock pool vivid with seaweed, purple urchins, flitting shrimp. Something to do with Selda. But like the other memories that have begun to come back, I can't connect it to anything else. There are other sounds, too, in my immediate surroundings. Whispers in the sigh of traffic, in the tick of an unseen clock. I'm still not sure what we're meant to be doing here. Sitting, listening. Waiting. For what? So far, nothing out of the ordinary. Nothing heathen or spooky. Just candles, hushed voices, flowers. We could be in the waiting room of a spa, or in an alpine sanatorium two centuries ago. Why the bell?

She never recorded the piece, the sheet music was never published, it was performed only once. As far as I know, she never gave it a title. Accompanying Flora and I are two musicians who worked with Selda moons ago, cannonball-bodied old geezers who could be brothers, with their check shirts and smoky hair, seated at opposite sides of the circle of seats with their instruments in front of them. One, I'm not sure which, grumbled at length to me over email. The piece calls for him to play on the thirty-second partial, using a thumbnail and only a few strands of the bow, which he declared 'not impossible exactly but bloody difficult!'

It was written for an exhibition by Paweł, the Polish sculptor with whom Selda was briefly involved. Dead now, I wonder. I scan the crowd half-expecting to see him. Would I recognize him if I did? That man in the cafe, stocky but vulnerable. His unbuttoned canvas shirt was like a tent cut open by a bayonet. He was bearishly handsome back then, but bad news too, with his smoker-toothed grin and his hell-raiser hair, the grey hands hard as rock. And those planetary eyes, vast and melancholic, the eyes of a young boy whose postwar world was eclipsed by loss. But in the most recent photo I've seen of him, taken a few years back and with an unforgiving flash, he's shed his definition and colour, swollen and bald as a grub. He believed the intrinsic barbarism of the universe, which western culture had been mendacious in obscuring, had been exposed by the horrors of war, and was in need of aesthetic purging of artifice, adornment, pretention. Can't see him here, anyway. Can't see anyone I recognize, really. He designed the stage sets for *Snow Trio*. This was years after the split. Soaring panels of scuffed white plaster, slopes evoking the barren moors, sheets of glass for frozen rivers, and a few dead ash trees. When the fake snow fell across it, the set became a picture of isolation and cold. Then, out of the blizzard, a sound emerged. A bell. A woman alone on stage, striking it, sending out a message.

Without any instruction, a shift in the atmosphere takes place, a collective acknowledgement, and the crowd falls silent. They stay like that for a few minutes. My mother stands up. She thanks everyone for coming and says a few lines about Selda, but there's a thumping in my ears, I can barely concentrate on her words. The Agnesian custom is to sit in silence. Which we do. Then my mother looks over and nods. My throat feels glued shut. I clear it, swig water, clear it again. Then I look over at the cellists, over at Flora. One, two, three. I open my mouth. Nothing. Clear my throat. People are watching. My skin prickles with heat. Another mouthful of water. Clear my throat. Again.

'C-c-can you hear me?'

Flora picks up the cue. 'I am here.'

The lyrics of the piece, like those of *Counting*, are so simple that they may have seemed childlike, even embarrassing, in their original context of a contemporary art gallery. Each singer repeats a refrain for the duration of the performance, which lasts for perhaps ten minutes.

We sing these lines individually at first. Over the first few bars, our statements overlap, until we're singing in unison. The counterpointed melodies form two-note chords that shift like steps in a dance, forever close but never touching, moving near but never reaching the tonic, semitones, fifths, and sevenths which refuse to resolve, G minor modulating to C major but never reaching F major, tension, tension, and never release, the four beats of the question shifting with the three of response. Our voices are multiplied by the reverberant chapel, no curtains or carpets to deaden the echoes. Melodies repeat and in doing so change. The phrases' meaning seems to alter, too, despite remaining identical. An acoustical fluke of the chapel, or maybe the gift is singing too. The sound registers as much as a physical sensation, a vibration in the bones of my feet, my shins, thighs, and chest, as music heard by the ears, a music that moves in the flesh. By the end, it is impossible to tell which of the singers is singing which line, who is asking and who is answering, *here* or *hear*, *hear me* or *here I*, *can you* becoming *I am*, or which of the hundreds of voices are from our throats and which the third or the thirtieth echo. We sing the final repetitions of our given refrains. The piece ends. The echoes fade to almost-silence, reverberate in the dome.

Someone sniffs. Another coughs.

For a long time, no one says anything.

Then a woman stands up. She starts humming. A man follows. Then a boy. Three chords. Others take to their feet. Soon the room fills with the sound of voices striving to find a chord, a tone that will unite them. My mother stands, then Todd. People I do not recognize sing. There is no hymn sheet. I don't know where it comes from and part of me thinks it's all stupid and embarrassing and that nothing could be worse than this tone, this tremble in the collective throat, this karaoke of the collective soul. But there's the other thing, the hum in the marrow, in the bones of my feet. The sound pours and pours into the space. It grows louder and more complex, taking on a life of its own. I can almost see it happening in the air, the tones jarring, overlapping, interfering, creating moiré patterns that coalesce into triangles, circles, chords, which bring the sounds together, amplified by this hollow of stone, flowing upwards and surrounding us.

Reluctantly at first, I start to sing too. The weight in my chest, which has been there all day, kindles, catches fire. Whatever distinction existed between inside and outside, lungs and church, dissolves, the air in my mouth and lungs continuous with the sound that surrounds us, not heard so much as felt. For a flickering instant it seems that Selda will sit up and join us.

Then I spot Hernandez. He smiles sadly and taps his wrist.

155

IV. SPOOKY FLUENCY

The A road traces the peninsula's spine. As we drive, the quilt of mismatched fields and villages give way to bleaker, flatter expanses across which spidery structures loom. Hills of grey waste from old clay mines. Quarries stippled with broken stone. A landscape that hasn't changed all that much in two or ten or twenty thousand years, that might have looked like this when Wessex invaded, a fact of which certain residents must be proud. We pass flooded fields whose brown waters reflect the pylons over them, RAF bases built in the Blitz and marked with high fences, rusted planes and fields of caravans, petrol stations by the roundabouts. Saint Piran's flags adorn fences, bumpers, windows. Suddy clouds float on the dishwater sky, which is touched in places by the turquoise of guillemot eggs. My mother and I have been silent since dropping off a relieved-seeming Todd at the station. The satnav repeatedly lies, sending us down dead ends and into strangers' farms and private estates.

A short while later, we spot it. The road itself is winding, the driveway camouflaged with tangled growths and trees. The gate hangs limp off its stump, transfixed by bindweed. I remember it differently: granite columns either side, BELL HALL emblazoned in the Gothic wrought-iron gate. I ease the car up the driveway overhung by trees. We step out, boots crunching on wet gravel.

'Bloody hell,' says my mother.

'I know,' I reply.

The windows are set defensively deep in the granite. Algae blooms across the stone in shades of chalk and sage. The roof is misshapen, slumped to one side, but it hasn't yet collapsed. Webs of ivy creep across the closest wall, wet petals so green they look black. You can feel it

scheming, seething into everything – a religion of stillness and rain. The woods nearby are both lush and stern.
They stand like a phalanx or fortress wall. Further off, I
remember now, are acres of squelchy fields and forests
dissolving in mist, scattered with granite schists and dozy
sheep but nothing much else to write home about. I understand why she moved here: no one around to bother
you, no noises to distract from the dead. I kick a pebble
across the yard. It collides with a rusted petrol can with
a dull *thunt*. The sound reminds me that I used to throw
stones at it as a kid – the can has been here all this time.
To my left is a row of empty chicken hutches, stray feathers twitching on latticed wire. I don't remember chickens, can't imagine Selda keeping them. Further off, a low
wall divides the driveway from a cluster of stunted trees
that, centuries ago, was an orchard.

> *he's hunting for something*

> *he doesn't know what*

> *skeletons in the piano*

> *accumulated lucre of all our sweat and*
> *tears, bonds and wise investments flowing*
> *into that mighty river of molten gold*

I open the boot and unpack the bags. When I was a
child, it was a vast and sturdy castle wreathed in opaque
mist and impenetrable forest. It's smaller and drabber
now, but still something to look at.

As a child in post-war Coventry, so the story goes,
Selda ate treacle on stale bread for dinner and scavenged
coal from the streets, bending her mucky knees, plucking

the back stuff off the street, and feeding it into the stove. She played piano to help with the gas bill, didn't own a pair of shoes until she was nine. Selda almost never spoke about her childhood – rarely spoke about herself full stop. 'Coventry was my conservatoire,' she proclaimed (half serious, at the very most) whenever someone expressed surprise at her upbringing – she would have always preferred if they'd never found out. Everything she knew, she told an Italian magazine, could be traced back to her childhood in that city. Having dropped the hint, she declined to say any more. That was her style at home, too. Either way, and by the end of her career, she'd received enough in commissions and royalties to buy a place like Bell Hall: not a grand house, but the image of one – something that her parents may have dreamed of, but come no closer to, owning.

There is one last item to fetch from the trunk. I've been saving it 'til last, I didn't want to touch it. A duffel bag. It's lighter than I remember. My mother hasn't moved. I call out to her and ask if she wants us to start. Her arms are folded tight about her chest.

'Need a minute,' she says.

I don't tell her we don't have a minute. That we're already late. I drop the suitcases on the welcome mat and bury my hands in my pockets. I don't think she's blinked since she got out the car.

'You alright?'

Her gaze is fixed on a point on the roof.

'I'm going for a wander,' I say. My teeth creak as I set my jaw firm.

Paving slabs lead around the side and into the garden, where I jump. There's someone in the bushes. He has dark, hollow eyes and greenish skin. His open mouth choked with vegetation.

It takes me a moment to recognize him – one of Selda's singing statues. It, or he, warbled softly in the night as the wind coaxed tunes from his open throat. Selda found him, I guess, comforting: a technological chimera, a hybrid of animate and inanimate realms – it had something to do with Renaissance gardens, too. I pass the living room's shuttered windows. I loosen the latch and peer inside: the sheen of brass, a harpsichord on a carpet that used to be blue, now faded to beige. I can't see any corpses or rubbish bags or mouldering newspapers stacked in towers, no feral droppings or roosting owls. Just a musty old room and no Selda.

> ♫*o can you wash a sailor's shirt?*
> *o can you make it clean?*
> *o can you hang it on the line*
> *beside the village green?*♫

The lawn is overgrown in places, bald in others. At its far edge are clumps of bracken and a wall of firs. A short distance behind them is a Neolithic standing stone, a hulking monolith on the side of a path. Selda liked to take me there on morning walks before my mother was up. Leading me by the hand, Selda swore it murmured, on certain nights, with voices from the depths of the earth. They belonged to ghosts whose flesh and bones had dissolved into other ages and epochs, ice and iron and stone. They were victims of famine and slaughter, poets and nobodies who'd multiplied without record but who at some point procreated, the result of which facts led to her and I standing there together in those cold bright mornings, dew at our feet. *That stone is like a tuning fork*, she said. I believed her then. I don't know why. Or maybe I never believed her, and our staged declarations of faith in something that we knew was untrue became the basis of our intimate conspiracy.

The South Wing was the name for the extension she added to the rear of the house a while after she bought it. It was here that she wrote all her music. Until she stopped composing, anyway. It was my favourite room in the house, all the instruments laid out, the synthesizers, computers, stringed instruments, and the old upright with the missing front panel, the one she left me in her will. The door is locked. I press my forehead against the window.

he believes this codswallop?

more likely she hated to think that you'd grow up to like her

like us

multitudinous mumbler with the grave dirt on your breath, the blood glueing up the teeth

In the middle of the long, double-height room is a patchwork of carpets dotted with desks, lecterns, armchairs, a desktop computer and instruments. There's an upright piano, a cello, cymbals, a gong. On the far wall is her ARP 2500, a grand wooden box inset with silver panels, grids and dials. Closer to hand, a dining table is piled with books, a reel-to-reel recorder, statuettes, a dead fern. In a far corner is a spiral staircase. It leads to a walkway that runs around the edge of the room, midway up the height of the wall, like you might find in an old library, shelves stuffed with books and binders. I remember taking books from the shelves as a kid, the abstruse contents of which baffled me. There were guides for the acoustically afflicted, copies of the *Rigveda* and the *Nāṭya Śāstra*, business cards for celestial chiropodists, Rosicrucian alchemists, and founders of myriad bells, scribbled notes and phone numbers, a pressed thistle in a plastic sleeve, textbooks on sign language, piano-tuning, remote viewing, vibrational analysis, radio waves, acous-matics, military history, crystal matrices.

The books were arranged according to a system whose logic I could never make sense of.

Now, it looks like a whirlwind has passed through, blowing folders from the shelves, disgorging their con-tents everywhere. The floor is white with pages, which have built up in drifts in the corners and against the fur-niture, so that it looks as though snow has fallen indoors.

I'll need a rake to shape it, whatever these pages are, old letters? orchestral scores? the 'papers' she referred to in her will, surely, blown into disarray. I cup the window with both hands and peer at the pages below the door – dots and dashes, scribbled words – but I can't make any sense of them. I'll try to find another way in.

Round the corner, beyond the lawn, a neighbour's field slopes to a row of trees. Those firs mark the edge of a shallow valley, which leads to an inlet, on the harbour of which is a pub, beyond which stretches the coast. Judging from where she was found, that's the route she will have taken.

My phone buzzes: *where are you x*.

*One sex / ffs / sec**

I walk past the rose bed and the garage that reeks of turpentine and round again to the front of the house. For a moment I watch my mother, expecting her to speak. She pauses at the door and digs in her bag.

'Sorry I was just, uh... did you know she still has that weird statue?'

The hallway smells of cold stone and stale air. Straight ahead is a corridor that leads to the kitchen. To the right is the living room, door slightly ajar. Dust has accumulated in thick layers on everything, lending the room the look of a diorama cut from beige felt. An accordion hangs from the coat-stand, cobwebs in its concertinaed folds. By the door, in lieu of a table, is an upright piano on which are placed unopened bills, a pizza leaflet, a ceramic pig, a half-empty bottle of green-tinted surface cleaner. My mother heads towards the kitchen with the shopping bags filled with supplies. She tells me she's 'gasping for', positively 'unable to live without' a cup of tea before we start. I head into the living room. It was Selda's favourite place in the house, besides the South Wing, and part of me – a child part, a boy who needs to see and speak with her – expects to find her sitting in her armchair, glasses perched on her nose, pencil in hand, glass of whiskey at her feet, frowning at me with those mismatched eyes, wondering why we didn't call to warn her we were coming.

The room's emptiness seems to mock me. I pull back the curtains to find that the clouds have parted. More of those thick, mossy layers of dust. The room floods with light. I set the duffel bag down on the floor, just in front of Selda's chair.

'Welcome back.'

The room is crowded with instruments. In the corner is a stringed instrument, a cello maybe, cloaked in its fabric case. Nearby is a stack of manuscripts with a Dvořák concerto on the top. Selda was sometimes compared to him on account of her reworking melodies from murder ballads and drinking songs, but the comparison was lazy. On the walls are hung dozens of small instruments of polished bronze and brass, spoons, cymbals, triangles, metal castanets, gongs and silver jingles, Chinese and

Krishna bells. The polished instruments reflect the sun with crossed beams of hay-pale light. Beside the fireplace is a harpsichord. I lift the keyboard's lid and cast my mind back to the songs that Selda sang to me. I can only remember fragments, phrases, cadences. I improvise to fill in the gaps. As I do, a sudden rage roars in me. I bash the keyboard with my fists.

> *he's not inherited her touch has he? his notes, they grate the ear*

> *yes but she was a once-in-a-lifetime talent, that's what everyone said, including us, and all the more remarkable because she was...*

> *well...*

> *a she*

> *yes we did rather doubt her*

> *initially, yes*

> *from the get-go, in fact, we must admit it, but we understood soon enough that here, o, here, yes, HERE was the best among us, a rare voice, once-in-ten-generations*

On the instruments' top is a framed black-and-white photograph. A young Selda stands in front of a sandstone building. She is gawky, her blondish hair stirred by a breeze, her expression alert, downturned, scheming – she must know the person behind the camera. She has her arm around the shoulders of another young woman who has a round face, dark hair, and a crooked smile. Carved into the stone above her is a frieze of winged musicians playing trumpets and drums, and that name: Agnes's Hospice for Acoustically Gifted Children.

Of course. Mystery, to some, what took place there. Sometimes got mistaken for a church. Attached to one side is a fancy auditorium with a painted ceiling, red velvet seats.

> *believed all kinds of claptrap like we*
> *drained corpses of their vital fluids and*
> *knocked the liquor back like brandy*
>
> *well... not being funny but some of us kind of did*

There's music on the stand, a sketch of hers. I sit down and pick out the melody, bring in the chords, my eye drifting again to the photograph.

It was not the only institution of its kind. She sometimes spoke about Greenland's School of Silence, where students were electively mute. There for a brief stint in the eighties, I believe, she had a breakthrough, or was it a breakdown? She almost lost her fingers to frostbite, may have come close to death, but it marked a new phase in her music. Or the Ospedale della Pietà in Venice, the all-female orphanage of *figlie di coro*, or chorus daughters, for whom Vivaldi wrote many pieces. Or the Conservatorio de fortaleza acústica on Chira Island, or the Resonant Temple in the mountains of Laos, or The College of Wandering Voices, and all the other splinter groups, societies, and clusters where the gifted would gather.

> *cavorted with the Devil and spoke his forked tongue*

harpsichords make nasty noises

and all the ones we die to sing

surround us now

he cannot hear

the flap of wet linen, the rattle of shutters, the
baa-baa of lambs, the clattering attic, the axe, the
lads, the gadflies, logs tumbled in heaps, the farmer,
his boots, piles of wood in an outhouse, matches,
pine-cones, twisted headlines aflame in the hearth,
chimney-tops burning, stars in the dark

She spun tales of wards that MI5 recruited, others who were subjected to vivisections and experimental medicines that precipitated mania or fugue, and those who hid their gifts and lived 'normal' lives. These tales of singing schools and harrowed children weren't designed to impress me, but to let me know that having the gift was, if not common, then at least precedented. The older I got, the easier it became to associate her, as opposed to myself, with a darkness I would rather deny.

The woman beside her is dimly familiar. A singer, I think, or a cellist – but why put the photo here, pride of place above the keys?

we drank death, by which we mean life,
distillations of the old, poured into the young, to
revitalize the flesh, to celebrate the cycle

what's he playing there? Bach?

There is a crashing noise in the kitchen, a harsh clatter of metal on stone – and then the sudden, wrenching sound that I remember from outside the chapel.

I jog into the dingy kitchen at the back of the house. My mother is standing beside the oven. Selda's old stovetop kettle is on the kitchen floor. A puddle is spreading across the flagstones, silvered by the light of the windows.

'Everything okay?'

Her cheeks are pink and swollen, wet with tears. 'Stupid fucking kettle. It flew straight out my hand.'

My mother's plan is simple. Before she can apply for probate, and handle the transfer of inheritance to the beneficiaries of Selda's will – my mother and I – we need to *value the money, property and possessions ('estate') of the person who's died*, according to the government website I consulted, reading off my phone in my mother's kitchen a few weeks ago. Until we look around it, top to bottom, we have no idea of Bell Hall's condition: if the roofs are sagging with damp, the attic crawling with bats and vermin, the beams abuzz with termites, or whether, conversely, a Stradivarius is gathering dust in a disused practice room and the mattresses are stuffed with cash. Pages and pens are laid out on the table, battle plans and maps. My mother has divided our days to the minute, so as better to conquer their uncertain terrain. We eat sandwiches and allocate jobs.

'*Papers*,' says my mother.

> *we've forgotten more than he'll ever know but he hasn't the brain cells to ask us a simple question – to summon us to speak*
>
> *young people, honestly*

166

his head's buried so deep up his hole he's got arsecheeks
for earmuffs, he'll not hear a word

We spend the rest of the day working through the house, performing tasks on autopilot. Counting, noting, shifting, holding. Picking things up and putting them down again. Opening and closing cupboards, doors, drawers. Walking up and down stairs, drifting into rooms and standing gormless, forgetting what we, what were we doing again? I avoid the South Wing and so does my mother. These are acts of recognition. A violin, a nightie, a book about thermodynamics, dirty shirts bundled in the depths of a wicker tub. I forget why we're here, what we're doing. We are box-tickers, auditors: this could be anyone's house. Our province is spare rooms, the cobwebby damp-smelling basement, the outhouse, the garage, the attic crammed with bundled boxes, the study. I write lists.

2 x tin-can telephone hanging from a hook on a roof-beam
? x loose bar chimes, bundled in a sports bag under the stairs

Up the stairs, into the main top corridor, the walls hung with watercolours and pressed wildflowers. Her bedroom door is closed. Softly, I rap my knuckles against the wood. No answer. Don't know what I was expecting. Clean room. Made bed. Light from the window catches a bottle of eau de vie containing a whole pear, fat and pale green. A shirt draped over a chair. Look at the bed a while. Sit on the end of the mattress.

1 x Rooster of Barcelos figurine
1 x copy of *Conversations with Stravinsky*, the

composer's name crossed out in biro and
replaced with *a psychopath*

Early one morning I knocked on this bedroom door.
Selda called out in that camp and operatic voice she only
ever employed on our secret mornings. The high-wire
trip of the second syllable, *hel*-oh-*oh?*, like a Gilbert and
Sullivan walk-on. It's a large and sparsely furnished bedroom, its rustic feel enhanced by walls of milky orange,
almost terracotta plaster she never got round to repaint-
ing, or the appearance of which she preferred. Rasping
underfoot were floorboards, warped and grey, gasping
for polish. Directly opposite her double bed was a row of
windows, against which she had pushed a narrow desk. It
was lined with bottled perfume, tubs of face cream, earbuds. The combined effect of the low, beamed ceiling, the
windows, and the creak and shush of the wind-turned
trees, gave the room the feel of captain's quarters at the
rear of a galleon, and I often liked to fantasize, or more
simply believed, that she and I were on a voyage. The
floor was dotted with uncomfortable furniture. Like the
applewood chair in the corner, over which she draped
her clothes. From her bed she could see the South Wing's
roof, the fields, and trees I could not name. Wildflowers
were in bloom. I climbed into bed beside her.

'What's it like?' I asked.

She had extinguished her cigarette and was sitting upright, her legs on the top of the duvet. Nettle tea in her
mug.

'It's not always like you expect.'

She had been telling me, as she sometimes did, about
the gift. One day, when she was dead, it would pass to me.

Why not to my mother, I wanted to know. To which
Selda replied, why should it?

Not everything is passed down automatically. Hair colour, eye colour, the breadth of the brow, high or low cholesterol: some variable is always unpredictable, changing, mutating. It's in the nature of such traits, sometimes they skip a generation or two, patterns straddling the branches of the family tree, which is more of a copse or forest. A newborn isn't always the spit of its parents. It might resemble a grandparent, great-grandparent, great-great, and so on, not that photography has existed long enough to confirm how far back the similarities rhyme. Inheritance was a bit like music, that way. Or one aspect of music at least, which is that it almost always involves repetition, perhaps the most basic organizing principle of the form, and that every repetition brings change, whether harmonic, rhythmic, or merely perceptual on behalf of the listener. The gift helped her to understand the correspondence.

Most of this flew directly over my head, of course, but I pretended I understood, nodded solemnly and peered blinklessly into her eyes, the irises of which were flecked with rusty brown.

She herself had received the gift, she was sure, from her uncle Charles, who was badly injured while fighting in Sicily, wounded in his head and throat, and was considered by my mother, who had a tendency to project onto Selda's immediate male ancestors images of stability, benevolence, and strength, to be a 'true hero of the war'. He had been a talented tenor before he left for Sicily. Her parents, she said, told her that he'd died in the war, heroically and definitively. Only after she received the gift, which had been with him, which had, in the end, tormented him, did she learn that he had lived several years longer, in what was then known as an asylum, scribbling notes about ghosts which his orderlies took as further evidence of his madness. Eventually, Selda said, he vanished from his room. He was found a week later, face-down in a lake.

Dust conquers everything. Folded clothes and curtains, yellowed books, bottled white spirit, bundled wires, stacks of old newspapers, sandpaper, utility bills from '92, a dead mouse, a bird's skull, a pestle, a dumbbell. Maybe my mother is right: all that's left is junk, dust enough to keep me sneezing. She has costed all the works that will need to be done. Mildew all over the ground floor. Cracks spiderwebbing the plaster. Broken beams in the South Wing, missing roof tiles, leaky heating, dodgy electrics, the upstairs loo, infestations of moths. The more she lists, the more despairing she sounds. When you factor in the fact that it's in 'the arse-end of nowhere', Bell Hall is likely worth less than it was when Selda bought it.

never been the absolute very best at the accumulating

I seem to remember some kind of castle, no?
unless we were pages or squires or

tortured in the tower! hot poker up the backside!

Dark already. Stars are out. Unsure whether we have achieved anything since we arrived, I shower, open some wine, make pasta in the chilly kitchen, and carry it through to the dining room. The table is crowded with instrument cases, which my mother clears away. In glass-fronted cabinets are bows, mallets, drumsticks, plectrums, pots of wax.

all the old friends and foes

Midway through a bite of spaghetti, she bursts into tears. Pasta slaps the table, mixed up with spit. She reaches for her napkin, clears it up, pushes her plate to one side. I crack a weak joke about my cookery, which makes her laugh. Sort of.

It has been like this all afternoon. Sodding kettle. Fucking puddle. Cracked vessel leaking its water, spilling its guts. I tell my mother that memories are coming back, glimpsed things from childhood, and each one a reminder of how much more there could have been if we'd kept in touch.

I do not say that one reason for my regret is self-interest. I wish that Selda was here to offer advice. In her absence I feel an urge to do something extreme and anarchic. Smash a window, hack the table to pieces with an axe, pour gasoline over everything, stand in a field with the stars at our shoulders and watch the whole place light up, Selda's manuscripts, memories, mysteries, music, all of it burning to cinder, carried to sea by night air. I do not set the house on fire. A breath later, the feeling subsides. I pick another song and turn the volume up so loud that for a moment the gift is drowned out – until my mother tells me to switch it off because she's got a headache, is going to bed. Alone in a silent room, I set about clearing the plates.

Earlier today my mother put Selda's ashes on the kitchen table, beside the fruit bowl. There's dirt against the side of the tub. I carry it over to the sink. Only once it is here, in the light of the cooker-hood, do I realize what it is.

I check the duffel bag. In the bottom is a spoonful's worth of ash. I pour Selda out onto the work-surface carefully, but she's already over my hands. When I pour her back into the tub, bits cling to my fingers. In attempting to fix it, I make the mess worse. Soon Selda is all over my hands. I can't just flush her down the sink. That would only deepen the indignity. The gift berates me for having been so clumsy, so disrespectful, but it also has a suggestion. Selda, who is dead, lives on in my mother and I. She can live in me again, nourish, sustain, permeate me, closing the cycle of death and renewal.

    do it properly

they say.

      make it official, her to you, a ritual of inheritance,
      Agnesians practice it all the time, no need to be so
      modern and squeamish, where do you think your cells
      are from? flesh begets flesh, minerals flow from sea to
      soil to body and back again

So I fill a cup with water and clean the ash off my hands. Selda swirls before my eyes, a galaxy in a glass. I feel dizzy, watching it/her spin, as if the swirl were a form of hypnosis. And then, because the gift insists I do, because it calls this an act of love, I lift the glass to my lips and drink.

      atrocious behaviour

        drink it up joining us yesssss

      I expected rather much better than, uh, conking
      out cold on the flagstones

        cold floor applecore rottencore hardcore

he's not d-d-dead is he? he'll wake eventually, yes?

he's in the in-between. in a manner of speaking

well that's just it you see, the living ones keep telling us we're dead, but I don't remember dying, so who's to say it ever happened? or to put it another way, how can I be sure I was ever alive?

do you remember being born?

no – and I wouldn't want to! but it must have happened, cos here I am

how so?

if I forgot it, it must have happened

no wonder we send the lad postal, I'd be driven up the pole by our endless jawing, shouldn't we be here to bestow the crown of ancestral endorsement? surely we can put our self-interest aside for a moment and, if we can presume, offer him wisdom

somewhere back in the endless oral annals is an account of my decease, but unlike my birth – of which there are none – when it comes to my death, too many! can't tell which is mine

let's face it, we're shit at our job, we're supposed to remember but mostly we don't, we improvise when we're meant to recite

173

yes but see, it gets a bit repetitive, telling the same old
myths for eons, stale tales worn so thin the words wear
out, get numb with repetition

forgive me for feeling aggrieved that this ingrate can
wither and dither and wander and wonder for days over
Selda's old tripe and I can't even chit-chat except to you
deadfolk, halflings, spectres and echoes and shimmers of
souls long-rotted to nothing, no offense

no one's blaming no one, people is what they is and
they do what they do, and you can't say fairer than
owt

well, listen, hear that? breathing, he's not dead
– and neither are we

V. DARK EARTH

My skull rings with the gift when I wake the next morning, my joints stiff and my extremities numb. The condensation-clouded window is mauve with the unlight that comes before dawn. It's far too early to be awake. I wrap the duvet tighter and turn on my side, which movement, and the creak of the wooden bedstead, brings vividly to mind the mornings I spent with Selda.

She never seemed to sleep. And since I was always up early, the first thing I did most mornings was seek her wherever she was in the house. Most likely she would be in the South Wing, where, unless she was busy composing, she would be sitting quietly at her angled desk with manuscript paper in front of her, pen in hand or gripped between her teeth, her body tense with concentration. She would teach me simple pieces on the upright piano, murder ballads and bawdy songs. The lyrics described how babies are made, others murdered by jealous lovers, what sailors get up to at sea, tales of villainy, debauchery, calamity, featuring charismatic pranksters and legendary thieves.

Other times, unable to find her in the house, I would spot her walking in the fields or heading towards the woods with an abstracted look on her face. Her bony frame and posture resembled a stork or a scarecrow, and her head, tilted to the right, directed at a sound I could not hear.

Whenever this happened, I would become convinced that she was in desperate trouble, from what I could never be sure, and that I had only moments to save her.

In the course of that short journey, a couple of minutes at most, as I ran downstairs and fumbled at the door-handle, which sometimes was locked, meaning I'd have to double back to the key-cupboard in the hall, or else leave through the front door and run what felt like miles around the living room, I would be consumed by an irrational terror that every step was having an elastic effect on time, turning seconds into years, minutes into centuries, and that, long before I arrived, she would have vanished, crumbled to dust blown away by the wind. Burying my face in the folds of the long wool jackets she often wore indoors and out, and which carried the scent of her morning cigarettes, served a double purpose, providing tangible evidence that she was alive and hiding my tears of relief from her view. Sometimes, though, she would express her irritation with a tut or hiss, at which point I would wonder, with a pang of egotistical horror, if the thing she needed saving from, the monster in her meadow, was me.

Not all mornings were so fraught. If she was in her bedroom, I would knock on the door, wait for permission, push open the door, and grin, whereupon she would fold away the paper or her book or whatever happened to be diverting her attention, and pat the duvet beside her as you might, I suppose, for a dog. It was our time. I've never felt closer to anyone than I did on those mornings, not even my mother. Selda would tell me stories about the gift and recite what the voices around us were saying, and mostly these were idle or mundane things that were muttered to her in passing, about tilling fields or combing lice from a child's hair, though sometimes they were as obscene or violent as the songs.

'Do you ever hear them?' she asked one morning. I can still hear the raspy, whispered tone, the cracked warmth of her voice, a living voice, the hushed tone of which suggested conspiracy, an adult world of secrets into which I was being initiated in advance of my understanding it.

176

'Who?' I replied.

'The dead.'

Her tone suggested that this was the most natural thing in the world to tell a boy not yet seven, and the smile on her face convinced me that I had encountered these people, these dead, several times already and knew them well. But I couldn't remember meeting them and so I told her the truth. She would have known if I was lying.

'I think you *can* hear them,' Selda said. 'They might be quiet at the moment, and they don't always speak in the way you expect, it isn't always words or sounds. But they'll need someone else once I'm gone, and then you'll know for certain that they're with you,' she said, pressing a finger to my sternum, where, now I think of it, a heavy feeling now sits. It was one of those summer days that sometimes graced us amid the usual fog and rain and the world beyond the house felt unnaturally still. The leaves through the window were golden. Birds and insects clicked and sang as if to signal the interest of the natural world in our conversation.

'It's a feeling I have sometimes,' she said. 'And I have it with you. Not everyone notices the people who notice, but I do.'

I felt equally pleased and troubled by this endorsement. Even then, I understood that by bringing Selda and I closer together, this talk had put distance between my mother and I. When Selda spoke about snowstorms in second-century France, or siblings butchered by jealous heirs in a village north of modern-day Hull, or spectacular stage lights in a Dublin theatre concocted from dried berries, ochre, and lime, or an arson attack on an Agnesian chapel on whose burnt earth a Tesco Metro now stands, and claimed these scenes were not only historically true but the story of how we got here, the odyssey of us, my mother, most often, nodded and smiled and laughed, but sometimes rolled her eyes, too, as if to say *enough already, change the tape.*

I looked up to Selda. Not just as a second parent, my only living grandparent, a replacement father-figure, or as a famous composer, but as something harder to define. We spoke with spooky fluency. I sometimes wondered whether she was my imaginary friend, though I could never tell if she was mine, if I was hers, if we were both my mother's, or if such distinctions even mattered.

Selda, without whom I wouldn't exist, was a mischievous genius with snowy hair and mismatched eyes. She was thin with big hands and long feet. Her brow was broad and noble over a high-cheeked, imperious face. She grinned and gasped and grimaced, but only when playing music. The rest of the time she was poker-faced. Her inscrutable manner put strangers on edge.

On stage she wore tailored suits that emphasized her androgynous frame. At home it was garish late-eighties aerobics sweats or floaty shirts over old jeans. In the seventies she had an epiphany: a neck-length bob was the cut for her, covering her sticky-out ears, framing her angular face, long enough to skim but not bother the shoulders. Prime Ministers came and went, wars were won and lost, the Soviet Union collapsed, but she stuck to that haircut as the colour faded, burnt-chestnut to white. I sometimes wondered if it was stuck on, like a piece of Lego.

She fumbled cutlery at dinner and was hopeless at sports. At the piano, however, she would glide through Schubert, Gershwin, Chopin, Glass and every note was newborn, weighted with just the right grace and pressure to bring the composition to life.

She dined on Snickers and Mars bars half the time and foraged fiddleheads and bladderwrack the other. Down at the shoreline, swinging seaweed into a bag, whipping us all with salt water. Deep in the woods with a paring knife, snicking mushrooms at the root.

You could bask in the golden warmth of her unconditional love for days. Then, within seconds: the switch. Her expression would harden – and you were out. Sniping, cussing. When she was angry, her voice spattered like fat from a pan. It drove me crazy trying to work out what I'd done to displease her. A word, a look? Did I *smell*?

Always recording, collecting, collating. She sampled sounds relentlessly. The old kettle's cricked whistle. The sop and simmer of conversations in crowded pubs. My mother's laughter, my howling games.

I must have drifted off again. Now the light is stronger, the sky a flat laptop-screen blue.

I dress and open the door as quietly as I can and burglar-step my way along the dark corridor, past the spare room my mother is sleeping in, past Selda's empty bedroom, from which no smoke leaks, stepping softly on the staircase. The flagstones are hard as ice under my socks. The grandfather clock in the corner clucks as the pendulum swings, a solemn, wood-brown sound, reminding the gift that certain people in Selda's family believed she was a chime-child, born at a magic hour, as David Copperfield was, and able to perceive ghasts, spectres, all manner of go-by-nights. Sometimes I wonder if the gift is an august system of healing beliefs centred on finely wrought chapels and transcendent song, or a sack of superstitions we should chuck in the trash.

I pull on a coat and boots and head outside.

The garden smells of copper and peat. Rain sizzles on slab and gravel, sluices down the gutters. There's another sound, a hooting, neither human nor animal. Then I notice him plonked in an overgrown hedge. The singing statue. His open mouth overflowing with rain, his hands outstretched. Lightning illuminates the raindrops for an instant, picking out the statue's eyes – I forgot how quickly and severely the weather here can change. What were you doing here alone, Selda, surrounded by trees and grass, with only this garrulous tin can for company?

can you hear us too or–?

Something happened in the night. Shapes, movement, a swirl of dark water. A thirst.

he seems somewhat... repressed? conking out, drifting into gardens and so forth... swallowing valerian

I slaked it. The gift's idea. It felt at the time like a medicine, or a tribute. Truth be told, I don't remember how, or if, I justified it to myself, drinking a fraction of Selda into my body like wine, like a life-giving elixir, isn't that what they said about Agnesians, that they drink the dead the way plants do, they didn't mean it literally, did they? Then why – and what, on the journey though? Gah, can't think. I need to get out of this place.

one of us now

or the other way round

This was you. Your idea. But I did it. Quiet. I need to think.

if only he listened, attended, attuned, he'd be able to

Someone a few fields over has lit a bonfire at this strange hour. Spring now smells like autumn as I cross the gravel drive.

The garage door croaks open. Other autumn smells: cool brick, sawdust, wood oil, petrol. Cobwebs everywhere, billowing, littered with husks. And in the middle of the breezeblock space, the shelves of which are lined with rusty saws and ancient tins and, strangely, not one instrument, is the tarpaulin-covered car: Selda's, bequeathed to me.

I pull back the sheet, open the driver's door. Inside, the car smells of the late-twentieth century, smoke soaked into the pleather, pulverized crisps in the footwell, pine-fresh thingy hanging from the rear-view, a muddy boot on the back seat. The engine groans, shudders, dies, then chokes to life on the third attempt. I ease the car into the labyrinth of hedgerowed lanes.

What is the aim of this pilgrimage? Up to this point, planning the trip in my head, setting my alarm, consulting the map, I have described it to myself as an *investigation*. As if being there will reveal clues, hints in the landscape that only I could perceive, which will reveal what Selda was doing the night she walked out of the door, whether she had lost her mind or was lucid, and whether, relatedly, I am keen enough to observe clues that others cannot, hear the pattern in the noise. Not everyone notices, Selda said.

The drive is not long. How long would it have taken her, heading into the blizzard which rendered visibility zero, piled snow upon snow, inch upon inch, and transformed a landscape she'd lived in for years into an alien planet? I realize how stupid it was to have taken the car.

181

Walking by foot would have given a more accurate under-standing of the route she took, the conditions underfoot, the rhythm of the journey.

I turn at a crossing, pass a farm-gate, and arrive at my destination: a car park within view of the sea. This can't have been her intended destination. How far beyond this point was she intending to get?

Grass flutters at the tarmac's edge. On a bench sit a middle-aged couple in matching jackets and waterproof trousers, squinting amiably at the wind, a tinfoil chrysalis on the man's lap holding two slices of buttered malt loaf. A scruffy terrier shivers at their feet. All three watch me as I pass.

The path leads close to the cliff-edge. Far below: black rocks, grey surf, white foam.

She wasn't planning *that*, was she?

No, I can find the right place, it must be near. I check the map on my phone, the GPS coordinate, which I ex-tracted from the Devon and Cornwall police. The right spot, the wrong time. So long as I do, then the gift will perform a revival, summon skeletal emissaries, disinter spectres from graves of thin air, open an invisible door to wherever Selda is – right beside me, probably – and let her speak again.

Double vision again. I feel certain that something, which I know will not happen, will happen. The com-peting beliefs don't cancel each other out but coexist in tension like a root and its ninth, in the same epistemo-logical twilight, or is it a metaphysical one? I forget.

I walk on, past gorse and heather.

Selda told stories of Hermes, Orpheus, Eurydice, of murdered turtles transformed into lyres, severed heads that continue to sing as they drift downriver, echoes that outlive their maker, journeys to the underworld and

sometimes back again, pillars of salt. These stories never sounded morbid to me at all. They made me think of
her piano, a casket in which each struck string hummed.
When she told the myth of Echo, among the saddest in
her repertoire, she was pleased to note the correspondence between the human ear's hollow and that of a cave.

Maybe those tales were the message, a code to be broken only after her death. She was preparing me to follow
her, so that she could sing again. But I need to find her
first, further along the path, into the headwind's forceful
chill. And instead of her last moments, the gift bickers
about her childhood, an issue of controversy even to
those who were there.

> *the cardinal sin in child-rearing, and a common
> one, is the indulgence of whims, and as such it was
> proportionate to have resorted, now and then, to
> corporal punishment, to r-r-r-rapping of the knuckles,
> chaining to the bed*

I halt for a moment, dumbstruck by a thought that only
sounds trite in retrospect: how little I know about her,
how much there is to learn, how fluently she withheld her
origins even as she spun tales of our collective ones.

> *o, that poor girl! wet towels wound into whips, soap
> in a sock, this being when she was ten, living in that
> mansion on the hill with her nanny Yuliya, who had a
> peg-leg and a glass eye and smelled of burnt chestnuts
> and crackling, who fed her herbal tinctures to keep her
> stupefied at night, always stinking of borscht, I like
> that word,* borscht, *and vinegar*

Selda didn't grow up on a hill, and in what, *Russia*? The

183

description is absurd.

I laugh abruptly: it sounds like a bark. A dogwalker passes by. I pretend to have seen something hilarious on my phone.

Path, heather. Clouds keening inland. I'll know the spot when I find it, can guide my way by sea and stars, it's easy, ancient knowledge, ancestral wisdom: the gift knows how. Aren't we from round here?

we're from here there and everywhere

— it says, so incredibly helpful, describing mountains, plains, and villages, though I know from both my mother and Selda that a branch of our line is descended from Somerset miners, into which young boys, skinnier and more flexible than the older men, would descend with nothing but a candle for light and a hammer for the coalface, heading down naked and dry and returning glossy with sweat and streaked with coke, if they returned at all, which stories, like so many in our or any family, seemed designed to flatter us, to elevate our stature by confirming a horror we had survived but not endured.

I strike off towards the cliff, close enough to hear the dry puffed plosive hisses of waves exploding on the rocks. The rhythm hauls the voices in, wave after wave, they talk about the swims she used to take in the bay near the pub we were at last night.

oh yes, she'd be out by the rocks in all weathers, rain, fog, sun and snow past the boats and bobbing buoys, her sleek head the only visible part of her, gleaming like a seal's

we listened and skimmed the liquid flitting about

184

as the bay shocked her system, electric cold that
made her feel more alive because closer to death

we sang into her ears, trilling and clicking our tongues
as she pedalled the water – do-re-mi-fa-so

The path isn't much more than a slightly muddier strip in the grass. Overhead, the clouds move swiftly, pierced in places by blades of blue light.

I've taken a stupid route, looping back on the spot rather than heading in a straight line from Bell Hall.

I ask the gift for answers. I get accounts about Selda swimming alone in the ocean.

plunging, dunked, resurfacing, baptized and
capsized again, she loved it out there, good for the
heart and lungs, though she ought to be careful, the
tide could drag her rag-doll body down

but she knows these waters

she's at home in the treacherous peace of the water, tow-
elling herself on wet rocks, drawing titters and glares
from the squinting locals, giving precisely zero toss

Details, details, how could it know so many? Selda, drunk on whiskey, would tell me of her father and her mother, how she sang to her in the bath, running firm fingers through her hair, the smell of carbolic, hot suds, stale bread softened in milk, jellies cooling on the sill, the honky-tonk gulls in the park, a lucky shilling rubbed smooth, a bottle cap buried for luck, laughter at her over-sized hands, canvas sacking hung over the doorway to shield the wood in high summer, porcelain dogs in the

185

windows, sparking wires, dresses, heels, tape deck whirring, escutcheons and buses and bowls of cherry jam, the bells, yes, those too, ringing tomorrow, today, and yesterday, the sound cutting through time, all of it piling up in a heap of nostalgia and noise, amounting to nothing, to silence.

'I wish you'd settle down,' I say, 'this isn't helping at all.'

what do you want?

Answers.

to which questions?

I follow the path inland, the sea wind pressing at my back.

Is that the problem, that I haven't asked the right question? Truth is, I don't know what I'm looking for. Clues, I think, but how will I know when I find them: a dropped note, a trunk into which she carved her final words with a pen knife – it won't be that blatant, surely. She could have made it easier for me. Instead she left an old car and her 'papers', that snowdrift on the South Wing floor.

Everything here is the same. Grass and gorse. Sketchy fences describing the limits of identical fields. Horses fixed in place as if by oil paint.

I tug my coat's hood over my head and keep walking, cold seeping into my bones. The wind is bitter, tastes of snow. She was figuring something out. That much is obvious, part of the plan. But if that was the answer, what was the question?

beating like a metronome

never alone, never separate, even at the end

Over a turnstile, left through a bush. Getting closer.

The leaves draw in and darken the sky, the path follows a dip in the land. Raindrops flit and spiral on the breeze, prickling my face. The gift ducks under the subject, pirouettes past the point, its digressions leading it further away from the heart of the case. I need discipline, I need a conductor. All this stuff about jolly swims and lonely afternoons, a murmuration singing softly in her ears like lovestruck starlings – it's all a diversion. What use were the dead when she opened the door, the ground frozen stiff under shoeless feet, snow falling so thickly she wouldn't have seen her own hands in front of her face. I should turn back, call my mother and tell her everything, or take another pill, drown the gift with gin, sink into dreamless oblivion, a place without language. That's one definition of sanity – that it's a skill, not a state, of being able to forget the right things. Or better yet, to never have known them in the first place. But the gift has given me an idea. I follow the path around the cove and quicken my pace.

she was following something if only a song

and not all of it was known to us

Footsteps thump in my head as I jog. The flat light lends the fields a greyish, weightless look. The gift changes. Less crosstalk, fewer rants, more repetition and melody. It grows hushed and chant-like, sung with a pulsing rhythm, as if the voices are marching in circles around me. Part of me thought that sound, a clear high ringing, could be a car alarm blown in on a breeze, but it's stronger now, distinct against my footsteps. The path leads to the right, the forest dark breaks open, and I see it up ahead. A clearing overhung by a tree.

This is the spot. I slow and catch my breath and walk towards it. I place my hand on the soil where the hiker in snow-shoes found her.

I should have known sooner. Guessed quicker. The gift is what killed her. The voices. You.

rumble in the bloodline

The we who are me, the others without which I wouldn't exist. Murderers. All of you – guilty. Every one. You persuaded her into the cold. Led her out. If it wasn't for you, she would still be alive.

you can talk

There's a rustling flock-like sound of a thousand small shapes rearranging themselves into sequence.

As a child, I could imagine the voices so clearly I seemed able to see them, a ghostly retinue in my wake. Now they are countless midges, winged idiots harassing my thought.

I spend a few moments at the solemn spot. There is nothing much to see. I lie down where she was found, half-covered by snow. The couple with the dog walk past. Their dog sniffs eagerly at my right boot. Once they have gone, I open my rucksack and take out the box.

This is the last thing Selda held before she died. I feel reluctant to touch it, as we did back at the hotel. I lift it with both hands. There's a heft to it, a weight I hadn't been expecting despite having lugged it here. In a houseful of instruments, she chose this item to carry, over tussock and crag and ditch, with her aching hips and stiff fingers, in a blizzard. An attempt has been made at a pattern, a frieze or a series of runes. The metal has eroded so badly, or was so poorly cast to begin with, that I cannot read what the images signify. Bodies in profile, I think. Figures marching merrily round the rim: harlequins, pilgrims, or skeletons.

I place the bell against my ear. There's a pock-marked, pumice-like roughness to the metal. There isn't any loop at the top to hold it from, whatever those are called. I hold it awkwardly, pinched, and, not knowing what else to do, feeling very much like a fool, a trainee town-crier who has forgotten to pack even the most basic bellringing gear and as a consequence remains incapable of making a timid dink let alone a resounding clang, I flick it.

pathetic

doesn't understand the mechanics of the thing

The sound is dull, as if the hollow is stuffed with cotton wool. I try again, murmur made-up spells, summon Selda with the language I have, remember how we used to sing together, oh can you wash a sailor's shirt. I wait.

The wind whispers. No voice comes.

I flick it again, aiming for the sweet spot, the resonant bull's eye, the note she would like me to strike, but nothing. Another dull tump.

Selda

Yes. Hands like Rachmaninoff's. Bullied at school. Drunk in the afternoon, working all night. Whizz with a scalpel and a soldering iron. My ancestry incarnate.

she was

I wait. The ringing grows louder the further I move down the path. A needling sound, high-frequency.

The night of the storm. I remember. Late night, a chiming woke me and drew my attention outside. The snow was moving with a wildness and ferocity reminiscent of a forest fire. Yet there was none of the crackling menace of conflagration. The sky had solidified into a magical, muffling substance, and fragments were whirring, whirling down to bury earth and subdue vibrations, pixel by pixel and layer by layer. I found myself thinking of Selda. The morning after, and the day after that, I rationalized that ringing sound as many things. It was a house alarm or a fire alarm, tinnitus or imagination. It was never a message. When I heard she'd been holding a bell, it made no difference. And now that I've stood on the spot, played the instrument, listened to the muffled sound it made, or rather the absence of the note I'd expected, it has only confirmed it. It could have been anything. It was not nothing.

Voices take flight in the quiet. Others fall in step with my breath, curious feeling, the world expanding and contracting like that.

she was holding

Snow settles in flecks on dark earth.

she was holding a bell

Yes, I know. In her hands. Beside mine, playing Chopsticks. Her skin liver-spotted and complexly creased, deltas of delicate lines. Where it caught the light it had the faintest iridescent sheen, like the mother-of-pearl buttons adorning her white linen shirt. Clutching a glass of wine, sitting in the living room, she fixed me with a look and struck the bell. A sound rang out, spilling into the hallway, the kitchen, the South Wing, the evening, the orchard, the fields, moving into the ground beneath us, the depths of the earth, into the compacted sediment of dead settlements and pulverized bone and eroded mountains, of successive extinction events, where the tectonic plates splinter and melt. What was it the voices told me, driving down with my mother, all those days ago? Bells in the night.

ringing singing walking

talking treading deadly through

the snow

There are too many of you to focus on, dead strangers, a snowstorm of voices. You're not shy of talking, either. Champion debaters and pot-bellied yodellers, the lot of you. Not one shy soul among you. Too many to make sense of. Dodgy business, anyway, looking for identity here, among this squabble and silence, this too-much and too-little, this disorganized sound. If I could cut you out, I would. What was that old drastic surgery, the one that sounded medieval but was invented last century? You're with me, always will be, you might as well help. I don't know what you want, what you need. Do I have to slit a lamb's throat? Haul my son to the top of a hill? Marry someone who looks like me? Take me with you. I'll follow you anywhere.

There is a fluttering sound of dry whispers and startled wings. Leaves snicker overhead.

why?

Something isn't right.

Selda didn't set out for no reason, unless she had lost her mind after all, like my father always said she would. The South Wing: look there.

The path back to the car park, says my phone, plunges into a stream-bed. I cross it and head into the dripping darkness of the trees through which I glimpse steely grey water, emerging at the edge of the fishing village. An old man in an oilskin coat is dragging a boat up the concrete jetty. The white houses look shuttered up. Picket fences, thatched roofs, gutters clogged with pink petals, a chip box crushed by the wheel of a motionless Volvo, 'Beware The Dog' signs on dogless lawns.

No you means no me, and no me means no you. Selda taught me that. Not that I understood her at the time. She died and you went with her, snuffed to silence. You were silent for a time. I was in my mother's garden, or tearing tickets in the theatre, or asleep in the quiet of the night, you were nowhere to be heard. And now you're a fire inside me. I'm talking to you, you're talking back. But she isn't, despite what you promised about the ash, drinking death to complete the cycle. Where did she go that you aren't?

VI. THE SOUTH WING

There is a scraping noise behind the door. Piled-up pages slide to one side as I force it open.

I'd forgotten what a state this place was in. I flick a switch and the halogens come on. Pages are scattered everywhere, on the floor and the desks, blown across the carpet, piled up at the vases of house plants, drifted against the black cases of stringed instruments. They lean against the wall like sarcophagi. When I see the grand piano across the way there's a jolt of longing as keen as if Selda herself had been there. At the centre of the room, a huge angled desk is stacked with piles of manuscript pages, most of which have slid into disarray, the banker's lamp casting a localized light: she wrote most of her music here. Her papers. Strange word. A joke, maybe: she wrote mostly by hand, on paper. The word brought to mind correspondence, to the letters and archival documents which contextualize the work, which are donated to superannuated institutions for scholars to pore over, or ignore. A stiff breeze blows into the room. Pages chatter as they shift. The window I peered through yesterday afternoon is open again. I take off my shoes and tip-toe across the room, past the desk, the piano, the double bass, the spiral stair leading up to her wrought-iron balcony, her enviable selection of books, the peaked eaves in which straggled spiderwebs hang, taking such care not to tread on her pages that I barely see what is on them. The latch is loose: I force it shut, reaching down for a stray page to fold into a wedge and keep it in place. In doing so, I spot the edge of a stave, a dense cluster of jarring, irresolute chords.

Buried memories of Selda's sight-reading lessons return. As I scan the staves, the music that sounds in my head doesn't sound like hers. It's nothing like the metrical complexity of her early work or the looser, expressive euphony of her choral phase. I paw through more pages, crawling on hands and knees to fit the pieces together, then crossing to the piano.

Like a stabled horse in winter, the piano wears a jacket, black plasticky fabric on the outside, a soft felt interior. I pull it back to reveal its high shine, then open the keys and settle the pages on the stand. I play a note. Middle D.

When I was a toddler – or so my mother tells me – I became fixated with the fact that Selda was her mother, and grew suspicious that she was withholding a truth from me. Something about her true nature. I ran into the South Wing one day and threw a bizarre tantrum – to this day my mother finds it hilarious, she often teases me about it – during which I accused a nonplussed Selda of hiding babies in her butty and her nano, my words for her arse and piano, respectively. What was going through my mind? That her piano was a womb? That, when she played, not just music but people were brought to life by her hands, as in an origin myth about the universe emerging from her music? When she, the accused, showed me the interior of the box, I saw only wood, metal, felt, all mute and motionless. Yet there was something aloof, almost threatening, in the instruments' mysterious varnish,

194

which promised and then rebuffed the possibility of infinite depth, suggesting dark infinities yet screening them from view behind a narcissistic surface: my own reflection staring back. The instrument's generous curves, the soft velveteen runner under the lid for the keys, were connected in my mind with the shape of Selda's body, her thighs and breasts in the bath and the public pool, her damp hair after the shower. And even her eyes, in whose surfaces I could at times see my own silhouette – proof that she and I were close. It was odd to me, and obscene, that other people touched similar instruments, bodies of wood and wire. Where did it leave me? Thereafter, I would approach the piano I'm sitting at timidly and with my head bowed, the way I might have a queen, afraid the piano was aware of me, understood my intentions. Once, when she was out, I pulled a footstool against its side, lifted the lid, and climbed on it. The strings left my tender body horribly marked by red lines, a body-length bar code of guilt. I utterly ruined their tuning, damaging a part of the mechanism for good measure. When Selda found out what I'd done, it was the first time I'd seen her direct her anger at me. A fierceness my mother had warned me about, which she could deploy in rehearsals, but which I'd never before experienced myself. It's not an exaggeration to think that, subjected to the full force of Selda's merciless rage, it seemed impossible that I would survive.

With my foot against the pedal, I play D again, but an octave lower. I press my ear against the wood to hear the notes meld and fade. Then I play the rest of the piece. Clumsily, though, struggling with a few of the chords.

I find other pieces, stacked manuscripts labelled in the top-right corner with her fastidious numbering system, which makes no sense to me. I organize the pages as coherently as I can, which, in a lot of cases, means wadding them into plastic bags to deal with later. Some are paragraph-long fragments, sketches of songs and scenes, others are pages long and look like fair copies. At the piano, I play through them as best I can. The first piece, that angry outburst of thumpy discord, was unlistenable. It was the most alarming of the lot, too. Those melon-fisted chords and broken tempos suggested their author was mad, and that the room, these chaotic pages, were littered with musical ranting. Other pieces are more carefully crafted. Selda admired Schubert. He was among the first freelance composers, before he died at thirty-one, and she identified with his mercenary spirit. There was more than a little of the *Winterreise* in her writing for piano, too, and of her fondness, most prominent in *Snow Trio*, for imagery of isolation and ice. Whatever happened in that blizzard, I feel increasingly sure, she was working on a song cycle.

My mother is in Selda's room. Late-morning light in the wide windows. A row of trees, a neighbour's field. On the bed are a few of Selda's dresses and suits, laid out over the mattress. My mother is holding up a jacket, black linen, vaguely familiar. I cross to the bed, floorboards rough under my bare feet. The desk at the window is empty, its contents likely downstairs in a bin. She's been going through Selda's wardrobe. There are clothes that date back decades, from dinner dresses to old shirts, the suit she wore to collect the Varèse. She hands me the linen jacket. I expect its rich odour to summon memories. Instead it smells faintly of camphor.

'Do you recognize it? She wore it in Portugal for *Snow Trio*.'

As soon as the connection is made, I can see Selda in the jacket, beside a pool, or the ocean, or an underground lake, with her arms folded, and a necklace at her throat, as the twilight – artificial, we were inside, surrounded by a biscuity smell of cold stone – fills with the sound of an orchestra tuning, all the instruments straining towards middle A.

'Listen,' I say, 'I need to show you something.'

We spend an hour sorting through the pages in the South Wing. Soon we have two intact stacks of new works. Among them are scraps and sketches of older works, including what reads like a dream-journal entry for *Snow Trio*: 'dead country / nothing but snow / the low soil of landscape / air tips fall of forest / black rise days / barely anything moves on moors solid with ice / roofed cart wooden kicks the air / dark stretches the north-east frost.' Which cryptic, gnomic style fits the way Selda spoke about – avoided speaking about – her own music.

Most of these pages, however, seem to be new. If each of these pages is part of a work, there are almost as many pieces in this room as Selda ever published in her lifetime. No one has ever heard these works, whatever they are. Standing at the desk, I attempt to reassemble a composition, following the melodies as I go, the sharp ticked edges of her notes, the slant of Italian words, rare fluffed passages and hasty rewrites. Imagining her working on these pages, I feel close to her in a way I haven't since I was a child. One page has more text than the rest. I skim-read from top to bottom, see notes about instrumentation and melody, the outlines for a drama. In between, there are enough sketches resembling the first I found, chaotic and disordered, to suggest other forces at play in her mind. That whatever formal clarity she was hoping to achieve was won at the expense of, or haunted by, its contact with something darker, more disordered – but no, too tortured genius: she was systematic in her work, collaborative too. Yet these pieces are the closest thing I have to clues about her frame of mind. Hard to shake the sense of some conspiracy at play. (If she was here, she would tell me the answer is right in front of me.) Pieces in a vast unfinished work, the scale and ambition of which match anything else she did.

I point to the desktop computer, chunky, clad in beige plastic, almost as old as I am, in whose hard-drives there may be a map, a plan, a logic to it all.

'What do you think we should do with them? Sort them, first. Obviously. But then what? We could start an estate.'

'We *are* the estate.'

'Are we?'

'Who else would be?'

I pace around the room. 'I mean like the estates that famous dead artists have. Heirs throwing lawsuits around. Refusing permission to put on exhibitions, that sort of thing. Vampire millionaire killjoys. That could be us! Guardians. No? Policing a legacy. Making a packet. Why are you looking at me like that? Who knows, she could become a star again, don't you think? Streaming contracts. We could contact one of those hologram companies. Turn her into a real cash cow. That's what sells, now, right? Sequels?'

'Wolf – enough.' That tone of hers, which thrills me with its power: a muscular mid-range she perfected after my father left, cutting through my fury like a tractor beam.

'And these are her papers?'

'I think so.'

'It's an odd word, no? She didn't leave instructions, a letter, anything. Why?'

'Maybe she was hoping to tell you in person. More likely she ran out of time.'

'Hmmm.' I play a cluster of chords on the Steinway. 'Hear that? Sublime! There's a hint of Gershwin in there, weirdly, don't you think? That F seven to B-flat six?'

'They do sound beautiful. And so different from anything she wrote. I can hear that. But we don't know what it amounts to. And I don't agree about how to run the estate, even if we technically *are* one, because–'

'I was *joking*.'

'I know. But there was a hint of truth there.'

'I just think that... Okay, so I *do* think we should put it out there, get people to play it. Eventually. But she was *doing something*. Sending a message. And you're right, she didn't finish it, but we can do that for her, can't we? Isn't that the point? Surely she wanted it out there?'

'The point of what?'

'I don't know – *generations*? I haven't thought that through.'

'Let's just sort through it first, alright? Then we'll see what we're dealing with. I'll finish upstairs. Don't forget our plans later. See you in about an hour.'

Once she's gone, and the door is closed, I fall into a trance.

The gift takes notice. I feel it pressing in around my thoughts, chatting to itself, wondering what I'm up to.

Do you know?

about what?

What all this music means?

altered distorted contorted cavorted

ever repeated and never the same

199

Those aren't exactly the answers I'm looking for.

she was finding a pattern

to unlock a door

from us to you, living to dead

I drop a handful of pages. If that was her motive, she must have been unwell. Unless there was some truth in it. Whole thing could be a metaphor. If I could find a way to follow her, to find a route into her gift, to an underworld that anyone in their right mind would dismiss as fantastical – if I could reach her there, she'd tell me.

what are you *looking for, son?*

I pace around the room, restoring order, putting the pages back where they belong. It feels strange being in this room without her expressed permission, no Selda behind the door to say *come in* or *not now* in response to the knock. That the South Wing was prohibited when I was a child only increased my desire to come in. I snuck in sometimes, and waited for her to enter, in order to be closer to her routines. On one occasion, I found a spot where she would not see me, a crevice behind an armchair in the room's far corner, the floor of which was mossy with dust, dead spiders, and bone-white moths. I peered through a crack of light between the armchair, a cello case, and a bookshelf: a porthole the size of a penny through which I stared for so long and with such intensity that I forgot to blink, tears leaking down my cheeks. I did not wipe them away. If anything, I encouraged them to fall. They were proof that I adored her, confirmed I was a martyr for her love. I didn't know which prospect scared me more: that I would be caught or ignored. In anyone other than a child, my vigil would have seemed devout, perverse, or criminal. But to me it seemed proportionate. Perhaps an hour passed. My knees began to ache. I watched Selda tuck her hair behind her ear. Scribble a note. Stare at her own reflection in the window's dark glass. Drink tea. Pace the room. Mutter to herself. Play a note. Scratch her lower back. What had I been expecting? Backflips? And yet it was everything. To see her play a note. Stare into the middle distance for a while. Write a long passage holding the page firm with her left hand and the pencil in her right. Or was it her left? Remember. Yes. Left-handed. A sinister woman. No. Ambidextrous. Then – a cry from the house, not a kettle-clatter this time, but a beckoning. My mother appeared. 'Where's Wolf?' she asked. Or: 'Is Wolf in here?' 'No.' 'I'm getting worried, I can't find him anywhere.' A tremble in her throat. I wanted to jump out and reassure her, but that would give the game away. Besides, I soon began to enjoy my newfound power, watching them, invisible: it reversed a differential to which, since I was a child, I'd been subjected my whole life. I waited until she left, with Selda following. Then I snuck out and into the kitchen, where they discovered me a few minutes later. 'Where did you go?' I said I'd gone for a walk in the forest. My deception was complete.

Waking me from my reverie, two temporalities clashing on top of each other, like dissonant tones in a bell, my mother appears in the doorway, just as she did however many years ago. Has an hour passed already? Maybe time has shot in the other direction. The light is darker, redder at the windows. She is wearing smart clothes, make-up, necklace, her hair combed and pinned.

'Come on. We'll be late.'

VII. ORCHARD TO OCEAN

Selda thonks against my thigh as I carry her into the orchard, medlar and apple trees crooked in overgrown grass. Dew soaks the hems of my jeans as we trudge. My mother lifts her dress above her knees and picks her path more slowly, avoiding the squishy bits where the rain turns lawn to marsh. I stand beside a tree whose trunk is scaled with emerald and tangerine algae. I remember this place being neatly shorn and golden, fruit fat on the autumn branches, the cider smell of those that fell and browned and grew white dots on their creased skin, a place I liked because it has a clear view of the South Wing, so that, while pretending to play, I could spy on Selda through the windows.

'I won't have time. Not if we're leaving tomorrow.'

'How long will it take?'

'Hard to say. It's a lot. I could take her car and drive back on my own.'

'I don't like the idea of you in that thing. I keep imagining it falling to bits on the motorway, screws and bolts flying everywhere. Just shove it into bags. We can sort it out later.'

'There's tonnes of material there, though.'

'It can't *all* be music, can it? She retired. Made a whole song and dance about it. How many symphonies is that, all added up? It can't be right.'

'That's what I thought, too. But I heard from a few of her friends that she was working on something, in her secretive way, though no one really knew what. And I'd rather not leave any of it here.'

'Of course, of course, I wasn't suggesting...'

We pass through a ruined gate and cross the tarmac road that marks the limit of Selda's land. The land across the way belongs to somebody, I guess. The royal family, a double-barrelled aristocrat. Whoever they are, they don't do anything to maintain the place, it's a wall of tangled wilderness.

'Through there, I think. That gap.'

'That's not a path.'

'It used to be.'

'Fucking hell. I'm being attacked by plants!'

We head along the narrow strip between two leaning trees. A bramble snags my mother's dress. It was treacherous going when I was a kid, spiny canes nicking my shins as I walked beside Selda in summer shorts and flat-peaked cap, heading for the quarry.

'Exciting, though.'

'I know. I wonder what's in it. I don't want to count our, er, chickens yet, but we could think about performances, maybe even recordings.'

'We'll have to look through it first. Are you volunteering?'

'She *did* leave them to me.'

Rain doesn't fall so much as hang, evenly diffused through the air. It lacquers leaves deep emerald, brings out the shine in the crow's-eye berries. Soon the path, a strip of flattened grass and tawny mud pressured by vegetation on both sides, opens.

In front of us is the first of the scattering sites: a giant bowl of granite open to the sky, with sheer grey walls of rock forming a kind of theatre, with brambles instead of balconies, and sheer curtains of striated rock in which the blast-holes are visible. The quarry itself is filled with water so dark it looks black. This is the source of the stone from which Bell Hall was built. We stand for a moment and watch the sky reflected on the surface. I set the tub down at our feet. My mother and I stand around for a moment, taking it in.

'Would *you* want to hang around here for the rest of time?'

I tell her that it's strange being back. Memories keep floating up. I mention, by way of example, how our voices are resounding against the far wall of the quarry: can she hear the faint echo that ghosts our words? It used to scare me as a child, the darkness of the water. I never knew what was stirring down there. Whenever Selda took me to this place, I would fall into a paralysis, momentarily unable to move. I could never escape the irrational fear that the water would suck me into it, and that I would drown, my bones absorbed into the rock. I could enjoy that fear, too, I suppose, because I knew that with Selda near me I was in fact safe. But the grand terror was when I convinced myself that Selda would turn to me and re-move her face, taking it off with one hand to reveal it was a mask all along. Beneath it, I feared, would be a stranger who wished me ill – a grey-skinned imp who would grab me by the neck and throw me into the water. The remedy to this predicament was noise. I would shout at the top of my lungs, delighting in how the echo mimicked and dou-bled my words. It made Selda laugh. Her sounds would blend with mine. Together, they formed a kind of spell. If the quarry was a giant mouth, we could force it to speak in our voice. It no longer seemed so scary after that.

'Hmm,' my mother says. I regret the confession. In the pauses between our words the only audible sound is water sliding off branches and leaves and hitting soil and stone. I've popped a pill. But even so, the gift seems quiet-er, more settled.

'I was wondering about something,' I say, and the thought of saying it tightens my throat. 'Did you ever talk with her about – I mean, later, towards the end – I don't

204

know what to call it. That's silly, isn't it. The gift?'

Only now do I realize what my mother's outfit reminds me of. Over her dark blue dress is a black velvet jacket and a crimson shawl. From her ears hang two silver teardrops, matched at her throat by a chunky necklace, the kind of smart outfit she'd wear to Selda's concerts when I was little. Around the edges of the water, lily pads like oversized emerald dining plates are laid out on the flat, dark water. I chuck a pebble in and watch the ripples spread, and picture it sinking through the dark to bury itself in the silt at the bottom.

'Are things alright with you, Wolf? You can't have slept much last night. I had a shock, waking up to the empty house this morning. It reminded me of the time you went missing. Or I thought you did. And then we found you in the kitchen.'

'That's not what I meant. I don't remember much about it and how it affected her.'

'She was born with it, as far as I know. So were you. I thought the hospice put it into her head, when I was younger. It was one reason I moved out so young. I guess everyone thinks that their mother is crazy. Other than you, of course.'

I laugh. 'You don't any more?'

'I think it helped her. She could fall into these states. Trances. Like your migraines, in some ways. It could be a moment, it could be days. It wasn't always fun. That's why I preferred to live with my dad, until he moved out of the country with Thingy. But I was older by then and could make my own mistakes.'

'You think that's what happened to her?'

'It's the best explanation I have. I always thought it would be how it happened.'

Inside the tub is a pouch of diaphanous plastic

containing Selda's ashes. We agree that it's time. I open the plastic wrapping. The wind stirs its surface, lifts flakes off the grey, clumped ash. I scoop a portion of Selda up with my fingers. Amid the soft and almost weightless ash are bits that nick my skin: thigh, skull, sternum, I think, whatever fragments of bone survived. I wonder how much of her I lost last night, drinking her death. Do I feel different after it? Side by side, saying nothing, my mother and I dip our fingers into the tub and take a handful of Selda and scatter her onto the water, saying goodbye as we do. She lands on the surface and floats. Charcoal, chalk, flecks of lilac and red. Much of it dissolves immediately, sinking into the water. I wonder if Selda chose this spot because she remembered our visits, too. The wind stirs the water's surface. The larger clump drifts past the lily pads and across the reflected sky. Water soaks into the ash, which relaxes. Unstuck, it sinks. We wait for a moment, watching. A moment later, the last is gone.

The garden's end is overgrown with ferns that outlived the dinosaurs, fragrant bushes our ancestors might have pestled into balms. We walk along the border, heading towards the gate. In the midst of the growth are statues, a wooden head, a stone sphere, though both are so fuzzed with moss it's hard to discern their shape. Standing upright in the midst of a bush is another singing statue, its body segmented like a suit of armour, and with the prim, upright posture of a butler. It leans towards us lopsidedly, hand raised in salutation. I open the tub. We haven't rationed wisely: only two thirds of Selda are left. I stare at the singing statue, its flat eyes streaked with moss.

Another handful each. We scatter Selda over the bushes and onto the grass. The wind picks up. It activates hidden mechanisms beneath the statue's metal skin. Its open mouth emits a sound, a two-note melody. My mother and I stand before it as the amber sun catches the rust, the dinks and dents, the open eyes, the singing throat, the verdigris. When I drove down the coast earlier today, and lay beneath the tree, I kept expecting to hear Selda's call or footsteps. The weight in my chest, the sadness I feel, is shot through with moments of thrill. Maybe I *have* been acting oddly. My mother seems to think so. She hasn't said it yet, but I can feel it coming off her, a worry in her gaze. How long have I been back? It's been less than two days. Whatever change has less to do with nostalgia than it does with memories which are not mine. Back home I'd not have mentioned it. But since we're here, with the statue as witness, I attempt to explain it to her.

'I know what you mean,' she says.

'You do?'

She nods. 'Come on, let's go. You booked that table? Good. I wonder who'll turn up. Maybe a few old faces.'

'Local friends, I think. Couple of musicians want to send her off.'

Rain prickles my skin. It gathers in drips and drops whose plinking rhythms interrupt the otherwise pristine quiet. Over in the bushes, the copper statue watches the low, grey clouds. As my mother and I leave, I remember the story Selda told about the origins of her name. In the eleventh century, a girl was born on the border of Cornwall. Her name was El. She had six children, one of whom had a son – her grandson – who called her Elda. The nickname stuck, not least because it homophonically referred both to her status in the village and her favourite tree, whose purple-black berries she often picked, the juice staining her lips dark purple. The tree kept the Devil at bay, too, and when she burned its branches she saw him dancing in the smoke. She gave the name to her daughter, who gave it to hers until, three generations later, a cleft palate softened it to Selda. And as the name was handed down by the whispering gift, it became talismanic. The story was mixed up with the other myths of singing trees and fiery giants. I've no idea if the name came from the gift or not. Most likely her parents gave it to her.

Between Bell Hall and the bay is a nameless forest so dense that, even in high summer, to walk through it is to enter a kind of twilight. A stream runs through it, shaping a channel in mealy soil, the water running clear and swift over pebbles and sand, reeds leaning over the water as if to admire their own shaggy reflections, as I did with Selda's piano. The trees above are ancient knock-kneed things, some cloaked in ivy, others in moss, the low branches strung with parasite vines and the higher ones tufted with birds' nests. Lichen covers stone and fallen log alike in velvety splotches and offcuts. Selda may have walked this way. I wonder if the snow would have hit the ground or formed a roof overhead. The earth is dank and mulchy, a rich, peaty smell rising up off it as my mother and I head deeper into the forest. The wooden posts that mark the path grow soft and rotten and fall away altogether. We reach a clear stream clogged with leaves and stones, and slow down beside it. 'I think this is the spot. She took me here once. Not sure why she liked it here.'

My mother tilts her head and squints. 'It's not the most picturesque part of the forest.'

'Dingy.'

'I mean, we can find somewhere nicer.'

'You think so? She said here.'

'I like down there better. So long as we're in the woods...'

'You're not worried she'll come back to haunt you?' I

mean it as a joke.

'She already has!'

We step and slip down a path made treacherous by rotted leaves and mud, the kind of unstable terrain that Selda, whose joints were arthritic and who was known to lose her way on long walks, who spoke to people who were not there, referred to places not on maps, events unrecorded in history books – the kind she would get lost in. It is dark enough already. If she walked this way, through the snow and the gloaming, without deciding to turn back, she was pursuing something with a need that exceeded her will to survive, or was led this way, or was on her way back, when the metronome stopped.

We reach another broader stretch of clear water where the current slows and pools, eroding a basin in which a few fish, the colour of wet pebbles, swim.

'Look – life! I was beginning to wonder.'

'We should say something,' I suggest. 'We haven't said anything so far.'

My mother gathers herself for a moment. Then she says a few lines. She talks about Selda as if she is with us, addressing herself to the stream as it carries dead leaves and reflections towards the bay. She speaks with tenderness and feeling about how much she has to thank Selda for. But most of what she says passes me by. A ringing has begun to fill my ears, the result of an incipient panic. I pat my pockets for the last of my pills, check my wallet, pockets, jacket, check my wallet, pockets, jacket a second and third time. Images flash through my mind, each as vivid as the rest, of the packet on my bedside, or on the bathroom shelf. A moment ago, I felt elated and free. Now my tongue feels strange and heavy in my throat. I breathe deeply, slowly, smell the cool green of the leaves, and feel the gift quicken to verb: rolling, swilling, stirring through the branches, the murmuring streams. At a bend in the path we pass a man in an oilskin coat: slim face, doomy blue eyes, boots creaking as he takes the incline. He nods at us. Why do I feel like I've met him before? I watch him trudge off up the path, in the direction of Bell Hall, then take a right fork, towards the fishing village, disappearing behind a curtain of ivy. My mother, who kept walking, turns to ask why I'm dawdling.

'He look familiar to you?'

My mother turns and squints into the forest's thickening dark. 'Who?'

'A man just walked past.'

My mother shakes her head. 'Really? I doubt I'd have noticed if a ten-foot purple elephant walked past.' She places her hand on her shoulder and we walk in that fashion for a moment. I am reminded of the years we spent together between the acts – after my father left, before Todd came into the picture – how it was just the two of us and how it could feel, sometimes, as though we weren't mother and son but friends, comrades, thieves. I take deep breaths, remind myself how I felt at the quarry just now.

'Listen, Wolf, about earlier. The gift, I mean. You and Selda.'

I ask her what she means. When she repeats herself, with that tone of hers, telling me that she *knows*, I tell her that I don't know what she's talking about, haven't a clue, no idea. Which is to say I overreact, and in doing so betray myself. 'Well, I just wanted to say that I know what it's like. From the outside at least.'

'I'm fine. Look – the sea.'

'You're changing the subject.'

The path leads out of the trees and onto a slatted walkway half buried by sand. After the sepulchral forest, with its dark dripping liquids and smells of decay. We follow the path over a bay whose ashen sand is scoured flat by the wind. I've spent so long denying the gift that I lack the language to discuss it. She asks me if I can hear individuals. By which she means people with names. Ancestors that I could look up in the records and prove they lived, if I wanted to try. For years, the subject was taboo. Any mention of it was met with a refusal to countenance Selda's faith as anything more than a superstition. All that heaviness – a background feature of my childhood – has vanished in a weekend. So rapidly, in fact, that I wonder if I have been mistaken all along. How much of that prohibition was just in my head? My mother's eyes are bright and searching and there is a tension to her lips, the suppressed quiver of an incipient grin. I sense a door being opened or a tree being felled, empty space, sudden light. After the last few days in the shadows of this house, my mother's interest surprises me almost more than anything else.

'I'm sure I've told you this before, but for a time, before you were born, Selda and I tried to join forces. She told me things about the gift, and I researched the tree, going back as far as I was able to. At a certain point, the records became unreadable. Everyone was called Smith or Jones or Brown. Sons took the names of their fathers, who took their names from their fathers, who took their... This would go on for five, ten generations. Some would be named after the village they came from, which made it look like they were all related. Which they might have been.'

'Like the royal family. Everyone marrying their cousins.'

'The way she went on about the monarchy you'd think she hadn't heard of the Civil War.'

'Or wanted another one.'

Rock, flight, ferns – they spin and blur as I tumble forward, my toe caught. The tub drops loose, smacks the sand. The lid pops off and rolls away. Wind catches the edge of the plastic and lifts Selda out. Ash scatters weightlessly into the air and across the beach, a swarm of grey flecks on grey sand, wind gusting in from an ocean without end. I scrabble back and snap the lid shut, but half of Selda has gone.

told you

My mother gasps. I look at my hands.

fingers crooked with a lifetime's playing

For a moment we stare at each other. Selda flies off. She's a flock. Too late to put her all back. My mother brings her hand to her mouth. I think she's about to scream at me. Burst into tears. At the same moment, we laugh.

♫o can you wash a sailor's shirt
o can you make it clean?♫

We stand at the water's edge. The waves rimmed with stiff, brownish foam like something a brewer might pour down the drain. Seagulls caw overhead. A few tankers are out at sea. This is what she wanted? I guess it traces a journey. There is a sense of the infinity of the ocean and the sky but most of all the slapstick error of my clumsy tumble sending her scattering into the reeds and the ignominious sand littered with crushed cans and plastic. There isn't much Selda left for this part. My mother lifts the lid and the wind kicks up. A sailor's dirty shirt. Her hands as she played it, fingers crooked as the roots of old trees, every note weighted and placed. Spindrifts of ash falling into the waves. The sea steals the song from my throat.

VIII. ABSOLUTE MUSIC

Night falls quickly. So does rain. Lightning through the clouds far out at sea, purple, pulsing light amid the black mountainous vapour. Then thunder's mighty rumble, like boulders rolling over the sky.

'A bit wet out,' I shout against the roar.

'Is it?' my mother cries back. 'I hadn't noticed.'

The street takes us around a promontory, the coastline's jagged shadow veiled in rain. We pass a row of squat grey houses. Sheer rock glistens to our left. Spectres of spray drift across from the right. Tarmac streams with runoff racing downhill. Only a gnarled bar of rust-bitten steel prevents us from keeling into the sea. Silver light plays on the swell. The moon, visible through gashes in the clouds, is full and bright. My mother and I trudge on, cursing Selda for having dragged us here. I start laughing. 'No-no,' I tell my mother, 'not you,' though she does look funny. 'It's something I remembered earlier. About something I did in the South Wing.' And I run through the story, laughing at the image of me imprinted with piano wire, trembling with love and pain, begging Selda to forgive my attempt to transcend my corporeal form and become continuous with her music.

'When was that?' my mother says. And my frenzied self-amusement drops a gear upon seeing her sceptical face.

'Must have been... five? Dad wasn't there, but I was small enough to get inside a piano and close the lid.'

'Are you *sure*?'

'Yes. I'm certain. Why? It's funny. Don't you think it's funny?'

The Boatman's Rest is set back from the street. Boats heave and sway in the harbour below, loose lines clacking the masts. Inside we smell woodsmoke and vinegar, carpet musty with spilled ale. Low white ceilings sag over the rooms, tankards dangle from warped black beams. The walls are hung with framed maps, photos of fishing boats, bearded saltdogs, Victorian illustrations of deep-sea fish. We put Selda down on our table. Our jackets drip onto the floor. Denim clings to my thighs and shins, my boots squelch as I walk.

'What would you like? Other than a towel.'

A drunk man at the bar asks about the tub and makes a joke I don't follow. He's a kingly chap with a plump ruddy face and a hefty belly, deep creases in his forehead and neck, and the puffed ears of an ex-rugby player, sleeves rolled back on smudged tats. Something to do with genies in bottles, worm-bait. 'She used to live up the way,' I say, 'place called Bell Hall.' Sharon the landlady pours a white wine. The man's stance stiffens. 'Holiday home, is it?'

'No, she lived there.'

I've heard she came into this pub, perhaps he even met her. She was a well-known composer, her music famous from Prague to Paraguay, but he might not have known it: she wasn't always credited in the films and adverts her music moved through. She had a face like mine, I say, not exactly sure what I mean by it and much less sure that he's listening.

Sharon sets our drinks on the bar top, beside the fibreglass piggy-bank shaped like a boat livid with plastic flames. 'Selda Heddle is in *that*?'

I nod. She tuts. 'No way to treat her remains.'

'We're following her wishes,' I say. 'She left very specific instructions.'

Her magnified eyes blink behind thick-lensed glasses. She moves her head in nimble, perceptive jerks, picking up every last detail, from the dog in the corner to the croak of the door, from the man hoisting up his belt to the woman biting her nail as she looks at her phone. I ask if Selda visited often. She nods, topping up vodka with tonic. 'She sat over there, by the window.' Selda ran a song group. An amateur opera in the snooker hall over the harbour, connected to the school she ran at Bell Hall. 'Of course,' I say, acting as if I know this already, why wouldn't I? She was my grandmother. I could only be her dutiful heir. Through the window and across the harbour is a Victorian building stark against the moonlit night, stocky block and chunky spire. A wave thumps the harbour wall and cloaks the whole thing in spray. I ask what kind of music they performed, Puccini? Verdi? Sondheim? Gilbert and Sullivan? Sharon shakes her head. She isn't certain, but it was something new. Selda planned to perform it somewhere near here. Where? Sharon shrugs. The gift murmurs, sub-linguistic, like a burbling stream.

the deeper music

the ditties she wrote, rewrote, and wrote again,
hot-blooded songs and sangfroid

It wouldn't feel right to eat greasy fish and chips with Selda at rest on the table beside us, and so, while my mother is outside speaking to Todd, I set the tub down beside my shoe on the flagstone, near a tacky patch of evaporated lager. Then I put her on the seat beside me. But that doesn't feel right either, she isn't a child, so I lift the tub again. I resolve at last on a three-legged stool, acquired from a mutton-chopped gent who approved its removal with a baritone growl. I want to speak with the voices directly, with the ease with which they presume to speak to me. Demons claiming an ancestral relation I've

216

never heard mentioned before. I want to question them, line them up in a ghostly parade, but where to begin, what questions to ask? I cannot tap their number into a cognitive box and speak with them directly, as individuals, if there even are any. As their clamour rises, with the cacophonous pitch of an open-air market, or a trading floor of coked-up ghosts in skeletal pinstripes, so does a countervailing sense of, what to call it, sharpness? Keen edge. If only I could speak with them, the way I might a family of flesh and blood, if I had sisters, brothers, cousins, they might unfold before me like a painting of hell, a dinner party to which all possible relatives were invited, our differences colliding at last.

There's a singed, acrid smell. The edge of the plastic tub has softened and browned in the heat of the fire. I pull the stool away from the flames, closer to me.

Was Selda looking for them too? When she comes back as a voice – if she comes back as a voice – I must be ready to find her, to hear her, speak with her. I don't need all these voices, cold comfort for the absence of hers. Not that this will ever be possible. In darker moments, of which there were many, the solution is easy. I could jump off a bridge or a cliff and be done with it, but what could be worse than waking up in their limbo, a voice without a body, outside of time, talking of things you can barely remember to ghosts who won't quit? The thought gives me more than pause, it makes me shudder, but that might just be the rain. Or is the issue something else? Selda made peace with it. Somehow. She may even have worked with, and not against, it. In whose head will her words reverberate? Will they even be 'her' words or just echoes, residues, epigenetic mimicry? The closest I've found to a solution are the pills, which leave a bitter taste on the tongue, though I have come to enjoy them.

Try another way. Talk back.

I mutter softly under my breath, barely moving my lips, shifting my perception just so, intending them to hear me, and as I talk my voice grows louder, and I forget the gift's not there.

So I've heard, I say. Or so Selda claimed.

To talk with you would be madness, or one common definition of madness, which is to say a prejudice, I should talk to you after all.

> we were real enough once as no cunt never asked
> us to defend it, real as spit in your eye

> we worshipped false gods and we sat in the pillories,
> tarred and feathered in town squares, hung from
> bridges first light

And you're me? I would say we're quite different.

Did you speak to Selda too? Are you the same voices she heard?

> we set out for China seeking glory, died of frostbite in
> the Urals, made penitential offerings in Ripon, Whitby,
> Jarrow, confirmed our holiness by parting heathens
> from their heads, stood at rivers before they were
> named, lowered our tugs and pissed on crickets, worms

> we were remembered until we weren't

I don't want proof. What use are you to me?

> we've been walking this land since before there
> was a language to divide it, hence our tendency to,
> um... hiccup and, gah, gargle from time to time

218

My mother appears. Phone by her side, rain dripping off her hair. She looks from me to Selda and back again. 'Hello?' she says, waving. 'Anyone home?'

> does your chest ever clench in the heat of the sun?
> does rage ever rise at the sight of a stranger? does
> terror hit you when a shadow falls just so? has hate
> ever twisted your gizzards for no better reason but
> whim? do you own these sensations? will them into
> being? or did they just arise? from where? whose
> are they?

She sits in front of me, rolling her eyes in a good-natured way, but there's the faintest tremble in her voice.

> some of those are we, us, the sediment in the seams
> of your being, bitter rage and lifelong love

> only now that you have the gift

> our singing gift

> the heavenbell

> ringing

'Sorry, daydreaming.'
Quiet now. Shut up. Quiet.

> you summoned us at last

> son of the unnamed plains, the painted caves

> we remember a time when the land was all tropic,

hippos in that water-course you call the Thames

'It's been a long day. I'm *exhausted*. Let's just relax, shall we? Are the musicians here yet?'

The gift quickens and the room slows down. Smoke hangs like a ghostly mobile, beer stands rigid as an icicle under the tap, lighting cuts a livid crack in the sky's dark glass. The gift speaks of marshes, disasters, in accents so rapidly mishmashed I can't place town, county, century, until one half-familiar voice rises out of the throng.

> *we had teeth, too, once, births and battles*
> *before the bones*

> *if you'd only just give us a minute, sir, we beg*

> *fuck begging*

> *beg, fucker!*

LISTEN

'Not sure. Can't see anyone with an instrument.'

I order another round, hoping booze will calm the voices. It doesn't work like that, though. Intoxication by spirits rarely helps subdue the other kind. I lean from side to side, feeling queasy, stewing in the room's sudden heat. Sharon stares sidelong over the taps. I ask her if she recognizes any musicians here. 'Sorry, strange question. We're just expecting a few. But actually, don't bother. They're not due for another hour. Losing track of time.'

I take the drinks back to the table. 'Do you ever think Selda was making it up?'

My mother exhales. 'Sometimes, yes.'

jealous old bitch

'Weren't you ever curious about what they sounded like, where you came from?'

'Well, sometimes she did try to show me.'

> *those visits down to Bell Hall, the lonely woman in the forest, isolated, fearful of outsiders, weaving music like a spell*
>
> > *how the sounds and smells and textures of that farmhouse, those fields, returned you to moments you'd buried, laughter in the afternoons, terror in the evenings, craving your grandmother's company, and how she told you to go*

When she was young, Selda would tell her stories about our ancestry, and my mother loved to hear the strange and wonderful things they, or 'we', had done. She has forgotten a lot of the details, but she remembers the stories' auras, in which the magical and the mundane sat side by side. Stars reflected in buckets of water, an angel dancing on a chimney at midnight – a sparrows' nest that caught fire in an up-draught. They sounded embellished to her, if not improvised on the spot. And they were tangled up in Selda's tendency to claim that her Coventry childhood was harder than the one my mother had experienced under her care and at a different point in history: an observation tainted, it seemed to my mother, by intergenerational envy. Eventually, inevitably, scepticism tarnished my mother's wonder. It became impossible for her to believe that she was directly descended from the people her mother told her about. But Selda insisted that we *were*, just as surely as my mother was descended from Selda. She admitted that, from time to time, she would embellish for effect, excise the steamier passages, heighten the comedy or the tragedy, compress the time-lines – but that, despite all this, nothing she said was *invented* because the gift could never lie.

all we ask is to be listened to

I laugh. My mother blinks. 'She told me that,' she says. 'She said it didn't lie. It was sometimes mistaken, but it never deliberately bent the truth, because it wanted us to remember.'

'So you do think it exists?'

My mother doesn't answer directly. Instead she tells me that, when she was little, she would ask her mother to tell her certain stories over and over again, and how moved she had been to observe me, when I was that age, do the same with Selda. Back in the house in our mornings together.

'Which stories did you ask her to tell?'

Drowned sailors appeared in Selda's tales quite often. Ancestors who roamed the ocean's sunken highways, bluely looping the lightless depths. Selda identified with them. As a young woman at university, where she met my father, who like *her* father was a scientist, my mother used the library and records services to track down what information she could find about our ancestors. She became a genealogist. Property records, certificates of birth, marriage, and death, the indexes of richly sourced histories. She drew diagrams in which our family's history was plotted – in so far as it could be from ghostly hearsay – and compared it against what she remembered from

222

the stories Selda spun at bedtime, or driving down the motorway, or in the anecdotes she told over roast beef on Sundays, when one of her friends – a singer, a musician, some other gifted person – would come over, and it was my mother's job to lay out the plates, decant the sauces, and top up the wine. One of the middle-class rituals that Selda felt compelled to perform.

'What did you find out?'

'A lot of what she told me was accurate,' my mother says. 'Some of it wasn't – the dates clashed, that sort of thing. Or a record noted that such-and-such ancestor had died from tuberculosis, when Selda had claimed, say, murder by slitting the throat. The vast bulk of it couldn't be proven either way.'

'Did you speak to Selda about it?'

'I did. I got a little obsessed with it. Folders. Copied documents, family trees.' She researched our lines going far back as records allowed. One clan were farmers until the Highland Clearances drove them south, where they went into service. Farther back, one of our ancestors came into a large parcel of land in North Riding shortly after the Norman invasion, which suggests we are descended from at least one collaborationist. That was my interpretation anyway. My mother admires this man from afar, doing what was best for his family. To say that both of us are projecting is to understate the case. There was just an entry in the Domesday Book for a taxable value: nine geld units, seven plough teams, eight acres meadow, one acre woodland. 'All this evidence. I was building a case.'

'Against Selda? You wanted to prove her wrong?'

'No, not against her.'

'But you thought she was lying, that the gift wasn't real?'

'At the time, yes. I thought that no evidence meant no proof, and that no proof was proof that the gift wasn't real.

I was a zealot. But at the same time–'

'You wanted, I guess–'

'I called her up, arranged a meeting. I hadn't seen her in a few months and we'd not been so in touch – it wasn't a good time between us generally, I'd run away from home a few years before. She was up in town, rehearsing for a show of hers.'

My mother and Selda met at a London rehearsal studio complex that was mostly underground, a warren of soundproofed cellars in which musicians were running through trills and punk and dub bands were playing behind shut doors. At the farthest end of one long, dark corridor that smelt of wet socks was the rehearsal studio's largest room. Selda and a group of musicians had set up in that dank stuffy space with its low arched ceiling, where mildew had blackened the plaster behind which a pipe had burst, leaving green mucus like the trail of a slug. They had been rehearsing *Songs of Innocence*, which I hadn't heard of before. It wasn't one of Selda's successes. When my mother arrived, Selda was in furious flow, commanding the horn section, while a bearded tenor stood still and stern as a beefeater. My mother waved at Selda, who acknowledged her daughter with a grin and a swipe of her baton, then sat behind the grand piano, which wasn't being used, instinctively pulling her legs up to her shoulders and hugging them, just as she did when she was little.

My mother had been living away from home for almost a decade by then. She had just met my father. It had been a few years since she'd sat in like this, as she had throughout her childhood, often hungry and bored by these rehearsals, but thrilled by them too, by the swagger of the musicians, the way they welcomed her into the fold, the late nights, the pranks, the licence to do whatever she wanted, so long as it didn't interrupt. The musicians were attempting a fiendish stretch in the second phase, where the time signatures alternated so often – in some places thrice in two bars, seven-seven tessellating to five-ten to two-four – the musicians believed it was devised as a form of punishment. They were worn-out, stroppy. Selda was too. The air was thick with sweat. Bass was pounding through the brick, dust falling from the ceiling in rhythmic sifts.

'This sounds like a piece from her early career, though. When she was working with mathematical formulas and all that. Looking for order. Pattern.' She was always going on about pattern, in the interviews from the period, as if everything was just a matter of sequence, one thing after another. 'Very purist, wasn't it? Absolute music.'

'It had elements of that, I think, but she'd written the score half by chance, and there were improvised passages.'

Eventually a skeletal flautist came in a half-bar too late for the sixth time in a row. Selda howled and snapped her baton to splinters across her knee.

Did she really? I don't ask.

The room fell silent, save for the creak of a chair and the plink of damp from the ceiling and the whirring of the feeble fan, which did nothing to freshen the air. Through a glass panel set into the wall my mother looked as a whiskered, wizardy recording technician in a purple waistcoat raised his eyebrows and tilted his head as if to signal, *told you so*, though she didn't know what. Selda took a deep breath and apologized. She gave the musicians the night and the next morning off. They packed their instruments away, *like a battle-weary regiment*, heading variously for bed and the bar, leaving Selda and my mother alone amid the stiff chairs and music stands. But Selda was scribbling notes, talking to herself.

'She forgot I was there. Just for a moment.'

'She wasn't ignoring you on purpose?'

'No, I don't think so, she was never that petty. She was talking with herself.'

My mother cleared her throat. Selda jumped and spun round and that's when my mother noticed how gaunt and thin she looked, her eyes sunk in ashen sockets and red around the irises, a turbulent, unfocused energy to the dark pupils. The anger had faded, and with it the colour had too: *the musicians looked dead, but Selda looked like a ghost.* And the moment she saw her daughter, remembered she was there, and in the present, she flung her arms wide and hugged her, and pressed firm dry kisses onto her cheeks and forehead, and smelled her hair. *My prodigal daughter!* She opened a cello case from which she removed a bottle of J&B and set it atop the piano. She poured slugs into cut-glass tumblers and topped them up with soda, then whined about the musicians, the venue, *we had a lovely place but some idiot double-booked it and so here we are, rehearsing in a wheelie bin*, but mostly her own music, which, she felt, was *lifeless, horrible, I can't do this any more, maybe I never could.* Then my mother stopped her short. She had come for a reason, after all. To present her grand project, a historical counter-document, researched pages and pages. She felt, she says, extremely anxious. What would her mother make of it? Would it read to her like an attack? Selda lifted the top page off quietly. Thought for a moment. Lifted the next page. Then she said something like *come on, let's get out of this tomb shall we? I haven't eaten since yesterday.*

'She needed looking after.'

'She was in her own world half the time. She liked

company. Interaction. Life. That was how music was made, she always said. She wrote it alone but it came together with people.'

living, dead, and livingdead

'Which makes the end – I just accepted it at the time. I thought, she wants to be alone, so let her. And I thought – I don't know what I thought. It's a mystery even to me.'

not really, you liked it that way

'Why would she retreat like that, you mean? I did ask her, but it was always a time-of-life thing. *When you get to my age it will make more sense. You only have so much time left...* the whole spiel. I'd sort of blown my fuse by then. We were different people. I just accepted that. Anyway, as I was saying...'

They went for Chinese, took a table for four on a vast table at the back of the restaurant, near-empty at that late hour. My mother turned what she joked was the Lazy Selda until the real thing told her to stop. Once they'd eaten – roast pork, rice, beer – they returned to the chilly flat that Selda was renting on the second floor of a redbrick townhouse. It had high ceilings and windows, the walls bare except for a large gilt mirror, its surface blotched with imperfections, and a painting a friend had gifted her, unframed, raw canvas edge, of a figure in a garden. Separating the living room from the bedroom, the front and rear of the flat, were not doors but curtains, heavy, faded crimson where they hung from an unseen rail where, less stunningly, clothes were drying on a rack beside the radiator. As she set down her things and headed to the kitchen, those curtains unnerved my mother, as

227

though she expected them to part, and for a circus top to appear. Instead, in the kitchen off the side, was an empty soda siphon in the fridge.

'No instruments?'

'Not then, no – that shocked me more than anything. I knew what they meant to her, they were a kind of protection. She believed they had souls.'

'She was an Agnesian, though.'

'Independent life, then. She had some electronic stuff on a table in the corner. I think she moved out shortly after. But she was productive there. It's not important really, but there was room for us to lay it all out.'

My mother refills her glass. My thoughts turn with sinister ease to incest and to murder which, if Selda is to be believed, are as integral to our story as the mountains and the mills in which the unremembered lived, the beds in which they perished, the livelihoods they won and squandered. Growing up with Selda, such transitions seemed, if not always welcome or natural, at least expected. I do not tell my mother that, unlike Selda, I can't yet shape the voices, parse the noise. Selda may have been doing just that, attempting to set down in song what would otherwise go unrecorded. I rest my eyes on the window, the sea beyond it. My mother's left eye is half-closed, the lid sagging slightly. She's tired. Tears glisten at the edge of her eyes. The cold from our soaking trip lingers in my skin, despite the heat of the fire and the warmth of the others in the pub.

'Do you think the gift was part of it?' I ask, convinced of the fact myself but uncertain if my mother agrees. 'That it led her outside?' That may be where I need to look for her, not here, in the landscape, but there, in the gift. To put the pieces of her life together and understand how it led her astray.

My mother doesn't answer directly. 'I saw a preacher once. A friend was trying to convert me. He was very hammer-and-tongs. Homophobic, lots of spittle. *Hated* it. Was about to leave. But then he started on about the gift. I froze. It was like a spell. Said the voices were devils. Evil things. I didn't believe him. Of course not. But I couldn't shake it. Not for months after.' Then her face brightens. 'Anyway – be back in a tick.'

So we left her alone with her devils, I don't tell the empty seat.

I picture red-eyed shadows in the snowbound trees, beckoning through the blizzard, *join us, join us*.

Then I see Selda. She is standing at the doorway of Bell Hall. It is dusk. The sky is the stone of a plum, wood-yellow and purple, a few red-tinged clouds. She watches it darken. The clouds draw in. The first flakes fall, sweet and weightless, lilting to the gravel at her feet. Within minutes, the air is teeming.

> *what do you see?*

She's alone in a storm.

> *what do you hear?*

That's just it. Nothing.

My mother and I will leave tomorrow. That's the plan, at least. But the past two days have had the opposite to expected effect, raising more questions than they have answered. Selda's friends trickle into the pub. They approach our table and introduce themselves, offer condolences and memories, remark on how much I resemble her. I try to listen to what they say. I have questions for every one of them. But the heat, the drink and the gift render everything woozy, hard to grasp. I speak to locals, singers and musicians about their afternoon walks with Selda, the rehearsals across the way. One man excitedly remembers hearing 'the most extraordinary' music floating across the fields from Bell Hall. There is singing, much of it drunken, some of it tear-jerking. Then the last-order bell cuts through the uproar. My head is thumping. It's time to go. Sharon gives us a number for a, or the only, cab company. When I call, we hear the ringtone right away, because the cabbie's right there, in the corner, nursing a pint of ale. We really shouldn't, but we're drunk and exhausted, so we do. We stagger into his minivan and he drives us along the meandering road, away from the ocean and into the trees. My mother rests her head on the window. Within a minute, she's asleep. The storm has cleared at last. No more lightning, just a fine rain that blesses the windshield. Bell Hall appears ahead. Gravel crackles under the cab. Once we're back inside, in the living room, I stoke the fire. My mother makes tea and lies down on the sofa. The brief nap has revived her, she says. She suggests that we finish the story.

Fixed with clips and staples, typewritten notes, post-its, labels, colour-coded folders, even its own index, it was clear how much effort my mother had put into her project, how completely it had consumed her. After years of shunning the gift as an embarrassment, she had now, and to her mind unwittingly, produced a comprehensive response: her attempt to make sense of a sense she did not share. As my mother watched her mother read, her motivations at last became clearer to her. Presenting these materials to Selda was tribute and provocation both. It was also the product of another, more secret need, which until that moment had remained obscure.

'The first thing she said to me was, *Do you ever hear it too?*'

'The gift?'

'She'd never asked me that before. Not once in my childhood. I didn't know what to say. I told her I had to go. She looked exhausted. And I had things to worry about. I'd just met your father. So I stayed at a friend's for a night and took the train back in the morning.'

A month or so after that meeting, *Songs of Innocence* was performed. Selda had worked on it for a year. It was her first real flop. Critics savaged it. They said it wasn't clear how or if this sequence of songs, nominally inspired by Blake's poems, related to one another in any narrative or even thematic sense, because the words were scrambled, and so were the musical patterns, jarring, atonal, and so rhythmically dense as to sound at various points as though the musicians were out of time with one another. In public, Selda showed queenly indifference, claiming she never read reviews. In private, a bad one could trigger a days-long breakdown, a months-long sulk. For all her imperious self-belief, she was equally capable of despair that her music was worthless, that she was a failure and a fraud. And so, after *Songs*, when she disappeared for two weeks, people were understandably concerned. No one knew where she had gone. My mother was worried by the absence, but exasperated too, because it wasn't the first time. One day, my mother says, the phone rang.

'It was her. She asked why I hadn't flown out to meet her.'

'Where was she?'

'South of France. Never mentioned she was going.'

My mother flew out the next day. Selda paid for the ticket using the last of her money from *Songs*. A friend had given her the run of a family home.

His name was Lambert van Klampt. She'd met him at Agnes's. He was the wiry scion of a dynasty and could trace his fortune to the early thirteenth century, when a distant, gifted shipbuilder in the Low Countries – himself descended from Assyrian merchants who migrated through Mesopotamia and eventually settled in Hungary – succeeded in his desire to become a vassal to King Phillip Augustus of France by supplying the warmongering monarch with timber, having forcibly seized, from his drunken, indebted supplier, ownership of a modest teak plantation. That merchant had three sons who each had three children, all of whom worked for the burgeoning business, as did their children's children – and so on. The gift allowed them to ensure generational return on investment, building, over the decades, a merchant fleet which for a time was highly active in the Mediterranean, augmenting William the Silent's forces with a considerable privateer force during the Dutch Revolt. By the seventeenth century they had a dispersed and diversified set of business interests including timber (which they now traded for largely sentimental reasons) and the transatlantic trade of tea, sugar, rubber, and enslaved people, amassing a vast fortune which they dispersed across multiple European banks, investing in properties in Amsterdam, Rotterdam, London, and Rome, which, over the next hundred and more years, went up vastly in value, so that a family whose wealth had at one time consisted of a modest shipbuilding company became, over the centuries, an internationally powerful dynasty whose influence permeated various governments.

'They'd call it a conspiracy theory these days,' my mother says, 'but for Selda this was something different. Which was how the gift, something immaterial, all whispers and rumours and voices only few people could hear, could reveal the material basis of inheritance.'

She herself had no idea about this hidden history until Selda told it to her, as they sat one afternoon on the patio beside the pool and in the shade of the plane trees. The fields around them were audibly sizzling, my mother says, in the heat of the midmorning sun.

Selda was wearing shades, an enormous sun-hat equivalent in size to a dustbin lid, and a hot-pink, canary-trimmed swimming costume somewhat resembling a tutu, an ensemble which made my mother cringe despite there being no one nearby to see it. Selda's friend – the gifted, tortured scion who was off in Marrakesh – had one ambition in life: to liquidate his entire family fortune. The publicly stated reason was that he believed his family's ill-gotten gains should be repaired to historically wronged parties, including the descendants of enslaved people, workers who'd been swindled in the timber yards, anyone who had been wronged. But Selda believed in a baser motive. The scion wanted to anger his mother, who had tormented and abused him as a child, lashing him with her tongue, making him parade in front of dinner guests for his own humiliation. Having suffered two strokes, which left her able to think and feel but not to write or speak clearly, power of attorney had been signed over to him, her last surviving relative, whom she believed she held in an iron grip undiminished by her infirmity. Liquidating the empire before her eyes, in her dying days, was a feast served cold. He was fond of Selda. They'd met at Agnes's. She was rude to him. For whatever reason he took a shine to her. They were friends right up to his death.

'She wasn't sulking about the bad reviews?'

'She was upset. She said she planned to retire – even

back then she was fatalistic about the end of her career... She was drinking Pernod and having an affair with a sous-chef at the local brasserie. We went there for dinner one night and the kitchen sent us calf's head stew. After which he delivered to our table a sickly pudding which was mostly prunes in Armagnac. Looked like Marie Antoinette. The pudding, I mean. He was handsome enough but he was younger than I was. Made me feel a bit sick. The situation, not the pudding. The pudding got me drunk. I excused myself and stood outside trying not to cry, smoking a cigarette. I was convinced a man younger than me would be my new father-in-law.'

'He might have wanted to be.'

'He thought *we* were van Klampts. Or maybe he'd taken one look at that tutu costume. I told Selda how uncomfortable it made me. She didn't seem to care. Two days later, she called it off.' Over the course of that week, my mother says, she and Selda put their disagreements aside. They enjoyed the kind of holiday they'd never been able to afford when she was younger, when Selda's devotion not just to music, but experimental classical music, often left them close to poverty. In France, though, they sat on the veranda, ate fatty rillettes, pastries, baguettes, and creeping cheeses. At night they set the citronella candles out on the outdoor table and drank heavy reds. The air swam with synthetic lemon and acrid black smoke which did little to deter the licentious mosquitos. Flames flung unsteady light across the documents on the table, which Selda had brought with her and had annotated.

'You were talking about the gift in theory,' I say, 'or as told to Selda?

'Both. But mostly what it told her, and how it compared to the evidence. There was a discrepancy.'

'How bad?'

That my mother and Selda hadn't reconciled as much as she might have hoped grew clearer over that holiday. As she relates these stories, she is telling them to multiple people: me, herself, Selda – and the gift itself. She believes it exists and is listening, recording, all ears. Or she thinks she's better off hedging her metaphysical bets and acting as if it is. A marriage in the seventeenth century between a landowner and a seamstress – there was a record of that in the parish register, so that part must have been true. Her uncle Charles going to Sicily in the Second World War: there were records there, too. (Her own father, exempt on account of a blind eye, worked for Dunlop, until he lost his job.) Charles's admission to an insane asylum, as it was then known, eighteen months later: a letter from the psychiatrist. His apparent suicide by drowning: a register of death. A waterside mill in which a great-great-grandfather lost an arm: footnoted in a two-volume history of the British textile industry. The existence of a tin mine in Somerset: two history books (though no employment records link our ancestors to it). These were facts. The rest was inference, embellishment, if not downright invention. The gift, she sometimes thought, is 'no more trustworthy than any old soak down the pub.'

IX. LAUGHING IN THE PAST

Late coffees, hungover lunch. We give the rooms a final once-over. I check the windows and doors, lug boxes of manuscript pages from the South Wing and into the cars, my mother's and mine (formerly Selda's). We can only take so much of her work. I feel tetchy about leaving the other boxes behind. As if in briefly desiring the house to catch fire I had condemned it to that fate.

We lock the front door and stand on the gravel drive-way, staring up at the house, pausing to listen, taking it in one last time before it's sold.

'Alright?' I ask my mother.

'Alright,' she replies.

Then we set out in our separate cars, my mother in her sensible hatchback, me in Selda's clapped-out judder-ing box, through spring rains and light traffic. We reach home before nightfall.

Normal life will resume a few weeks from now. Before then, I put in calls to solicitors, estate agents, auctioneers, antiques specialists, music charities, instrument makers, a structural engineer, removals men. I request quotes, post keys. Everything is in order. Bell Hall is tied with a bow. It goes on the market. It will be months, if not longer, before it is sold.

At the Everyman, I sell ice cream in darkened aisles, pluck litter from seats after curtains down, and watch an identical script play differently every iteration: fluffed notes and missed cues, jokes that belly flop into the stalls one night and cause widespread hilarity the next. The main character's rags-to-riches-to-rags-again arc is com-ic in the Sunday matinee, tragic on Wednesday night, tragicomic the rest of the time. In the theatre's backstage corridors, ferrying macchiatos and ibuprofen to dressing rooms, I daydream that it will be there forever. Bell Hall like a snow globe, pristine, hermetic. It's morning. I walk down the corridor. A smell of cigarettes leaks under the door.

Then, a pair of offers come in. Remote bid from Connecticut, another from Milan. A text from my mother. *GONE!!!!*

Cash buyer. Connecticut. Handled remotely. Video-tours, local surveyor. The guy's British by birth. And a 'big fan'. The exchange will take place in six weeks.

'What about her papers?'

'We'll have them sent up.'

'Who by?'

'Movers.'

'You think it's fine, leaving her *last work* to – to *strangers*?'

'To professionals. They know what they're doing.'

'I don't mean *that*.'

'What do you mean?'

Now for the regression...

Over the course of a night and a morning, I tantrum at my mother and Todd, accusing the former of betrayal, the latter of gold-digging, both of cruelty, disrespect, and a 'lack of imagination'. Time-out in my bedroom, a walk around the block. The gift. It keeps tapping me on the shoulder, nagging at me to go back.

there's a lot you haven't realized

Next day, after an undersold matinee performance, during which a wizened tortoise of a man in row K begins to snore five minutes into the first half, I return home with a bottle of wine. In my best tail-between-legs tone, I tell them I'm sorry. It's over now.

Todd sad-smiles and pats me on my upper arm. I brace myself for him to call me *kiddo* or *buddy* until, in the backs of his eyes, I see something of my own mood now reflected back, a sadness or incompleteness. 'I'm going to move out tonight,' I say, turning from Todd to my mother. 'I mean, if that's alright. I could stay if you'd like...'

She says I don't have to, there's no rush, I've done so much already. And so on. We both know it's the right thing to do. To get back to normal, as planned.

Earlier that day, during my shift, I asked for a week off work, citing a death in the family – not untrue, as it happens. A day or two should do it, that's all. The gift insists I missed something. A clue, a hidden music. After dinner, my suitcase packed, I say my goodbyes and leave my mother's house and get into the car. Instead of driving north, to cross town, I head west, towards the main road leading out of town.

Selda's car struggles down the motorway. It feels like plate armour patched together with solder. Engine chugging, windows humming. I try the radio: crackle and hum. The window panes steam over. Black trees, sudden rain. The gift no longer seems trapped within me, buried, muffled, as it did for so many years. Instead it seems an active, restless force in the world around me, a kind of invisible fire. Laughter rises like exhaust in the moonlit air. I feel the gift at the edge of the motorway, walking in single file.

hey listen boy listen hey listen

I sense it sitting on the branches of trees, watching my headlamps pass.

238

it's something of a boon, this, a real responsibility

Sooner than I expect, I am back on the peninsula. A brief spring storm passes overhead, pelting the car with snooker balls of greasy rain.

we've been having a long hard think amongst ourselves

Up the path, the gravel driveway jumpy in the rain.

a great idea, marvellous in fact, for you

I let myself into the hallway. Flagstones cool underfoot. A tape-measure on the side table, muddy scuff-marks on the floor.

to visit, see, to come where we are

Upstairs, downstairs. Opening doors on empty rooms.

so we can show you it, all these acres of heredity, the whole delta, get in and paddle around

Half the house's contents are gone. The instruments have been evaluated, itemized, priced. Most of them, anyway. Some remain: the grand piano, for instance, under its black jacket. I pull it off and reveal the dark gloss, my own reflection staring back. The beds are gone. I hadn't bargained for that. On the bedroom walls are rectangles of darker plaster where framed prints and photographs used to hang. Her empty desk is still there, by the window overlooking the garden.

a song

Fog thickens in the fields. The smoke from all her cig-arettes. Captain's quarters, sailor's shirts. Out of and into the sea.

it guides you home

The boxes in the South Wing are still there. All the manuscript pages I've yet to piece together. Moments from her life, I wonder. That's the impression I get. Vignettes, a kind of autobiography. Things she could remember. Candles reflected in rainy windows. A lone voice in a cave.

I turn her desktop on, try password after password, bash in birthday dates and song names. Nothing works. Someone will be able to crack it.

and the idea we have, you see – well, that's just it, we want you to see it

hear it

The synthesizer is in a van south of Calais by now. A French enthusiast made an offer for his private museum.

it belongs to you, after all

there's a lot we can't put into words,
but words are all we have

well, apart from the howling and yowling and such

All day and into the night, I work through Selda's pa-pers. Wildlife roams across the grounds. Birds alighting

240

and departing, foxes sauntering. Frogs emerge from the woods and parade all across the wet grass. Antlers which might be branches. And other forms, too, move back and forth, or perch here or there, under chairs or in the corners, wrapped in the shadows, hovering just overhead. My breath steams in the air, but my body feels warm.

but there's another way to know it

I set up a makeshift bed from cushions I found in the living room. The gift keeps dragging me into this place, to feast on Selda's music.

all it takes is a leap

I spend hours in its company. I ask it questions, trace stories back through the generations. It leads in so many contradictory directions that my skull begins to hurt, make me wish I could relieve the pressure. Meanwhile, distances measured by sound. Close at hand, the piano. The skeleton's rattling drum. In the distance, a chiming sound. Never once do I miss living friends or family. Should this be a cause for concern? The phrase 'living friends' is perhaps, in itself, a worry.

for instance, did you know about the

All the while, around me: signs. Items I hadn't noticed before. Carbolic soap, a tray of burning fairy lights. Shadows swaying back and forth across the wall. The singing statue eyes me through the window, open throat overflowing with song.

version of you who fought in the war

who committed a murder before he was thirteen

*this was, o, it was centuries ago, the world was so
different then*

Talking with the gift can have unexpected effects.
I'll wander around the house, as a sleepwalker might.
Sometimes I stray outside, beyond the boundaries of
Selda's land. No awareness of the fact until I bash my knee
into a coffee table or stub my toe on a log. I come to at the
edge of the orchard, down an overgrown lane, ankle-deep
in the stream we scattered Selda into days ago.

*going round and round and round she watched the
record spin, the fires dance, just captivated by it all,
really, as her appetite shrank and the tempo slowed*

*death is nothing, and there is nothing to fear from
nothing*

It can't be nothing if you're talking to me.

we don't expect it is easily understood

from where you are, anyway

One time, a living person's voice snaps me back to
reality. A lopsided giant with a bristly beard. He's growling at me to get off his land. Blinking, my gaze slides past
his gilet, his jeans, to the shotgun in his hands. He lifts its
snout until it's pointed somewhere near my left kidney.

To be fair, I *am* right beside the kitchen window of
a farmhouse. Late evening, it looks like. That under-
developed-Polaroid light. A young girl in pig-tails is

242

pressing her nose to the glass, a child's bike propped up against the outside wall. I back away slowly, hands up, staring into his narrowed eyes. What do I tell him? Sorry, sir. I'm not a burglar or a creep, sir. I was led here by the family phantoms.

The last thing I remember was a candleflame, but it might have been a laptop screen. A glow, anyway – and music. Dangerous music.

The man watches me leave, his barrel trained on me the whole time. Once I'm clear from him, I run.

under a poacher's moon

born to mechanical howls with avenging angels overhead

Later, I wake under a full moon as bright as a halogen, lying where Selda's body was found. Flat black trees like paper cut-outs. My head rings with a music that, minutes later, I am barely able to remember, let alone describe.

and you wish you could hold it know it for one more second

Next day, while driving into town for a few supplies, I pass a figure on the roadside leading to the harbour. Long dark coat, plastic bag. I think nothing much of it. Just some old drifter. At least he isn't holding a gun. At dusk, I return to the pub for some food and a few last questions. There are a couple there who sang with Selda across the bay. They tell me that her last songs were simple individually, but seemed to be connected by a grander scheme, something she planned to reveal, but for obvious reasons never managed to. What kind of music, and were there lyrics? (I have some idea already, from the pages on the South Wing floor.) They described small scenes. Some of them domestic, others apocalyptic. Skies on fire, lit candles, radio, television, holidays, lovers, caves. Returning home, I see again see the man at the edge of the forest, his pupils gas-flame blue. He raises a hand. 'Didn't I pass you here, a few days back?' Then: 'You knew Selda,' I add, which I know to be true only after I hear myself say it.

He nods. His grey, longish hair is combed back, glossy with some kind of product. He is taller than me by a foot or so, gaunt, his expression inscrutably hard except in the eyes, which roam anxiously over my own face, searching. 'I didn't want to interrupt while you and your mother were here, see. Then I realized you were gone. Sharon said you'd come back, so... Declan, by the way. Declan Fischer.'

in the dark nights writing at the lamplit desk

'Did you know Selda, then?'

a machine for translating pain

'Used to play music together. Live not far from here.'

into understanding

We set out the way I just came. The fabric of his oilskin coat, blackened by layers of wax, sways with his gait. His large hands are buried in pockets so capacious he could smuggle hams in them. At his side is the plastic bag. He clears his throat as if about to speak, and pulls a photo out of it. Has he been carrying it around the whole time?

It's a group shot of a restaurant table at which guests

with enormous hair and shoulder-pads are leaning forward, grinning over plates of seafood and glasses of white wine, garish colours faded by the photograph's age. A woman in the shadows at the back may or may not be Selda – the only clearly visible feature is her Cheshire Cat grin. I ask Fischer how they met.

It was back at Agnes's, he says. He was at the Royal Academy, and she was a young, completely unknown composer, a decent pianist with few concert credits under her belt. She was known for being frosty, spiky, funny, mercurial, hard to pin down – and in his view, she was nothing special, no indication back then of what she would become. He was more impressed by Ellen Montague, her inseparable friend at the time, who was devising all manner of powerful instruments: bells, which she claimed could heal the rift between the living and the dead, which could bring the gifted back if they had strayed too far into the underworld.

> *voices fall toward our realm like rain on the*
> *ocean's surface*

The photograph on the mantelpiece. One person I've yet to speak with. I make a note to find her.
'You knew each other, then?'

> *don't be afraid if the scheme reverses, if the bells of*
> *sunken ships and so forth sound above water*

Selda knocked on Fischer's door unannounced a few days before Christmas. She wanted him to look at a piece of music. No one else had a copy, she had no plans on releasing it, had never shown it to anyone before. It was handwritten on manuscript paper and dated a few days previous. Fischer played the piece through. She adjusted a couple of notes, asked him to play it again. He did. This time, she seemed satisfied.

'She asked me to play it to you,' he says.

'She did?'

He nods. 'She made me promise. I didn't think anything of it at the time. It sounded kind of throwaway, my end. But then I heard...'

'Now?'

'Well, yes. I know it by heart. It's quite simple, mind. All her last music was.'

'What's the instrument?'

'A cello.'

'There's one in the South Wing, will need tuning up.'

The singing statue's open throat overflows with melodious rainwater. Draped around its shoulders is a mantle of wet black leaves. Fischer salutes it as we pass.

In the South Wing, he hangs up his coat. He's dressed in an immaculate tuxedo, a little greasy around the lapel, perhaps, and smelling faintly of camphor, but otherwise tailored and dapper, his shirt pristine and his bow tie neat. I don't remember lighting candles, but they're glowing now, in candleholders and wine bottles, soft light on the polished floor and patterned rugs. Do I stand, sit? Fischer carries the cello to the seat in the middle of the room, sets the instrument in its stand and begins to tune the strings by ear.

'This was always my favourite part,' I say.

'Of what?'

'Her music. Well, any music like that. The bit where the orchestra tuned.'

I have an idea. The removals men have left a mess in the corridor, old bedsheets and tablecloths from the upstairs cupboards. A couple of these are red. I carry them up the spiral staircase, the sound of strings tuning rising into the space, and tie the sheets to the railing. Back downstairs, they almost look like theatre curtains.

I find it hard to picture Selda and this man playing music together. Seeing him with his cello, though, reminds me of something she said about her piano. Before she was born, she loaned a part of herself to the instrument, so that it could express what she could not, and that only when she found it again did she feel complete. Fischer's hands remind me of Selda's, things of wood and wire, sinews visible under the skin. He clears his throat and settles his posture. Amber light catches his cello's curves as he starts to play.

The tune – I've heard it before but can't place it. Something in the rhythm, the slowness of the notes, their interlocking structure, convinces me that this is a song that she and I sang together. It moves in a kind of counterpoint, rhythmically simple glissandos that slowly ascend the neck. Phrygian mode, possibly. Selda's hands guide each note as surely as Fischer's do. But it's the tension and release of his muscles and lungs, his skilful fingers moving up and down the neck, that feel most present and alive. I think of her body in the casket, how strange it was for someone to be there and not. Now her music moves in the air, a message from her to me. Hearing it, I burst into tears. Another strong wave of feeling, warping space and time. Not even in the days after, nor in the chapel, where everything felt muffled and unreal, nor on the night we returned to Bell Hall and I fell asleep remembering the songs we sang here – not even then has it hit me like this.

o can you wash a sailor's shirt

My hands in hers, over the keys.

o can you make it clean

Above the sound of his cello, I hear another high note. That silver sound again. I heard it on the night of the storm. I heard it the other day, walking to the spot where Selda died. Now I think I know what it is. Not her voice exactly, but a trace of it. She's laughing somewhere in the past.

o can o can o can

One musician. I wish there were more. A hundred orchestras. Ten cities' worth of musicians playing with note-perfect precision, aside from those moments when their grief overcomes them, when they drop to their knees in tearful, gasping awe. No expense shall be spared on the indoor fireworks, the rotating stage, parades of live tigers, peacocks and elephants, acrobats spinning, the flaming sabres arcing over jugglers' heads, a polestar burning at the apex of the firmament. The music brings images to mind. The window blows open. Pages blow across the floor. Candleflames flare and cast Fischer's shadow back against the back wall, the red-bedsheet curtains. Notes slide higher up the neck, plummet, rise again.

at a certain point you cut to the quick

go under

The tune comes to an end. I dry my tears and thank Fischer. Then I fetch us a bottle of whisky.

she felt at home in the treacherous peace of the water, towelling herself on wet rocks

248

'Are you *sure* we haven't met?'

'I think I'd remember. Now, what do you want?'

*fancy composer whose music you couldn't hum along
or tap your foot to*

which decade is it?

I tell him I've been looking for him. For anyone who
can help me answer some questions. Things I can't work
out, maybe never would. About the papers over there,
about her music. What was her plan, in giving that piece
to him? Was she in the habit of turning up at his doorstep
unannounced, practically flaunting her impending demise? Did she *know* she was going to die? What about the
storm? If it hadn't happened, then what? The illogic of
it, the self-erasing drama, may have been part of a score.
Or had she found something, discovered something?
Fischer's gaze rests on the windows behind me, beyond
the lawn and the trees. The South Wing no longer feels
cold, but warmed by the candleflames, and scented by
whiskey and woodpolish. Most of his answers are sullen,
others monosyllabic. My excitement at finding him fades.
He tells me that he and Selda were close. That he knew
her well, a long time ago, and that the present state of their
relationship was, he pauses, somewhat distant. Which fits
the pattern with my mother, with Ellen Montague, with
others I've spoken to. It brings us no closer to answering
why. Fischer falls into one of the gloomy, wordless rev-
eries that I have already come to realize are a feature of his
personality. The gift tells me about a swimming spot not
far from here, where Selda used to night-swim.

heating back the cold

249

This isn't helping. You're with her. And if you aren't, you have ways to find out where she is.

Fischer finishes up his drink, shakes my hand, shrugs his coat up. We agree to meet again soon. I watch him disappear into the rain, notes from the piece he played repeating and repeating in my mind.

I come to again near the water. No recollection of how I got here. The last notes fading in the air. The clouds move swiftly overhead. The moon is bright and full. Creep and suck of bladderwrack at my feet. Smell of ozone in the air. I'm on the concrete jetty in the village. Behind me, the white bungalows look blue in the dark. Browned, pinkish petals litter the water around my freezing ankles – I seem not to be wearing shoes – and the water, though black, is alive with swaying glows, like tea lights.

And all at once, I realize why I'm here. What I'm meant to do.

It would be mad, but it wouldn't be dangerous. Selda used to every week. Perhaps that's where I'll find her. Out there. Or under there. It will bring me closer to her. If I am cold and quiet enough, maybe *then* it will work – the gift will clear, her voice will shine.

Whispers mix with surf. I pull off my shirt and trousers, leave them crumpled on a rock, and step forward. The water, to my surprise, is warm. Then it is neither warm nor cold, I feel nothing, the water takes my weight, and I am swimming. Lanterns or fishing boats light the distant sea. Overhead, stars scatter the sky. Notation I cannot read. In the air, a bright insistent ringing. From beneath the waves comes a deeper, slower tone.

The trickling water that runs down the long concrete

jetty is a stream. It runs from Bell Hall all the way to the sea. We poured her into it. She came this way.

I still don't know where she was walking. If you draw a straight line on the map, it takes you back to London.

I see porch lights, blue houses, black forest, big sky. The polestar propping up the firmament. I think, of all people, of my father in Canada, with whom I rarely speak. He is under the same sky, in a snowbound station, satellite dishes tuned to heavens that never talk back. I swim further out. Towards the horizon, bobbing black boats. A night-bird screams and scatters points of light through the air, interference patterns with the stars. Along the shore, massed shadows. Ears open.

He turned too quickly, she was still in the underworld, looking back destroyed the object of his love. His head floated downriver and continued to sing his sad music. These stories she told to prepare me. The only way through is down.

in he goes, sploosh!

how many centuries of increase depend upon this hodge of a body and its will to live

if he goes and so do we

I come to again in Bell Hall. Hard to tell how much time has passed. Part of me thinks it might be days. Candles burning everywhere, red curtains draping the walls.

I realized something while I was down in the dark and the quiet. In half-drowning, I panicked the gift. The voices dropped their masks. I saw what they were.

not quite

251

Not ghosts. Something else.

if you could know the world like we do

My clothes still dripping wet, I wander around the carpet. Fischer's cello in the corner. The piano on the floor. Stillness. Music falls around me like snow.

listen under here

Selda told me that the gift were the dead, and that to listen to them, with skill and supplication, was to commune with our past. That's not what I hear in it now. I stand beside the window's glass. Under the poacher's moon, the falling flakes are luminous, cinder-bright. They extinguish themselves on the ground. In other places they build up, layer upon layer.

In the living room, I peel off my sodden tops and mud-caked trousers and towel-dry my skin, which is puckered and damp. I tumble logs on the fire, enough firelighters to burn the place down. The room heats quickly, chilblains itching at my knuckles and fingers, an incandescent red.

Fragments from Selda's music keep repeating in my mind. She was putting together a story, and it is up to me to complete it.

And with the last few days, the freezing cold, the sudden heat, the sleepless nights and strange dreams, the room begins to swim. Those shapes on the wall, are they shadows or seaweed? Jellyfish cymbals swim loose from the walls – no, light swaying in the play of the low-lying fire.

The curtains are half-drawn. The wind prowls about the old house and the fields beyond it. A high-pitched wail, an alarm or a night-bird, fills the sky with light.

III. SELDA

I. 1937–1956

Late evening in a two-up-two-down in Clay Lane. Small concrete yard but no garden. Stove to the right of the kitchen, cupboard to the left. At the back, a freestanding bath covered with a wooden tabletop, on top of which are a bucket of coal and a saucepan of milk. In the corner stands a shrouded cage containing Buttercup, the pet budgie. The windows are blacked out with sheets. Edward has done his nightly inspection to ensure there are no gaps or holes through which the glow of their paraffin lamp might be seen. It's a clear, cold night. Glancing quickly through the bathroom window, a full moon brightens an almost cloudless sky, glaring silver on the frost in the garden. He takes this as a good sign. The Germans would have to be mad to fly on a night like this: for the anti-aircraft gunners on the ground, he thinks, it would be like clay pigeon shooting. Pop pop pop!

The kitchen air, steamy with potato-water, smells of snuffed wicks and carbolic. Next door, in the living room, a large wooden dining table has been pushed against the wall, beneath which Edward and Maud sleep most nights, in what they've taken to calling The Hutch. Its sides are reinforced by a wardrobe on one end, a suitcase on the other, and a strip of rabbit wire to protect from splinters and other debris, should a bomb land nearby (if it lands on their roof directly, the table will form the lid on a mince-meat pie). The windows closest the bed are blacked-out and boarded up with removable wooden shutters, which Edward made by hand using screws and salvaged wood. On windy nights, the shutters' hinges croak and rasp. From hooks on the walls hang Maud's five-piece collection of zithers and lyre harps. Nothing Edward says can persuade her to part with them. Some are beautifully made from glossy wood, others cobbled together from petrol cans and screws.

The compromise: two suitcases, stationed at the front door. They are packed with essential supplies, with coats, hats, underpants, biscuits, a few pound notes, a tin of cocoa (Maud seems to think this is vital), two of pilchards, Edward's mother's necklaces. On the table beside them are gas masks, two for them and one for when the baby arrives. Edward finds the look of the latter, its cyclopic oval panel like the window of a furnace, more disturbing even than his and his wife's insectile plague-doctor equivalents.

He watches the stovetop kettle with dark, unfocused eyes with his hand on his chin, idly thumbing his moustache. Maud is at the table beside him. Hard to tell if pregnancy or war has caused more stress. Either way, she has barely slept in two weeks, and it shows in her pallor, her puffiness. She looks almost as dreamy as Charles does.

'I can feel something,' she says, resting her hand on her bump.

'It won't be yet, will it? He's not due.'

'You don't know it's a he.'

'I know alright. A man just knows.'

'Right. Yes. Well, a woman just knows something too.'

'What's that?'

'I think it's coming.'

'He can't be. He's not for two weeks.'

Maud rests her head in her hand, her hair – almost waist-length, she's barely cut it since meeting Edward – spilling down her back and hanging to the table, where a folded newspaper shows adverts for Avocado shaving cream ('The closer / the bubbles / the sweeter / the shave'). 'Look at these, Maud,' says Edward, pointing at an advert for Aurax ear protectors ('they take the "sting" out of gunfire and explosions'). 'Perhaps I'll get us some. They're approved by the Noise Abatement League,' he adds, though he's never heard of the league before, can scarcely afford the protectors: his solution thus far has been wadded tissue dipped in wax. Water gargles in the spout. Edward pours the kettle into a teapot in which he has scraped the last spoonful of leaves. He hums Handel as they mash the tea and sit down to a supper of boiled potatoes, tinned sardines, a few tomatoes grown in a neighbour's garden, which he's seasoned with salt and a little mustard powder (too much, in Maud's sneezy opinion).

Maud makes a sound. He thinks she must be singing along. Her tone changes. She leans back, touches her bump again.

'All alright?'

Maud looks at Edward, her eyes catching the light of the candle. They are grey-blue flecked with rust and charcoal. 'Probably nothing,' she says.

As he's clearing away the plates, emptying the kettle, they hear it: a wailing sound.

'Probably nothing,' says Edward, forcing a joke, half tempted to pull back the blackout curtain. Was he thorough enough during his round? What if he wasn't, and a bomber saw their lamp all the way from Germany. The night, when he looked, was cloudless and the moon is full. He imagines that, seen from the vantage of incoming planes, the city's streets will form a legible grid. That mournful and mechanical sound (the one which, years from now, he will attempt to recreate for his daughter) rises from the rooftops: hand-cranked sirens ululating over the streets.

'Into the Hutch then,' says Maud.

'Once more, yes,' Edward groans.

There is fear and there is weariness: if only the latter would soften the former. Instead, there is both. The deadness and the panic, recurring every night. Bombers sighted overhead.

The first planes drop flares and incendiaries. Turbulent points of light fall to earth with liquid grace to settle on the gas and waterworks, the power stations, the factories of Daimler, GEC, Humber, Armstrong Whitworth, and Dunlop too, and the shadow factories around the city's edges, where they flicker and die. The Germans' code-name for the bombing raid is Moonlight Sonata. (Selda will later claim that this fact explains her otherwise inexplicable aversion to the composer; why, excepting the Op. 132 string quartet, which she seems incapable of listening to without sobbing, she thinks Beethoven 'rots the heart'.) Incendiaries aren't too much trouble, except for now, when so many fill the air. They fall with a swishing roar like heavy rain, they smack into the ground.

Some stick upright in the earth like Roman candles. People run out with buckets of sand and water to extinguish them, or they pick them up and chuck them, but the things keep falling from the sky. The incendiaries catch the roofs of houses and sheds and shops and pubs until the city is aflame, not just manufacturing targets but the centre, its department stores, hospitals, spires, a conflagration widespread enough to ensure its passage, even as it happens, not just into history but into myth – the city's, the country's, Selda's. ('I was hardened in that fire,' she'll boast to her new friend, Ellen, years from now. 'I took a piece of it inside me. Yes, there's *fire* in me, alright.')

And still it comes, the last the heavy-duty ordnance: HE bombs, five-hundred-pounders and landmines.

The electricity goes out. So does gas. Water mains burst and flood the roads. Children climb into chimneys and huddle under stairs. Fires in the streets, churches, waterworks. Planes passing in the bright sky, cruciform against the glare. Now and then the ack-ack guns find them, the bullets sparking like fireworks on cockpit-glass and wing, but not enough to make halt the passage of the planes, which has the flow and force, yes, of a kind of migration – of deadly birds or butterflies passing through the sky.

The bombs find a sore spot, a symbolic wound: the cathedral, consecrated to Saint Michael the Archangel, defender of the Catholic Church. Roofs collapse. Pews and beams erupt in flame. At the crucible's heart is the grand organ, which Handel once sat at and played. The flames blacken brick and melt stained glass. Saints and angels, clouds, sunbeams, and streaming banners will liquefy, drain out of their molten webs of lead, and harden over the course of the dawn, when the morning light reveals the frozen waterfalls of glass, of carmine, sunflower, emerald, azure.

Hours before that happens, Maud clutches her stomach. She staggers around the kitchen, breathing heavily and spitting curses. Her waters puddle on the flagstones. 'Not now now not please not NOW Christ bugger I can't I can't *think*.' She should be in the hospital whose staff she recently joined, tending to soldiers back from the front and factory workers mangled by machinery they'd only just learned how to use, but if they try to cross the city now, they'll risk being blown to bits. The sky is rent by the roar of aeroplane engines, machine-gun fire, the swish of falling bombs, and the concussion of impact, of collapsing masonry, of shattering glass. Nothing to light that blacked-out city, with its countless painted windows and its boarded-up doors, but flame. They should be on a bus to Leamington, in an air-raid shelter, anywhere but here.

'Go round to Kirsty's, Edward, she might not've—'

'Who?'

'— gone yet. Kirsty. She's a f-f-friend, you've met her. A midwife. She'll be able to —'

'Here? You want to do it here? We don't have any of the, any of the ah, um, the uh, the — *equipment*.'

'Do you have a better idea?'

He opens the front door, closes it swiftly behind him. The sky is as bright as a cinema screen, alive with flame-glare, with tracer fire. He cannot see the planes but he can sense them. Fires glow down the road. The air is filled with itchy scent. Molten butter and acrid ash.

He heads right, and understands why. The dairy is on fire; butter bubbles out its front door, gushes along gutters and down the drains. A fire truck, far-off, upside-down. Tangled in the upper branches of a leafless roadside tree is a dark brown mass that Edward takes for a piece of masonry or a roof tile, until it resolves into the pointed leatherwork of a brogue, attached via a white sock to the lower part of a shin, all blown off quite cleanly: no other body parts are visible. Flakes of ash drift groundward like snow. Everywhere he looks, people's expressions mirror his: the eyes wide and the mouth immobile, the nostrils flared. The street is scattered with brick and wood and scraps of singed fabric. There are pools of fluid that might be blood or water; there is a puddle of burning oil. A few people are screaming but most are silent, moving as if drugged. They stare up at the sky's red chamber, alive with unsteady light. One grey-haired, slippered man, dressing gown over his shoulders and thick glasses on his eyes, stands in a doorway, sipping a mug of something hot. A girl, clothed in so much masonry dust she resembles a yellow ghost, picks her way over the rubble in front of him, clutching a tin of peaches as if it were a pet.

Edward was half expecting to open the door on a ground invasion, tanks rolling down the street, German soldiers storming into living rooms, skewering innocents with bayonets, children up against the wall, hoisting swastikas up telephone poles. Instead he sees hills of rubble where neighbours used to live. The street's far end is shrouded with tar-black smoke; turning the corner, a house on fire, the bricks glowing as brightly as coals. A roof beam cracks, sending a fountain of sparks.

He knocks on the door of Clive and Kirsty's house, farther down the street, still standing. When the former answers (he is wearing a tin helmet, is meant to be out working as an air-raid marshal) Edward opens his mouth but says nothing, is unable to speak.

Hours later, they are not dead yet. Light rain on the roof and against the windowpanes, the gargle in the gutters. Candles hiss and spitter as the wicks lick the wax.

The preparations are underway, the resources are limited. Edward has guided Maud into the Hutch, which he's reinforced with everything he can find, bedding, potato sacks, pillows, hand-towels, old clothes. He's filled a tub with warm water and brought out what soap he could find, and needles, thread, scissors, plates, kerchiefs, towels, paintbrushes: a helpless assortment of conceivably useful tools, offered up like a magpie's attempt to impress a potential mate. One item at least is of use. Kneeling on a cushion, her hair done back in a bun, Kirsty works by the paraffin lamp, the thin reek of the burning fuel mixing with the smell of smoke filtering in from outside. The labour is long; the bombardment begins to slow. Fewer thumps, quieter too. A high crack and sizzle of burning.

Light rains soothe but don't staunch the city's wounds. Edward paces back and forth, praying to a deity he has never believed in, counting the bricks in the wall, humming familiar music – this, at least, soothes him. He ducks at the mouth of the Hutch, beside Kirsty. He fetches water, reaches under the table to hold Maud's hand, struggling to see it in the dark rendered depthless by monocular sight. And he thinks to himself, *well, this will be one to tell the grandchildren...* if they survive, that is. How much better it feels to narrativize the event as it unfolds: the act is a hopeful one, he thinks, for it presumes a future in which a story can be told.

The city calming, growing quiet. Piano, piano...

Kirsty with the towels, the warm water. Maud cursing and breathing heavily, more heavily still. Heat flowing off her, the sheer force and industry of the whole process.

Please don't fall, please don't, not now, no more bombs, that's enough now, he keeps telling himself, soothing himself, as though he could filibuster his own mortality and that of his wife, his child, as if an unbroken internal monologue could dispel the image that keeps returning, that will return now and then for the rest of his life, of a blown-off foot lodged up a tree in a brogue: no blood, no body, whose was it? And it is now, at this still moment in an otherwise wailing night, that the grandfather clock strikes to announce the arrival of their child. Three strikes, din-dang-dong.

('I was a chime child,' Selda tells Ellen. 'Do you know what that means?' 'Let me guess,' Ellen says, not looking up from her book, 'you can talk to ghosts.')

And then it is over. The quick miracle. Sooner than Edward might have expected, having no other experience to go on. From under the table, his wife's howl – and then a second.

(Later, in a frank conversation with Selda, Maud will compare the whole process to death, or how she imagines death might feel: the body takes over, you sink down deep inside yourself and live there, lodged in the dark between bone and sinew; an ancestral process that unfolds without conscious thought, that subordinates the mind to something ancient, something primal.)

A baby, unmistakable. Kneeling, he see the shadows, the soaked bedding, Maud's glistening skin – and the child, bluish, minute, streaked all over with blood. Kirsty with her bunch of blood-soaked towels and kitchen shears, snipping the cord. Maud in a heap of pillows. Her face like he's never seen before. A sigh. No more sirens. She's looking down at their firstborn daughter and only child, and she has just begun to wail.

A few years later. Sicily. The landscape coloured with washes of dust and sand, with citrus, date, olive and fig. Dwarf palms, corn oaks, carob and tamarisk dot the dry plains. Pilgrim hawks, falcons and imperial crows pass overhead, their shadows gliding across the sand. Geckos and grass snakes flicker in the underbrush and the streams run black with eels. The brown fin of Mount Etna breaches a poster-paint cloud. Below it, the land is bleached by citrus sun. In the middle distance, convoys' wheels throw white dust into the air: it hangs like low, bright cloud. Closer at hand, a town sprawls on the top of a star-shaped hill. White, blue, pink and terracotta buildings crowd its ridges.

British and Canadian forces are camped in an archaeological site a few miles south. Infantrymen stand idle, smoking and sweating in the shade between tents and trucks, and ammo-boxes piled high among the ruins of the ancient town, tents pitched under the scalloped roofs

264

of thermal baths. From the distance comes the slow, soft drone of a bulldozer forcing open a narrow street, the yellowish walls of the houses audibly grinding, crumbling, discomposing into powder.

A broad-shouldered soldier stands apart from the rest on a bluff, squinting at the landscape through a curtain of shimmering heat. Perhaps he is chewing something, a juicy segment of stone fruit, or the brittle black casing of a sunflower seed. More likely he is smoking an unfiltered cigarette, the smoke as harsh and hot as the land he peers at. Sweat-stains have bloomed and browned his shirt, which is stitched up in two places. He flicks the butt and kicks a stone and whistles through his teeth, and all at once the tension in his face, which fixed his flare and creased his brow, evaporates. His expression is childlike with mischief.

Head flung back, he laughs.

Closer to the camp, a pair of soldiers and a journalist frown at him. The latter, sweat pouring down patchy stubble on a wide-jawed face, his gaze sharpened by his scintillating lenses, clutches a microphone and a tape machine, which, whether from superstition or negligence, he's not yet uncoupled from the life vest he tied it to as they came aboard two days ago. He's half-wondering whether to hit record. Call the man the Singing Soldier. Say look, listen, he's not afraid of the fight. Death scares him not a jot. Be more like him. 'When the guns are firing, he sings!' The journalist bats the air to rid himself of a meddlesome fly, which returns a second later, attracted by a day's worth of dry sweat. He's among the paler-skinned men whose necks, foreheads, hands and arms are burnt a lambent, blistered red. Almost as irritating are the fleas that jump and bite in the hot still nights, leaving prickling, needling pains which only swimming can relieve.

Charles, more darkly complexioned, has fared a little better. Locals beckon him from the dark doorways and sunbaked roads of the towns and villages they march through. He's no idea what their dialect means. They could be calling him a cunt, for all he knows. His hair is almost black, the bright bottle-green eyes deeply set over the hard round cheekbones, the lips smiling and full over a walnut-crusher of a jaw. He wishes his brother Edward were here. In his head, a melody forms, falls, high notes followed by low, then high, then low: the harmony swells, lifting off the sunbaked dirt, rising heavenward with the smoke of the cigarettes, the windblown dust... A few weeks after their great grand-uncle died, when Charles was twelve, a change came over him, which had nothing to do with the hairs on his chin and chest and about his cock, or his unevenly deepening voice; not directly, at least. He did discover a talent for self-control of the vocal chords. A limpid and resonant voice, the timbre and note of which he was able naturally to manipulate. It came with a great deal of information. Hard to have put it into words. He went under his brother's protection. He sought his love. Edward, of course, loved music. And so Charles would perform. His ambition was to play Orphée in *Orpheus in the Underworld*. He sang 'Tzing! Tzing! Tzing!' in the bathtub, bellowing arpeggios that drove his brother half mad, and another song he sings repeatedly, in babble-languages that sound made-up: three short high notes followed by two long, low ones, the sequence changing and repeating. He has developed a reputation here for terrific singing, but being over-keen about it, too, serenading the troops with songs from Somerset, Cornwall, Cardiff, some of which are familiar and others which appear to be his own invention.

They pay a group of locals to prepare a supper. It

feels to Charles like a feast: fried potatoes, macaroni and cheese, cucumbers and tomatoes in vinegar. After eating, they watch the sunset pinken the pock-marked cliffs in whose caves, they've been told, the enemy are camped.

'Go on, then,' says one of the reedy-looking, pale-haired soldiers standing around in the awkward time between supper and sleep. No one is particularly thrilled about the prospect of returning to their flearidden camp bed. 'Give us a song.'

The journalist presses Record, only to realize that he's run out of tape.

Charles sings 'None shall part us' and 'Questa o quella' and 'Tzing!' in the still heat of the August night. His song returns to him, fragmented and multiplied by the rocky crags and valleys on the outskirts of Centuripe, a cluster of boxy buildings on a sloped peak that juts from the arid scrub, from the blood and dust and lemon-groves. Dumnph! Bnt! Pntntnt! Planes overhead. Tank-tracks underfoot. Low thuds in the distance, felt in the bones rather than heard. His voice carries over the dry places, the sandy plateaus and parched slopes; it ramifies as a god's would, for miles and miles. The gift is with him. It surrounds his voice as a chorus's might. It fills his mind with terror and with ease, remembering battles fought, won, and lost in some cases centuries before this one. In the gift's endless retelling, these moments – stored somewhere in song, and somewhere in Charles – have a silky, unreal quality, vivid and strange as a dream. (Selda will attempt to describe this sensation, which she shares with Charles, to her grandson, only to discover that Wolf experiences it differently, or sometimes not at all: the boy seems in denial about the fact that he has it.) His mother's mother was an Agnesian. So says the gift, anyway: the family deny it. He does not count himself as one. Nor

267

does he believe that the gift is an ability to listen to death. To understand the presence of it, the immanence of it. It all sounds, to him, too sparky and alive. Too *musical*. The problem is, it lacks order. It lacks shape. He supposes this has something to do with improvisation. Which he loves. But you can have too much of anything. It is a clear night, the sky bright with stars, the dry ground skittish with lizards and insects. Charles finishes his song. Scattered applause. The gift lingers in his mind like an echo, murmuring to him of irrelevant things: the wise decision to purchase a waterwheel, a dismembered shepherd laid to rest in a hilltop cairn...

The soldiers who sleep through the fleas are woken by rattling patterns of anti-aircraft fire down in the valley. Ratatatatttttta! Ratatatatttta!

Charles, who has slept fitfully at best since he came ashore, sneaks out for another cigarette. If he needs a pep up tomorrow, Benzedrine will help, washed down with his morning coffee. On a dry slope overlooking a vineyard, twisted stumps in the yellowish dirt, he hums another song to himself. One that reminds him of home. Of the songs that his grandmother sang, high notes and low, *o can you clean a sailor's shirt*. He wonders about his brother and his niece, blondish, strident, with that over-serious frown and that wheezy laugh. He has only met her once, he is impatient to meet her again.

He manages a few hours' sleep. Next morning, low sun simmers in the distance. Crooked trees cast tangled shadows. Since he arrived a few days ago, moving through the naval blockade bristling with ships of all sizes, coming ashore in the amphibian vehicle, under clear blue skies, the fighting so far has been almost non-existent. The only evidence this country is at war takes the form of sounds in the distance: dull thunder of bombs, scattered crackles of

268

gunfire. Their own going, so far, has been a long, hot hike.

He senses that will change. Their objective is to re-capture the hilltop town. As they march through the morning's fierce heat, white dust floats up off the road to whiten their faces and uniforms. Charles keeps his gaze focused on the greenish distance, or at his feet, attempting to ignore the roadside corpses under grey shrouds, the dead horse abuzz with flies (a fragment of Mendelssohn returns to him, the violin screeching up the neck: the sound sends needles prickling down his thighs to the base of his ankles). Better are the hotels, outside which a table of well-dressed men sit drinking coffee. Or the roadside checkpoint, surrounded by bushes of yellow flowers.

Soon they reach the lower hills, which a first wave of Irish battalions have already succeeded in taking over. They advance up the sloped roads, past houses and shut-tered shops.

Now, at last, the bullets fly. Walls of houses and bridges pop and shatter. Charles scans the hillsides but sees no enemies to shoot. Instead, they move through the town, its crooked streets and bulldozed alleys, its dense textures of floating dust, thick shadow, sudden bars of blinding sun. He hauls a rifle down the cobbled streets as bullets ping and tufts of dust leap around him. Voices move above and around him. The fighting is bitter and chaotic. It is also slow. Shaking violently, he's barely able to move. Every shadow seems to promise death. The air itself smells burnt. He can smell something else, too. Acrid, scorched. A petrol smell, a corpse smell. He is certain he is doing no good, either. Training was one thing. This is quite different. He fires at random, hitting window shut-ters, roof-tiles, but mostly air, his aim erratic and dizzy with fear.

Looking around, he discovers that he is alone. As

though he has drifted into a forest clearing.

And out of that calm, a voice emerges. A woman's. Her words are slurred, but they captivate him. Why now, of all moments? He has never heard her in the gift before. An ancestor, individuated from the noise, striding towards him. She has a warning.

She sings of lights in the sky, angels in basements, snowstorms moving across the moors, and as her voice rises so do others: turn back, they tell him, turn back. Instead, he turns a corner. A skinny dark-haired boy leans out of a high window above him. He wants to tell the boy to get back, go inside, it's not safe out here – from the enemy, from himself: any stray bullet could catch the lad. But the boy is pointing at something. Pointing and shouting.

Charles follows the boy's finger. Over the rubble of a ruined wall, he sees a Panzer tank. It's the first he's ever seen with his own eyes before. The sight of which – its crude bulk, the snout's black maw, the turret grinding as it rotates – drenches his blood in adrenaline, quickens his heart but freezes him to the spot.

How long does he stand there, suicidally still?

His niece will imagine this moment. The pause between knowledge and impact. Selda will imagine it felt like a kind of miracle. Time stalling, the world filled with light. Between these hot walls is a place without thought. And something is indeed revealed to him. A kind of vision. A sudden intuition of a wide-open space, very gentle, vast and powerful, a kind of ocean or infinite sky – but it's just a sense, a hint of a realm both beyond and within him. He will forget it the instant the shell hits.

A second before the blank flash and the cloud, he regains motor control. He moves. But the shell is airborne, its trajectory assured. Muscles contract, pulling bone and

270

sinew, sending Charles to his right, his knees bending, preparing to jump – but his speed is no match for explosives. The mortar passes so close to his skull that, before it hits the brick wall of a shoe shop several metres behind him, it removes a large part of his right ear as cleanly as a surgeon might. Lights out.

Selda, older now, capable of babbling but not quite speech, is headstrong. She never seems to rest. When she isn't running circles, she drives her parents up the wall. She gnaws door jambs and bars of rationed soap, smears the corridor walls with boot-polish procured from the under-stairs cupboard (Edward swears it was locked). She lures stray cats, pigeons, once a badger, all manner of vermin into the house. From kitchen utensils, she assembles instruments, banging pots and her father's tin helmet at the crack of dawn, twanging elastic bands. Worst of all is her incessant, discordant singing at the top of her toddler lungs. 'La la la, oh oh ah ooh-heh-teh nehhhh,' goes a typical lyric. 'Oohaaaaaaaalala.' These melodies rarely delight her parents. They have neighbours knocking on the door or craning their neck over the garden fence. Some are eerily familiar, and all the more maddening as a result. Where did she get them from? Surely Maud didn't teach her. The other day, Edward came home with a wireless. Perhaps that is the source of it: speech from the ether, news from the front, and droning, churchy organ in between the voices. Maud is apt to pinch Selda's ear or send her to bed without supper. Sometimes, when anger overcomes her, she clips her child with a twisted-up tea towel or locks her in the wardrobe. Such punishments rarely achieve the desired effects. Instead they make Maud feel as though she has disfigured a part of herself, or revealed a latent monstrosity. (Her mother treated her similarly, if more harshly; she swore she'd be different with Selda, but then the feeling comes, sheer and vertical, and all the oxygen leaves the room.) Sometimes a handful of wooden pegs or an empty carton, more so even than a toy or a picture book, will focus her daughter's energies. Sometimes she'll bargain for rest by preparing a hot sweet cocoa, fortified by enough soporific whiskey or gin to conk Selda out for hours. She likes to help her mother hang up the washing, tottering from basket to line with a pillowcase or a slip across the wet, cold concrete of the yard, through which grass has begun to crack. As she holds the piece of washing aloft, Selda peers through the air as though she cannot just hear but see the words and music in the broadcasts. An unheard, unseen force, neither spirit nor electricity, moves over the roof-tiles and smog, through the rain, under the clouds and the stars, from the stem of her brain to beyond the horizon.

One evening towards the end of the war, V-2s falling on London suburbs, Edward leaves work and goes for a ride, rather than cycle home directly. His chrome spokes blur in the city's dark streets. He is clean-shaven and slim, his hair threaded through with white, the skin around his jaw and throat beginning to loosen and crease in a way his daughter, later in life, will compare to that of an ageing greyhound's. He isn't heading anywhere in particular. He is looking for something, he couldn't say what. Instinct takes him where it takes him. The world feels empty tonight. Clear and cool and patient, as some stone-built chapels feel. Few people are out. Now and then a grand car slowly passes, or he hears a clopping horse. The air is cold and clammy. He is glad of the freshening wind. He hears a muffled pizzicato in the alleys, of cats and foxes padding in search of a meal. A slow note of wind fluting through chimney tops and broken windows. His own rhythmic breath as he powers forward, chugging out clouds of locomotive steam. He hums as he cycles, finding that the tune he is singing was taught to him not by Chopin or Elgar but Selda. Her songs have that effect. They burrow into his mind. Perhaps all fathers feel this way. Their child or children the very centre of things, the clearest voices of all.

This afternoon, at work, he was overcome by a mood that has begun to grip him since the news came back about Charles. There seemed no way that his brother would survive. That he did was almost worse: he was kept alive to breathe and suffer, that is all. Edward finds the whole thing distressing beyond measure. Easier to pretend his brother died. Still the moods overcome him. Deep, black glooms. They have a strange quality, too, of gravity, of weight. He pictures them in terms of sound: waves of pressure passing through the world, like peals from a baleful bell.

But these states of being have an earlier origin. When his daughter was born, the night sky shuddered with unnatural light (in his memory, his walk through the streets has been drained of all sound, is completely and eerily silent). Something else was born then, too, something monstrous. The stench of burnt butter. Incendiaries raining down like meteors. What was revealed by their fire? A man's foot, bloodless, up a tree, its brogue like the beak of a grotesque bird. The foot itself was not so bad, but what it signified was harder to parse. The raw force of the world's disorder. Still, he wasn't on the front, was he? Charles shot him early, saved him from the real thing. This was the world he was bringing her into, where death was arbitrary, where your foot could end up in a tree.

He has nothing to complain about. He must regain a

sense of perspective.

Now he is passing a workshop's gates, a corner pub whose windows, blackout restrictions eased, cast yellowish light over a yard whose cobbles gleam like obsidian eggs.

The disturbing sensation that he wishes to shake, to run from, is this: he is pregnant with death. It lives and grows within him, day by day. It is not the sense that death is waiting around the next corner, sharpening its scythe, or looming on the horizon of his immediate future like a wall of smoke and flame. Rather, he has become attuned to something within him. A cellular process. Death is not an end, it is not a full stop, it is an active and ongoing scam, a dark bloom or a thief in the blood. It is insidious and inextricable from life.

And so this is what he goes in search of. A fire to burn the feeling from his chest. To remind him of where life resides.

Once, certain types of music did it. Mendelssohn's late concerto did it. Now, only opera can. Its excess, its overspilling, tumbling abundance of feeling, of sound pouring out of the throat, taps into something, allows it to flow, drains him of unwished-for blood. Opera lends musical form to his suspicion that life is not a defiance of nothing: it is the crescendo of death itself. The only remedy for this – the only recompense – is love.

Or to put it another way, life is the exception and death is the rule. Therefore life is a kind of obscenity. A beautiful one perhaps, but an obscenity all the same. Our awareness of this, he suspects, is what gives passion its reason to be. To keep asserting our obscenity – of love, of life – over and over again: this is the secret of the man of passion (if he would allow himself to be one).

He does not know where this paradoxical feeling

274

comes from. Needless to add, he cannot mention it to anyone.

Or there is, of course, one person he can talk to about it, but the last time Edward saw Charles, it left him shaken. His brother sat low in a chair. His face was stitched together, the right cheek sunken, like a crater, and the eye above it permanently closed. Charles's mouth was open, but unable to make a sound beyond whistling, laboured breath. The floor around him strewn with pages on which were written reams of gibberish, tales about snowstorms and ghosts. And he was thrusting them at Edward as though his life depended on it, a word in gappy caps along the top of a page: *L I S T E N*.

To what? The feeling has been with him since childhood. As a young boy, when he first saw a steam train, he felt a strange fear passing through him, like a shadow consuming a sunlit field. When he first saw the blue sea, the idea that it was bottomless transfixed him: where other children might have fantasized buccaneering, he imagined sinking down into the lightless depths. The feeling surges from his diaphragm, pushes into his throat. If only he could open his mouth, let it burble up and spill out; if only he could vomit this feeling and be rid of it, once and for all.

He takes a left down a long, dark street. Almost at once, he stops pedalling.

He has never been here before. It is one of those parts of the city that has yet to be rebuilt or redeemed, where bomb-weed takes root in the rubble and children love to play. He doesn't know what makes him stop in front of that particular boarded-up house, its roof caved in, its front wall torn in half. An intuition, no more. A sense that he remembers from dreams, of being compelled by something irrational and erotic, which finds its object in places it shouldn't, in busts and buttocks, in ears and chins, in body parts belonging to women and men, a noise and confusion of desperate, spun-compass longing. A dark and all-consuming attraction whose object – dangerous, electric with risk – is all the more alluring for possessing, on the face of it, no obvious allure. He has always felt some trace of it, in fact, with Maud. In the alley when they first met, noise from the nearby pub, the threat of being caught. And later, before marriage, when they met in that hotel. Even after moving to Clay Lane, he felt a trace of anger in his desire, hate in the midst of his love, pinning her to the bed as if they were animals. These moods come from somewhere. When they pass, when they are panting and damp and the sheets are a mess, how do they feel? Is *this* music?

Not that he expects to find a woman waiting for him here, in a silk and lace gown. Rather that, as he steps over the rubble threshold that was once a living room wall, and casts his gaze around the dusty furniture and shattered ceramic (dinner plates, they might have been), he senses his proximity to something savage and untamed. The danger of being here, in a house of death, excites him. That is simply the case. It does not edify him to admit it. He climbs the stairs, the carpet scattered with fragments of brick. He should not be here. He feels a thief, a violator. Still he steps forward, short of breath, onto the cramped landing. Who used to live here? Would he recognize them if he passed them in the street? Perhaps they did not survive, and that is the source of his prurient game: to get close to a thing he fears, to stare down the skull. If that is the case, explain this: it is only in moments such as now that he feels truly alive. Well, outside of music, at least. It all sounds very unfortunate, very Germanic: love and death entwined.

The left door opens onto a room that may have belonged to a bachelor around his age, rented, by the looks of it, and modestly appointed. (How many times did his landlady knock on his door to ask for rent or enquire about breakfast?) The wall is blown-open, a curtain billowing and collapsing, moonlight falling over the floor and the unmade bed.

That's when Edward sees it. On top of the chest of drawers. Its shape is unmistakable. He recognizes it from the newspaper adverts, from the shop windows he lingers outside some weekends. The closest thing one could image to having an orchestra in the living room.

Back home, he crosses another threshold. The dark air evaporates: he is himself again, a Dunlop man, a responsible father. The air smells of cooking dinner, he guesses plate pie. He calls Maud to the living room. 'Work ran late,' he says, 'but have a look at what the boss gifted me.' With a flourish he displays a black box resembling a suitcase which, when he opens its hinged lid, reveals a circular disc of padded felt and a chrome arm. He rests it on the table and fits a handle into a hole in the side of the box and cranks it, like he would an old car engine. Once the disc is spinning, he pulls a vinyl out of his satchel.

Selda appears in the doorway in a nightie Maud sewed for her from parachute silk. She pays the object no attention at first: the hems of her father's trousers, held tight by trouser clips, are of greater interest. In her arms is a dozy tortoiseshell tomcat roughly as large as she is, blinking in bemusement at the room. Her father kneels and sticks his tongue out.

'Right then, if I just... ah-*hah*.'

The needle finds the groove. A crackle fills the cold room.

The record spins, the music starts: a change comes

over Selda. She drops the cat. It shoots off meowing. She stands still, staring at the box, her mouth open and her arms relaxed at her side. A string section is with them now, a violin at the forefront, and it sounds to Edward like nothing so much as a voice, anguished, eloquent – he clears his throat to fight back tears. Selda will not remember this first encounter with recorded music. Years later, though, she will claim that she does. Her first memory. She will describe it as such so often that she believes it herself. The feel of raw floorboards in the gloomy living room in which she was born (the Hutch long since dismantled, blackout curtains down). She will recall a tin of cooking grease which is not here, stacked newspapers, the shrouded budgie-cage, brown wallpaper (in fact it is arctic blue). The memory-room will be steeped in a postwar spendthrift dinge, in which brownish air the music will appear less like sound than a form of illumination, sunlight reflected by malachite. Something beamed from the deep past and into future. Her future. Life itself.

'Edward, look.'

'What's...? – Oh.'

'Little one.'

'Is she alright?'

'I think so.'

'I've not seen her do that before.'

'You remember this piece?'

Maud shakes her head. She kneels beside her daughter, looking, with puzzled amusement, into Selda's wide and staring eyes. Maud tucks a stray hair behind her ear. She thinks her daughter looks hypnotized. Has some strange, suited man crept in, twizzling his moustache, and mesmerized Selda with his fairground psychic tricks? The child's concentration is so intense it begins to unnerve Maud (who only that morning, and not for the first time,

278

had secretly cursed her daughter). She lifts Selda into her arms. Selda's gaze does not leave the black, rotating disc from which the violin sings.

'Surely you do!' says Edward. 'It was playing at the Opera House the night we met.'

'It was?'

'Of course, of course.'

'Well, I wouldn't have heard it from the cloak room.'

This version of Mendelssohn's *Concerto in E Minor*, the composer's final work, was recorded in 1938. Six vinyls are handsomely bound in a book of records whose edges are tattered and frayed, the red-leather cover seamed with yellow dust.

'If I didn't suspect she was in league with the Devil I'd say she looks like an angel for once.'

From that moment on, whenever Selda is badly behaved, her parents will put on the Mendelssohn – for several months, they are the only records – and she will fall into a wide-eyed trance. She will forget to close her mouth. Saliva will build up and leak down her chin. But still she will not move. Her transformations confirms her father's sense that music, while connected in his mind to danger and disorder, to lust and death, is an instrument of social betterment. It civilizes the child. He notices how, aged two, she is able to hum passages. Her savage song is tempered, grows melodious. When the war ends, he will take her to recitals, and she will respond in the same way. He will take her to a recital of a forty-part motet by Thomas Tallis, a stirring work for voices staged in an Agnesian chapel. The following morning, he will come downstairs to find Selda seated at the kitchen table, pages laid out all around her, scribbled notes everywhere, and the image will chill him: he will remember his brother, in the hospital Edward hasn't been to in weeks, broken and

279

muted and surrounded by pages. He asks her what they mean.

'Music,' Selda replies, not looking up from her page.

'What music?'

'From last night.'

He lifts a page. It makes no sense to him. The notes might as well be hieroglyphs or military code.

Years from now, Selda's workaholism (Anya's name for it) will drive her daughter up the wall. She will interpret Selda's commitment to composing, above all other responsibilities, as a rejection; an abandonment, even. Her independence will emerge in response to her mother's, then, rather than in emulation or inheritance of same. Even after she has flown the coop, gone to university, met the rangy, over-confident man who will become her husband and father her child, Anya will resent this. Selda will dispute this account. She will attribute her dedication (Selda's word for it) to her character. There is, she says, a toughness running through her, both intrinsic to her being and a manifestation of the family line. A kind of compulsion, too – the artist's curse, subordinating all drives to its monomaniacal will, etc. In certain tellings, this aspect of her character will carry another nostalgic and dubious aura: that of the upbeat, tea-towel Blitz. In the national mythos (as Anya sees it, in her late teens), this silly 'spirit' draws attention to what it pretends to conceal: trauma, in the parlance; and repression – of national complicity in mass-scale death, of the fact of how lost and sorrowful everyone felt.

For now, though, Selda is just a girl. As of a week ago, her father is unemployed. The war is over: good. The Dunlop factory's output has plummeted, and they have made sweeping redundancies: bad. She often feels desperate to alleviate something. A pain she can intuit but not peer into. An ache that hides behind Edward's jokes and smiles, the pouchy eyes and the increasingly low, slurred voice, the growly laugh that bubbles at the back of the throat.

Tonight, while Maud is across town to look after her mother, who's sick with leukaemia, Edward has taken his daughter to the club. They have dined on toast and marmalade. Selda has a wide-eyed, watchful look in contrast to the men and women around her in the dim, low-ceilinged club, with its red carpet and murky mirrors in polished bronze frames. Smoke rises from the piled-high ashtrays and the Dunhill loosely clasped in her father's fingers; it hangs so densely in the eye-stinging air it might as well be highland fog. Yet it is – or becomes, by dint of repetition – a comforting smell. One reason why she takes up smoking, later in life, is that the habit reminds her of her father.

Selda is the only child in the club. She already has the lanky look that will carry through to adulthood, from Agnes's to the Varèse, from motherhood into old age: sinewy, beanstalk limbs, prominent knees and elbows, big hands and ears. She's a gangly scrabbler, born climber of trees. And yet her face, at rest, has a scholarly aspect: the narrowed, liquid, inkwell eyes are serious beyond her years (there is a trace of the toddler transfixed by the vinyl). She sits on the plasticky seat-cover in a clean blue dress with the cardigan thrown over, the moth-holes sewn up with red thread, and drinks blackcurrant squash. Her father is having a conversation with two former Dunlop men on the next table, muttering darkly of their ex-employer's plans to make rubber plantations in East Nigeria, where the Colonial Office failed, and meanwhile all the jobs are being filled by immigrants from the colonies. 'It's all topsy-turvy,' says one of Edward's acquaintances, to which he sadly nods assent.

Then the sugar hits Selda's bloodstream: a marmalade-and-cordial rush. Off she goes, ducking around the legs of tables and people, going for a meander, hearing snatches of song in the hubbub. She collides with the thigh of a tottering, red-faced man with white hair sprouting from his ears. Propped against the bar, he's struggling for balance as it is; gin soda slops over the rim of his glass. Edward crosses over, cigarette between teeth, and drags his daughter back to her proper chair. He's lost the moustache, but hasn't shaved since yesterday evening, and the light stubble around his jaw is flecked with snow.

'*Sit*,' he tells Selda, the Dunhill wagging. 'Don't move.'

'Sooright, sooright,' mumbles the magnanimous drunk, lifting a paw to placate him.

'I'll stand you another one, Steve. Sorry about that.'

'Sooright, Eddie. Sooright.'

Selda cries and cries. He pours her a finger of beer and tries to make her drink it, but she won't, so he pours it back into his glass.

He has an idea. He sees the piano, the stool in front of it. He sets her on the stool and lifts the lid. She plays a few notes, slow at first, with a rapt gentleness, as if aware of something – life-force, mystery, plaything, friend – at work in the interaction of hinges and strings. The piano hasn't been tuned in a while, the notes have a honky-tonk dissonance. But the sound runs through her like electricity; she throws her head back in laughter, *cackles* like Charles. She presses the fourth F-sharp, the string muffled by something invisible in the instrument – a mouse crept in before the war ended, died, dried, and now dampens the sound of this particular string: dnk, dnk, dnk. Pints hover between elbow and lip, heads turn. Men

282

are watching, some with amusement, others with irritation, indifference, curiosity, mockery, at the child and her noises, dnk. So. It was a bad idea, bringing Selda here. His daughter plays a note, another, another, dnk, dnk, three baby-step keys: a D minor, her very first chord! Then another note. Another chord. Within a few minutes she has picked out the notes to 'Happy Birthday'.

He brings her back again. Night after night. A routine. Gets a beer, sets her on the stool, 'Go on Selda, there's a good girl,' gets a beer, tells the bar his daughter is Mozart reborn, gets a beer, takes requests, and so on. In a few months she's taking requests from the Irish, Bangladeshis, Grenadians, Jamaicans. Sometimes, there is dancing; often, the audience sing along, tap their thighs, raise their glasses. Back then, Edward doesn't care who she plays for, white or black or destitute or a bona fide millionaire, so long as they contribute to the various receptacles he hands out, fresh coins slinking into an upturned flat-cap, clattering into chipped mugs, dropping into his open palms, the empty cups of his open eyes. He watches his daughter's hands move across the keys, with a fluency that, barring a few ad-hoc lessons in technique, seems almost entirely self-taught. Unless it comes from *there*, from the gift – but: to imagine her afflicted in the same way that Charles was? He'd rather not. Still, she is putting *something* into music. It isn't opera. It isn't the final concerto of a composer he hasn't been able to listen to since the war, hating all things German (he'll feel this way until his dying days, even when it comes to types of mustard or makes of car). Is it his daughter's soul? It may just be her skill. Every night, it seems, she knows a new technique, a new flourish, a new, strange chord. She improvises, she improves. And she seems to enjoy it. It becomes their game. Maud's mother lies dying in a hospital bed, Edward's father is losing his mind, but here is new life: this spectacular jukebox girl with her trancelike focus. She's only to hear a song once before she can play it, practically. Later in life, she'll remember the club as a kind of cloud, a heavenlike space in which voices floated, and music moved, and she felt, yes, *powerful*. And the money doesn't hurt. Free beers, gins, cigarettes, cordials, bags of sweets, once a loaf of bread. He has visions of national tours. He will be her father-impresario. Together, they will set the world right. And though he rarely describes these fantasies out loud, they do not go unnoticed by his daughter.

She is in town with her mother. Earlier that month, her mother's mother died. There was a funeral, everyone in black, some prayers and some singing. Selda remembers her grandmother as a doughy, solid presence, crinkly about the face and hands, quick to temper and fond of limericks. They are out shopping for the weekend meals. They visit the butcher, where Selda stares entranced at the wine-red livers and honeycombed tripe, the sausage-link necklaces hanging from hooks. The heavy leather-smell of dead flesh is so pungent she's convinced it will stain her nostrils. She can almost hear muscle and sinew speak. The words are muttered in voices like gargled blood. Maud buys a half-pound of lambs' brains and three chicken thighs. The butcher wraps them on the slab, where blood forms drooling staves on greased paper.

Back outside, sunlight blazing on the street, Selda attempts to explain. She has tried and failed and tried again and failed again and still she must try, still she must try, no matter the reaction, because her mother must understand. The more she doesn't, the worse Selda feels. She has done something wrong. Or *is* wrong. If her mother understood what it was like, perhaps things would be different. Maud does not want to listen. Why? Selda must make her.

'What is it, Selda?'

'I just think, I just mean, maybe it's not so strange, maybe it's normal, like now, what's so different about now? You can hear all these people can't you?'

'Selda, please, there's Manze's to get to first, then the Post Office before it closes at four.'

'You keep hearing things, speech, the radio, isn't that sort of the same?'

'I don't go pretending about any ghosts or spectres or whatever games you and poor Charles devised together, and it isn't the voice of God you're hearing either or you'd behave yourself at church.'

She begs her mother to listen. Listen to the litanies in Osburg's and Holy Family, in the Church of the Sacred Blood. Listen to elderly women gossiping on market day. A man repeatedly interrupting his wife's attempts to convey a story to friends at dinner, then tutting and rolling his eyes because she's not telling it quickly enough. Listen to drinks orders barked at the bar. Listen to a radio with a bent aerial, the dial being combed, the crackle between the stations. The more desperate she is, the more tenuous the comparison. Maud's heels clop the pavement in curt denial, no no no, as they go about their chores, no no, distracted by shopping they covet but cannot afford, no Selda no not now. Dried pineapple and fudge at Russo's, creamed cakes and rye bread behind Newmann's glass counter, counting coins and planning supper as they cross the street, waving at Hillary, avoiding Thomas, pausing at the crossing and adjusting her belt and correcting her hat and crossing herself at the sight of a dead pigeon on the

285

side of the road, she has tasks, tasks, tasks, has she forgotten the soap? is there enough left for two boxes of eggs? Selda is only a child. No no no. But if Selda could only do it, if she could find the right analogy... if she could write a tune that would capture how it felt, then Maud would understand, her father would no longer feel sad.

Home at last, slithering up and down scales, writing music. In her own hand, that is, using notation of her own device. As Selda will be proud to note later in life, she sketched her own musical shapes in her childhood, long before encountering those by Cardew or Xenakis or Cage. The branching lines, hollow circles, triangular legs reminded her of wire coat-hangers, electrical tape, her father's buttons, dinner plates, bicycle wheels, lightbulb filaments, split compass needles. Selda is on the kitchen floor while the neighbourhood kids make a racket in the street, sketching music on the back flap of a packet of baking soda.

These notes will help her to remember. (Why, she will later wonder of her child-self – why this melancholic premonition that she needs to remember, in the moment, what she will later forget, that these moments will fade to silence?)

Her mother in the yard, decapitating a chicken. The inky sneeze as blood spatters the dirt. Feathers floating, sunlit.

The zinc tub in the kitchen. Pink feet in soapy water. A crispy towel drinking the water off her skin.

Steam rising from the same tub midweek. Her mother bent at the waist, elbow-deep, washing the clothes, hands bright red with the heat of the water.

Her mother in the yard, chopping wood. The roar of the wood-burning stove. The ashy smell of it.

Bricks in the living room, blackened by time.

The crisp browned edges of fried Spam.

Boiled leeks and mashed potatoes. Her father's brown bottles of stout. The sound of car engines. Rubble. Then, suddenly: plastic. Plastic toys, containers, packets, itchy nylon jumpers.

Fires in the yard in the summer. Neighbours coming round for an afternoon of washing. Bedsheets, dirty linens. They threw the sheets and pillowcases into the bath placed over the fire, a kind of cauldron, which they stirred with a broom. The sheets hung out to dry on the line had never looked so white. The smell of fresh-boiled sheets left out to air-dry later that night or tomorrow.

Out of these sketches, she scribbles a song. It is a kind of love song, its intended recipient is Maud. The next morning, she reads it again, plays it in her head. No good, no use. She twists the pages up and burns them in the hearth.

Selda is unusually quiet. She does not sing compulsively or indulge her fantastical side, refrains from make-believing that she is one, or several, people that she is not, or that the very air swims with dead relatives. Instead she stares, in apparent rapture, at gold and bronze coins, at flint arrowheads and pottery. Could this be the civilizing influence Maud has been looking for, a *museum*?

They head through to the next room, which is filled with dead animals. Apes and gibbons squat on truncated boughs backed by painted banana-palms and vines. Wild cats prowl wooden boards dusted with sand. Maud sniffs. Her throat feels dry. Reflexively she scratches her left wrist with her right hand, blinking around the room. The animals' fur is dry and tatty, their dulled glass eyes point in odd directions, yet this is how such creatures appear in the wild. Nature's roaming threat safely framed, yet the likeness frightens her. A moment ago she had joked about breaking the glass. Now she thanks goodness for cabinet-makers.

Scenes from social history are a focus of the following room. They pause beside a display about the textile industry, which features a painting of a waterside mill.

'Your great-grandmother worked in a mill just like this,' says Maud.

The stories are a cornerstone of family lore. Her grandmother had worked thirteen-hour days in air so thick with heat and cotton-dust you could slice it, like steamed pudding. Colleagues fell flat with cholera, or were deafened by the roar of machines.

'No she didn't,' Selda says.

A frivolous denial, coming from the mouth of a child. It should not upset Maud. 'She did.'

'None of us worked in a mill,' says Selda, matter-of-fact. 'They're telling me.'

'Who are?'

'The dead.'

Maud ticks her daughter off. What if someone overheard?

Later that evening, while Edward is away, Selda has a fit. She begins speaking strangely and will not stop. Perhaps the museum is to blame. Who to call, doctor or exorcist? Selda spouts untruths about their family, worse even than calling Maud's grandmother a liar. She makes outlandish, even lurid claims that their family line is marked by incest, theft, and so on – impossible to account for and distressing to hear. Maud commands – and later begs – Selda to stop. Yet her daughter paces round the room as though it is filled with people with whom she has urgent business.

'*Listen*,' says Maud. 'Selda. *Listen*.' She grips her daughter's chin, slaps her lightly round the cheek. No response.

Words pour out of her. The only thing that has any effect is when she plays one of Edward's records, hoping to drown out Selda's speech should any neighbours be listening.

Selda casts around as though uncertain where she is.

'Are you playing a game, Selda? Are you? This isn't funny, it isn't funny at all.'

Then she is lost again. Selda begins to sing along. Maud has never spoken to, or at, or with the gift before: now, though, she addresses it directly – she begs it to leave them alone. She curses the damned meddling dead, commands them back to their rightful place, the graveyard, the past, silence.

Maud has no way of knowing this, but Selda is, in fact, aware of what is happening. She has not yet been lured too deeply into the gift: those maladies will come later. She is dimly aware, in other words, of the distress that she is causing, which causes her distress in return – yet she remains unable to stop it. The best that she can manage is to shape the nature of her possession. To inflect her speech and song so that Maud will hear her daughter in the sound.

Apparently, she does not. And looking back, Selda won't blame her. If anything, she will blame herself. She will even be grateful to Maud for what happens next because, in Selda's adult mind, this moment will mark her premature transition into adulthood, or a kind of adulthood.

Something snaps. Maud takes Selda by the wrists and drags her to the pantry, smaller than an outhouse, its shelves lined with tins and jars. She drags out the broom and the mop and replaces them with Selda. Then closes the door and presses a chair against it. Her daughter's voice carries quietly through the wood. Maud waits a moment. Then heads next door, where the record continues to play.

It is not the last time that Maud takes such action. On occasion, Edward will too. They do not do it out of a wish to punish or to discipline, they tell Selda, but to contain. When the gift becomes too much for them to bear – when their daughter wanders like a sleepwalker or exhibits distress – they will put her here, in the pantry, its dark, hard corners softened by heaped sheets, where she will sing and talk and howl until at last the trance subsides. At which point Selda will fall still, like a stuffed animal in a cabinet. Coming to in this cramped, damp box again, sometimes leaning on a wall but more often curled up on the floor, she will come to understand that this is where the gift belongs.

Edward spends his days looking for work. Odd jobs come through. They are far beneath his station but at least his family do not starve. Maud suggests he retrain, but what profession? Who'll take him? The whole point of moving to this city was security. He feels humiliated, betrayed. His mind drifts over Outer Mongolia, over the Volga, to a snowbound land of revolution: the common man rising up in a fever of liberty... He has fantasies of taking his former bosses into the basement: *that's* the part of the story that gives him a thrill, not what came after. Better still to picture oneself as a Roundhead at the scaffold as the king lays his head on the block. In the meantime, in the lax afternoons, he has time for a new hobby: schemes. Buying and selling whatever crosses path or palm, prospecting on the black and grey markets. It isn't pretty. But it tides him over. And it clues him into a different economy, one he first encountered in the bombed-out house with the record player. He hustles lessons for his daughter from local musicians. He writes to music schools, to the Musicians Benevolent Fund. Maud suggests that he write to that other place, the hospice. Not because they're certain about their daughter and not just because Charles has it too, but because they offer something they cannot afford: a musical education. All the same he puts it off and puts it off again, kicking the can down the road (every time he does, his brother's face appears in his mind: the open throat, the guilt that sticks to him like tar). One day, he and Jim Croghan go for a drive in a creaky-wheeled cart. Jim's famous for being stronger than he looks: he's shy of five foot six and has a boyish face, but there's unusual force in his arms and hands, you wouldn't cross him in a hurry. They steer about the rubble-heaps, the boarded windows, the gaping basements, though the city is already changing: many of the sites have been razed, repaired, replaced.

'It's about here somewhere.'

'Right you are,' says Jim.

'Plain as I see you now.'

They keep going, curb-crawl, moving with the clop-clopping sloth of horses half-knackered from hauling pipes and sheets all day, all week, all lifetime. Then he sees a scrap of lino that looks familiar – chess-board flap of black-and-white diamonds, mired in dust with a sweep of something black. Oil, he hopes. One last clamber over the brick, through a door in the back, down into a basement, and there: an upright piano, tan wood, nestled in the corner like a bird in cupped hands: a miracle.

This is Selda's first piano, she'll later bequeath it to Wolf. The casing has splintered and cracked in places, its strings are old and dull, the white keys are yellowed like a smoker's teeth, some are missing the ebony, and the lowest C's a dud. But it is the most marvellous thing that Selda has ever had the pleasure, the all-consuming cellular ecstasy, to interact with. It's better than the cinema, television, radio, chocolate, and cordial, better even than music as she has hitherto known it. The instrument completes her. It is, she'll later say, and mean it, the great love of her life. (Only later will it occur to her that this is a sad thing to say, and why did she reach for an inanimate object and not Anya, not Wolf? She revises herself: they, she'll think but never find words to say, are her greatest works, the best things she's ever created.) She hadn't known that she was missing something before. But here it is. The piano makes her whole. Her relationship to it is of a different order than friends or family entirely. It isn't an object, nor is it a living thing: it is somehow both. More than that. It is a part of herself. She never doubts that it has an inner life, and that it echoes her own. On quiet days she can hear the strings creak, the wood settle. When she plays, its moods move with her own. She likes nothing more than to rest her head against the box and hear the notes' reverb, the instrument's soul. When she was younger, she rested her head against something else: her mother's body in all its warmth, the gargling stomach, the beating heart.

II. 1956-1960

Selda's bag contains a heel of stale bread, spare clothes, and a bundle of cloves in a handkerchief. She has completed her schooling (good but not exceptional grades), has earned money by playing and teaching piano in bars, music halls, ballet classes and living rooms, she has washed dishes, pulled pints, and scrubbed floors. She can memorize a tune after hearing it once, has begun to compose entire motets, quartets and cantatas using little else than memory, arranging the notes in her mind such that they hang fixedly, constellations she can observe and change at will. But she has no real formal training to speak of and, until recently, it never occurred to her that it might be available. It was the gift, which whispered to her of a hospice. When she told her parents about it, they acted as though they had known all along.

She steps off the train. The station's bright glass roof is alive with echoes, the polished concourse glaring. A few men eye her as they pass. Can they tell that she's already lost? Is she really that legible? Leaving the station, she walks in a straight, brisk line, her gaze fixed on a chimney aloft in the sunlit smog.

With ambitions to walk, to save money on bus fare, she crosses the Thames at London Bridge. Sun scrubs the dirt from the world, makes everything fresh-minted, clean. The paleness of brick, the transparency of glass.

All the same, the city confounds her. She follows the map but the roads unravel under her feet. She loses her way, gets side-tracked by the sound of a record player, skiffle lilting from open windows, the jangle of electric guitar mixing with lavender oil and chip-grease, with petrol and American doo-wop everywhere.

She reaches a tangle of soot-dulled streets, public

squares thronged with overgrown bushes, front gardens strung with fluttering laundry. A radio on a windowsill, laughter from a sketch comedy. Sunlit squalls. The music in Selda clips forward, interlocked sequences that capture a heart beating fast and hard, she can't tell whether from excitement or fear. She hears the tick-tock rhythms of the street. Her shoe pinches her heel. A pellet of gravel has lodged itself under her sock. She pauses to jimmy it out.

There is something wrong with Selda. On top of being a tall girl with big hands, that is. People have told her so. Friends, her parents, her parents' friends have been saying so since she stood in her room while her father was sleeping and felt the voices stir. What rich smells in this city, too: boiled bagels, spilled beer, roasted spices, the leather-rot stench of hot butchers, alleyways ripe with piss, pipe smoke, a sweet and heady smell she'll later identify as hash. She looks down, scratching an itch on her forearm. More skiffle, worse skiffle, shambles out the open doors of a basement bar, a bassist who can't keep time, the snare drum out to lunch. She passes streets that remind her of home, a strip of tyre strung from a tree on a green, a horsey boy splitting an apple in half with his teeth. She hasn't eaten since the apple she ate on the way to the station this morning. Hunger sparkles at the edges of inedible objects. Just last week she fainted whilst walking to the park. And now her mouth is flooding with saliva.

She halts at the steps and cranes her neck. A sandstone frieze carved over the double doors depicts a crazed, continuous parade of musicians playing trumpets, bugles, violins, among gibbons, lizards, eagles, lions, chimeras, vine-leaves, flaming bushes, trees, the congregation watched by angels with harps and bugles afloat under outstretched wings. She peers at the squat pale towers further back, and the stained-glass windows above the frieze, patched with cardboard in places, lead hanging tangled in others. It's a Gothic concoction of slate roofs, turrets and arched windows with a taller, redbrick building towards the rear. Carved above the front doors is its name: Agnes's Hospice for Acoustically Gifted Children. Beneath it are a set of double doors, heavy oak, closed.

She stops in the sun. Waiting, watching. Thinking she should turn and head back.

The name of the institution frightens her. It has the grim Victorian ring of asylums and sanatoriums, places where illness was compounded, not cured, by ice baths, electrocution, confinement: 'treatments' that eclipsed the afflictions they purported to cure; where patients, mostly girls and young women, were strapped to beds in windowless cells, hosed down, dunked in baths of ice, fed stupefying tinctures. And what does 'acoustically' mean? Are the people who go to Agnes's simply competent listeners, good girls, silent girls, seen but not heard? Or are they gifted with sensitivity to waves and vibrations, uncommonly alive to sound? Is she ill or gifted or neither or both? Whichever the case, she is here, in her itchy hand-me-down jacket in the desolate sunshine, clutching a satchel with a heel of stale bread in it and not much else. She doesn't know why she's come. The place doesn't even look open.

She grips her suitcase and knocks on the door.

The hall has the feel of a chapel, with its checkerboard floor, dark wood-panelled walls, tiny high windows whose unloved panes let in columns of milky light, its enveloping smell of cool stone. She introduces herself at the reception desk. A woman resembling a stuffed owl, yellow eyes wide behind her half-moon glasses, consults an appointment book, makes a phone call, and directs Selda downstairs. She heads through a side door and down a flight of stairs into the Jensen Centre, an archive and library built in a basement beneath the hospice, the walls of which, lined with books and vinyls, hum when tube trains pass, as do the booths around the edge of the rooms, equipped with tape machines and headphones.

She takes a seat outside a glass-fronted office beside three other people about her age, two women and a man. They ask her to fill in a form. Does she communicate with her ancestors? How do they make her feel? What kind of things do they tell her? Do they ever sing, and if so, how does it sound? She fills the form in diligently. Perhaps she exaggerates here and there: she wants to 'do well', to ensure she gets accepted. Handing back the pages, she notices her hands are sticky with sweat, her heart rate elevated.

A tinny speaker croaks Selda's name. She is shown into a cave of a room. In the middle is a low table and two simple wooden chairs. No decorations, other than sheets on the walls of padded foam, and shelves on which a range of bells are displayed. She doesn't realize it yet, but this unprepossessing space will – as she'll later put it, only semi-hyperbolically – change her life.

'Let's see. Selda Heddle?'

'Yes – no – yes.'

'Is there some doubt?'

'Sorry. That's me.'

'Well, you wouldn't be the first, would you? No. Long journey?'

'Coventry.'

'Hmmm. Disastrous, what happened,' says the man, skim-reading Selda's form. 'Then again, look at Dresden.

Look everywhere. Those poor Japanese. Oh, whataboutism. How vague. Yes, sloppy, sloppy,' he continues, muttering to himself. Or to the gift. Is this is what Selda will become, an avuncular eccentric conversing with chairs in a basement cell? 'Still, we must keep an open heart. Not literally. That would be bad for one's health. What scares me more than the past, however recent, is the other direction. The future? Why, yes. The future's what harrows the marrow, alright. Now, where were we?'

Selda blinks. 'I've no idea.'

The man laughs. 'Quite, yes. See? That's very well put. Well. Names. Mine is Vaughn. Or Otto. Call me either.' Grey check suit, cornflower shirt. The man's wide domed head is mostly bald and pocked and licked with scars. He wears wireframe spectacles, round lenses the size of two bob bits. A lit cigar smoulders in a tray (a sense-memory flash of her father's Dunhill). An odd, short cape hangs from his shoulders, a heavy blue fabric, velvet perhaps, that is somehow both shiny and matt. On the table beside him rests a bell of polished bronze, though it might be gold.

'How long have you been here, Selda Heddle?'

'About an hour.'

'Oh, that's not what I mean.'

She waits for a while. Electricity hums in the bulb overhead. 'I don't understand.'

Vaughn Otto, or Otto Vaughn: whatever his name, he laughs again. A soft chortle. 'You must forgive me, of course. I've not left this room since this morning. Now, without further ado,' he says, lifting the bell from the table. (The faintest high-frequency ringing sound clarifies the air.)

At once, his demeanour shifts. He sits in front of her, all his concentration gathered in his twitching eyes.

'I'm going to ring a few of these instruments. They're not ordinary bells, I hasten to note. I doubt you'll have heard anything quite like them before. We make them ourselves, in the foundry. We've been doing so for hundreds of years. They're nothing to be afraid of. Nor is this procedure. It's certainly not an exam. But it is a test, of sorts. Alright? Now. Relax, if you can. Deep breaths, deep breaths... Good. It won't hurt. We're simply trying to understand a little better who you are. Understood?'

Selda nods. She feels the gift begin to move darkly around her, individual voices in one body, one shoal.

'Ready?'

The sound is sudden, startling. The shoal quickens, spins. Ordinarily, a bell tone begins to fade almost immediately. This one goes the opposite way. Like feedback, it only grows louder, ringing so harshly in the room that she can almost see it: a hard and blue-tinged music juddering in the air. The man says something. Selda doesn't catch the words. The light sinks down and down and down again. Everything begins to feel still.

When she comes to again, she is on the floor. Someone is singing. No, screaming. Someone is singing and screaming about the cold, about bells in the snow. Who is it? Otto is standing over her, a small bell cupped in his palm. His dark eyes are not narrowed in concern but fascination. Is lying on the floor really so interesting? Why is she down here, anyway? Who is singing? Then she realizes with a jolt who it is. She lifts a hand to her mouth to silence her song.

She isn't alone in feeling confused, confounded, bamboozled, bemused, her compass spun and her sextant scrambled. The gift has an arse-over-elbow effect, especially in minds so unformed. Worse, it can break minds entirely, confusing their sense not just of where they come from but who they are. Since arriving at the hospice, the gift has got louder not quieter, more unruly and powerful. She is more prone to trances than she was back home. The gift will snag her attention, lure her into a tale or two, and the next thing she knows she will be halfway across the hospice, or standing outside in the rain. Surely this is the opposite of the point?

A week after arriving, she joins an induction class with three other new 'wards' – the name given to the people, neither students nor patients, the hospice takes under its care. They go around the room, attempting to explain how it feels, a task none of them relish.

'Like a Punch and Judy show. It was funny for a while but then the puppets turned on me, started bashing my head in.'

'Like being in a busy train station, everyone talking, moving, pushing past, going somewhere else.'

'A concert. Sort of. But the musicians are playing different songs.'

She comes to one night on the edge of the roof. The city glistens under rain. Amber-stained fog in the alleys. She is inches from certain death. The courtyard is a footstep away. How did she even get up here? A ratty pigeon brought her back in time, flapping its wings at her feet. She must control these trances. Does the gift not want her to live? Isn't that its aim, to guide her, support her, so that Selda can continue their song? She imagines how her parents would react to the news. Her father's sad-proud grimace the night before she left. Her mother was cold and curt for days, until at last Selda was closing the door behind her, when Maud rushed forward and kissed her daughter so hard on the forehead she left a toothy bruise. It can help make sense of things to picture herself from the outside, to imagine a descendant who doesn't yet exist and describe herself to them. She narrates the moment as it unfolds, stepping back from the edge of the roof, narrowly avoiding a pointless and humiliating death, transposing horror into comedy.

There is a courtyard round the back of the institution. Sooty walls, leaky drainpipes. Flashes of colour punctuate the peasouper gloom: multicoloured bunting strung between the building's roofs, a sunflower in a pot. A young woman about her age approaches. She has a moonish face and burnt-hazelnut hair. Posh accent, goody-two-shoes smile, a slight limp in one leg. Selda could eat her for breakfast. She introduces herself as Ellen; she hands over a sheet of music, an unfamiliar piece.

'When did you know, then?'

'Oh, I've always known,' says Selda.

'Always?'

'I'm a chime-child.'

'What's that?'

'Born at *exactly* three o'clock in the morning. It's extremely rare.'

'You don't believe all that, do you?'

'No worse than what they've been telling us here, is it?'

'Well, there's a lot of books. And science,' Ellen adds vaguely.

'Bombs were falling all around the house,' Selda says, wishing for two things at once: that Ellen would listen, that Ellen would leave. 'I remember the sound of the air-raid sirens. Beethoven himself was in one of the planes.' Ellen snorts. 'I play piano. I'm really good at it.'

'Prove it.'

'You'll have to pay me.'

The demand is apt. Auditions for the choir are held

in her second month at the hospice. In the seventeenth century, a dean was inspired by the Ospedale della Pietà in Venice, administered by nuns, where orphaned and abandoned girls were sheltered and trained to perform for wealthy patrons. The class is a mix of ages, some thirty-strong, most but not all girls as young as twelve and as old as twenty, white British and Irish, Italian and Polish, Bangladeshi and Caribbean. The choir is rehearsing for the Christmas concert. It's several months away, but for years it has been the biggest money-maker in the calendar of this organization, which has only just begun, in the era of shortwave and shellac, to branch out into other income streams.

Selda and Ellen stand together at the back, near a drainpipe and a wall hung with emerald moss. They sing 'A Boy is Born', an early cantata by Benjamin Britten, chosen to placate a sceptical audience with its explicitly Christian theme. They stand serried in grim mizzle, wetness sheeting down from a low, grey sky.

'♪Wassail, Wassail! Lully, lulley, lully, lulley.♪'

The lyrics are silly. Worse, she has a terrible voice. She can't hold a note, hurts her ears with how they jar against her peers, and so she quietens it to a mime.

'♪Herod that was so wild and wode. Mine own dear mother, Jesu, Jesu!♪'

As she does so, the gift changes. She wonders if she can make them sing along with her too, if music might come from within.

The hospice is chaotic. At times, it feels sclerotic. Selda is absorbed into its rituals and accommodations: the steamy canteen, the hall with its creepy paintings. The auditorium, vast, regal, is a grand confection of splendid decay. She likes to play here, when she can, and hear the piano luxuriate in the space.

When she has a chance, she sneaks behind the stage, where all the staging and props are kept. She walks dwarfed beneath the stage-sets: facades, props, and building-fronts from pick-n-mix historical periods, brought together in storage. It's all bathed red by a warning light, a ruddy half-light like the sun through shut lids. There are marble columns from ancient Rome, a medieval graveyard, an equestrian statue from a Victorian-era London square, a pagoda from Japan, a Venetian bridge arching over bare floor, a pine tree, a gallows, a pig sty, half of a wood-panelled drawing room, a golden throne atop a plinth, all of it flat as plywood and light as cloth, buttressed by stitches and slats of wood. The houses are paintings, the stone is foam, the valley is a tapestry.

She moves between cities and centuries, from Victorian brothel to Egyptian tomb. A forest floor passes into an executive's office. She has a sense that she is walking less through space than the pages of books, or through her own mind: the dark roof, the silence. She could be asleep. She could be dead.

It is not so uncommon for children to turn up with bruises and burns. A few arrive with mutilated lips and ears, or (so the rumour goes about one particularly retiring, sallow boy) in a leather muzzle. Conversely, some wards have been delivered to Agnes's door as prophets. They pull up in grand cars trailing retinues, draped in elaborate robes and armoured with so much jewellery they require help mounting the front steps. However they arrive, the wards are eventually subsumed into the chorus, larger than the sum of its parts, charming and brutal by turns.

In the darkness, after lights out, it's not uncommon to hear muffled screams and beatings. Selda herself is targeted while brushing her teeth, dragged to the floor by her hair and stamped on with socks and slippered feet. The pummelling is softer than it might have been: the sound will remind her of heavy rain. It happens to Ellen in the corridor, shoulder-pushes, rough names, invitations for her to remove herself from the gene pool. Half a year before Selda arrived, a girl in her late teens was found hanged. If the hospice has grown more compassionate since then, as everyone claims, how bad must it have been? Several fights break out between boys, one involves a knife. For all the drama, however, it won't form a great part of her story. Some things stick. Others don't.

There are four full-time members of staff and an itinerant population of teachers, inspectors, musicians, composers, benefactors. The hospice used to be powerful, apparently, which explains the number of buildings it used to own, given that it courted royalty in the thirteenth century, received commissions to map royal family lines and secure hereditary transmission of power. Agnesians cut out the tongues of gifted natives after landing on the shores of the New World or while privateering in competition with Catholic Spain, for a giftless populace possessed a little less continuity, fewer whispering links with its past. Selda receives treatments of dubious efficacy: acoustic massages, silent retreats, listening sessions, herbal teas. Staff members pull her aside. They tell her to communicate with her gift, to speak to the voices, to plot their stories into graphs, to experiment with being a kind of ventriloquist for them, to speak on their behalf. It doesn't always go according to plan. Once a month, she meets with Otto Vaughn in his basement room. Always the same procedure. The mumbling intro. The hard bright noise. The stillness, out of which voices rise. Each time they do, they are clearer, more distinct.

She and Ellen wish to get to the bottom of it once and for all. What is the gift to each of them? They attend the lectures, scribble the notes.

The gift is the voice of God. The gift is a Russian doll. The gift is the dead in our bloodstream. The gift is madness, the gift is metaphor. To learn about the gift is to know how often it has been wrestled with, by superstition, religion, medicine, science. According to Lanworth and Murray, the gift is the result of microbial activity in the cochlear cavities. Their view is disputed by Nancy Chambers, who attributes it to 'electrical activity' in the 'overheated brain'. Clarence Royle, dean of Agnes's from 1887 to 1891, claims that the gift is evidence of 'genetic aristocracy', and advocates against 'miscegenation' between the gifted and non-. An anonymous collective distribute fliers that claim that the gift 'was invented by the H-bomb'. The radiation released by US nuclear tests in the atolls, they argued without evidence, bloomed across the sky, a flood of toxic pollen that diffused into the clouds, rained upon the populace, entered their pores and nostrils and warped their DNA. But if the gift hasn't been with us for years, Selda reasons, how else do you explain the yellowed books in the Jensen, the craquelured art on the walls? Aren't they evidence enough? Can a delusion be passed down? How many people have the gift? When did it begin? Agnes can't have been the first, but who was? Does the gift feed on death, does it harvest souls, or does it negate death by allowing the deceased to transcend their mortality?

The questions make her head hurt. She gives up.

Instead, she applies to the class in Advanced Composition, run by Leroy Loudermilk, the current dean. To her surprise and apprehension, she is accepted. There are seven students. She is the youngest, one of two women. It is to her surprise, a slightly ghoulish-looking young man, with a drawling, aristocratic accent, who takes her under his wing. His name is Lambert van Klampt. She teases him about his name mercilessly; she believes this is why he likes her.

The classes are demanding. They move too fast, use too much jargon, draw on reserves of academia and experience that she simply does not have. She considers giving up. They study scores, attend recitals. She sketches chamber music, cantatas, oratorios, fugues. She is adept, but they are lifeless exercises. Too tight. Academic. The forms don't suit her. Or she doesn't suit the forms. She gets bad marks.

The academic year passes quickly. She grows used to the hospice, in all its contradictions: the white heat of new music technology, rituals so ancient they feel arcane; feral energies and measured, stately schedules. There is enough for her to forget Coventry almost entirely.

Loudermilk's curriculum emphasizes chance, change, spontaneity, play. It encourages students to answer a question: what is music?

And they seem to think, almost anything.

At concerts of students' work, she might hear the sound of drum solos and angle grinders, voices howling from darkened aisles, hunched feral figures with bleached hair and neon eyeshadow, and the electrifying confusion of being unsure if she was listening to music or sonic warfare, a masterpiece or a mess.

Her peers incorporate new technology (tapes, oscillators, radios, punch-card computers) and approaches to performance (shock tactics, strange venues, compositions that lasted for seconds or days). For a time, she desires to antagonize the audience, almost exclusively white, bourgeois, and middle-aged.

It isn't just the lessons, though. Whether they take place in a coffee shop, the Jensen, or in the dorms, conversations with Ellen often feel more educational to Selda than the lectures do.

She begins to formulate a sense of what the form might be to her, at this moment in history. After empire, the war, the invention of the phonograph, the telephone, the oscillator, what's the point of music?

The question keeps her up at night. Shouldn't she do something useful?

One selfish reason she writes music is to get rid of the patterns that lodge in her mind, and which the gift picks up on. Sometimes, she thinks, it guides those internal melodies, so that she often feels as though her head is an upside-down ballroom, in which the ghosts are waltzing. (The phrase Hell Ball, from which she derives the name of her final home, in turn derives from her attempts to describe this feeling.) Music is not a higher art, rarefied, perfectible, separate from everyday life. It is woven through life, integrated with the substrate of chaos out of which all activity springs.

And please, none of this crap about music *transporting* the listener. A song is not a subway. A tune is not a train. Music's purpose is not to remove us from this world in order to make us *feel better*. Before the eighteenth-century monarchs and emperors employed court composers, Selda tells herself while stamping angrily round the park. The idea that music was an art would not have occurred to composers. Music served a purpose. It was functional.

Music, she comes to believe, is inseparable from the rituals of life.

No, more – it simply is life.

The year's pivotal incident does not involve encounters with her peers or teachers but her dreams. One night, she opens her eyes. The dorm is pitch dark. From the corner of her eye she spies other wards asleep in their bunks.

She sits up. Or tries to. However hard she does, she cannot move.

An old woman is standing on Selda's chest. Her feet are on Selda's sternum. She wears a heavy, many-pleated dress with a brooch at her throat. Her eyebrows are thick, her eyes sorrowful. But she is smiling. Her hands are lightly clasped.

Selda's paralysis extends to her throat. She cannot raise her voice.

The woman smiles more broadly. Now, she opens her mouth.

Instead of language, music spills out. Music flows like water.

A chord flows into the air. It hangs suspended, does not decay, like the organ music she used to listen to through the radio. Only the sound is much softer. Quieter. The gentleness of the music, when she attempts to make sense of it later, will surpass all description. Won't stop her trying, though.

An expression comes over the woman's face. A playfulness that wasn't there before. The music flows and flows. And now the chord evolves. She begins to hum a simple melody, the way a mother might to her child. Selda feels wood against her cheek. Her mother's skin. A pang. As well as the sound itself, the music expresses an emotion it would be impossible to put into words, a contradictory longing. It feels like heartsickness and falling in love, a fire being lit and extinguished. It is in this state that Selda drifts back into unconsciousness, the woman smiling down.

The next morning, Selda wakes just before midday. To her immense relief, she can move. Birds are singing, someone is brewing coffee. She gets up and writes down the melody she heard in the night. It covers sixteen bars.

A letter arrives for Selda in her second year, a manilla envelope heavy with folded pages. She heads directly to the Jensen Centre and sits in the darkest, mustiest, most neglected and private carrell she can find, one crammed between stacks under a jittery bulb, the wooden desk scrawled with signatures and obscenities. She opens it.

'Dear Charles...'

The words send a thrill through her, a shock of pleasure and transgression. 'I read with interest your latest chamber piece. The modal influence of Hawthorne is stronger here than in your previous works, which decision feels well judged...' She skips ahead through the typewritten pages until she finds the manuscript papers, her own, the notes as neatly written out as she can manage, now scribbled and scratched over with red ink: a fresh crop of James Mycroff's notes and corrections. He is stern in his assessments, always chastising 'Charles' for the dissonance of his harmonies and the rigidity of his rhythmical structures. A few months ago, at Ellen's suggestion, Selda sent her music out to her favourite composers, asking if they would consider teaching her. Only two replied, declining the invitation; neither appeared to have read her pages. She changed her name to Charles, in tribute to her uncle, and had more success. For the last few months, Mycroff, a once-famous composer whose pastoral symphonies are now considered old hat, has been coaching 'Charles'.

Amid the older parts of Agnes's, the wood, brick, paper

and iron, are rooms containing glimpses of the future in all its humming, brushed-steel promise: the recording studio with its monumental mixing desk, the anechoic chamber with its floating floor of suspended mesh, the nameless room with its banks of oscillators, the punch-card computers whose matrixes allow composers to automate orchestras to the second, an oscilloscope whose flickering screen dances with mesmeric shapes, ballet-flowers, supple ovals, jelly-soft zigs and collapsing zags. Those machines are left on day and night, humming in unison, holding a note.

Best of all is the editing suite. It is tucked in the back of an office beside the notorious toilet whose flush sets the pipes rattling like prisoners shaking the bars of their cells. The floor was littered with strips of cut tape, brown confetti; the desk's wood a blizzard of scalpel-marks, each the trace of an incision, decision, revision. A famous Belgian is working at the desk. He was a composer of sorts, known as much for his dense philosophical texts as his jangly, jarring music, often used in challenging ballets in which dancers variously leap, faint, walk on all fours, abruptly jerk between postures, and stand still. Not much taller than she is, he stands at the desk in a baggy woollen jumper over a shirt, greyish hair tumbling from the bald dome of his skull, finessing the finicky rhythms of a new piece which he is due to perform in Agnes's concert hall later that week. The looped tracks are played, rewound, replayed, refined, the machinery clicks and hums, the air smells of hot metal. When Selda asks him what he calls this kind of music – she has never heard anything like it before – he tells her that he is making concrete. He loops recordings of radios, trains, humming tops, and bells with speech and snippets of improvised music. Standing in the dark small room, she is momentarily distracted by Ellen asking her if she knows that the chlorophyll in Clorets 'eliminates mouth odours'. The capstan motors rotating the reels of the tape are a form of hypnosis. Ellen's words blend with those of the concrete man, with his spliced and looped tape, and with the gift.

Selda takes as given that all sounds exist on a continuum. Those within her head and those without it. The cello's smooth tones, the ugly rumble of a pneumatic drill. The voices of the living and those of the dead. They all exist somewhere. Notes combine to form motives, motives evolve and combine to form phrases, phrases combine to form periods or double periods. If it is not sound, then something else. Consciousness maybe. Or history. Or even *time itself*. Though it will be a few years before she reaches for these abstracted terms.

For now, it is just a feeling of ascension and vertigo, like running up a skyscraper's shiny glass.

It has something to do with her understanding of every melody as a sculpture – a relational sequence of discrete sonic objects distributed in time – and that this feature connects all melody to memory. The brain understands music as sequential. The memory centre lights up to anticipate the next beat, the next note. Kick, hat, snare, hat: rhythm comes from what came before. Two high notes followed by a long, low one. A C major chord, on its own, is insipid: at the end of a soaring symphony, the same sound is a triumphant release, a spillage of gold. Art is in the sequence; every sequence is a series of deaths. Time falls into line. Songs shape the cerebellum, trigger the amygdala, and the prefrontal, auditory, and motor cortices light up like fireworks over Brighton beach. Some bed themselves in the hippocampus, others fade for good, but all derive meaning from time.

In her last year at the hospice, Otto Vaughn summons Selda to a room in the Jensen Centre. She's usually here to pull empty vinyl sheaths from the shelves and carry them to the desk, where the sour upper-middle librarian-bachelor, whose pallid skin and sunken eyes suggest he lives as well as works in this bunker-like space, asks her every time to display her ID, despite her coming here most nights. She knows that he knows that she knows that this routine is a power-play, putting a Midlands shrew in her rightful place, and for this reason she has never once taken the bait. He will eventually hand her the records, remind her to return them fifteen minutes prior to close, and she'll head to one of the booths round the edge of the room and lower the needle. This time, she asks him the way to a room she's never been in before. He points across the stacks.

Otto moves slowly. His sockets are smudges, his skin is tinged yellow and grey. Selda doesn't realize it at the time, but she'll only see him once more. The room is similar to the one that they normally meet in. Still, it is different enough to unsettle her almost as much as her teacher's appearance. Concrete walls, a thin window at pavement level: court shoes clipping past, bus, van, and bicycle wheels, the occasional horse.

'I'm going to play you something,' Otto says. 'This isn't a test.'

So far, so familiar. His hair, never much to begin with, is thinned and whitening, his lips dry, his skin dappled with liver-spots. They remind Selda of her mother's squashed-penny mole. His hands are what get her, though. He's had to punch a new hole in his watch-strap. The fingers have almost no flesh on them at all.

'There are no right or wrong answers. I would like you to listen to the sounds closely, but without judgement.

Can you do that for me? Simply let your mind – relax. Don't force it. Refrain from imposing categories. Music or noise. Good or bad. That sort of thing.'

'Of course,' she says. Already, her mind has settled. She can feel them around her, the dead, *her* dead, from which she draws her breath, into whose music she will one day dissolve.

She clears her throat; she nods. The gesture conveys the understanding that, even now, she feels she lacks.

'But they'll come naturally, won't they? Associations. If I hear a trumpet, I am going to think *trumpet*. And then I might think, *music*. Such thoughts are banned?'

'No, I am not saying that. When you put it in such blunt terms, indeed the exercise sounds absurd. Allow the sounds to be whatever they are for you. Does that make sense?'

It doesn't. She nods.

'Yes, everyone says it. A talented musician. Excellent. We've had a few, no? Yes, of course. Even so. But a word of advice. Leave your pianist hat at the door. Do pianists wear hats? Some do, perhaps. Per-hats. Ha. Well. This is not a test. It is not a measure of aptitude, talent, skill. I would simply like you to *listen*. We are simply seeing what we find. We might find nothing at all. *You* will find? That would be fine. So relax. Easier said than done, I realize. Listen to the tape, then tell me what you remember.'

At the top of her vision, through the bright strip of the letterbox window, she can see a man's brogues, scuffed on one side, clumps of manure, the wheels of a passing car. It is a bright dry day. Tepid sunshine. Early March.

'I'm sorry. You want me to remember?'

'Yes. It's quite simple.'

The man is still preparing the tape. Or, he is attempting to. He has clumsy and fumbling thin-fingered hands.

Twice he has dropped the steel spool in which one half of the tape is stored, causing it to run along the floor, the inky strip loosed like a yo-yo string. 'I'm going to record our session, unless you object?' He looks over at her. It's the first time he's made eye contact. She nods. How could she object? She has grown fond of him over the years, has come to think of him as an uncle. 'Good,' he says, sounding pleased with himself. 'Thomas Edison said that the phonograph knows more about us than we know ourselves. It remembers more than we do. He might have said the same about writing, but no matter. Ho. Ho ho ho.' He chuckles and sings to himself, turning the tapes, flicking a switch. An amber light comes on with a dull hum of electricity. This machine remembers. But so, in a way, does a song.

'Aha! I have tamed the infernal device.'

In other circumstances she would have offered to help. She knows her way around the machine and could have loaded the tape in less than half the time, with none of the huffing and puffing. Men tend to bristle whenever she offers them technical help, so she neglected to mention it.

For the second time that morning, she consciously relaxes her spine. Nervously she folds a stick of spearmint chewing gum into her mouth. She feels queasy. Otto's questions do not help. He plays tapes: smooth sine-waves, choristers' trills, the glug-glug of tropical wildlife, ribbits, clucks, clicks, the rusty yawp of an opening door, a crackle of distant gunfire, another of logs in a hearth. She remembers the small room beside the toilet, the one with the tape-strips littering the floor. She's been frequenting it after dark, assembling her compositions from the floor-scraps others leave behind, excited by the possibilities, but knowing she preferred to assemble them in her head. None of the sounds Otto plays her make much sense to her.

'Tell me what it reminds you of.'

So she does. The opening triads of 'It Ain't Necessarily So.' The jingle for Murray Mints, the too-good-to-hurry-mint. The shuffled-deck sound of a bird taking flight. The questions lead nowhere. This doctor is an imbecile, the gift tells Selda. Don't listen. Run away. When Otto sighs and pinches the bridge of his nose, Selda feels, obscurely, that his disappointment is her fault; that she has failed a test despite not knowing the point of it all; that she has again proved unable to find the right words, the right analogy, to bridge the gap between herself and other people.

The voices don't change, they just question what Otto is doing here, stirring them up with his sounds, who does he think he is, what is he trying to force? He strikes a bell. It is smallish, roughly the size of a mug, cast from a smooth, reflective metal, chrome perhaps, embossed on its rim with the number twelve.

The voices grow calmer, quieter. The sound of it soothes them; they settle into groups, and as the moments pass a series of images come to mind, vague at first, just hints and flashes. Moors white with snow, frozen rivers, empty villages, hunger, someone missing in the storm... It will be years before she writes them down, but this is the moment she hears them: the first fragment of *Snow Trio* falls through her mind. It will be years before she hears the full melody, the seeking of which will almost kill her.

314

III. 1962-1963

It was Ellen's idea to holiday after their graduation. To celebrate the end. And it was her idea to take the Invacar.

Someone in the government, she's no idea who, has decided she is incapable of driving a normal car. And so they've given her this. The vehicle is small, slow, flimsy, with a chassis of nurse's-uniform blue that creaks and crackles as the engine struggles to reach its highest gear. Ellen doesn't need a licence to drive this glorified motorized bucket. There's only enough room for one person: the driver, Ellen, with a space in the back for luggage. The crevice is only just ample enough that Selda can curl up in a ball, close to Ellen's feet, while she guides them up the slow lane.

In that cramped space, tucked under a rug to hide her, Selda hears trucks and cars zooming past, exhausts so close to her head she is certain they could scalp her. She harangues Ellen to drive carefully, to stop the car, but her friend pretends she can't hear above the sound of the motorway.

The gift is active in Selda's mind, not as voice this time, nattering and distracting, but a mood, an emotional temperature, guiding her observations.

Which marks the first time since she started Agnes that the gift presents a theme. A broad sense of how things are, or were. Of traits, generally conceived, leading to herself. Not the pixelated, pointillist jangle of all those overlapping arguments and claims of being. Not harmonies competing and colliding in a kind of cosmic soup.

A harmony, perhaps. The first suggestion of coherence.

These voices stir but do not speak. Instead, they fill Selda with a sense, eerie yet comforting, that she has lived in other places, other centuries. The closest thing she can compare it to is déjà vu, but that doesn't cover it at all.

Ellen, who hasn't driven before, is discovering that she loves it. Neither have her ancestors, of course. Unless you mean carriage and cart and all that muddy stuff. She seems completely untroubled by the fact of her amateurism, gleefully yelling:

'I tell you WHAT – this is FUN! No one told me that driving was so amusing! Toot toot!'

Which prompts Selda to bite Ellen's shin.

In truth, she's been wanting to do that the whole journey. Her tongue lingers a fraction of a second longer than it might have if she merely meant to punish.

'OUCH.'

'Concentrate.'

'You're not driving.'

'I don't want to die.'

'It will be quick and painless, I assure you. Crikey, these trucks are really enormous actually.'

'I don't want to die in a fucking footwell!'

'At my feet? I like you there.'

'Fuck off. Just fuck off.'

'OUCH. I think you drew blood that time.'

Ellen steers them off a juddering ramp and into the gliding sunlit holiday-poster lanes. Dapple is a welcome change from the parched harshness of the motorway, during which Selda tried and failed to make peace with her imminent death, squashed to bits in a blue plastic egg. She wasn't afraid of dying so much as leaving a work unfinished, a symphony on her desk, which, if she was killed, would remain that way, imperfect, incomplete. They set up their tent at the far edge of the camping site, near a stream and under a tree. It's neither a school holiday nor high summer, so the place isn't too full, just a family in the corner, flat-capped dad and toothy kids, and a

316

smart young man and woman in tweed. They set up the tent and promptly fall asleep.

Next morning starts early: a walk through the nearby woods. It's pleasant in a drifty, dreamy way, like how the Romantic poets might have felt while their wives and mothers stayed at home. But Selda quickly grows bored and anxious. One of the clearings makes her think of blood-soaked clothes, corpses littering the dirt, a smell of burning on the breeze. She thinks back to her father. How he walked about in cold sweats in the dead of night, sleeping rough in the park for fear of new bombs, barking at strangers by the end. The unease that took a hold of him out of nowhere, as if he was possessed: perhaps he was gifted too, but differently to her, not hearing the voices but feeling their fear. Ellen is on a path a little further up the hill, heading towards a felled tree blotched with lichen. Its interior of rotted, crumbled wood is the colour of powdered mustard.

'How many times are we born?'

Ellen laughs.

'I'm serious.'

They walk the stream's edge barefoot, Ellen in a skirt, Selda in trousers rolled halfway up the shin, the cold water flowing over the soft silt, the burnt-tan and pigeon-grey pebbles that press into the soles of their feet. Trees march into moss-green distances. The campsite feels very far away, let alone the city and Agnes and everything else. Further still is Coventry, her mother and father in Clay Lane, whom she has not seen in months and whose letters are sporadic, whose voices she has not heard in months. Does she miss them, or is she glad to be free of them? They have been wandering for over an hour, discussing, as they tend to do, the gift, their respective ways of relating to it, and to the other wards at Agnes's, and to the question of their future, and to that of the world in general: Selda remembering her father, who more than once decreed the dissolution of the empire would lead to an invasion. But what did it matter anyway, given the bombs would fall, the sky would blacken, a man's foot would appear up a tree, clad in a brogue. Ellen hates it when Selda brings that detail up. They spent a while arguing about communism, too, Ellen of the opinion that she would like to hand down whatever money she earns to her children, thank you very much, while Selda is more of the opinion, having witnessed her father's decline, that the Soviets might have a point. After one of many longish, comfortable pauses, during which they each examine the forest in relative silence, she opines aloud about birth: its frequency in a person's life.

'Once, Bunny.'

'Stop calling me that.'

'It's your name.'

'It's *your* name. You gave it to me. I never asked for it and I don't like it. How'd you like it if I called you Guinea Pig? Or Hamster? Dog? Here, Dog! You think that's alright?'

Ellen thinks that she wouldn't mind if Selda called her that name or any other, so long as she called her something.

'It's a serious question,' she says. 'Or do you mean something more abstract? I mean, we can discuss the Tibet question with Toby if you like.'

'Ugh. Forgot about him. Pass that stick.'

'This one? Why?'

'I just fancy it. Pass it over, will you?'

'I guess you can call me Dog after all.'

Ellen hands her friend a long blonde branch. Filtered by the trees, as if on cue, the sound reaches them of a dog owner crying after their wayward pet. Selda takes the branch, her long hands clasping Ellen's for a brief moment, bringing the slightest shift into the look in Ellen's eyes. It passes just as quickly as Selda strips the leaves and stray branches to form a crooked staff. Ellen crosses her arms and wades into the centre of the stream where the currents run deeper and more quickly, the sand pressed flat as suede.

'It's not so bad, is it? Whining all morning then off with the shoes.'

Silt rises and is carried away. Sunlight catches it and makes it spark, Ellen guesses from the minerals and crushed glass. She daydreams briefly about fighter planes having crashed in the war upstream, weather-punished hulks of rust gnarled and softened by the wind until they crumble into glinting flecks of brown and silver that feed the roots of trees, the river into which the stream flows. The dog-owner shouts again, this time from a point to the east. She steps further into the water. The forest stands still and quiet and very much alive, with its own massive and ancient and inarticulate and collective presence, a mind of many mute parts, which if it or they could speak would do so at such an arboreal tempo that a human lifetime would rise and expire in the space of a single word. She walks upstream, guiding herself less by sight than by the feel of the stones pressing into her feet. She embraces the round dulled jolt of pain each pebble brings, guiding her course upstream.

'Here,' Selda calls, 'take this.'

Ellen's gaze is fixed ahead, not behind her. She turns to see Selda, who was very gung-ho at the start of the walk, lingering on the water's edge with a scared look. Her hair, recently cut short, is scruffy and wind-rubbed. Her trousers are damp almost up to the knee.

'I thought I didn't need help?'

'Don't be silly. It's tough going even for me.'

'In a while, Bunny. All things in time.'

She walks further. Clouds overhead screen the sun, casting the forest in a fresh, greyish light; a moment later it's racing and bursting again, gold-tinged. She wishes she could collect and preserve the moment like stream-water in a bottle, but there would only be so much water in it, and she'd have to ration her sips. Something better, then. Something self-replenishing. A memory she could return to whenever she likes and which doesn't run off and drain away and grow cold.

Distracted by this thought, which she will quickly forget, she loses awareness of the dull pain in her soles. Her left leg, the weaker, buckles and slips on the sand. The sky tumbles into the stream and she plunges into it, head below water, eyes open, seeing a dark shape, perhaps a fish sliding away as the water foams. It's shallow, so she's back on her feet in a matter of seconds, and she's soaked from head to toe. She looks back, gulping like a beached fish, to see Selda on the shore, wizard staff in hand, bent double and laughing, laughing.

Later, dripping wet with the branch at her side, Ellen walks down the endless-seeming, treelined roads. Her teeth chatter. 'You were s-saying s-something earlier, until I t-t-talked about cremation.' Selda keeps step beside her, hands in pockets. She kicks an acorn across the road. Behind them they hear a car engine and stand to one side. Selda's face is unreadable. Has Ellen said something wrong?

'I don't know, really. It's just a feeling I have. Can't really explain it. I don't mean – reincarnation. I think I mean... versions.'

'Of o-ourselves.'

'Are you alright? Don't die on me. Take my jacket.'

'I'm f-fine.'

'Just take it. Here.' She drapes it over Ellen's shoulders. 'It just seems obvious to me,' says Selda. 'It always has. It's not something that I could talk about before Agnes's.'

'It's not something that those who don't have the gift understand,' says Ellen, attempting to walk a fine line – appealing to Selda's egalitarian mindset, as well as her sense of exceptionalism. The car passes. They continue to walk.

'I suppose, well, I think, oh, shit, it's hard to explain. I think of it in relation to music.'

'Something similar to what Lyle and Davis say?'

'I just mean stages. Phases. Mewling, puking, the rest. I was born. Obviously. Stands to reason. I was born again when my grandmother died, and again when I played piano the first time. New Seldas.'

This new if occasional illeism amuses Ellen. Alarms her, too.

'And I don't feel continuous with them all, but I am. Much the same with these voices, which aren't me but are me, which can't be removed without destroying who I am, destroying me. It feels like a paradox.'

'Like the Ship of Theseus?'

'What's that? That chap who fought the Minotaur?'

Ellen explains the thought experiment, leaving out that she heard it, in turn, from a first-year philosophy student who was seeking to impress her at a cafe, something from Plutarch via Hobbes. The hero's boat had been at sail for so long that every piece of which it was composed, every plank and oar and sail, had been replaced one by one: was it the same ship as the one that set off at the start of his journey?

321

'It makes me think about musical form, anyway, although I can't think how yet, and Agnesian chanting, and the feel of it. Like what Loudermilk talks about.'

'The *duty*.'

'Stuffy. Hate it.'

'But you feel something? Even if you want to break it. How else w-w-would you know w-what it is?'

'I don't feel duty towards it.'

'You ever wish, y-y-you know, you didn't have it?'

'All the time. Mostly I'm glad. Can't imagine it another way.'

They walk in silence for a minute, turning it over in their minds.

'It does make you think, doesn't it, that there must have been an origin. The very first. Whatever that might be. A place where you began. And if you could just trace it right back—'

'You've been smoking dope, is that it? These ideas of yours...'

'You're shivering again.' Selda grips her friend's dress. 'Bloody hell, you're soaked through.'

'I'm f-f-f-fine.'

Half an hour later, the sun below the tree line, they accept that they are lost. Stress levels rise. They bicker. Ellen's legs feel weak and sore and she leans on her stick for support. They see a wiry hiker strolling up the path, stop him and ask for directions. He tells them that they have to double back on themselves and follow an alternative route all the way around a reservoir, a walk of an hour or so. Without realizing it, they have strayed far off course. Selda blames Ellen's poor sense of direction; Ellen blames Selda for storming ahead in whichever direction she pleases. They curse their city instincts and trudge on in the gloaming. Selda hails a passing car, which ignores her. Night coagulates, thickens to solid black between the trees. Then they see it up ahead: salvation – light. As they quicken, they see a low building with sloped roof. It is nestled in a bend in the road beside a low redbrick bridge that crosses the same stream they walked down earlier.

The pub has a table beside the fire. Heat makes Ellen's clothing visibly steam. They don't know how exactly they'll get back to the campsite and for the first hour they decide to ignore that technical issue. Instead they focus on refreshing themselves and warming up. They empty their pockets and purses onto the table and count out their coins and consult the barman. Selda buys a pork pie and two halves of local ale. They eat and drink. They feel relieved and uneasy. The isolation of the forest, where a wild animal might have attacked them, where poison ivy lurks, felt safer to being in here, with eyes on them. There is something comforting in it, too, for Selda at least, reminding her of the trips she took with her father. They eat and drink and feel at least partly restored, but bone-tired too, Selda is sleepy and frustrated at her inability to explain in words something that feels urgent and complex but which when put into words makes her sound very stupid indeed. They order whiskies next. On a whim, as neither has drunk whiskey before. It goes to their heads quickly and marvellously despite tasting utterly foul even when watered down. The drink makes the room, which feels warm and half liquid, swim. 'I think we're the same,' says Selda. 'Forget the Greek man and his ship. You and me. We understand each other because we know what it's like.'

Another whisky. Full dark outside. Selda is overcome by a feeling. She places her hand on Ellen's and tells her: 'When I was trying to say earlier, about being reborn,

God it sounds so stupid. I wasn't able to explain it at all. It sounds so stupid.'

'It's not stupid at all.'

'But it happened when I got to Agnes's, it happened when I met you.' Very briefly, and unnoticed by Selda, Ellen's eyes water.

Even when drunk, Selda finds this kind of talk intolerably maudlin, and she wakes up in the moment, newly lucid, aware of having shared too much, or said something she shouldn't have, and so she excuses herself for a pee that she does not need. She sits in the stall and stares at the tiles and feels dizzy. On the way back, a man with a red beard, all bristles, talks to her, and she finds herself trapped in his odorous aura of pipe-tobacco and tweed, but somehow, in the course of her evasions, she persuades him to buy her and Ellen two whisky sodas, which he carries over with a chivalrous flourish, smoothing his dry hair across his scalp before lighting his pipe.

They drink and plan their futures. They will make music together. Ellen will write books about the gift and bells. The room sways like a ship. Selda sits beside her friend in the wooden alcove and rests her head against her shoulder. 'I do mean it,' says Selda, slightly babbling now. 'Shanged. Shayned. Chaynged. We met you. I you. Wehn you an me.'

'Haahahah.'

For a while they sit breathing, saying nothing. Ellen stiffens in her chair. Her heart quickens. Selda squeezes her hand, buries her face. She asks Selda if she means what she says, but Selda doesn't answer.

How do they return to the campsite? Do they walk through the dark forest, drunk under the stars? Maybe the redheaded man who bought their fatal whisky sodas drives them in his Cortina. What happens when they do at last get into the tent? Selda and Ellen will remember it patchily, and differently, and those memories will fade and change, grow less and more significant with time. For Selda, it's a confusion of shadow and rain. More impactful than the events themselves are how they are retold, by the separate, respective parties; how this alters their view of themselves, their formative friendship. Selda will feel something at her ear and wonder what it is. Only later will she realize that Ellen has taken her earlobe between her teeth. A moment later, she stops.

Is it the same for her as it is for Ellen? She'll barely remember the incident later, but other aspects of the evening will stand out. A beaded cover draped over a leather car seat. Smudged privacy glass. A fag stubbed out in a bowl of whipped cream. Rain, endless rain, from a sky the ill tint of old bruises. Broken branches forming unreadable glyphs. It's true, they are closer now than ever before. They are like family. Ellen is her sister. Closer even than that. Like finding the piano, a lost part returned. And this is why Selda will feel uncomfortable about it all. It is easy, after all, to hate one's family, to lose them.

When she wakes next morning Selda will feel as though she has been hit by a bus and hung up to dry in a kiln. Ellen will lie embalmed in a tangle of tight-wound sheets. A miasma of sour breath and alcohol will pervade the tent's trapped air. Selda will tug on some shoes and stagger outside heading for the concrete hut in which the campsite's toilets and showers are housed. Before she gets there, she will vomit in full view of a family frying eggs for breakfast. She will stand beneath the tepid sputter of the camp shower as the gift swims in her head and she feels like she's about to pass out. Ellen, when she wakes and finds the tent empty, will feel different. She will feel as though a new life is starting, one she could not have dreamed of just a day ago. A future that feels tender and frightening and raw, so bright her first instinct is to flinch from it, regret everything, did she really *say* that, *do* that? She has never felt this way before. Almost the moment she sees Selda again, she senses it was all seen differently by her, which puts the events of the night into different arrangement. Hard to say what about her friend, who looks like death, articulates this, but it does.

IV. 1969-1971

The bike's spokes blur in the autumn air. She thinks about her father as she rides. Or the stories he likes to tell, about the night he fetched her first piano. According to his account, he single-handedly carried it home. In some tellings, he juggled it back on a unicycle. The street forms part of a suburb. It is lined with bay-windowed townhouses, the pavements obscured by heaped leaves leaking a brownish, fermented smell in the cold autumn air. Her expression is vacant, her lips slightly pursed. The gift is quiet this morning. Her thoughts drift already to supper alone in the one-bed flat on the second floor of a cul-de-sac townhouse, which she once found gloomy and bleak but has begun to love. It has a stove on which she likes to fry eggs, chicken livers in sherry, potatoes in foaming butter. It doesn't have a piano, but it does have a suitcase equivalent: a Rhodes. Before the long rehearsal, she drinks in her life: the gift subdued and the wind in her hair, the morning's cool light and the smoke from the chimneys dissolving.

She rests her bike against the railings outside the crumbling pre-war concert hall. As she does so, she feels a pressure on her shoulder. A man is watching. She watches back, from the corner of her eye. A clarinet case is tucked under his right elbow, a lit cigarette loosely clasped between the ring and little fingers of his left hand. (Looking back years later, she will remember this peculiarity and scold herself: *I should have known*.) She doesn't pay him much attention at first. When she notices he is staring at her, she begins to feel uncomfortable. She gives him a proper look.

He's a well-dressed bundle of stalks. Skinny and straight all over. Long neck, thin nose. She can picture him playing cricket or lounging on a deck chair, leeringly drunk, sloshing pink gin hither and yon. He wears a pea-green V-neck jumper over a white shirt undone to the third button, horn glasses, cream trousers that stop short of the shoe. He has a moustache, or an attempt at one: a downy shadow on his upper lip, which is curved in an ironical smile as he crosses the pavement, just as she is bending over to remove her key from the lock. And in that moment of indignity he greets her in a manner that, since she has never seen him before, is presumptuous. Threatening, too. But in her experience, not so unusual.

The gift murmurs. Silt is disturbed at the bottom of the pond of her mind, and sleeping eels uncoil in the reedy depths and turn their gazes to the light. What they say, if indeed they are saying anything, remains beneath the surface of the water. All Selda can discern is motion, activity.

He introduces himself as Garth Martin. 'We've met before, actually.'

'Oh,' Selda says. 'Well.'

'I expect you don't remember. A friend of yours introduced us. Briefly, it must be said.' He knows a little about her, it seems, such as the fact that she composes music. 'Perhaps you'd be so kind as to show me?'

Selda has written dozens of pieces of chamber music; experimented with amplifiers, tape machines, plate reverb units, oscillators; attempted to capture the sound of that piano she played with her father, the dead mouse dampening a string, an accidental prepared piano; and although it will take many years for her to fully realize this shift in her music – it will take, in fact, her divorce from a man she has only just met – she has begun to devise new ways to incorporate the gift into her music, to take cues and ideas from that chorus.

The other musicians pass them by, chatting, filtering into the lobby. She follows them, wishing this character, Garth So-and-so, would take the hint.

She is at a stage in her training, if that is the word, when the gift has begun to offer advice. Not all of it can be deciphered. She cannot tell if it believes this man should be avoided, a member of a family with which hers were former rivals, perhaps, or whether their activity suggests the opposite, a leaning over-keenness. More than once the gift has whispered to her in dark conspiratorial tones about the Marchams, Smythes, or some other dynasty, imploring her never to do business with Mr Such-and-such, never accept an invitation from Madame This-and-that, always on account of some ancient grudge, an unpaid debt, a stolen heifer, a slight so glancing it might as well never have happened. (The gift doesn't think this way, however.) Some of these burdens, bred from sectarian contempt, involve successive and apparently meaningless murders, fathers whose sons and grandsons kill each other, cyclically, almost formally, as if fulfilling rituals (until they all die out, and *fin*). Others feel petty and depressing.

Easier to think of the gift as background noise. The sonic texture of the past. Ancestors she may or may not wish to listen to. She has grown out of that disorder, but she has had no say in its progress. Is this, she later wonders, why her early music ends up so tightly regimented and tooled: an attempt to tame the noise.

The man continues to stare as she loosens the strap on her horn, which had begun to ache. As she heads inside he walks over to her.

'Nice bike. Good way to get here. Walked myself. A nice day for it.'

'Thank you,' she says, her tone polite but icy. 'I must

be getting along.'

'For the rehearsal? I'm going there myself. What's with your horn?'

'Excuse me?'

'I said, what's with your horn? It's not your instrument, is it?'

The pair of them pause at the doorway. He nods at the instrument over her shoulder. Selda curses Ellen for having suggested she take on this gig.

Stalling: 'It's not mine. I'm bringing it for my friend.'

She doesn't much like the look of him. Pities him, really. He isn't exactly striking. He is at once sharp-featured and slightly chinless. All elbows and bones. Are the teeth a bit buck? She leans away, busy with her pages. He stands beside her, inert as a telephone pole. A pause while they wait for each other to speak. The gift in Selda stirring, stirring, warming like embers, blown ashes.

'What's in your friend's horn, then?'

Wedged in the instrument's cone is the scarf she had been knitting all week, and which she plans on continuing during the lulls in rehearsal. It's a modern piece with long fallow stretches during which she will not have to play. The conductor is a bore, he can't see her behind the piano.

'Oh. That.' She explains.

'Well, at least it didn't get blown out.'

'I suppose not.'

None of this is funny. All the same, the man chuckles. The gift does not warn or belittle. It sounds oddly serene. It begins, in fact, to sing to her. She pictures its music as a golden, steady hum, interrupted now and then by a quick red biting jump of melody: she wonders what it all means. Garth opens the door, steps into the lino-floored lobby, where the other musicians are milling about and a radio is playing. A bell dings over the tannoy. The rehearsal must begin. She waves the odd man goodbye. He could do with a bowl of hot stew.

They meet again weeks and months later. His accent drips. Those buttery, rounded vowels, the drawn-out yaahs and laahs sliding off the hard-top consonants. When he mentions that his family run a series of mills and factories whose flours, with their cosy logo of the wheat-sheaf and the lamb, are sold on supermarket shelves up and down the country, she is not surprised. He carries that dynastic air.

On their second date, after a greasy Greek meal in the shadow of a flyover, he takes her out dancing. He wears wool slacks held up by suspenders, a white shirt, brogues and Coke-bottle specs.

One o'clock. The pair have just left. The streets are filled with mist and skittering echoes but not much else. They look for a cab but can't find one. Stalking through the pre-dawn fog, he is sinewy and long, his features gaunt and faintly skeletal. And yet, she finds him handsome. This walking, talking bundle of stalks and canes. He puts his arm over her shoulder. They kiss. They press their bodies together. Through his trousers, she can feel his erection against her thigh. She wonders if they'll go somewhere right now. Behind an iron fence, or down an alley. Instead, they part and continue walking, hand in hand.

He asks Selda what she made of the music. She enthuses about the electrical hum in the air of the basement bar, the thumping bass and the crackle of the circuitry. She has recently begun to work, she says, with synthesizers.

'I see,' says Garth.

'You disapprove.'

'I prefer real instruments. Electric ones are nasty.'

'A composer uses whatever's at her disposal.'

'I'd dispose of synthesizers, for a start.'

'You're atrocious at clarinet you know.'

'You think so?'

'Yes. And so do you.'

'Well, that's harsh.' He does sound hurt.

'I was only teasing.'

'They were a man short,' he says. In the streetlights his cheeks look hollow. 'I was making up numbers. I've never once claimed I was a professional. If you made that assumption, more fool you.'

Later, she will learn that his harrowed look has more to do with a genetic predisposition to high blood-sugar than disastrous dancing (to which he may also be pre-disposed). A few years from now, once their daughter is born, and their relationship has begun irreparably to break, this dissonant strain in his DNA will prompt him to collapse outside a concert hall. For the time being, he eats indiscriminately, excessively, endlessly, even alle-gorically, as though his true name is Gluttony. He stuffs jammy scones, battered sausages, pastries and pies, heaps of spuds and peanuts and crisps and beer and wine down his neck. Yet he never seems to gain weight. Which makes Selda jealous. And a little suspicious. He has his secrets, his private urges, and she has hers. She is selective about her past, dissembles her education, and since childhood has perfected ways to suppress and disguise the gift, to pass off its interventions in her mind and speech as the trappings of an eccentric, an artist, or simply a certain kind of woman. It will be months before he even begins to suspect that she might be gifted. When eventually she confirms the truth he will hold it against her, when it suits him. By then, however, they will have already begun to grow apart.

They are drifting through a park one weekend, their sixth or seventh date, the second since they'd first made love in a hotel bedroom Selda struggled to think of as glamorous rather than sordid, the curtains stained brown by spilled tea, wallpaper beginning to peel. As they wander through the park after recent rain, puddles reflecting trees and sky, Garth tells Selda about his childhood. He was the youngest of three brothers. He often felt overlooked, unloved, desiring his parents' affection but uncertain how to win it, often attempting to in ways that backfired, drawing (accurate) accusations from his stentorian dad that he was seeking attention. She slips her arm into his.

'I used to be quite pious, you know. Wanted to outperform my bloody do-good brothers. Impress the man upstairs, if I couldn't impress my parents.'

'Hmm,' Selda murmurs. She wonders how or if his background will alter his reaction to her newfound Agnesianism and, more to the point, the gift itself.

'Until the day that I decided I didn't need to any more,' Garth says. 'I didn't think much of it at the time. Perhaps I should have. My poor old parents *died* a few years later, you see,' his tone bouncy, almost upbeat. 'And in rather a silly way. Boating accident. On the Thames, near Henley.'

'Oh shut up,' Selda mutters. She is better at controlling it now. But sometimes, the gift pierces through, and at the least appropriate moments. But Garth didn't hear her. A child flies a kite on the green. She wonders if she and Garth will have one together.

'So, that was a bit rough.'

'And the life of science,' Selda asks, 'was that a rejection of them? Was this before or after they died?'

Garth nods. 'I'd already gone up to Oxford,' and Selda winces at the fluency with which he says it, *up to Oxford*, as though he was describing a trip to the shops. His family can't have been *that* cruel, if they'd supported his education. She loosens her hand. They might as well belong to different species than classes.

Their next date, Garth arrives at the restaurant wearing a lab coat, so absorbed in some problem or other he's forgotten to remove it. Selda still isn't sure about him. She considers it wise to order a large gin and tonic, to start, as they take a seat in the bar, the air of which is itchy with cigarette smoke.

It is the first (by no means the last) time Garth speaks to her at excited, hard-to-follow length about his work. 'It's part of this great ongoing effort to lend a bit of evidential heft to our good friend Darwin's theories. Post-Watson and Crick, you know. And one might hope, in doing so, to solve a bit of this mystery about being human.'

He takes a swig from his brandy. Selda shuffles in her seat.

'Where we came from,' he says, 'all that. Diseases. Skills. It does strike me as a touch ironic that the genetic mechanisms for perpetuating our finest abilities and our knack for survival,' he swirls the wood-hued fluid with a finger, 'should be the same ones that perpetuate defects. And I dare say pain.'

Should she tell him now? Will she ever tell him? He places his hand on her thigh and squeezes it. In the corner, a pianist strikes up. It's the kind of confused upmarket restaurant that considers it classy to display a colour television behind the bar.

'I say, how many cells are in your body? Oh, I should guess, taking a close look at you, yes, hmm, let's see here... quite tall, a reasonable bust... Yes, I value this specimen at between fifty and seventy *trillion* cells.'

His area of research – so far as Selda can tell once they

334

move to the table, and over her bowl of onion soup – is the impact of mutation on genetic expression in purple sea urchins. He shows her a photograph of the things, which for whatever reason (another prop?) he has in his pocket. Clad in mauve-and-lavender spines, they look to her like sunken pom-poms.

'From fertilization to adulthood is fifty days. Relative eons, poor things – you've heard of mayflies?'

She blinks. 'Have I heard of mayflies?' Sometimes, it's as if he's never met a woman, let alone her, before.

'Quite, quite.'

'Blasted man,' she mutters.

She doesn't grasp why it should be sea urchins and not some other animal. How months and years of detailed study of these bristling things could illuminate the mysteries of human suffering, which pass from age to age, ever repeating and never the same. Isn't it, to put it bluntly, a waste of time?

'Mendel had his peas. I have my bundles of purple pins.'

Selda hears *son of*, as in Mendelssohn. Her father. His face when he played her the E minor violin concerto. 'I'm not sure...'

'Gregor Mendel. Father of genetics. Augustinian friar, as it happens. Anyway, the purple sea urchins are a red herring,' Garth cracks. 'I'm not interested in them, as such. What do you take me for? Do you see me with a net, a bucket?'

No. And yet she can picture him on the beach.

In studying them, he explains, he is able to observe how trivial changes express themselves repeatedly, over generations. He can model how cells are fertilized, controlled, and differentiated; what happens when they die. Nematodes are useful for this, too. His colleagues work on 'the squirmy little things. They reproduce ferociously. The nematodes, not the colleagues.'

She nudges him under the table.

Before the dessert, he goes off on a tangent: 'You know, I do see death and life in a different way than some might. Including my parents. Well. Before they. Before they died.'

'How so?'

'The pace of it, you know. All those urchin-lives and nematodes... I suppose the gods look at us with a similar almost-pity. But, I don't know... Loss is a tragedy. But death – the fact of it, a natural death – it just isn't.' She wonders where he is going with this. How it relates to his parents' malfunctioning boat, which collided with a bridge in high summer. Garth despatches a last piece of wine-stained chicken. 'Without it, there's no advancement.'

The waiter clears their plates. Dessert? No. A couple more brandies.

'Isn't death the end of advancement,' says Selda. 'Almost by definition.'

'Only for the individual.'

Selda, abruptly uneasy: 'I consider myself a socialist...'

'Oh, I won't hold it against you.'

'You're sounding rather more like a National Socialist.'

All that gin and irritation. She can't tell if she means it as a glib provocation or a serious point. Garth turns red from the bottom up, blotches staining his neck and ears. Then, a change. Whatever fury he feels, he throttles, bottles, and buries – these powers of self-restraint will allow him, in time, to underplay the symptoms of a serious blood condition.

'On the contrary,' he says, forcing a smile, 'it would have been more accurate to accuse me of being Victorian.'

Speaking with Garth, often late into the night, after

336

rehearsals and concerts, they will discuss the correspondences between their worlds, as if no one had hit upon the connection before. Both are predicated on repetition and change. They share a formal similarity, however loose: inheritance has cadence, DNA a kind of musical score, every life a cover version of the striving primal song. She at one point attempts to transpose genetic material into melody. G and A and C write themselves. Where to put T on the scale? The exercise is corny, its results terrible – proof, she'll later think, that she and he were never meant to be in the first place. She never shows it to Garth, whose responses to her music devolve from admiration to bitterness over the years. She is wonderful. A genius. Who is she playing with? When is she coming home? Shouldn't she find a real job? A teacher, he'll say, is more her speed: she has a child, after all. For the time being, though, there is conversation: where to draw the line between the human and the animal, animal and vegetable, vascular plant life to jawless fish to trilobites, minerals, atoms, quarks – why not? Was it simply easier to throw up their hands and say, 'there is only process?' What was the original?

They marry in the Agnesian chapel: a domed, musty structure of sculpted stone, posters for after-school art classes on the noticeboard out front. It is a modest occasion: Selda, Garth, and the requisite witnesses, friends from Agnes's and Oxford, respectively. That afternoon they hold the ceremony on the beach. A string quartet plays, they exchange vows at dusk. Guests totter on the pebbles, smoking pipes, cigars, and cigarettes, pressing bonnets and fascinators to their scalps, swigging from hip flasks and blinking at the lowering clouds, which threaten but do not dispense rain. Some stand barefoot, toes splayed on the pebbles, coloured teal, piebald, tan and ash. Others stand walleyed as the pier-lights come on or stare into the distance, paying no attention to the couple's vows, in which Selda requests that Garth accepts not only her but the others she contains, and vice versa. Garth's brothers, aunty, and two surviving grandparents are there, the latter with matching zimmerframes watching from the vantage of the promenade. His two brothers, wedged into ill-fitting suits, are shorter and wider than whippet-thin Garth. His aunty stands purse-lipped in a purple suit, her cinched and tinted hair shellacked into a solid, protective dome, a kind of helmet, her powdered cheeks and creased lips softened by talced fuzz.

A friend has provided fireworks. They shoot and bloom against the night. They pulse with gold that fades to ember that darkens and fades to black, with midnight blue that blends to rude fuchsia before the dusk swallows them whole. The faces of the crowd blush. There's Edward, retired since he injured his back, flinching at the popping noises, which remind him of the night of Selda's birth, and Maud, crying quietly, she can't tell whether for her daughter or something else. Herself perhaps. Or nothing, or God, or a boat out at sea.

Garth, who has been grinning so stupidly long that his jaw has started twitching, is contending with a rare and meddlesome fact of his physiology – namely, that his body tends to confuse nervous and sexual agitation: the odd, contorted-looking angle he's adopted is designed to conceal the growing bulge in his trousers, which hasn't escaped Selda's notice. And Selda, her hair pinned back with winedark lipstick on her lips, faintly drunk from a few midmorning glugs of scotch, and feeling like she might throw up at any second.

They lean together, kiss again. Fireworks arc and pop, golden world-trees branching over the ocean and gilding the waves. Distance splinters the harbour lights. Sea-wind disperses the smoke emitted by guests, hungry and parched, turning to head back to town. They trudge up the beach towards the banquet hall, pebbles slipping under their shoes like pennies in the seafront casino's coin-pushing machines.

The party is in a music hall, chosen in partial homage to Selda's father. It's a rundown late-Victorian place on a coastal road, the floorboards warped and shiny, gold foil curtains on the stage, a mirror ball fracturing the glow of the candles on the tables and floor. A table pressed against the side wall heaves with breads, biscuits, cheeses, apples and grapes and dates, cut-glass bowls laden with thawed pink prawns slathered with marie rose wearing tiaras of curly parsley, chicken and pineapple chunks suspended in green and yellow aspic, sliced white bread and baked ham and punnets of butter and jars of pickled whelks and perhaps a few cocktail sticks on which cubed cheddar and Spam are skewered as if by a lepidopterist. And booze, oodles of booze, dozens of bottles of red and white plonk but mostly ale and beer and gin, a bottle opener attached to the handle by a length of twine.

Garth's schoolfriend Leslie is best man. He is short, portly, and bald on top but with a wizardy ring of red-brown hair that hangs lank to his shoulders. He grew up in Meath but as legend has it he lost his accent within ten yards of the Dún Laoghaire ferry: it fell from his hands like mislaid luggage with which he's yet to be reunited. There's an air about him of a surfacing mole as he staggers onstage and blinks into the stage-lights' glare. He grins at the crowd, ruddy-faced and having reached a level of intoxication that feels, to him, cellular, the vapours of eight pints of ale and whiskey chasers almost visibly shimmering around his neck. He drank to calm his panic but he's still as nervous as hell, not least because he's aware – dimly but certainly, which is to say with dread – of how pissed he must look.

He stands at the microphone, clears his throat, and says: 'Ladies and gentlemen, good evening.'

Which the guests hear differently, as a toady burp followed by: 'Rr'adies anneltelmen. Goo'reevering.'

His view of the audience doubles and reforms, doubles and reforms, less a visual distortion than a temporal one: he briefly wonders if he is living this moment or remembering it after the event has occurred, the feeling he has sometimes when, privately, he will begin to narrate a humorous or extreme event midway through its unfolding, *I tell ya, I was standing right there, on stage, beer pouring out me boots...* He does so now, one part of his mind narrating his predicament to another part of his mind, making it funny and thereby redeeming it, *so there I was, utterly fucking trousered...* From an inside pocket he tugs out a folded, sweat-damp piece of paper and extemporizes off of the notes he scribbled upon it last night. And a change comes over him. He describes Garth's gracious magnanimity, his prowess at cricket, badminton, and wooing, his fondness for Jimmy Stewart movies and Stilton cheese. He ribs his old pal for his ineptitude at the bassoon, then pivots to praise his love for music – when he might have followed his brothers into insurance and made rather more money – because it led him to Selda.

Applause. Yes yes, well said.

At which point, in a tonal swerve prompted by desperation at the impassive faces of the crowd, he describes an afternoon at school during which the deputy headmaster opened the stationary cupboard to find Garth masturbating over an April 1953 edition of *Playboy*, which had found its way from America via an underground network of adolescent males.

No one but Selda laughs. The scrape of cutlery on plates is the only other sound besides her giggle-sneezing into her tissue – it's the sourpuss look on other people's faces that sets her off more than the anecdote itself. A moment later, Leslie is escorted off stage mid-speech by a frail-looking Edward, who takes the mic and proceeds to sedate the crowd with schmalzy reminiscences of darling Selda as a cherubic child. He tears up midway through, blows his nose on a handkerchief. Selda's glee at Leslie's disaster-speech darkens. Her father isn't lying exactly, but nor is he telling the truth: sugar-coating memory in order to protect himself from something he would rather forget. She grits her teeth and reaches for her glass.

She is upset. But how to care when there is dancing and short skirts and high-heeled shoes, when wet eyes glimmer with desire?

A band assembles on stage, drums, electric guitar, organ, and brass. They are rakish and sweat-sheened, shirt buttons undone. The tables are pushed back, forming a dance floor. Garth and Selda take up their preordained place in its centre, the immovable heart of the room's attention. They meet, press palm to palm. And they kiss: the audience erupts into cheers and sighs. *One, two, three...* The band strikes up, the newlyweds take their first steps, laughing at the daftness of it: Selda stiff-legged and self-conscious, Garth with a limber, lascivious grace, all loose hips and shimmying feet. And it is clear from the music that they are in love. Their song ends, the uptempo tunes begin.

'Oopsie!'

A knocked glass smashes. Lashings of fizz, warm gin, whisky soda, the room aswirl with skirts, hips, lips, as the music hall's doors are flung open on the warm evening air. One or two local jack-the-lads in loose shirts and twill caps askew on their haircuts saunter in from the street, hello, what's this, a party? A disco ball dazzles the sweat-softened air as the dance-floor pounds under dancers' feet, as foreheads drip and shirt-buttons pop and bra-straps fall loose from shoulders.

'Heather – your foot – it's bleeding.'

A hash cigarette is surreptitiously lit, its raggedy owner seeming to have forgotten that other people have noses. Drinamyl and benzedrine do the rounds, too: see the glazed and pepped-up glare in a few guests' eyes. Cheeks and shoulders and hands and mouths are kissed. Love is declared and rescinded. A fifteen year-old kid in a red velvet suit heaves up kirsch-flavoured vomit in the alley outside whilst another guest pisses triumphantly into a phone booth. Suited men sit in the shadows and steadfastly refuse to dance.

'Frick's sake, Jim, you're a junior clerk not Al Capone.'

A bunch of helium balloons is loosed from its tether. They float upwards and nudge the ceiling, some of them popping as they touch the chandelier's overheating bulbs. Bridesmaids on the upper deck scatter handfuls of confetti on the crowd, gold and silver twists falling on the dance-floor below. And when a few hours from now all the guests have left, and the house lights come on past midnight, those trampled pieces of paper, beaten white under the soles of dancing feet, will resemble fallen snow.

Through densely shadowed forest, past swift and shallow streams they glide. Sunlight licks the rim of Garth's glasses, haloes his grouse hat's tweed. He insisted on bringing it with him with boyish alacrity (his father took him shooting more than once before he died). He hums 'Wild Mountain Thyme'. The forest flickers like a cinema reel. Selda squints at the wind, quietly regretting her own insistence that the roof stay down. She can picture herself in the film of her life, hair streaming, sunglasses on. The reality is different, the wind so fierce and cold and it wicks tears from her eyes. By the time they arrive at the manor, the sun has retreated, rain has set in. It will not lift for several days.

They pull into the grounds of a country pile. The building has steep and grey-tiled roofs and towers with bell-shaped apexes, outer walls painted the pale yellow of powdered custard. The high, narrow windows are shuttered and inscrutable; those which aren't reflect the greying sky and admit no view of the manor's interior. In front of them is a stone bridge that leads to a hooded front door. Between the drive and the house, there is –

'A moat, Garth. A *moat*. Garth. Look.'

He does not. His expression is darkly preoccupied, as though contemplating a grave mistake.

They step out of the car and head onto the bridge. Selda looks down the steep stone sides of the moat. Shaggy weeds erupt from the brick. The depths clotted with weeds through which black fishes swim. She fights the impulse to take her clothes off and jump into it. Sometimes, in the bath, she will submerge herself in the water. As the noise of the world retreats, the gift will take its place.

'The chap said he would meet us here, didn't he? Do you suppose he'll be here any minute or...? Perhaps the door's unlocked.'

Garth is clutching his stomach. Earlier that day he told Selda that he was feeling 'a little bit off', then had to pull over for an emergency stop, jouncing into the bushes whilst undoing his trousers with one hand, then returning to the car with a harrowed expression. After which they had driven around a smallish town looking for a shop. What they encountered first was a fancy department store around whose marbled atrium smart women were shopping for silk scarves and perfume and luggage set to the somnolent tempo of piped Haydn, and with whose manager Garth negotiated to purchase their entire stock of toilet paper. Since which time her husband has been somewhat on edge.

As if in answer to Garth's question, the manor door opens. A man shuffles out and raises his arm in greeting. He is younger and better looking than Selda had anticipated. (Lambert had described him to Selda as a kind of potato-gnawing hunchback, a shuffle-footed farmer's son who could barely count to ten.) She notices how she straightens her posture, adjusts her smile. She wonders where this automatic behaviour originates from. It feels preconscious, animal. Seen from another angle, it is a trained behaviour, a kind of etiquette. Thinking this, she slouches again.

Garth whispers harshly in her ear. 'Deal with him. Code red. Emergency.'

He mutters something at the housekeeper, then waddle-runs into the open door.

The Czech housekeeper's name is Jan. He speaks scant, heavily-accented English. He is an inch or so taller than Selda, with shiny black hair and bright brown eyes. His hands, she notices, are smooth and muscular. As she takes the keys her fingers brush his. He guides her through the keys, telling her which open which doors. She and Jan are already skinny-dipping in the moat, sun on their faces, weeds warm against their skin.

'Mhnn-hmmm,' she tells him. 'This one? Yes. I see.'

They are sharing a candlelit supper, and he is reaching for her cheek.

344

He gestures at the manor with serious eyes to indicate that certain wings – entire houses' worth of rooms – are out of bounds. She sees an emblem, perhaps the family crest, embossed onto the side. A shield, crossed swords, a bell. She squints at it a while, remembers her friend, Ellen. The trip they made to a forest. Is this one a repetition? On a long enough timeframe, will the two memories blur?

Too late, she notices Jan gallantly stomping round to the back of the car to open the boot. It is stuffed full of toilet paper. Dozens and dozens of rolls squashed into every available crevice, several springing out and onto the gravel at their feet. Jan looks to Selda in alarm and confusion. Selda's face prickles with a sudden blush.

'You have party?'

'Party? No party! Mein Mann, herr ist... Oh, why am I speaking German? I can't even speak German. Well he's having a, oh,' she gestures at her stomach and pulls a face.

Jan raises his eyebrows. 'Hmmmnh,' he hums. He quietly closes the lid of the boot.

The manor is vast and creaky. Selda wanders down the halls. Giant mirrors. Motheaten curtains. Whole areas given over to shrouded furniture, to storage. Later, it starts chucking it down. Cats and dogs. Thunderclaps booming over the forest, rain drumming onto the roofs and waterfalling down the windows, seeping in through cracks. In the huge bare bedroom with its four-poster bed, its pale green walls and its mirrors, they fall asleep to the sound of rain. They wake to it next morning. She loves it. Garth hates it. The whole point, he thought, was to soak in the English sunshine.

At Agnes, in the Jensen Centre, Selda read through Cage, Morton Feldman and the American school. Her admiration for aleatory music, the music of chance, shifted her perspective on where composition ends and the world begins. Birdsong in the morning, the crackle of pylon wires, the jarring harshness of unoiled machinery – all of it is music. But the sound of her husband shitting in the midst of a rainstorm? If everything is music, what to select? If music is a form of attention, where to focus it? How to shape and arrange it? This is an artistic question. But it is also a question of how to live.

Garth insists that he is suffering from 'a mild case of the jips', and no more. He refuses to let Selda call a doctor or visit the pharmacy. She sometimes wonders if he is phobic of GPs. He tenses up whenever doctors, hospitals, or medicine are mentioned. He once alluded darkly to having been 'seen to' as a young boy. Whatever is the matter with him, it shackles him to the toilet, and any attempt to inquire if he has, for example, an infection of some kind, or heaven forbid something worse, is met with a thigh-slapping breeziness. She spends her time thinking not about his health but about Jan, her fantasy now extended to a lavish, candlelit meal in the abandoned ballroom, in which she serenades him with piano, and he strides towards her, puts a hand under her chin, reaches down towards her throat, the top of her blouse (she is wearing one, in this particular scene).

Meal times proceed as follows. A shivering Garth will take a seat at the dining room table in a vast, sombre room overlooking the moat, and take a mouthful of whatever meal Selda has prepared for him – weak broth, rye bread, porridge – before dashing upstairs again. A brief pause. Then the fundamental obscenity of it: noises amplified by a porcelain horn, their volume undimmed by the thin walls and rickety floorboards.

Still, his incapacity, when it stops being repulsive, funny, and frustrating, has its uses. So too does the endless rain that fills the sky, surrounds their manor, and drowns the black woods. The empty days give her time to think.

Garth tells Selda that he needs a new pair of glasses. Aside from the bowel trouble, his vision is blurry. He rubs his eyes.

'It's like I'm drunk,' he says. 'If only!'

'You must see a doctor.'

'No, no. It'll pass.'

'It's been days.'

'A bad sausage. Not my first.'

She wanders around the rooms, many of which are out of bounds, according to Jan's gestures, but she walks through them anyway. Those that are open at least, with their shrouded furniture and empty cupboards, spider-webs softening the edges of rooms, dead flies dotting the floorboards. The house smells of old fabric, damp plaster, and the coolness of the stone walls, the thickness of which derives, Selda presumes, from a time when the nobility dug moats to protect them from the peasants whose labour they stole. She spends the mornings reading, the afternoons with Garth, the evenings and nights drinking Himbeergeist and soda, smoking Dunhills, and listening to the gift, asking it questions.

Sifting through the hearsay, she has a better sense – still not a clear one – of patterns in the past, her place within it.

Motifs emerge. Stories are told and retold, returned to and modified. Rhythms quicken, stall. The long, slow settlement of a riverside village near a sacred hill, for instance, modulates to the brisk adagio as, centuries later, a descendant returns on a steam-powered train to take up a post as an actuary, at which firm he meets his future wife: their grandson opens a pharmacy, the tiled façade of which survives to this day.

The roar of rain reminds the voices of their time in

the foothills of bleak grey mountains – they've forgotten which – where they farmed the slopes and herded goats until a blight drove them south, where they went into service, working as kitchen porters, maids, and butlers, telling anyone who'd listen that they didn't feel right in dingy basements and stuffed cupboards because they were 'mountain folk', forgetting that before the mountains there were plains, before which there was forest.

Most shifts are gradual. History outpaces them, the changes so slow that they induce a kind of amnesia. Others are abrupt.

Whatever the relative tempo, each shift is a question of status and wealth: of employment, of ownership, of the injuries of work, the welts and scars and aches and scabs, how much sweat is shed and how much gold is left once the body is buried. She detects a kind of music in these sequences, an emergent form. It's nothing fancy or ornamental or even necessarily pleasant to listen to – although it is preferable to Garth's backside – and no doubt that it derives from her own way of making sense of the world as much as anything else.

There it is: the gift is a kind of music. It sounds nothing like the stuff she has written thus far, with its tap-dancing rhythmic complexity. It is a kind of pulse or tone, blood-heat, a thump in the temple, layered and rich with timbre. It isn't always exquisite. Often ugly, in fact. Harsh, or so chaotic as to leave her feeling queasy, not just because of the Himbeergeist, which she found in the back of a cupboard.

She remembers, too, the snow, which is connected in her mind with a feeling she has had since the gift became part of her.

Until the gift revealed itself to her, then. Though she can no longer remember a time before it, before the

348

feeling of inner contradiction and multiplicity, of separateness and desire, complicated her development, set her apart from her immediate family by bringing her closer to their predecessors.

Loneliness isn't the word for what she feels, sitting in an armchair on her washout of a budget honeymoon, watching the forest's black canopy steam. Aloneness might be better. The world of objects, other people, small talk, shillings, sanitary pads, bus tickets, post office queues, all of it at one or ten removes – a distance often clouded by the gift, which connects her to times and voices which are and are not hers. Her awareness of this distance is inseparable from the desire to cross it. Which desire is inseparable from the knowledge that she won't be able to, that every attempt will fail. But she can't stop trying.

Out of this tension, which is tragic in form if not in implication, emerges her desire to write music. Music, patterned like memory, bypasses the rational brain: it is the closest thing – closer even than language – that Selda has found to communicate what it feels like to be her.

She hears movement at the door, a soft rapping of knuckles on wood. Selda blinks out of her daydream and turns to see Garth's head poking in through the doorway.

'There he is, my little invalid.'

He shuffles over, kisses her forehead, and lies on the sofa with his head in her lap. She strokes it, running her fingers through his slightly greasy hair, as supple and thin as a mouse's fur.

'That's nice,' he says. 'I could get used to this. And I'm feeling a lot better now.' They remain like that for a few minutes, comfortably silent, Selda idly stroking her husband's head. Thunder crackles in the distance. Garth kisses his wife on the thigh. 'I'm as right as rain,' he says.

Garth is stabilized, sticking to a diet of rye bread and boiled rice. He whistles as if he has never been ill in his life. Hands on hips, game hat on head, he tells Selda that he feels in *fine fettle*. They still have three days until the end of their honeymoon. The rain has stopped. The forest lies gleaming, liquid light dripping from each leaf. They stand beside the windows in the manor's drawing room. On the cover of a volume of Romantic verse is an envelope, on top of which are four small squares of perforated paper. They look to Selda like little stamps, the azure ink soaked into the rough fibres. She asks Garth where he got them.

'I know a chap in a lab,' he says, boyish with the glamour of transgression. This from a man who always crawls at the speed limit and has more than once doffed his hat at a passing police car. 'A little wedding present.'

Selda isn't sure. She tells her husband she'll consider it.

They pack a bag with bread, cheese, apples, water, a rolled-up carpet from an upstairs room, two large brown bottles of beer. Apart from a few short walks and a drive to the nearest town to shop for food and drink, Selda has spent the past week indoors, under itchy wool blankets, cocooned in the rumble of rain, drinking, smoking, writing, and thinking about her mother, whose voice is sometimes louder in her mind than the gift, or attending to the sound of the rain, each individual drop blending into the multitude of those surrounding it until they form a unified drone, like horse's hooves or applause.

They walk through the woods for an hour. They pass a few cyclists but no other souls. In Selda's mind, her mother is telling her how shameful it would be to ingest such a thing. Is she not a grown woman? Why is her mother still such a feature of her inner life? 'Alright then,' Selda says out loud to Garth and to the Maud in her mind, 'if you think this scientist of yours can be trusted.'

Garth grins and removes his grouse cap, tucked into the inner band of which is the envelope. He tears two strips off the blotting paper and hands one to Selda.

They are lost in a forest of dripping trees under creaky branches, Garth in shorts with his game cap hiking healthily down the paths, the sunlight golden, leaning on mysterious trunks in whose blue shadows rodents shuffle and midges itch.

It comes in waves. First she notices colour. An intensity to the green. Prismatic shimmers dress the stones beneath her feet.

Someone is laughing. A broad stream runs with clear water and wavers with weeds.

Oh. The laughter is coming from her. Which makes her laugh again.

The weeds are the hair of the maidens who sleep on the riverbed. She recognizes them from the moat. Paused on the path, she watches their dark locks swaying slowly in the liquid. If she adjusts her ears, she can hear them singing, murmuring a song just below the forest's threshold of noise, under the hum of insects and the seep of soil and the sizzle of sunlit grass. It sounds less like the opening bars of the *Ring Cycle* than gossip in a drowned launderette. Garth is squatting by a mushroom, stroking its smooth brown, seal-like head.

Soon they are deep in the forest. The rivermaidens' song has given way to the courtly conversations of the beech trees that tower over them. The newlyweds reach a clearing hot with dappled light, which is also colour television beamed live from outer space, Andromeda, the flash of the sun on a Russian satellite. They spread the rug out and bask on the grass mostly giggling and laughing at trees, which are scholars and paupers with arms outstretched, their wigged heads nodding sombrely as they discuss the latest rumours spreading through the soil. They have shaggy green dogs at their feet. Oberon and Titania appear above them, looming higher and more darkly than the trees surrounding, their presence consecrating the union of Selda and Garth, who linger dumbstruck on the grass as the gift merges with the voices of the river and the forest, which speak in hushes, plosives, crackles, sighs, Germanic glots and stops of sound, prehistoric murmurings, the radio and television signals blurring in the multicoloured air. They do not touch their picnic. Other than the beer, which foams over their hands. They lie around and run their fingers through the long warm grass, which quivers and ripples, and peer back at the dark eyes between leaves.

Selda blinks.

She sees her father in the woods. He is cycling towards her, his wheels two spinning vinyls, his white hair a mushroom cloud. The ground rises up in a crescendo of leaves and loam, scattered soil exhaling smells of death and cocoa, and there he is, changed again: Edward, a heavy boar with coal-eyes a smoulder of fur, a blazing hot coin screwed into its forehead, exhaling a smoke of factory displeasure, of mercury-fumes and coal-dust. Her father's tusks gleam. The boar is a deer, or a passing shadow. It grunts into the undergrowth. A bush, her audience, chatters like canned laughter.

Selda blinks. Dusk falls and rises and falls and rises like a bouncing ball again. She cups the sun in the palm of her hand.

Wind-chimes. Looking up, she sees Garth. He has become a prince of the woods, his deer-eyes golden, his noble head crowned with a miniature solar system, his shoulders decked with mushrooms, twigs, chestnuts, and leaves, with a cape of ivy at his back and squirrels swirling round either leg. Selda cracks up. She runs at her husband, heartless with laughter, and a riverbank declares itself beneath her feet, a dry scree of pebbles shading to sand. She stands at the water's edge and hears the maidens underwater, braiding their soft green hair. There is only one thing for it. She peels off her clothes and splashes into the river, whose cool green water persuades her to dip her head and linger underneath it, where she can hear her mother's and her mother's mother's singing. The sunlit forest fades. There are clouds of green and darkish blue, cathedrals of smoky weed, tracts of liquid clear as glass through which the voices flow. She passes maidens who sing to her, whose hair brushes her skin. Just before she surfaces for air, she catches sight of one for long enough to recognize her. Ellen, wreathed in weeds, a black bell in her outstretched hand.

V. 1973

One winter's night, on a motorway in Wessex, an eighteen-wheeler jackknifes on black ice. For several metres it slides serenely. Then the driver hits the brakes; the carriage swings, reversing the jackknife, making the vehicle spin, and spin, and spin, until it howls to a halt. Other than nausea and shock, the driver is completely unharmed.

He unbuckles his belt and opens the door. His boot, which he'd unlaced for comfort, hits the sill. He plummets a few feet onto the tarmac, at which point his luck ends: he breaks his left wrist on the frozen road. The snap of bone is audible in the dry, cold air.

Fog brightens with the light of an approaching vehicle. A moment later, a canary-yellow car materializes out of the fog. The driver sees the truck and hits the breaks. For a suspended moment, one that seems to defy the laws of time and which has a sculptural, graceful quality, an arrangement of forms and angles and ways of seeing, the drivers of the truck and of the car make eye contact. They watch each other with the same blank gaze: perfect strangers united in an unforeseen catastrophe. It came upon them both within seconds and yoked their fates together. A second, no more. Both men will remember it for the rest of their lives, one of which will end very shortly indeed.

The car hits the side of the truck. The driver is instantly killed.

Another car hits the first. Then another. They brake sooner, are travelling more slowly. A pile-up begins to form as the lorry driver, superhuman with adrenaline, vaults over the dividing strip and into the path of traffic coming the other way.

Damage spreads outwards, like a bruise. Two, three

more cars crash into one another, fenders crunching, front-lights cracking, air bags whooshing. An engine catches fire. Doors open onto flickering fog. A couple of dazed passengers stagger out. Others lie slumped, concussed in their seats, broken glass on their laps. Call it a miracle. Thanks in part to the relatively cautious pace at which most were driving, partly on account of the darkness, partly from a misguided belief that slow driving would make the cheapest use of petrol, no one besides the first driver is killed in those collisions.

Does the truck driver, who has dodged the path of a car and a motorcycle on the opposite side of the road to make it onto the prickly ridge of the embankment along the motorway's side, believe in God? Until this moment, he had only believed in a cold pint after a long drive and the feeling when a woman takes him into her mouth, moments which however brief seem to flood the world with pleasure, which wash it clean. Now he senses something altogether more edifying. Hidden music.

He heard it flowing, a buried stream, beneath the surface of his terror. The look in the eyes of the driver of the yellow car: he had seen it too. Not all are guided to safety by the song. Some are knocked off course by it. Others, like that driver, are destroyed by it. Only now does the truck driver realize that he survived, the other man didn't, and the accident was his fault.

Other cars have crashed, are crashing. He turns to run, scrabbling over the slope on all fours. But his broken wrist fails him, he falls and gets up again, stumble-running into the darkness of the trees, he doesn't know why, he isn't thinking, he has to get away.

Oblivious to the accident a kilometre ahead of him is the captain of an amateur five-a-side team. Duties include the kitty, booking pitches – and driving the coach. Earlier that day, on a rain-wet pitch in Bristol, they beat their rivals six-nil in the tournament semi-final, and given the drubbing his boys subjected the other side too, well, could anyone blame him for wanting to celebrate. He takes his eyes off the road for a moment. The boys are singing on the back seat, and he wants to join in. When he turns back, he sees a lit fog. Red and yellow, muffled glare. The way the lights pulse reminds him of those in a disco. And if he wasn't so open to the beauty of the thing, he might have processed sooner that those lights belong to flames.

Then the sudden definition: a tangled mess of vehicles. He turns the wheel, but overdoes his correction. Seized by adrenaline, he forgets to remove his foot from the accelerator. Even if he had hit the brake, the speed of his approach, its angle on the frictionless ice, would have made what would follow inevitable, set in motion minutes if not hours before, when the referee blew his whistle.

The coach clips the side of a cherry-red hatchback, spins, flips and tumbles over the side of the motorway, crashing into a line of trees. Its roof concertinas. The windshield blows and scatters diamonds over branches and tarmac. Not long before the accident, a power cut came into effect. The motorway lights went out, and streets, shops, houses, cinemas, pubs, pool halls, and the motorway were cast in darkness. Those who were able to fill their car engines were barely able to see, squinting through the fog and hoping nothing would come out of it. The driver and four passengers die instantly.

A few hours before the accident, in a community centre north-east of the crash site, Selda is conducting a choir. Heavily pregnant, she wears a loose-fitting dress of dark-green cotton, flat shoes, and a tartan scarf. Her hair is in its by-now customary bob, tamed on the right by a tortoiseshell clip. On a stool beside her is a two-litre bottle of sparkling water, a bottle of milk, and a packet each of biscuits and Dunhill cigarettes. On a small table close to this are sheafs of manuscript paper, pencils and pens.

She moves from the music stand to her chair and back again, with slow, swaying steps, wincing often. She excuses herself to the toilet several times an hour. Her left hand rests on her belly at almost all times. As her drawn skin and the doughy bags under her smudged eyes indicate, she has not had a night of unbroken sleep in the past two months. It has prompted some among the choristers and musicians to worry about her, more still to gossip. Is she alright? Is *it* alright? If she notices them discussing her – in the locker room, in the corridor, and indeed here, in the rehearsal hall – she shows no outward sign. She has been known to snap at musical errors, none of which seem to get past her. What could this silence signify? Opinions differ. Some attribute it to arrogance, others to resilience, others to eccentricity.

The performance, at the Festival of New Music in Bristol, is five days away. The piece is far from ready. Selda has repeatedly been advised that she does not have to work, that an understudy can take over, one who will accept instruction over the phone. But since the baby is due in four weeks, Selda has decided to press ahead. When the piece is complete, she will take time off. Only once the piece is complete, however. Otherwise, she fears, her life will drop into a hole from which it will never climb out. She is a well-regarded pianist, but she isn't interested in the concert stage; in any case, even if she wasn't too lazy for all those drills, it's far too late: the childhoods of most concert pianists are overtaken, aged five or six, by the militaristic discipline of the conservatoire. Barely anyone knows who Selda is. The budget and profile of this commission are not huge, but they are the biggest she has received by far. If she doesn't get this right, no one will. She can't risk it. Standing, she rests her right hand on the corner of the upright piano behind her, partly for balance.

'Thank you, everyone. Better. We're not on top of it yet but sharper all round. Particularly from you, Oriana. But from bar thirty-six onwards – mezzos, tenors? You have diaphragms. Please use them. Good. Now, Peter, if I may.' She quietens her voice to address him directly. 'Small note here. The trills in bars twelve to sixteen are in fact a semitone. Easily done.'

A rather short man in a brown jumper and thick plastic spectacles, seated on the second row with a viola in front of him, blinks at Selda. 'Yes,' he snaps, without consulting the page. 'I can see that.'

'Well, as I say. It's a small thing, easily missed. But you were playing a full tone.'

'I beg your pardon. I was playing a semitone. It says it right there on the score. Your score.' Now his voice swells to the occasion: 'Are you meaning to suggest that I am unable to read music?'

Murmurs ripple through the string section. Peter, the most senior member of the whole ensemble, has his supporters. 'Of course not.' He appeared in one of Selda's dreams in the guise of an oversized guinea pig; it was of vital importance that he be fed, but he bit her fingers whenever she tried.

'I have been a professional violist for twenty-three years. I trained under Yanlin Gao. I would submit to you, Mrs Heddle, that you misheard my playing.'

Always something with Peter the diva, Peter the not-so-great. Yesterday, it was timing. He repeatedly joined the fourth bar of the second movement a quarter-bar behind the soprano, throwing the whole piece off kilter. He did it three times in a row. When Selda raised the error, his response was almost identical. Twenty-three years. Yanlin Gao. (Selda doubts that Peter has met Gao, a retiring, softly spoken man widely regarded for his creative interpretations of Schumann's *Violin Concerto in D Minor*, let alone studied under him. Perhaps he sat in on one of his masterclasses.)

For a second, she considers how best to react. At first, she wondered whether Peter's bluster was deliberate (an attempt to undermine her authority) or defensive (knowing he was wrong but too ashamed to admit it). Now she feels certain that, in the reality that Peter inhabits, he makes no mistakes. In his mind, in his memory, he played a semitone; he came into the fourth bar of the second movement at exactly the right juncture. It is simply beyond Peter's powers to conceive of a world in which Selda is right and he is wrong, never mind that she wrote the damn piece. The corollary to this lack of imagination – namely the presumption that he is almost always correct – is diffused so evenly throughout his consciousness that it has ceased to seem like a lack at all. Which is why he doesn't even bother to consult the page in front of him, or to examine his recall of the immediate past.

Selda would very much like to throttle Peter into submission. Aside from the chronic insomnia, bad back, hot flashes, fatigue, needing to pee every three minutes, how heavy and unwieldy she feels, how tender and swollen her breasts are, the anxiety about how much her life is about to change and how trapped she will shortly feel, not to mention the gift and its demands on her attention – asides from all that, she is at times overcome by a desire to inflict extreme violence. Now is one such moment. At the very least, she would like to be a fraction as rude to him as he has been to her. More pressingly, however, she forgot her pad. Her main priority as regards Peter is get through the rehearsal without accidentally urinating in front of him. That would really add piss to his mill. It has happened a few times at home. Selda has sneezed or been startled and pee has come out. Just a little. She doesn't care about Peter's opinion of her; not in itself. But she does care about morale, without which *Theseus* will be ruined.

She would like to tell Peter that, since she will soon have to care for a baby, she is glad that she has met him, because it allows her to get some practice in. But she – or the music – needs him. And he knows that she needs him. The thought makes her shudder.

Whatever the case, she concludes (the decision takes less than a second) thinking about him a moment longer would be a waste of a limited resource: her energy. And so, although she hates herself for doing it, she placates him.

'Yes, you're quite right. But no harm in checking, is there?' She smiles at him and turns back to the choir. 'Another half-hour and then break, alright? From the top, please.'

They run through the second movement again. *The Ship of Theseus* is woven from quotations of other composers' pieces, Mozart, Chopin, Brahms, from Strauss's *Ariadne auf Naxos* and the lament from *L'Arianna*, the only surviving fragment of Monteverdi's lost opera. She adores not one of these composers. Yet their work is, to put it one way, available. So much music has been written and recorded, is available at the fingertips: the composer's job may now be to lend it shape, to alter and mix what's already there. No more religious or regal or anxious music. Information music – that's the future. It is the first and so far only work that Selda has composed using this technique. She wrote it specifically for the festival's open call.

She had planned to submit a piece she had been labouring over for months and whose looser form, its simpler, more yearning tone, were based on the listening techniques she practised at Agnes's. Then, at the last minute – crisis. She swapped it out for *Theseus* which, then and now, she thinks of as a kind of armour. She can justify her every move intellectually. She can make coherent claims about the relationship between the canon and recording technology, of the role of originality in a cultural climate dominated by the reproducibility of the work of art, not to mention the irrelevance of the classical canon, confined to spaces which would be dismissed as utterly marginal were they, and their audiences, not so wealthy. But these ideas, interesting and valid though they are to her, do not get to the heart of things. There is something defensive about this piece, each quoted melody a link in a tightly wrought chainmail.

When, last year, she opened the letter telling her that *The Ship of Theseus* had been accepted, her reaction was ambivalent. She was delighted. Yet it confirmed deep fears about her other, more personal – to her mind much better – work: the suspicion that no one wanted to hear her music at all. She had submitted works of that nature on twenty-seven separate occasions. All had been rejected. If *Theseus* had been rejected too, she would have taken it as a sign.

'Good,' she says. 'Improvements. Especially Bleddyn, who really took my note about oomph.' By far the largest member of the group, towering over the other singers and taking up double the width, is this son of a Welsh miner. When Bleddyn grins, the skin of his vast head creases in complex ways, making his tangled black beard lift up off his shirt collar. 'I felt the floor shake, Bleddyn. You almost knocked me off my feet.'

Titters from the singers. Stony silence from Peter's gang.

'But bars sixty to sixty eight – and I don't like to bring these up again – but the emphases in this sequence are on the third and fifth beat of each phrase, not the first and third. Like so.' Without looking at the piano behind her, she reaches out her right hand, finds the keys, and plays a few notes whilst singing them, to demonstrate the emphasis: 'Pom-pa-TUM-tum-TUM. Not POM-pa-TUM-tum-tum, as some of you had it. And Victor, if you'll remember, I added a seventh to that G-flat. You played a ninth.'

Again without looking, she plays both chords.

'I want that dominant feel there. Something jarring, almost bluesy. Not that rounded, romantic sound the nine brings. Alright?' Victor nods. He is a thin, vampiric-looking young man all of nineteen years old, his narrow skull inset with two enormous and globular prawny eyes. Barring a few fluffed notes, he is precise. *Too* precise at times, closer to a player piano than a piano player. That there is nothing remotely amusing about him makes him an object of her amusement. She has never once seen him smile. 'Now, if everyone is ready, shall we try again from the top of bar fifty-four?'

To those who know Selda well – few do – her behaviour is in keeping with her character. Under these strip lights, on these polished wood floors, with jugs of orange juice and pots of tea and sandwiches on the side board, she is not one of life's delegators. She is known for her talent at piano, her remarkable span on the keys, her memory for melody, her inventiveness. Perhaps more so – at least now, at this early stage in her career – she is renowned

362

for her dedication, which eclipses all other qualities. To some, she moves through life like a bullet down a muzzle. A straight path. Clean, direct, unswerving, not a person you'd want to obstruct. One word for this is determination. Another is rigidity. Stiffness, a kind of deadness. She appears to know, or to have always known, that she is destined to become a composer. Meaning, according to some, that she is destined for obscurity and poverty, in which she will quietly die of some old-timey pirate disease like consumption or scurvy.

They run through the piece. Until, in the middle of the third movement, the room goes dark. Overhead strip lights, lamps, heaters, the fridge in the far corner, all go in a click of the fingers. The music stops. Everyone starts talking at once.

'Bugger.'

'Another one.'

'Candles. Candles. Where are the candles?'

'Language, gentlemen.'

'This isn't part of the score, is it?'

'Warned you.'

'Didn't.'

'Did. Told you there'd be a cut at six o'clock sharp. And lo.'

'Paraffin. Love the smell of it.'

'I've been looking forward to a drink all afternoon. A nice quiet pint or two down the Cathedral. It's not too much to ask, is it?'

'Could it be a blown fuse? My uncle's an electrician.'

'Cathedral'll be open, Jim. That place is like your pie hole. Never shuts.'

'Any objections if I light a cigarette?'

'Oh, so *someone's* got light, I see. Kept that one quiet.'

'I'm sick of these work-shy unions ruining normal

folks' lives. How'm I meant to get home with the main road dark?'

'Candles? No? We had a box of them. Candles. Anyone?'

'Steady on. It's not our boys' fault. It's them, the Arabs, manipulating the market.'

'If she says *candles* one more time I swear to God.'

'There's a reason for all this dark. War's coming. Big war between us and the Arabs. Will make the last two look like pillow fights.'

'Can! Everyone! Please! Shut! Up!'

'No candles then. Fine. Let's just use our sparkling wit to illuminate the room, shall we?'

Bleddyn to the rescue. The big man brought a generator down from his brother-in-law's farm. He sets it up just outside the side door of the community centre, a flat-roofed building on the edge of a new estate. Candles glow in a few of the windows of the flats all around. A puttering, shuddering thing, the generator kicks out fumes of petrol. It also makes a racket. Loud enough to render a rehearsal difficult. And with the door ajar to let the cable into the hall, it gets cold in here, and fast. Those with poor circulation start complaining; the first violin pulls fingerless gloves from his pocket, which gives him the look of a subway busker. But without the generator, the musicians and singers can't read their scores. Only a couple of candles have been located, despite Lucy's faith that there are enough to adorn all the chapels in Canterbury.

Should the rehearsal continue? Of course. Power cuts are nothing special. For the past two years, they have been integral to the texture of daily life. When they come, candles are lit, matches are held to the wicks of paraffin lamps, no choice but to get on the bike and ride to the shops, trudge to work, fry the bacon for the supper, read a comic by candlelight. She thinks about the stories her mother and father used to tell. They'd used candles back then, too, her mother liked to say. She wasn't romantic about it, but Selda was; in fact, she had imagined the scene so vividly and in such detail that she had tricked herself into believing that she can remember it. That she was *there*, observing her birth in third person: the incendiaries falling like rain, the sky a fiery cinema screen, planes like metal angels overhead. Selda feels a tickle of something, a twitch in the gift. The more comfortable she gets with it, the closer to what her teachers, some of them excited by Freud, called 'integration', the less concretely she understands it. Sometimes there is language, the dead with their red tongues flapping like panting dogs. Just as often there is something else, something pre-linguistic: call it intuition, but the word doesn't quite fit. *Music* would be closer, but not exactly right either.

She watches the figures move amid the darkness like in a Renaissance painting. She must decide. A prudent person would call it quits. Stay, the gift tells her. Talk to us. Sing to us. Is she perfecting this piece for herself, or to please something or someone else? She is exhausted, tender and sore from head to toe; she wants to cry and laugh and scream her head off, and she needs to pee for the thousandth time since they started rehearsing.

Then she thinks about the performance. Five days away. That is all. Five days of struggle. She could spend ten times as long on the piece and still not be satisfied. She understands this. All the same – the decision was never really in question – she rests her right hand on the upright piano again.

'Everyone! If I could – yes. Thank you, thank you.' They settle down. 'Yes, it's dark and it could be warmer. Yes, it's all very frustrating. But we have to crack on.

Like we did last time. Now, if we could pick up from bar seventy-six and run through to the end of the movement – if we can get that right, we can all go home.'

'I can't see the score,' says Peter. 'How do you expect us to read the score if we can't see it?'

Bleddyn moves the lamp. Peter seems both pleased and disappointed by the harshness of the glare burning onto his stand.

'Right,' says Selda. 'One two three four...'

The musicians strike up. They run through the bars.

Selda isn't satisfied with the performance, but more so the music. It is flawed beyond repair. If this was a ship after all, it would sink. Fifteen minutes in, and overcome with dizziness, she calls a break. Oriana glides over. This commanding Welsh mezzo-soprano, who sprinkles her blouses with rose water, whose favourite pudding is dry sherry and custard creams, has become, if not yet a friend, then a kind of mentor. She took Selda under her wing within moments of meeting. In almost their first conversation, she told Selda that her first husband, Cedric, had been killed in the Libya campaign and that, regrettably, she has yet to lose her second.

'Can I interest you in a small sherry? I have a bottle in my bag which I'm bringing over to a dinner later. Don't tell Peter.'

'Oh, no. Thank you.'

'I think it's fine, you know. With the baby I mean. I'm no doctor, but I do know that my mother had the occasional dram when she had me, and I turned out fine.'

'Better than fine, my dear. Might cave in and have a cigarette though. To take the edge off.'

'Go ahead. How are you getting along?'

Selda lights a cigarette and immediately feels dizzier but calmer. 'I'm not a woman. I'm a whale. A beached whale. They should put me in an aquarium.'

'I remember my first. They keep telling you to get some rest, get some sleep, but how? When?'

'If I get two straight hours in a night, I count my stars.'

'We understand. Well, the women do. I'm amazed you power through it. Custard cream?'

'No. Thank you.'

'Where's the hub, if you don't mind my asking?'

'Work.' Two days ago Garth took the ferry to Amsterdam for an academic conference in a genetics institute. Around now, he will be delivering a paper about his latest experiments into the structure of marine DNA, its behaviour over successive generations of urchins.

'Hmmm. Nauseous?'

Selda sips water, nods. 'Yes. Slight pain.' The wavering candleflames make her feel snoozy. She sips at her cigarette, watching the glow.

'Are you sure you *want* to power through it? Are you sure it's wise?'

'The piece isn't ready. I worry it isn't good, either.'

'Bunny, stop that. The piece is marvellous.'

That nickname: Ellen's name for her, too. Is there something about Selda that gives this away? Her front teeth? Her gait? She is torn between the desire to explain what she is trying to achieve with her music and a pre-emptive understanding that she will never be able to. She wants to unburden herself on how hard it has been to write it, and everything she's written these last few years. Once, when she was young and lacked self-consciousness, she lived in a state of grace. Everything came easily, felt exploratory. The gift would guide her. It kept her company. Now, the gift hectors and berates. Each new piece is an arduous task, wrestling something unstable and invisible into form, like fitting the west wind into a duvet cover. Before she can explain any of this to Oriana – if indeed she wants to – or talk about pattern and ancestry and repetition and change and love and death and all the other ideas that storm around her brain, not to mention the images – for some reason, snow, how it falls, the magic of it – before she can begin to tap into these disordered thoughts, she feels wetness spreading. One benefit of the darkness, then.

'Shit. I'm sorry, I'll have to excuse myself.'

'Oh, I see. Yes. Happened to me all the time.'

'If I can just get past Peter.'

'Sour little gnome, isn't he? All that chuff about Gao. Here, let me help you up.'

Oriana offers a hand. Now that Selda is standing, they can both see it on the chair. The puddle catches the glow of the lamps and the candles, glows like molten gold. Selda unwinds her scarf. Unthinkingly, she throws it on the puddle before anyone else can see.

'Bunny?'

'Yes?'

'Are you sure that's, you know.'

'What else could it be?'

'Oh dear.'

Selda follows Oriana's eyes. Running down her leg and pooling by her left foot is more liquid.

'Bunny. Look. Your waters have broken.'

'They have? They can't have. It's *pee*,' she whispers.

'It's your waters.'

Selda is angry now. And embarrassed. Across the room, she can sense Peter's eyes watching. Drinking in this scene, which must confirm all his suspicions. 'What are you talking about? This happens all the time. It can't be, the baby's not due for weeks.'

'Bunny, I'm sorry. Yes. Yes, I am... quite certain.'

'But—'

'It's alright, it's quite alright. But we should probably get you to the hospital.'

Grace's shift begins at six a.m. It's an hour to reach the hospital from her house by foot, a journey she only makes if she absolutely has to; sometimes, late at night, when she least wants to, she has no choice. She doesn't have a car or a bike. This morning, she takes the bus.

It only runs once an hour at that time of the morning. To make her shift, Grace must leave the draughty bedsit she shares with ten others at a quarter to five. Factor in needing to wash herself and her clothes, having to cook something, eat it, and clean the dishes, she doesn't have much time for sleep. Yesterday, she arrived home at midnight. When she sets out this morning, the sky black and the streets frosty, everything feels weightless and unreal.

She stands at the bus stop and rubs her hands together to take the chill off the tips of her fingers. A few metres away is a stout old man. Briefly Grace considers waving or saying good morning, but his posture advises against it. His boulder-grey head is buried in his collar and his hands are stuffed deep in his pockets; the steam rising up from his scarf is the only indication he's breathing. Grace notices a bull's eye on his cheek, a scrap of toilet paper red in the middle to staunch a shaving cut.

Sometimes the bus runs late. Other days it's cancelled. This morning, though, the 22 is right on time.

She lets the old man on first, then follows him on. Once she's in a seat to the left, she rests her head against the window, and instantly falls asleep.

'Grace, we're here.'

The bus driver, a friend of a friend, knows where she works. She thanks him and steps off and, yawning all the while, signs in at reception, heads to the ward on the second floor, and gets changed. She works all morning on her feet, preparing beds, cleaning floors, signing in new mothers, showing them to the waiting rooms, cleaning up spills, refreshing stocks of medicines. Two babies are delivered during that shift; Grace is present at neither birth. The obstetrician and the ward sister never call for her if other midwives are present.

At one o'clock, Grace breaks for lunch. Five minutes to eat a ham salad roll. She makes a tea from the urn which, needing a treat, needing the energy, she sweetens with three sachets of sugar. Then she carries the mug outside.

The afternoon is humid. Fog has begun to form. The trees and buildings look paler than usual, as though their colours, like her steaming tea, are diluted by milk. Harriet, one of the other midwives, stands near a steel picnic table in a brown coat, smoking. She gives Grace a cigarette and a strip of matches from a hotel up the road. Grace slips them into her pocket for later. They nod and smile without exchanging words. Some days, you just want to be quiet.

That afternoon, like the morning, Grace spends on her feet. Same routines. Endless small jobs. She makes a cup of tea for a man who accepts it gratefully, then looks up and sees her face, at which point he recoils, throws it on the floor. No one else will do it. She cleans the spill with a mop.

An hour or so after dark, the lightbulbs fade. They turn a jaundiced yellow for a minute, then brownish light, then nothing.

'Alright, everyone. Candles out.'

Grace's next meal, at eight o'clock, is again in the cafeteria. There's a splat of brown stew, a clag of dry mash, a steamy heap of mixed veg from the freezer bag. Cover

370

the whole thing in butter and pepper and salt, in the flattering glow of the candle, and she can almost believe it's delicious.

She carries her plate to the corner, fills her plastic cup with water from the jug.

Realizing she's forgotten cutlery, she heads back to the counter and reaches for the last remaining fork. But a junior doctor snatches it before she does. He doesn't look at her; it's as if she isn't there. Everyone in the queue saw it. No one says anything. So nor does Grace. She clenches her hands into fists and stares hard at the floor. Then she takes a spoon.

On the short walk back to her table, she hopes for two contradictory things: that no one will see her, and that someone will talk to her. She scans the heads, looking for Harriet.

The canteen occupies a long, windowless basement. It has the claustrophobic feel of a submarine. Hazy with cigarette smoke and candles, the kitchen hatch exhales dull odours of bleach and boiled vegetables. Around Grace nurses, doctors, cleaners, and surgeons argue over the power station workers, curse Heath, blame the Arabs for hoarding oil, crack jokes and explode in laughter, some of it forced.

Grace looks forward to the first weeks of spring. Some warmth. A little sunlight. Most of all, she would like to have a party. To have a friend come round with their car and take her to a place where there is food and music and maybe some punch and she can dance and forget all this.

She returns to the second floor, where she works for an hour or so, though she finds it hard to tell in the dark. She's still not used to it. Blackouts, rationed power. Always the same cycle. The lights are on. The filaments dim to dull brown. Then they go out.

371

The hospital has to make do. Candles stand askew in glass bottles and mugs. Paraffin lamps on lino floors emit a faint noxious smell into the corridors. Nurses and surgeons work by candlelight and battery power, tending the sick and wounded in dark wards. The army has loaned them a generator, which thrums and rattles in the basement: it kicks out petrol fumes worse than the lamps, but nowhere near enough power for a ward. One of the nurse's husbands has an ice cream van, and he's loaned it to the hospital – no one's buying ices anyway, this time of year. The generator is only enough to keep a few machines going, mostly fridges for blood. Every time the lights go out, decisions are made about what to power and who to save.

The ward sister stops her in the corridor. It's dark in here, the candles reflected on the lino. The sister, Grace's boss, reminds her of army generals and iced buns. Her round cheeks white with powder, her lips are glacé-red. Yet her strong arms are dead-straight at her side, and her chin juts out like an accusation.

'You're on the evening shift, Grace.'

'I started at six this morning.'

'Ruby called. She's stuck at home without a voucher for petrol. We're short of staff. We're down to the obstetrician, two midwives, and yourself, and we already have two in.'

'I was hoping to have the night off.'

'Yes well we all want things.'

'I just say because, I'm very tired. I did a double yesterday. And the day before. And before that too. So it's four in a row. I'd need someone to drive me back. The bus don't run past ten on Tuesdays.'

The ward sister doesn't reply. Instead, she glares at Grace.

'But I'll stay,' she says, 'if you need me.' She can't afford to say no.

'Good,' says the ward sister. 'We're out of gloves and we could do with more disinfectant, and we've had two women come in the past hour. That can be your first job. Make it quick.'

What did she mean, *first job*? Did she not hear what Grace told her? Does nothing go in?

The second-floor supply cupboard is practically empty, save for a ratty mop and a box of plasters. Grace will have to look further afield.

She takes the stairs to the ground floor. To reach the supply room means going the long way round, via the labyrinthine corridors of cardiology, or taking a short cut through A&E, which for superstitious reasons Grace prefers to avoid. To be present at a birth, to help bring a soul into the world, is to be touched with grace and fortune. To be present at an injury or an accident, by contrast, feels like a violation, not to mention bad luck. This troubles Grace. If she had more faith, was closer to God, she would feel differently. She would understand that she was needed here, more than anywhere else.

Ordinarily she'd take the long way round, but the thought of the walk makes her weary, so she pushes open the doors to the emergency rooms. The corridor is dark, lit here and there by torches and paraffin lamps and a few candles.

Her breath catches in her throat. Many more people are injured than usual. She steps over a man on the floor with a broken leg. A young man lies on a gurney in the corridor, groaning, sheets soaked purple, his lower right leg at an unnatural angle. A paramedic, green uniform black with blood up to the elbows, bites the tourniquet's rubber thong to tighten it. Grace asks a passing casualty nurse what happened.

'Accident on the motorway.' The nurse says it briskly, as though she was relating last night's TV.

She continues down the corridor. The door to an emergency room swings open, and she glimpses pockets of activity illuminated by torches and a battery-powered lamp: metal implements flash like Morse code. Grace grabs gloves and Dettol from the supply room feeling like she's about to be sick. Instead of heading back to the second floor, she goes outside. The fog is thicker now, solid as a wall. Somewhere beyond is the power station. In the last three days she's helped deliver how many babies by candlelight – eleven? twelve?

She is seeing things again. In the ward earlier this evening, in the corner of her eye, she saw a creature composed of pure light. It was a brief, golden vision. When she'd looked at it directly, startled out of her skin, she saw what it was. Candles reflected in a window at the end of the ward, their glows vertically elongated.

The world played tricks. She was hearing things. Voices echoed down the lino-lined corridors, and she'd begun to hear music too. A portable radio had been playing ghostly melodies. Someone was practicing flute, swift trills and breathy snatches of song. And now she heard something else – a clear, high note, like a bell being struck.

Grace remembers Harriet's present to her. She lights the cigarette with a hotel match and glances up at the building behind her. Through the windows the unlit corridors are eerie and theatrical. Shadows swing as torchlights roam the corridors. A child's white face appears, vanishes. Shadows grow and shrink with a pace like breathing. Grace takes another drag of her cigarette and blows it into the cold night air. She leans against the awning, closes her eyes, longs for bed. For clean sheets and dreamless sleep.

'You're alright, Bunny. You're alright. Plenty of time. Could be twenty-four, twenty-eight hours. Could happen tomorrow, Bunny. Hold on. Good girl. Good, good. Look – road's nice and clear. A nice little ride. Steady on.'

Selda is in the passenger seat in Oriana's car, the footwell a midden of wrappers and tatty magazines. She winces and grits her teeth. Something doesn't feel right. It's frosty and foggy outside. Inside, the car feels like a warming oven. She opens the window a crack, fresh air seeping in. No matter how often Selda asks her to give it a bloody rest, Oriana will not stop self-soothing with her obsessive, repetitive words, filling the silence with rambling.

'When I had Matty, my third, it was exactly like this – well, not *exactly* – we had power in the hospital at least – and well yes Terry was with me – oh it was twins of course too, but it was raining that night, or I think it was – and anyway – oh, I'm talking too much again, am I? Aren't I? No? Why *are* the workers striking, anyway? It's all so far away, why should it affect us over here – can't they understand *we* have lives to lead, babies to deliver?'

'Orie, please.'

'Oh no! It's a nerves thing. Trevor hates it.'

'No, Orie – what's that?'

'What's what?'

Now Oriana sees it too. Blue lights pulsing through the fog. She screams, hits and then releases the brake, causing the car to spasm and eventually slow.

'Oriana!' Selda cries, her arm flung out to catch the glove box and cushion the jolt. Now the car crawls forward. Selda starts talking in repetitive ways, 'It's happening, it's happening again,' to which her friend asks: 'What's happening? What is it? This is your first, isn't it? Oh, darling – I had no idea. No idea.'

Then Selda, upright again, with a sharp tone: 'I don't mean the baby, I mean *this*. It's like before but different. I can't escape.'

Oriana hasn't been so close to a gifted person before. Is this what it's like all the time?

The scene becomes clear through the haze. Several cars have crashed into one another on the rightmost lanes. Behind them is the blackened bulk of a truck. Traffic cones have been laid out to funnel traffic to the slow lane and the hard shoulder. Cars creep along, slowed as drivers rubberneck the crash. Whatever work was being done by the emergency services has passed into the clean-up phase. There is one ambulance, its lights strobing blue, but no injured people to be seen. To one side, part-screened by a police car, a body lies under a sheet. To the left, a policeman with a torch waves the traffic forward. Oriana winds down the window and calls out.

'Hello? Yes? Hello? Officer! We need help here.'

He looks up. Points the torch at her face. Holds it. Lowers the torch. Turns back to his work.

'Officer! We have a pregnant woman! She's about to go!'

Does that convince the recalcitrant young man? Or do they have to wait as the cars creep forward?

He stands at the open window, elbow on the roof, his heavy black torch loosely clasped in his hand like a baton. A nasty burnt smell pervades the air. Selda feels delirious and very afraid. The gift roars. Her heart beats hard. Torchlight blinds her. Sharp chin, thin moustache. He might be all of twenty years old.

'Paramedic,' Selda says, the words like wet tissue in her mouth.

A message is passed. A paramedic jogs over, a bulky man with greasy black hair and an alert, hunted look in his eyes. Oriana explains the situation. The paramedic asks a few questions. Cars creep forward, inch by inch. He jogs round the car, opens the door, asks Selda a few questions, takes her pulse, holds his hand to her forehead. Then delivers a verdict on their approach which in its helplessness, its philosophical air, its invocation of both resilience and passivity, convinces Selda that this isn't really happening.

'The best way out,' he says, in a know-it-all tone, as if reciting an old saw, 'is through.'

They do get through. It takes a while, but they get through. Oriana remembers the car horn and beeps and beeps and beeps, the fog burning red with brake lights, her window wound down, shouting, beeping, bellowing again. The lungs on her! This renowned mezzo-soprano putting her gale force, Royal Academy-drilled, Fricka and Carmen voice into her pleas, so loud and piercing and expertly aimed it's a wonder the windshields don't crack.

As news gets round that a woman is about to give birth, cars begin to part. Men doff caps and children wave. Antagonistic car-horn blasts become cheerful ones. Whatever helplessness, horror, and frustration was aroused in the group of commuters by the crash and its repercussions is sublimated into the celebration of this woman's, this madonna's, this daring darling's safe passage through the jam. Anyone would think she was a royal and this VE day. Oriana steers the car along the hard shoulder, one wheel lurching and bucking on un-even grass, the fender catching the barrier, until they are free, out the other side. The fog is beginning to clear. The motorway's lanes are empty.

It takes another twenty minutes to reach the hospital. Oriana pulls into the front, headlamps lighting up the big blue sign, her engine making puttering noises indicating that the petrol is dangerously low – too low to make it back home, but that's a problem for another time. First off, where to take Selda.

'Is this the hospital?'

'It's right there.'

'I can see it yes but – where is everyone?'

'Park, please just park.'

'I can't see any lights on. It's shut!'

'It's not shut.'

'The next – I don't have enough petrol to reach the next one.'

The building looks deserted. No lights are on anywhere, it's a silhouette, dark against dark, surrounded by other buildings and a few tall pines, patches of unkempt lawn. The windows are black but Selda can hear a low humming sound, a generator, and there are lights in the windows, torch-beams and lamps that give the hospital the look of a series of alcoves, reminding Selda of the house shrines in the lobbies of Agnesian chapels. As Oriana steers them down to the car park out front, parks, and climbs out, rain begins to fall. Quietly, then quickly. Soon the downpour is upon them. They mount the front steps.

There are people under the awning, people in the candlelit lobby. None of them appears to be in charge. Oriana asks where to go. She scans the gloom for signs. Selda stands to one side, breathing heavily.

'We'd better try A&E.'

'No. Maternity.'

'I can't see a damned thing, it's like bloody Hades.'

'Don't say that.'

A nurse in a paper gown appears behind tempered glass. Oriana cries out to her. 'This is not fucking Saigon! Can somebody please do something!'

Selda has never heard Oriana swear. But the word doesn't register. Another wave of contractions almost brings her to her knees, but she steadies herself on the reception desk. Her sense of time and space begin to loosen, to liquefy. The room recedes. She sinks deeper into her body. A short nurse with a button nose and grey eyes appears. Everyone passing out of and into shadow again, like shades pacing through the underworld. 'Everything was fine until the fog came,' says the nurse, guiding them at a steady clip down the corridor. 'Then the power cut. All hell broke loose.'

'Anyone would think that we'd gotten over this kind of thing,' says Oriana, 'it's barbaric, absolutely barbaric! It went wrong after the war, my dear. We won that but we lost the bottle. Not the battle, the *bottle*. Utter dissolution. We fought off the Germans only to be invaded by, well. One doesn't like to say.'

Oriana is ranting again, and in a new, furious key. Selda tells her to shut up, but cannot, will not, articulate a more nuanced response because she lacks the breath. She is at the world's mercy. The nurse conjures a wheelchair from somewhere and guides Selda into it. She has to admit that the conditions of the hospital put her in mind of war zones and previous centuries. She thought that by the time came for *her* to give birth, history would have come good on its promise, everything would be clean and sterilized and monitored by machines and multiple, trained professionals. Again her mind flies back to her mother, giving birth under a table. This hospital, by comparison, is a fun-house. Its dimensions seem unstable. Dark corridors slide with shadows. Echoes run riot like loosed prisoners. Walls recede and race forward. The gift roars again. All the ancestry gathering in one place, in her womb, between her legs, leaking out. All that pressure on the hip-bones, the lower spine. Her mind flickers with visions of mountains and streams and battles and bread. She sees a boat on a roiling ocean. A maid in a basement, polishing boots. A composer driven mad by a ghost. Barely able to breathe, she is desperate with fear for her unborn child, and for all the unborn children who depend on her. The unending chain. It's all too much. Her body takes over. The gift is within her, prising her open. Something rumbles down the corridor. The wheelchair, the rain. She is helpless. Cracking open. Is that what she's giving birth to, not her child but a legion of ghosts? Not new life at all, but new death. The hospital dims. Life is no longer where it used to reside. Now it is somewhere between her and the gift, a dim flicker. She can do nothing to change or improve the circumstance other than reach out, follow the light.

'The quickest route is up the lift,' the nurse says, 'but it's not running because of the blackout. We'll have to cut through A&E and up one flight to Maternity.'

She leads them through double doors. Selda's vision is bleary, fast heart, breathing shallow. In the darkness she hears laughter and weeping and sees silhouettes and a few scattered flames. On the floor is a broad cloudy patch like spilled ink hastily mopped. The nurse opens another door and directs them upstairs.

'It's only one flight.'

'How's she supposed to get up.'

'I'll walk.'

'Oh no you won't. We'll carry you.'

'You can't carry me. I'll walk.'

'No. The nurse will come down to you. Stay there.'

Selda sits in the chair. She calls out after Oriana. But her friend doesn't listen. She bounds upstairs. A moment later, she appears again with a midwife, a young black woman with cat eye glasses fixed at the end piece with a strip of surgical tape.

In the basement are a pair of backup generators loaned by the army. One packed up this morning. The other, a rattling, rusted thing, is reserved for essentials, defibrillators, computer terminals, heart monitors, and fridges for blood. As a result, the room in which Selda gives birth has no power at all. It has candles. Years later, Selda's daughter Anya will remember these candles. She will first describe them to herself, whilst telling stories on rainy days and idle afternoons. The mother had the bombs, the daughter has the smaller, gentler flames, whose light connects not to international conflicts on the continent of Europe but fossil fuels and global flows of capital. Then she will tell her father, who, whilst reading a paper or a book, will nod and remind her he was not there at the time. At school, Anya will talk about the drama of her birth to impress her friends, make herself sound special. She will mention it in bed with the man who will later become the father of her own child, Wolf, telling him in order to reveal something about herself, and her relationship to her mother; to make herself intriguing, but vulnerable too. That she was born in those conditions, and prematurely, gives her a certain glamour. Once Wolf is old enough, she will talk about the candles to him. It will set the scene of her entry, the perilous voyage, the brush with death on the motorway. He will find the story boring at first, and roll his eyes. Until, by dint of repetition, he'll believe he can seen them, too: the way they waver, reflected in the rainy glass. And then he, in turn, will pass the story down. In time, his young

381

daughter will see the candles glimmer as if at the end of a tunnel down which she feels compelled to walk, not knowing how far it stretches into the past.

'Surely there is someone more qualified.'

'We don't have anyone else on staff tonight.'

'What about the obstetrician? The registrar? Where's the senior registrar?'

'They're busy with the other two–'

'Go get him.'

'Miss, they are busy. I have been working as a midwife for three years.'

Oriana turns to Selda: 'I don't think she's qualified, do you? We need someone to look after you properly. Not... her.'

The ward sister appears. There is an argument. Selda tells Oriana to stop being so stupid and judgemental and frankly racist and to please leave her alone, go away, she isn't helping, it's dark and she's scared. Oriana goes quiet. She steps to one side as Grace and the ward sister push Selda into the nearest ward.

Grace helps Selda to undress and change into a blue gown, and heave herself onto the bed. One by one she lights the bristling wicks, left there since an earlier labour, and again feels as though she is back in the church of her childhood, lighting prayer candles with her grandmother. Screwed into glass bottles and placed in empty cans, the candles burn on the bedside table, on windowsills, stools, shelves. Noises drift from other wards: rubber soles creaking on lino, the rumble of a gurney's wheels.

The ward sister takes the lead as Grace assists. It isn't a breach birth: the top of the baby's head is visible. There is no time to shave the pubic hair, even if they wanted to. The obstetrician isn't here, but he always insists on it when he is, he claims it's more hygienic. But to the ward sister it has the air of an assault or punishment. Selda's consciousness feels as though it is sunken so deeply within her body and its processes she might as well not be conscious at all. Only she is, and in ways she's not experienced before. The pain is extraordinary. Something about the world is revealed, though she can't say what it is. The gift is roaring, singing. If only it would shut up. Do they need to conduct an episiotomy? The question comes from Grace. The ward sister considers it. She comes from a line of midwives who delivered babies by firelight. And that is what they do. An incision is made. There is exertion and bleeding. The baby is born agleam with blood and mucus. By candlelight they cut and seal the cord. They check breathing, heart rate, muscle tone. They weigh it, measure the cranium, and lift the child into Selda's arms.

Flute music lilts down the hall from an unseen source. A battery-power radio, maybe. It has a crackly sound.

Oriana appears at the doorway, clutching a steaming plastic cup.

She sees the windows twitch with rain. Flames in the dark. The gleam of steel.

Selda holds her newborn daughter against her chest. 'This is the best thing I've ever made.'

Garth will not discover that he has missed the birth of his firstborn daughter (privately, he had hoped for a son) until tomorrow morning. At the moment, he is in the bar of a chain hotel in Amsterdam, more drunk than he yet realizes. The lights are low and the air feels sculptural, a solid volume of smoke. His eyes are sensitive: the smoke stings them and makes him slightly, and constantly, weep.

It is the first night of the conference, and excitement is high. Half the auditorium headed here from the centre attached to the university, after a long meal at which the food was so unappetizing (huge lumps of grey meat) that he restricted himself to a Biblical pairing: red wine and bread rolls. Over the course of the evening, couples formed. Now Garth and Helga, he thinks her name is, a lab technician, he thinks her job is, are the only ones from the conference left.

He might have been a pilot, had he been born a generation sooner. Tall and thin, he has a classically proportioned face, although his eyes are perhaps a fraction too close together. The most attractive things about him, however, are his hands, which are shapely yet muscular, with long, tapered fingers. Prominent on the back of his hands are a few sinuous veins, which imply vigour and sensitivity. He senses all this about himself, as he did when he met his wife.

He is holding forth about the beauty of the double helix, the proteins twisting like steps in a dance, cytosine, guanine, adenine, thymine, isn't it bloody marvellous, just beautiful? Animals, plants, fungi, protists, mitochondria, chloroplasts, bacteria, archaea, cytoplasm, eukaryotic chromosomes, chromatin proteins, histones, transcriptions, base pairs, grooves – is he losing her? He must be drunk. This is the seduction equivalent of filibustering. He catches her eye again, tries to remember what she told him about her own research. Haemophilus influenzae?

Anyway – this is it, the hidden pattern. The *key*. It's a kind of music, doesn't she think? These – two – strands – coming – together. (He summons the inward glint in his dark eyes, adjusts his cadence and his tone to imbue his words with all the innuendo he can muster.) He lifts a whisky soda to his lips as the pianist, in a crumpled tuxedo, tinkles at the keys.

The lab technician – her name is Helen – smiles at the man she has only just met, but who conforms to a certain template, which she has come to regard as desirable: broad at the shoulders, quick-witted (if a little too drunk). His attentions, not exactly solicited, are not entirely unwelcome either. They're even reassuring on some level. She is nursing a wound, has been hurt. Anyone can see it.

Garth laughs and leans slightly forward. His hand drifts down to her knee with such a studied gentleness as to seem a passive transition, a leaf finding its natural rest on the soil. She clears her throat and (imperceptibly to Garth, who has caught sight of his devilish reflection in the glass) twitches. She composes herself. Leans into it, slightly, too. Their eyes close, their lips meet. Garth shifts his position, places a hand on her shoulder, draws it closer. In the corner, the pianist wraps up a song. No one applauds.

Or maybe the betrayal is timed more bluntly, more brutally? Not that Selda will ever know exactly when it happens. Not that Anya will realize either. Likely it makes no material difference. When Selda and Garth eventually separate, it will not be because of this incident, or any other in the pattern of behaviour of which it forms a part, a cycle of gestures repeated like the notes of his favourite song. It will be something harder to define. Sadder, more fatalistic. This kind of separation would not have been possible for Edward and Maud. For them it may have been in the true sense unthinkable. Selda will realize that she hates the person she becomes in her husband's company more than the husband himself. The feeling will be mutual. Garth will avail himself of the time-honoured techniques for a man to belittle his wife, the slights and dressing-downs arranged for him like bottles in a liquor cabinet, behaviours observed and condoned. Controlling her seems an easier task, after all, than controlling himself. Which is to say (of this he will be all too aware) that he is a coward.

He will undermine her ambitions. He will play to her self-doubts. He will suggest that if she pursues her career, he will divorce her, which will cover her in calumny. She will respond, in part, by retreating into work. By becoming lost in music, as in a blizzard.

And she will do well, she will prove him wrong. Her independence and success will wound him. He will feel rejected, will mourn a loss. These are ways of coping, but not with marriage.

With what? Well, his sense of rejection, his sense of loss... but these long precede ever meeting the woman outside the rehearsal, the one with the actual horn. It has something to do with a malfunctioning boat and a christening sixpence. With the neglect of a youngest son.

So, he has found ways to cope: being upbeat and greedy; nursing the classic passions, women, music, drink. Always mobile, ever-moving. He wants to make his mark on the world – but hurry. Be quick about it. The shadow is there, a sunken thing, under his feet at all times. Move on.

In several years, it will be Selda who leaves him, not the other way round. It will feel better this way. Cleaner, somehow. Humiliating, though, of course. (He will tell his colleagues that it was mutual and amicable; he will convince himself they believe him.) It terrifies Garth to think that he is losing his daughter in all this. He sees Anya several times a week. He does the right things, as he sees them. He takes her to the park and collects her from school. Years pass. Anya grows up, she grows into herself. She is a serious girl, but not so serious as her mother. There is a flexibility and a pragmatism, alongside the humour and self-restraint. He meets another woman, accepts a prestigious post at a German university, has another child, a son. He and Selda drift apart. Of course there is an awkwardness between them, when they meet, that is preferable by far to the rows. Gradually, they forgive themselves. The silence between them drains of tension. They are better as distant friends. When he hears that she has died, he will feel as though the sky has been ripped off the planet, a gaping, howling waste where sun and clouds once were. Most of all, he will mourn for his daughter and his grandson. But he will not return for the funeral. Partly because he is busy, partly because his health is poor. And partly because he never sat comfortably with all that. The gift. It was too much to deal with. Too many people in one.

That comes later in the score. Does simultaneity matter? It does in an orchestra: music depends on it.

Say they are upstairs already, then. Selda pulls into the hospital. It's a hotel room – no need to describe it – except briefly to note the travel-sized bottles of whiskey and soda water on the side, the watch and the ring bundled carelessly up in a white shirt. Traffic shushing past the window, which is open a fraction, the customers leaving the bar below, laughing as they depart, the headboard tapping at the wall.

VI. 1984–1985

Selda runs a bath with half a bottle of Matey. *Concentrate*, she tells herself as the room fills with fragranced steam. The gift has been restless for days. It prats and prances in the corners of her mind, spinning her life into tangled yarns that dizzy her sense of time. It wants to ruin her evening if not her life, and to steal her away from Anya. *Snow*, it sings. *Snow*. A moment from a distant, otherwise unremembered past. *This is real*, it tells her. *This is who you are*.

'Anya!' she cries, standing over the heap of stiff white bubbles that fills the tub. Her daughter appears in the doorway, face creased in an irate frown. 'Oh, yes.'

'Privacy. Look it up.'

'I've heard of it. I was just leaving.'

In Selda's mind, Anya is still young enough to want help with shampooing her hair, to press wet foam letters onto the tiles and need towelling down once she gets out. She closes the door and waits a moment, listening. Anya begins to hum.

It is just a flicker. A few bright flakes fall through the air, carrying fragments of melody. This tune has been haunting her lately. It remains just out of reach, a few high notes followed by low – what next? Her thighs are aching, her vision blurs. *This is who you are*. Snow from another century begins to settle on her hair.

Darkness.

Next thing she knows: a garden fence. She recognizes it.

'Mum. Mum.'

She is outside in the garden, clutching a cushion to her chest, and singing at the pear tree. The air is cold and damp. She is not in a snowstorm after all, but a residential street. Anya is on the lawn in front of her, forcefully yanking her hand.

'Mum,' she says. 'Mum. Come back.' Mixed with her panic is weariness: she has done this before.

A light comes on in a neighbour's house. Where has Selda been? All she can remember is a broken melody, each note a cold and fractured thing.

'I'm here,' she says. 'I'm here.' Together they head back indoors. Anya's head is bowed.

That she loses control is bad enough. That she is losing her daughter is unbearable. Yet she bears it. This is living with the gift. At its highest form, relating to the dead is a kind of music. It is art, which is the best she can hope for.

Over the following weeks and months, Selda arrives at a decision. She must spend more time alone. That is the answer to her recent distress, brought on by the gift's new restlessness. The dead want her. They have something important to tell her: the answer to who she is, buried deep in the distant past, encoded in the form of a melody she cannot grasp.

She tries to listen, she lacks the skill. Whatever she learned at Agnes's was not enough. She must go further into the past. It is risky but it is the only way. If she cannot rid herself of the dead, perhaps she can work with them. To do this, she needs more than the usual isolation. She needs to get as far away from her life as she reasonably can. And yes, perhaps the extremity appeals to her temperament. She applies to the School of Silence. They offer her a residency the following year.

A week before Selda leaves, Ellen heads over for supper. They have not seen each other in months, partly by Selda's design: she cannot shake the sense that Ellen, trapped in a torturous marriage, wants something from her, or is foisting onto Selda a responsibility that she does not accept. It is a black spring night. Rain has been falling for hours by the time Ellen arrives, her cane in one hand and an umbrella in the other. They eat spaghetti bolognese and share a bottle of red wine. Ellen has joined the faculty at Agnes's, she has reason to hope they will appoint her to dean. Selda reels off a summary of her recent auditions, recitals, pieces, performances, in an attempt to defer the inevitable confrontation. Ellen piles the plates and pans up in the sink. Selda opens the window and lights a cigarette. Rain sputters into the kitchen.

Here we go, Selda thinks, as Ellen clears her throat.

'I wanted to talk to you, Bunny. I'm feeling confused. About us, I mean. So much has gone unspoken.'

'Like what?'

'The fact that you hate me.'

She laughs. 'Don't be ridiculous.'

'You can't stand me. You flinch when I walk into the room.'

'Not everything is about you, Ellen. If you realized that, perhaps you'd be happier.'

'I'm glad in a way,' Ellen says. 'At least it's out in the open now.'

The conversation turns to Selda's imminent trip to Greenland.

'You shouldn't go.'

'Of course you'd say that.' It isn't quite accusing Ellen of jealousy.

'It's the right decision at the wrong time.'

'Stop talking in riddles.'

'I have to ask you something. Have you had any episodes recently? Trances, maladies – whatever you call them.'

Selda stabs out her cigarette. 'Not this again. We're not

still at the hospice. Getting a job there? Move on.'

'Didn't you hear about the School of Silence while you were at Agnes's?'

'That's completely different,' Selda says.

Ellen rubs the head of her cane, a hare's head in polished brass. She sets it to one side, opens her bag, and retrieves a bell. Selda recognizes it right away. Ellen made two at the hospice foundry. Selda's half of the pair is on the mantlepiece in her bedroom, beside a photograph of her father and Charles.

'I know you, Selda. I can see that you're in trouble. There's surely no harm in it, is there? It'll be like it was before, only I'm better at it now. More skilful. You'll hear it ringing and you'll find your way out like you did the last time, and the time before that.'

Selda stands abruptly. At the kitchen counter she pours herself a sherry, knocks it back, pours another. Rain drenches the house in its sound. *This is who you are*, the gift tells her, so often that she has begun to believe it. 'No,' she says, returning to the table with the bottle. 'No listening. No bells. I'm doing fine, it's all under control.' She almost tells her friend: *I've begun to write music with it, like nothing else I've yet produced*.

'Hmm.'

Ellen presses again, but it's no use. She pours herself a sherry. They sit in silence for a minute. Two minutes. Then: 'You're writing me out of your life. You're attaching things about yourself to me, things you want to get rid of, and cutting me off like I'm some kind of tumour.'

'Ah yes. Your great theme. Poor Ellen.'

Tears start in Ellen's eyes but don't fall. She lifts the bell off the table and, in doing so, it rings. The strike is inadvertent, the tone correspondingly quiet, yet it resonates sharply in Selda's mind. She knows what she should say, she cannot bring herself to say it.

'Well,' says Ellen. 'I did try.'

Selda follows her down the hall. They stand at the front door open on the street, trees hanging their lank, wet heads over the streaming asphalt. Looking back on this moment, Selda will conclude that it was the gift that led her here. The gift, which insists that Ellen is not real family, twisting Selda's thoughts, convincing her of a half-truth: that she is a sackful of echoes, no more, lacking sound or substance of her own. In this, the gift is a great deceiver.

Ellen puts up her umbrella. She steps into the rain.

'Wait!'

Ellen turns.

Selda steps forward. 'Promise me something,' she says, not knowing where the words are coming from or where they are headed, her voice already beginning to falter. 'If something happens to me, if Anya is in trouble, sick, whatever, needs help, and I'm not there, if I'm if – I'm gone, promise me—'

'Look out for her?'

Selda nods.

'Have you really forgotten?' Ellen says. 'Maybe I read everything wrong and have been living in a fantasy world. If that is the case, so be it. It is a fantasy. But it gave existence meaning. The gift means nothing compared to our friendship. You are where my life begins. Do you remember that night in the forest? I expect you've forgotten that too. I love you, Bunny. I hope you understand what I mean. It is not a burden. It is a gift, another kind of gift. You do not feel the same about me. That is simply the way it is, for now at least. I will have to make peace with my lot. Now, I have a train to catch. Goodbye, Selda. Take care.'

She watches Ellen walk into the downpour and

disappear at the end of the street. Only then does she close the door and head back through the house.

Halfway down the corridor she halts, lifts her hands to her face, and weeps.

She dries her face and heads through to the living room, where she sits at her piano and rests her head against the case.

Selda calls home from the bar in her Copenhagen hotel. Last night, Anya begged her not to leave. Today, she talks in sullen monosyllables. 'I'll be back before you know it,' says Selda. A moment of quiet. 'Anya? Are you there?'

Next morning she takes the once-daily flight to Kangerlussuaq. From the small plane she looks down on a sea whose colour she has never seen before, a blue darker than slate. Greenland's coastline is a shattered spray of rocks, floes and tiny islands. Low sun slants through oval windows. She peers into the distance where the land aggregates at last into a mass of light so vast and sharp it hurts her eyes to look into it.

Reaching the School of Silence involves a bus and a sleigh – the 'best' way to reach the school, according to the letter from the dean. They meander through scenery of spectacular desolation. Ice floes the size of yachts bristle in bays of dark blue water. Rust-brown fields are smudged with shocks of yellow, gorse-like flowers. Here and there stand houses painted as brightly as wooden toys. The air is vivid with cold but in places veils of mist hang over the middle distance, solid stone and rough grass ethereally pale. All the while, the sky darkens. Stars come out.

A craggy peak juts from the ice like a monstrous broken tooth. The bus comes to a halt beside it. Among the buildings around its base is a radar post or science lab

– she half expects Garth to step out of a door – with a reception building attached to the side. It isn't long before she finds a man with a sleigh for hire, an Inuit who seems to have known she was coming. They set off over the ice and snow, heading away from the broken tooth. Cheerfully the man explains things to Selda, indifferent to the fact that she does not speak his language. She nods and smiles and watches the pack dogs' bushy wagging tails and clouds of breath. Snow effervesces in the air, prickling the skin of her cheeks and nose. The driver points up – a shooting star. The sky is livid with constellations, with the smudged glimmer of the Milky Way. Immediately she sees another shooting star, a brief bright etch of gold. She has never seen a night so clear, the stars so plentiful. If only she could share it with Ellen and Anya both. Until the gift corrects her. *This is who you are.*

The driver halts at the edge of a small town. He will go no further. Selda doesn't understand why but believes it has something to do with the weather. Flakes have begun to fall, yet she sees no clouds.

She climbs off slowly, joints creaky with cold, and watches him ride back to the broken tooth. What if this is the wrong place, or a ghost town?

The town's wooden huts, painted those same toy-bright colours, are raised on stilts and organized into three or four streets. Wind thumps towards her. It sends out concentric ripples of flickering, powder-white snow like sound waves rendered visible.

She walks lopsided, lugging her suitcase. No one but her is deranged enough to be outside. Smoke is pouring from several chimneys. Electric light glows in lit windows. She spots a bar or restaurant and heads up the short flight of steps. The low-ceilinged room feels like a sauna. It is lined with communal benches where people in dark jackets, felt hats, striped shirts and jeans sit eating and drinking. A few more are seated at the bar. The air is milky with cigarette smoke. Its walls, painted a faded aquamarine, are thronged with photographs, maps, banners, and furs hung salon-style. A narwhal tusk mounted like a ceremonial sword. Has she been here before? She can't have. The gift's old tricks again. On the counter, a sixties-era television is tuned to a sitcom, or so she guesses: the image is mostly white noise, in which actors are vague shadows. Faces turn her way. A hot blush itches up her neck and cheeks. A bell rings somewhere outside.

Selda orders a glass of whatever the next man's having. A kind of schnapps. She knocks it back, feeling chilled to the marrow and completely exhausted. A large man with a red, beaming face, his black hair in a feathery centre-parting, asks if she's Selda Heddle. He introduces himself: Per Magnússon, the School of Silence's dean. He's delighted to welcome her, he says. Would she like something to eat? He can recommend the fish stew. He beams at her from over the raised collar of his coat yet his eyes are mellow, curious: he is sussing her out, this woman who has burned her bridges to commune with the ice. She declines.

'I'm exhausted,' she says. 'But perhaps a quick schnapps for the road?'

They head back into the night's raw chill and totter up the high street, heading for the shadowy expanse beyond the edges of the town which, to Selda's eye, has the appearance of an empty stage. Magnússon carries her bags and guides her past the school itself – a warren of wooden buildings, some on stilts, others half-buried in the tundra – towards the cabin in which Selda will spend the next two weeks, mostly alone and in silence. Ice has built up on her lashes and her nostrils' stung-red rims. Now that

395

she is here, she wants to turn back. *This is where you are.*

'Here,' Magnússon says. 'There's wood for the stove, bedding, hot water. I'll check in on you again in the morning.'

He closes the door behind her. She thinks back to the pantry in Clay Lane. Is this where she belongs, contained in a box on the edge of infinity? Still, the place is comfortable and sturdy, a solid, sculpted thing of seasoned wood and zinc appointed with a stove, a double bed in an alcove, a desk, a table, a kitchen of sorts. She peers through the cabin's windows as an astronaut might. Here she is. Or here they are, Selda and her dead.

Days at the School of Silence are organized according to cycles: supplication, meditation, exercise, study, much of it done in solitude. Silence is recommended, if not policed. Meals and meetings are exceptions to this rule.

Over lunch in the school's cafe on her third day, the windows offering a view of the sunlit and snow-bitten town, Magnússon explains that the practices he teaches emerged in the Bering Strait tens of millennia ago, passed down by the gift in unbroken chains of inherited wisdom. As they talk, Selda begins to suspect that 'silence' is a byword for something grander and more complex than she has believed before. 'Reality' perhaps: inexhaustible, unknowable. So far as she can tell, making sense of this silence means spending lots of time on her own, and in a climate so hostile that if she goes outside for a stroll, without sensible clothing, she will turn into an ice lolly. The conversation makes her head spin. She is forgetting how to speak.

Over the next two days, the weather closes in. Once-clear skies are smothered by diffuse unbroken clouds that cast a smudgy half-glare on the colourless ice, on the colourless stone. The tundra's magnificent nothing appears so uniform, under this glare, that it resembles emptiness itself, a kind of visual silence.

Selda sits at her desk, as she has done almost without pause. She has barely written a thing. She begs the melodies to return. *Which melodies*, the gift teases. Selda: *You know exactly which*. The gift: *I'm afraid we don't...* Selda: *Snow, damn it, snow, the song that arrives with snowfall, you sang it when I ran Anya's bath...* The gift: *That is taking us back, isn't it? Yes, an important moment, but a long way back...*

This is what I need, she thinks. Peace at last. Solitude. A clear channel between me and the dead.

If only they would play ball. What more does it want from her? *Everything*, it says. *That doesn't narrow it down*, she replies.

Another day passes. The weather does not change. She eats another meal of bread and pickled fish and conducts the same listening exercises, hears a few glancing notes, no more. She came here to find her true music. It stays just out of reach, hidden deeper in the gift, somewhere in the land of the dead. *Bring it to me*, she says. *Find it*, the gift replies.

Another day passes. Perhaps two days. She is losing track. The isolation has begun to play tricks. Is the residency working? For the first time in her life, she does not just hear the gift, but almost sees it. It happens in the twilight between sleep and wakefulness, when she languishes in the morning, or wakes startled in the depths of the night. Spectres appear and vanish so quickly she wonders if she ever saw them at all, these mirages flung against the air, particles burning as they pass from one state to another. They wander past her cabin or appear in the corner of her room. If she looks at them directly, they vanish. The trick is to hold them in the peripheral vision.

Even then, she feels uneasy about what she is seeing.

Is she awake? Perhaps she has died and not noticed.

Maybe this is how she becomes one with the gift, makes peace with it – dying alone, and she didn't even notice.

But no: she bites her hand. Pain shoots down her arm. She hears her steady heartbeat, feels the warmth of her skin.

One night she wakes in a daze to find she has a visitor. A shadow under clouds of grey-white hair, the twin stars of his searching eyes peering at her across the room. He sings of hills and mines, journeys north and south across river and plain.

'What happened?'

But it isn't Charles, could never be. Her mind is playing tricks: the shape vanishes when Selda flicks the light on.

All the same, she is disturbed. She meets with Magnússon next day to relate her frustrations and fears. 'I've walked into a trap,' she says. 'I don't mean the school, obviously, I just mean – I came here thinking solitude was the right thing. That the living were the problem. It isn't, they aren't.' According to Magnússon, such responses are normal. So, too, are occasional visions: the gift cannot be seen, but in rare moments the brain will conjure images to give ancestral memory a recognizable shape. It is a 'good' sign, in a manner of speaking. A marker of purification. Unconvinced, she tells him that enough is enough. She must go home at once. Magnússon shakes his head. A storm is coming in, she won't be able to leave until it passes.

She waits at her cabin window and watches it approach. The horizon darkens in premature night. Clouds gather force as they move towards her, their heavy, dense appearance at odds with their speed. The silence grows more acute, weather smothering sound. Until, at points around the school, from low hills and cabin roofs, from somewhere underground, music emerges. People play and sing as though to herald the coming snow, bells chiming, horns blasting as the flakes scatter down like bright fragments from a crumbling sky. In less than an hour, the blizzard is upon them. It is a kind of conflagration: her cabin is engulfed in white fire. If people are still playing instruments, she can no longer hear them.

The blizzard's din is so total, the wind so harsh and howling, that she cannot sleep later that night. Time has already begun to feel elastic. Now it snaps. She tosses for seconds, turns for days. She falls asleep tomorrow and wakes up yesterday. Instead of dreams come half-waking visions. In the corner of her room, figures appear again. 'You are my brain's attempt to make sense of a past that has no shape, no form,' she tells the room. The gift comes and goes. She senses them around her, the dead, like nurses at her bedside. They are concerned about her.

She half-dreams conversations with her uncle. *Are you really dead? Ooohhh I should think so, yessir.* Remind me how you died? *Drowned I did, like the composer.* Which? *Scchuuuumann the huuuumannn, the German fella.* How? *I broke the lock on my door and kept on walking to the lake, tulley tulley, a la o la la, north o'er dale and south via underground river, under and under I drowned.* The gift is doing its best impression of Charles. Selda is not convinced.

She is searching for something. Pattern. To understand who she is she must understand where she came from, is that it? Why look there, to Charles, and not her parents, not family myth? She was gangly where he was stocky, she lacks his oil-black hair – yet he is gifted, so is she: that must be the reason. White flame rages all around, its roar mixing with the murmur of the gift out of which individual voices emerge before dissolving again, figure and background blurring. Music is pattern. She must find pattern. This is how memory speaks. Sings. Selda confuses herself and the distant dead. She wakes in a ditch as snow falls down, gathering on her clothing, building up – it buries her. She, or a version of her, has walked this earth before: there is a rhyme in that, a music. What was the original song? She hears the bell ringing again – it must be Ellen. Selda's friend here to save her, to bring her back to the land of the living.

Darkness, silence.

Selda comes to again. Night. It feels to Selda that she is dead and the gift is holding vigil, not the other way around. Fragments of a tune begin to fall.

She dashes to the desk and scribbles the half-melody down. How much time has passed? The gift draws closer, closer. *This is who you are, this is, this is, this, this*, repeating the phrase until it breaks, *thisthisthis*, meaning drains from language like water from a sieve, *thisisyouisthis*, until she can no longer think. 'Go. Away.' She paces tight-wound circles in the cabin, *this is, this, this is you*, the storm roaring against the window, blanking it out with snow. Under its roar, she hears music. From the low hills, from other cabins, people playing instruments.

Since her father died, her mother has been bedridden with an illness no doctor can name. Half-sleeping on a pyramidal heap of pillows scented with lavender and eucalyptus oils, singing ballads to keep herself entertained, the bedroom's air suffused with music, candle smoke, radio waves, and steam from her bedside soups and teas. Selda hears them now: she hears her mother's voice. Wasn't it true that Maud often spoke of Charles, when she did at all, with sorrow and affection, with love?

Confusion: the gift is too loud, disordered – rains, mountains, rivers, plains, where does she come from?

On the limit of the land, peering out at sea, drawing lines between the stars...

There is no pattern there, beyond the one that she imposes. What good is music, then?

She tries to force the gift back to where it belongs. She is an undertaker to the dead, will bury them all in snow and silence. And she tries. But her energy is spent. They are too much for her, too noisy. If only she had a sound to guide her, if only her friend was here.

Exhausted, weeping, she tries something different. Kneeling on the floor, resting in her bed, she begins to hum. The song is intended for Maud, whose voice Selda knows well enough that she can summon it in her mind. The song does not reach her mother. It reaches the dead.

Now she is surrounded. Her voice and those belonging to the dead at last reach an accord. As soon as they do, she feels better. A lilting chant fills the cabin and spreads beyond it. A music into which her voice dissolves, becoming part of something larger, older, deeper, wider than the sky.

Somewhere in that chanting, she hears it – the melody she has been looking for all this time. It flickers in the space between her and the gift. She follows it footstep by footstep, note by note, until her mind is engulfed in white fire.

Darkness. Then light.

She comes to again. The sky is bright and clear. The storm is over. Magnússon is shaking her shoulder. Beside him, a young man is ringing a bell, its vivid note painfully loud in her skull. Other figures are standing all around her. They are real, living people with bristling stubble and stray hairs, with woollen scarves and snow-dusted gloves.

'Can you hear me?'

'We can,' says Magnússon.

'Am I dead?'

'Not yet.'

They cover her with blankets, lay her on a stretcher, and carry her into the School of Silence. Over the following days she will learn what happened. Magnússon was peering out his cabin window once the storm had abruptly ended. He saw a figure out on the tundra, heading away from the school and towards certain death. She can't have been out for long or she'd be stiff as ice already. As it is, she's only halfway there. What does she remember of her trance? Very little. Less, in fact, than she would like. She remembers vaguely, and of all things, warmth.

She stays in the School of Silence for days and nights. Magnússon and his students ring bells and sing chants. Selda needs their help but feels unbearably embarrassed by her feeble condition, which is all her stupid fault. They feed her bone broth and herbal teas. She fears she is becoming like her mother. Yet these states feel specific to Selda. She falls in and out of trances – maladies, they called them at Agnes's – of which she remembers little. Charles is there, until he isn't. He never was. She plays the melody from her dream again in her mind. Hour by hour, step by step, she returns to the land of the living. She has failed. The gift has lured her here. Its reward for her betrayals and estrangements is this: a fragment of music, a few notes scribbled coldly on the page. As soon as she has the strength, she will call Anya and tell her she's coming home. And then she will write to Ellen.

Wolf is on the back seat of the hire car when he senses it: a snag in his mind. The delayed departure, the suspension of flight, the presence of his mother, the play of sunset on the surface of clouds, their journey through the dark of a different country. The smell of sea air. Lush heat. All these elements combine to shift something, unlock a door. He feels them around him, now. His old friends. The familiar dead. The sensation frightens him enough to sink lower in his seat, to tense his arms tight around his body. Since it is a familiar feeling, one that has come and gone since before he can remember, it comforts him, too.

Reeds flicker at the motorway's edges. Concrete buildings, shopping centres, lit billboards, towering hotels. A port appears to their left: blazing lights and giant ships. Crickets cry, the motorway drones. Beyond both sounds he can hear a glassy laughing, like dripping water or sleigh bells. He needs to pee.

Anya instructs him to wait, but Wolf insists: he's about to wet himself.

She pulls into the hard shoulder. Hazard lights flash. Wolf unbuckles and totters to the edge of the road, where it meets a field. Anya stands beside him, arms folded, anxiously watching the traffic. He pulls his shorts and pants all the way down, to his ankles, with a firm but weary gesture, as though he's been doing it for decades. She finds this habit amusing and peculiar; it gives her son the air of an eccentric old man, fastidious, cranky, set in his ancient ways, the bean-counting kind who'd read the paper with a magnifying glass and carry his change in a zip-lock bag. Wolf, for his part, watches the urine arc and catch the amber lamps' light. His piss patters on sloped dirt, mixing with the soil, snaking down and pouring into the field of corn that edges the motorway. He watches the cornstalks spring out of his pee: his urine is their mother, he is giving birth to all this growth. He pulls up his shorts and clears his throat. This, too, strikes Anya as amusingly odd. It must be innate, not learned. Where would he have witnessed this behaviour in order to imitate it? Was he born with an octogenarian soul? She is in the habit, still, of taking him into a ladies' cubicle when he needs to relieve himself. He rubs his eye with a knuckle and sighs. Then totters back to the car.

'Not long now.'

'Are we there yet?'

'We're not staying on the roadside, Wolf! Just a bit further.'

'I want be there now.'

'I know. So do I.'

'I don't want go down this road.'

'Which road do you want?'

'I don't want! This! ROAD!'

Anya does not respond. She knows that her young son's contrarian energies peak before they crash: he will be asleep soon, she senses.

They rejoin the traffic. Soon the lights, the sky, the monotonous engine combine to irresistible effect. Of his dreams Wolf will remember only vague forms and feelings: a dark cave, a dormant animal.

His mother wakes him at the hotel. It's past midnight, their arrival delayed by her circuitous route through the labyrinth of streets without signposts. They empty the boot and check into a sleepy hotel, whose lobby is clad in shiny, popcorn-coloured marble, a rotating fan stirring the air. Anya asks the concierge about the room service. He nods sadly: 'The kitchen, is close.' If they wish to eat, there are restaurants in town, which may or may not be open. Instead they wander to the kiosk at the far end of the street, where they buy bottled water, crisps, chocolate, a bag of nuts, which they bring back to the hotel room, where they eat on single beds beneath an air-con box that hums like the motorway. They half-watch a black-and-white Hollywood film dubbed in a language neither understands. Wolf asks his mother if his father will be at the concert. She reminds him that he lives in Canada now. Wolf can call him, if he wants. He'll still be awake.

As he often does, Wolf pictures his father in a castle. He is surrounded by forests thick with snow and ice, the pines crowded with his deadly namesakes. His father sleeps on a frozen throne. Machines, computers surround him. But they never make the call. Mother and son fall asleep in their clothes.

Next morning they head downhill towards the older, flakier parts of the city, colonial buildings colonized by ferns and vines. A garbage truck clatters past, trailing bin-smell so pungent it discolours the air. Wolf looks at billboards of politicians and satellite phones. The scrubby plots and unfinished concrete villas give way to palm-lined avenues whose reddish bricks and cracked stucco are tufted in places with more tropical plants.

They find a cafe on the corner of a shady square. At an adjacent table sits an old sun-beaten man with a deeply creased face and half his teeth missing. He thoughtfully loads a pipe, thumbing the damp tobacco into the bowl, lighting it with a lazy motion of the wrist. Anya stands at the bar stirring brown sugar into black coffee. A TV in the room's far corner shows Formula One. She watches the cars run circuits as she dials the number her mother gave her. The marble under her elbow is refreshingly cool.

It is meant to be a direct line to a mobile phone, one that only Anya has access to. A man answers. Selda can't make the phone, he claims. She is in rehearsals, too busy to attend the family lunch they booked five weeks ago.

'Can I speak with her please?'

'She is very busy.'

'I won't be long.'

'She is very busy.'

'I heard. Can you pass on a message?'

'... I don't know.'

'What do you mean you don't know? Listen – who are you? I'm her daughter. I need to speak with her. It's important.'

'... I see.'

'You do?'

'... Yes.'

'Let me speak with her. Who are you? Is this some kind of prank?'

'She is... very busy.'

After more of this humiliating back-and-forth, Anya hangs up. Hands shaking a little, she asks the barman for a brandy. Through the glass doors she watches Wolf watch an old man smoke. She wonders what her son will look like at that age. She found she missed her father more acutely after her son was born, not less. She considers calling him. Likely he wouldn't pick up either.

So she tries the phone number again. The same man answers. She's being mocked. Summoned and rebuffed by her important mother's important work. She is relieved, in a strange way. Almost giddy with freedom, in fact. Why are the rehearsals so fraught? Even allowing for Selda's high-wire perfectionism, something seems off with the call. She wonders, briefly and not seriously, if Selda is being held against her will.

'Enough,' she says, brandy burning in her throat. '*Enough*. You aren't her first idiot toyboy. And this is not my first fucking rodeo. Got that? Can't wait to meet you.'

She slams down the phone.

Wolf takes his bottle with him on the hot, bright tram as it glides down the leafy streets and into the city. He conveys his pleasure by regaling the carriage with verbal impressions of the sounds it makes, the keening squeaks, the clack and crackle. Since the twitch in the gift last night, the ghosts have been wandering with him. He senses them now, on the roofs, in the drains, riding the electric wires overhead.

They disembark and drift around the old town. As noon approaches, the heat becomes too much. Anya locates a payphone and calls the restaurant. The maitre d' excoriates her for having cancelled at such late notice. As she hangs up, she feels both unfairly and proportionately punished. She assigns the blame to Selda. That the error is not her fault does nothing to assuage the feeling that she has done something wrong.

'What do you want to eat?'

'Dog poo!'

'Interesting. Anything else?'

'Ice cream.'

'Maybe later. What about proper food?'

'Spaghetti.'

'More like it.'

After lunch, desperate for shade, they seek refuge in the cool dimness of a church. The lower half of its interior is clad in panels of heat-warped wood whose dark brown varnish reminds Wolf of conkers; overhead, the ceiling's sandstone exhales chalky-smelling, cooler air.

Only once her eyes adjust does Anya realize what it is. Icons haunt the eaves in their dim gold, beaten-flat frames, the smudged impassive faces of the venerated, gifted dead. It's a different style of chapel, here. If indeed they call them chapels too. Their narrow hands are raised in mysterious benediction, their eyes as wide as startled foals'. At the front, on a table draped with purple velvet, is a statue of Agnes. Or a version of her, at least. She stands in an ink-blue gown, her face turned to the sky.

Anya sits in a pew and fans herself with a folded-out leaflet. Those sounds. Like mouse-squeaks or laughter. But no one's there. Spooky acoustics. She's not getting it too, is she, so late in the day?

As the church shivers with sounds from outdoors, snatches of speech, mopeds' thrum, which blend and multiply around them, it would be easy to believe that more than two people, she and Wolf, are in here. Indeed she could almost believe she can sense it, too: the gift, scheming in the shadows, seeping from the gravestones that form the floor, the letters of which are worn smooth by countless feet, mythologized pirates, forgotten merchants, despised explorers, envied queens, marauding around the chapel, mobbing the space between breaths, swinging from the golden frames, the lectern, Agnes's elegant nose.

And these other sounds, these spectres, have invited her son to play. He clutches the glass bottle of orangeade like handlebars and runs in screeching circuits round the pews, singing made-up songs and yelling at invisible enemies.

Time to leave. Anya worries about her son, the connection he has with her mother. A region of his mind, his experience of life, is strange to her; it will only become more so, the distance between them greater. She wants him to grow into whoever he is, to be himself. But that person may end up like her mother on her bleakest days, and that thought frightens her. Anya calls him over, guides him back towards the glare of the open door. On the threshold, he pauses, turns, and sings into the room. The sound hangs for longer than it should, echoes exploding and swooping and chasing each other, accelerating towards their end.

Anya bought Wolf a new linen shirt for the occasion, crisp blue-and-white stripes with a wide, pointy collar, navy shorts and sandals. She wets her comb in the hotel bathroom and tames her son's hair into a slick side parting. Immediately, he scruffs it up. She tells Wolf off and fixes his hair. He looks so smart, so cute, she wants to grip his shoulders and take a huge bite out of his head, which is probably filled with custard. She thought for weeks about her outfit, her choices guided by her inner Selda. In the end she played it safe: a blue dress with a silk scarf thrown over it, black leather sandals on her feet.

Applying eye-shadow in a handheld mirror, she tells Wolf, as she has many times in the build-up, that tonight is *special* and *important*. It's a *major commission*, Selda's biggest yet. Her son watches her in the bathroom mirror, with a diligent focus, as she applies lipstick, purses her lips. When she asks for her mascara, Wolf hands it to her. Same for her foundation and eye-shadow. He knows exactly which item is which. Lots of practice. He has always found her make-up routines fascinating. For a time, if he needed distracting, she used to let him apply nail polish (messily, of course), let it dry, remove it, and start over again. Today, he asks her a question. He wants to know how often Anya did the same for her mother. She runs through her memory.

'Oh, now and then,' she says. 'Not as often as my own special helper.' Wolf grins. The white lie seems to reassure him, but of what, she isn't sure. That Selda was attended to? Or that she had as close a relationship to her mother as Wolf does with her?

'Shoes on? Good. Off we pop then, my cub.'

The concert is being held in some secret and spectacular location Selda has revealed almost nothing about, other than that they absolutely cannot under any circumstances whatsoever miss the shuttle bus, on pain of death. It leaves from a car park a short walk from the hotel. It should take five minutes; Anya leaves fifteen. Trees around the edges of a square are draped with strings of lights, while music lilts from speakers in the darkened, cave-like bars. Kids do their thing in the playground. Dust rises as they scuffle and run. Wolf is desperate to join them. He hasn't interacted with another child since they arrived. Anya wants to let him. Few things would please her more than to take a seat there, under those lights, order a nice cold drink and watch him play. She takes his wrist and tempts him across the square. The minibus is waiting. Its driver is a fleshy, balding man in a thick black jumper too hot for the weather. Indeed, Wolf can count the three distinct drops of sweat on his brow. He smokes a cigarette while a group of premiere-goers gather, most of them with whitish hair, creased skin, and linen suits and dresses and jewellery. Wolf's hair has already sprung loose from its parting. As he runs around the pavement, Anya notices his brand-new trousers are dust-smudged up to the knee.

The landscape changes as they climb, becoming harsher and more barren. As the road winds deeper into the range, dry slopes close behind the bus and obscure the distant ocean from view. The dirt is terracotta, not brown. It is dotted with lakes whose waters, a surreally vivid,

410

chemical blue, are rimmed with white sand. Higher up, beyond the distant peaks, the sky is the colour of grape juice.

'Couldn't they have put it on in the city?'

'It was the television station's idea.'

'I thought she was against all that. I thought she *hated* it.'

'She does. In theory. But—'

'Let me guess. Money. Sure, everyone has their price.'

Wolf doesn't understand why his mother sustains such boring conversations, especially with this older woman in her satin blouse, her creased, sunken eyes, her hair permed into bronze.

The journey is taking forever. Morale begins to waver. A vocal minority among the bus, filled with opera patrons and the luxury fug of their perfume, have begun to grow suspicious that they are being led up the garden path, instead of the mountain; that the driver is a criminal, an idiot, or both. Anya clears her throat. Raising her voice, she informs her fellow passengers that their road is the right one.

How does she know this? the passengers ask. She takes pride in, and laments it: 'I'm her daughter.'

A round of questions from the other passengers.

What is the piece like? (Anya doesn't know.)

What's the venue like? (She isn't sure either, it's all hush-hush.)

It isn't long before she is asked the inevitable question. So, what's *she* like? (Anya means to smile, but pulls more of a smirk: 'Selda is Selda,' she shrugs brightly. To her relief, the conversation moves on.)

Wolf is attuned to other conversations. Purplish light in the mountain's teeth. The blue lakes are unblinking eyes. These rocky slopes aren't empty. They're filled with spectres, his friends. Ghosts of people, turtles, coyotes, birds, ghosts of rock and rain. As the bus winds past dry riverbeds strewn with white and grey eggs, they speak to him, tell Wolf where he came from.

'I need a poo,' he proclaims. He points across the aisle at an old woman who has a friendly face, distorted momentarily by her surprise at being singled out by the boy. 'And I want YOU to wipe my bottom.'

Anya laughs; the woman does not. 'Can you hold it in? How bad is it?'

Wolf doesn't answer, he's already moved on. The ghosts are laughing, too. Their voices are sleigh bells trailing in the wake of the bus. He tugs his mother's elbow, and tells her Selda is far away, like Agnes.

'Not that far,' Anya says as the bus lurches over a pothole. Sensing the threat of a tantrum, she digs a book out of her bag. Her son is old enough to intuit the placatory motive even as he's pleased by its results: if he was younger, she would have placed a dummy in his mouth. He flicks through images he draws such pleasure from in part because he's seen them ten thousand times, coiled serpents and golden beasts forming out of washes of watercolour, as if they were born in pure vapour. The driver flicks the radio on, and the change in the bus is instant: Euro-pop thunders from the speakers. The driver slaps the steering wheel and jostles in his seat, bouncing to the rhythm as the bus takes a sharp turn, narrowly missing a truck that speeds the other way. Its horn dopplers down the mountainside, mixes with the shiver of sleigh bells.

One man gets out of his seat and stands in the aisle, lurching as the bus takes another hair-pin bend, the only protection from a plummet to certain death a wheel-high strip of metal that describes the corner's curve. The driver sits kingly with his curly hair and thick-ribbed nylon jumper. He gestures at his ears to communicate that he can't hear the complaints over the music. The ghosts laugh again.

But the game is short-lived. Or the point has been made. The driver turns the volume down to a background purr, another music to compete with those in the land and Wolf's head, then lowers the window and lights a cigarette. Cold, smoky air seeps into the bus.

'We're going to miss the bloody concert.'

To which complaint the driver utters his first words, barking into the rear-view mirror: 'It's only human to go astray!'

'Ah, so you DO speak English! Look at that. You were sitting there shrugging just a moment ago. Now, kindly answer my questions. Where are we going, and what is our arrival time? No? We'd better turn back. We can't just carry on with this lunatic, what if he drives us off a cliff?'

The driver erupts into laughter. So does the gift. So does Wolf. The sleigh bells chase the exhaust.

Now they are in the plains. As the light sinks and reddens Wolf feels the presence of the gift almost as clearly as the people on the bus. He can't see them but he can imagine them, often so vividly that they look just like living people. That lady walking the dog that he saw a few weeks ago. Or that boy in the branches, that young woman with the apple, that man in the oilskin coat. When the gift becomes this strong, it tends to make him feel dizzy, as though he is on a precipice, or slipping into something that will subsume him, like a warm bath or a deep sleep. On the barren slopes that flank the road he sees hard white powder, late snow, and shadows that stretch elastically, from horizon to horizon. Up in the mountains,

413

says the gift, true love sings. The valleys are all sorrow.

He looks at the book in his lap. A saint on a pyre, her eyes turned to the stars.

'Why in Christ's name are we up here in the first place?'

By now it is clear to Wolf that not everyone on the bus is united in uproar. The white-haired man – whom a woman, presumably his wife, has twice referred to as Eugene – claims to speak on behalf of a silent minority. But Wolf, for one, is enjoying the long, winding ride. He senses other passengers are, too. Perhaps this has something to do with Selda. She is waiting for them, wherever that may be, however long it takes to reach her – his first taste of the consolations of melancholy, maybe. He tunes into a different, calmer conversation than Eugene's. He recognizes the names from Selda, from his book, the stories she tells him in the mornings at Bell Hall.

'Agnes, more like. That's why they chose this location, is it not? An old religious site, pretty ruinous now. A kind of temple to the dead, at one point. Strange. I always had the Agnesians down as drifters. All those wandering choirs with their morbid bells and hymns.'

Someone wants to know what this Nowheresville they're driving to has to do with that superstition.

'They believed that she died here.'

'She was English, no?'

'Not by choice!'

At last the slope flattens out. Up ahead is a crossroads marked by what appears to be a farm, the dry land divided into barren parcels by lengths of wire. Emaciated goats nibble the scant grass. Beyond them, catching the day's last light, a structure appears. It is extraordinarily vast in comparison to the farmhouse that stands before it: less a castle than a town built from crumbling, chalk-coloured

414

stone. As they grow closer, the edifice disintegrates into detail. The walls resolve into houses, the windows into streets, and soon a sprawling town emerges out of what seemed to Wolf impossibly, excitingly, a single building.

Above it, a moon appears, less than a half full but unusually large.

'Hungry?'

Anya snaps a breakfast bar in half. By the time he's finished eating the sweet, dry gravel, the bus pulls to a halt.

The passengers mock their disbelief: a woman groans, a man cheers. They stand up on creaky knees and arthritic ankles and praise the day, shuffling down the aisle and alighting on the tarmac, where they yawn and stretch and blink at the darkening sky. Their faces express displeasure, unease and relief, except for one slightly younger man. Standing to one side, with long black hair and cowboy boots and mascara on his lashes, he flicks a cigarette out of a packet, lights it, and blows the smoke at the moon. Shaking his head, he drawls: 'Crazy, man. *Crazy.*'

A faction of the audience stay on board because, as one man barks: 'This can't be the place, look at it! What happened here, the plague?'

The driver shrugs and grins as he repeats his phrase again, this time appending a declaration: 'It's only human to go astray, my little masters.' He points at a print-out of a map, where the venue has been marked, then hands the page to one of the faction – its streets overlaid with frayed lines where the folded page has been abraded by the sweat of his breast pocket – then staggers outside to cadge a light off the man in the leather jacket. United in the solidarity that needs no common language, beyond that of their shared addiction, the two men exhale. With a nod the driver slumps down on the edge of a fountain, gesturing towards the street in a half-baked attempt to direct the group to their quarry. Most of them, after a huffing pause, set off.

The town comprises a series of narrow, curving streets, the pavements' whitish stone now satiny with age. Few if any streets are wide enough for cars to pass. Many of the buildings look empty. Shuttered windows, pad-locked gates. The festival demographic has throughout history skewed white, wealthy, and old: this group is no exception. Anya walks with Wolf, the youngest here by decades, and wishes he had a companion, some other kid his age with whom to talk (and to make her life easier). Having said that, he seems content.

As content as he ever does, that is. Often it is hard to tell, and this ambivalence troubles her. He wanders beside her, dressed with a smartness so unusual as to seem eerie – despite the whole costume being her doing – with his miniature suit, his dishevelled side parting. So involved in his own world is he that, when he was little, doctors hypothesized the cause could be autism, deafness, mute-ness, and other things besides. One suggested surgery to remove a portion of his soft palate. Is the child gift-ed, as Selda is? Of all the explanations, it is the simplest (direct inheritance) and, by the same token, the hardest to swallow (a family curse). Morgan, Wolf's father, long since self-sequestered in Yellowknife, left them, in part, because of the 'graveyard hysteria', as he once described it. The ornate, anachronistic phrase was doubly vulgar to Anya. Until she saw how camp it was. How glam. She had once revelled in Morgan's punkish disdain for a family legacy that Anya sought to distance herself from. Which effort led her to Morgan. Who led her, in a manner of speaking, to Wolf. Walking beside her, half in her world and half in a twilight she cannot hear, she takes his hand in hers.

'This way.'

'Hang on, isn't it there?'

The party have reached a fork in the road. Wolf senses presences on the roof. Angels? Ghosts? Neither. They gather and watch as the audience mills in a small, shady square beneath a sky awash with early stars. In the centre is a dried-up fountain – the town is dotted with them, Wolf has never seen so many in one place. After a long, dull drive, he is behaving remarkably well, hasn't wailed or gone ballistic and kicked her shin. But it will not last forever.

'It's raining,' he says. His mother looks up and sees a few clouds but senses no rainfall. 'It's Tuesday,' he says. 'It's Friday.'

'What about now?'

'Sunday,' he says, as though he's stating the most obvious fact in the world.

What is the point of this game? To test the limits of consensus reality and in so doing reaffirm them? Or simply to get her attention? It would betray the game to deny its non-logic. And so she goes along with it, nodding as her son announces his scrambled calendar. Sometimes she catches herself wondering if this is the graveyard hysteria talking. Or something else, a quantum logic. Until she pulls herself back to the waking world. Meantime she watches the group begin to splinter, debating among themselves which way to go to find the source of the music.

'It's this way – can't you hear it?'

'It's much, *much* louder down here. I can hear the lyrics. Tum-da-tum, dum-da-dum.'

For another few minutes they walk, taking alleys, ducking under low arches, pressing their ears to walls. A middle-aged man whose long, white hair pours down the back of his grey linen suit, took the driver's printed-out map. It's the only guidance they have to go on. Other than the stars, that is. But no one knows how to read those any more. They litter the dark in such profusion as to render navigation by their light absurd.

The moon is out, too. It's a sliver, not the full lunatic light. Yet its effects – amplified by the whitish stone, the empty streets – are evident. Each member of the group now seems fully and individually convinced that the town is alive with music.

They press their ears against walls, doors, windows, cock their heads and close their eyes, and point excited-ly towards the snow-pale peaks that thrust majestically over the rooftops. Even Anya, whose born scepticism was honed by her childhood with Selda, is caught up in the hunt for the source of the music. She can hear it, too: muted, bassy – it doesn't sound like Selda's music. In fact it sounds closer to a seismic event. She detects it not through the air but the stones at her feet, growing strong-er with each step. It isn't long before she begins to doubt the structural integrity of the mountain, and to peer more anxiously at the snow-capped peaks around which clouds have begun to assemble.

The group wander on. Some go missing down blind alleys. Others return from the gates of dark gardens. Eventually, on a narrow, curving road decorated by a single tree, they come to a stop. The man with the long white hair has convinced his peers that the music is em-anating from the second-floor room of a terraced house, as evidenced by the low thrum of a ventilation duct half-covered by a panel of loose-fitting metal. He lifts his hair to reveal his ear, presses it to the metal, closes his eyes, and gasps. A crowd gathers. Two blinking, crin-kled women, who might be twins, press their ears to the duct. A moment later, they each conclude that the white-haired man is right. The venue – at last! That sound is unmistakable.

Back then, Anya lost herself. Something to do with the soles of her feet, unsteadiness on these old stones. In any case, she is back to her senses. Wolf walks beside her, babbling quietly away, as she walks up to the group, smirking at their conviction. One of the twin women beckons Anya over. Despite herself, she presses her ear to the duct. And again to her surprise, she discovers that she can hear it. A strange sound, collective and faintly metallic, as of voices rattling round a small steel box.

'Has to be – has to.'

The white-haired man has already pressed the door-bell. When the door buzzes open, to audible gasps of excited relief, he pushes through and into a small hallway, with pigeon-holes on one side. The staircase ahead leads up to a lit doorway. A smell of fried onions drifts down the stairs. Soon the hallway is crowded with people who, squashed together like this, tottering in their black, starched suits, remind Wolf of flightless birds, dodos or penguins. At the top of the stairs, the white-haired man, at the peak of his triumph, steps into the light. Instead of a concert hall, or indeed a venue of any kind, he finds himself in a cramped, domestic kitchen. The walls are painted red. Beans are bubbling on the stove. An ancient cat sits on a cushion beside the oven. And a man in his trousers, his shirt undone, stares at the group of unusually well-dressed intruders, crumbs clinging to his stubble. On the plate in front of him is a half-eaten custard pudding in a plastic pot. Perched on a stool in the kitchen's corner a TV shows a football match, the picture mostly emerald glare.

So begins a protracted conversation between the

white-haired man and the resident, during which they struggle to understand one another. Despite this, the white-haired man appears convinced his interlocutor is not a citizen, but an actor; that he was hired to play a role, and that this whole charade was a part of the drama. Sleigh bells ring. Wolf sucks his thumb. Someone points out that they can hear no music, that the sound they heard through the vent might have been the television's tinny speakers distorted by the ventilation tubes. The white-haired man lowers his head.

The door closes, the group sets off again, heading north towards the mountain peaks. Now the music reaches them from other sources, on which no one can agree the true origin. Some people chase echoes down treelined streets, others knock on doors, most of which don't open, some of which belong to people who are baffled to the point of silence by the appearance of the group.

Following some vague herd instinct, they head past shuttered windows and derelict shops, incongruous fountains and gated gardens, the pale curbs. The farther they walk in this new part of town, the fewer residential buildings they find. They pass a chapel. Then another. Soon there are more chapels than other types of building, the spaces between them home to stooped almond trees. Neither Wolf nor Anya have ever seen so many in one place. Outside each small, domed structure – some of which are plainly plastered, others of which are encrusted with exquisitely carved reliefs – are placed dozens of house shrines. Their number seems excessive, given the sparseness of the population. Yet they are evidently well tended, each glass-fronted box decorated with toy rhinos, alligators, baboons, giraffes, and robots, with stacked pebbles and coins, gold-leafed icons and photographs, bundled clothes, ballet shoes, fresh fruit in glass bowls. Outside a few of the chapels are elaborately carved pyre-sculptures – not every sect condones them; some condemn them – depicting Agnes in her torturous song. Anya has half a mind to shield her son's eyes from these painted flames. But he has seen them before. Selda shows him them all the time. And besides, he is in his own world, still. He's singing to himself.

'Selda?'

'That's Agnes, remember?'

'It's Wednesday.'

'I thought it was Thursday.'

The group has splintered into factions, which have headed their separate ways. Wolf and Anya find themselves in a trio with Evelyn, the older woman from the bus, elected by Wolf to wipe his bottom. Her hauteur has given way to beatific confusion, possibly resulting, Anya wonders, from altitude. When she asks if she's alright, perhaps would like some water, Evelyn lifts the bottle to her lips the way a child might and pours, water trickling out from her thin, creased lips and down her throat, all over her dress. She doesn't seem to notice, let alone mind. As they continue, Evelyn launches into a brief, disconnected monologue about her forty-three year-old son.

'He went missing twenty years ago,' she says. She knows he's still alive, though. 'A parent just does.'

Unsure how else to respond, Anya clutches Wolf's hand a fraction tighter. They duck beneath a stone arch and emerged onto a large, paved square lined with trees and surrounded by a pale wall dotted with similar arched doorways. Across the moonlit expanse they spot several figures, other members of their group. And yes, the music is louder, clearer at least than it was before, only more complex too, not just several singers but several songs, the harmonies overlaid and incoherent, yet amassing, at

421

this distance and volume, into a kind of chant. Then the wind changes, the song fades.

At the far side of the square is what appears to be a theatre, though it might be a church or a palace, built from the same lunar stone as the rest of the town. Steps lead up to an arched doorway, the interior of which is dark. Between Wolf and the building is an expanse of wind-swept stone, the dust quickened into whorls that lift and spin into knee-high tornadoes.

Selda peers out the second-floor window. The expanse glows like a Greenland snow-field in the half-moon's light, a blank manuscript page awaiting the first notes of arrival: that she hasn't yet noticed the figures appear is a sign of both her panicked introversion and nascent glaucoma. She isn't wearing her glasses, either. Selda worries the sleeve of her linen jacket until a voice tells her to stop. At her age, she has lost almost none of her height, but her neck is more stooped, curved, she sometimes fears, like a vulture's: the result of contorted late nights bent over the pages, the keys. She wears a suit of dark satin, a silver chain, her hair nothing special, the usual bob. Her lipstick is a plum-dark red. They should have been here an hour ago. What kept them? Soon the cameras will turn on, their glare coating the stage, and the hall will be empty. She will look like a fool. When Vieira commissioned her, he requested 'light music... less an operetta by Lehar than a divertimento by Mozart', the meaning of which she didn't grasp. Never mind. She said yes, no problem, coming right up.

She tilts her glass, a gin and tonic (mostly gin), and Selda hears the ice cubes clink against the glass. A high chime. Who's there?

Two floors below, in the bowels of a venue carved into

the mountainside itself, an orchestra waits to one side of the stage. A television director paces circles, cameras stand poised, arc lights burn, a soprano fans herself, and the conductor snorts another line, which he swears will be his last, despite having snorted his last line over two hundred times now, off the porcelain shelf of the greenroom toilet's cistern, deciding, in the end, not to flush the plastic pouch containing, he estimates, a further gram-and-a-half of high-purity cocaine cut only once since reaching the nearest port, because, first of all, that would be a waste of money, and second (more important) he might need a pick-me-up before the show begins in earnest. *Really*, he tells himself, *you are doing this for her.*

Which would come as news to Selda herself. She watches the square in which a version of Agnes was burned to death.

There. In the distance. She didn't see them before. Two figures emerge. A woman and a woman. Or a woman and a child.

Anya and Wolf cast long shadows on the stone. She flies out of the dark hall and into the corridor and through the bar, down the carpet-lined corridor, along the rickety staircase that runs through the part of the building whose roof has collapsed in a picturesque, gestural scree. She is glad of the sensation on the soles of her feet: no matter how broken, the solidity of stone, like the rubble in the city of her birth.

A bronze plaque is affixed to the ground in the square's centre. That must be the venue, then. The steps outside are lit by candles. The guests who have arrived look wraith-like in the mingled moon and starlight, in their linen jackets, skirts and scarves, catching the wind and lifting, which, combined with their stretched faces and desperate, searching gazes – exasperation having reached an almost spiritual pitch, a kind of mortification – lends them the appearance, to Wolf, of people who lived and died a very long time in the past, or perhaps the future. And with his eyes he brings the moon crashing down on the mountain, where it explodes in a shower of moonlight so fine it resembles snow.

'We made it, Wolf.'

He nods.

'If this isn't the place just shoot me now, put me out of my misery, take me out there and put a bullet! In my brain!'

'They'd better hand me a bottle, no, a jeroboam of champagne on entry. A foot massage, the works. A frickin' *jacuzzi* of fizz.'

Wolf looks up. Selda is framed in the second-floor window, in a panel of darkness, surrounded by stars. He grabs his mother's arm. When they both look up, Selda is gone.

Something infinite finds expression in the movement of crowds, of swarms, of noise. As they gather at the town hall's steps, a stone's throw from where Agnes died, these festival-goers, some of whom won't live to see the turn of the year, appear to be returning, coming home, like prodigal children weary from a long odyssey. They mount the steps in pilgrim postures, browbeaten by gratitude. Low lights mark the glowing road toward the music. On the frieze above – the hall was a former hospice – are prancing lions, flayed corpses, winged mandolins, coiled snakes, bunched grapes, skulls, flames, harps and bottles. Wolf's eye roams, taking in each detail: monkeys stealing grapes and feeding them to the skulls. Anya tugs him by the arm just as the white-haired man bashes at the door with his fist.

'Open! Up!'

The man in the cowboy boots, his hair whitened by a pollen or dust of unknown origin, staggers up the steps. 'Did you try pushing it?' he says. And they push, and the door creaks open as if on hinges.

Wolf looks up at the ceiling. In contrast to the outside of the building, whose bleached stones gave no clue to its function, this room is lavishly decorated. The ceiling is set with wooden grids painted gold and midnight blue. Set into each square panel are portraits of people on fire. But this is an old building, the paints faded and dark. The walls are similarly decked out, this time with painted scenes of ponds, of factory flames, of willow trees, of boats. The hall is empty apart from the opera-goers he recognizes from the bus. Among them are a number of other people, similarly dressed, whom Wolf doesn't recognize, but who look just as lost, their drained faces conveying fatigue and forgetfulness. They blink and look around the hall, less in awe than confusion as though they do not recognize their surroundings. Now that they are here, the journey feels almost distant, as though it happened yesterday, or even last year.

'Where now?'

Fat candles glow on the marble floor: butter-light on milky stone. Wolf can hear the gift more clearly now. Maybe the others can, too. The voices mingle with the candle smoke that twists and thins, silver and black.

Just then, there is a wailing sound. Anya grips Wolf's hand tighter. The crowd turns back to the entrance where they can see, contained in the rectangular panel of moon-light, the expanse of the moonlit square, stars thickly slathered above it.

Halfway up the steps, on all fours, in the manner of a dog, is Evelyn. She hugs the steps, her arms spread wide, her cheeks wet. A few of the members rush out. Anya is among them, and soon a group has formed. Wolf drifts out and stands on the moon-bathed steps and blinks at a flash of light in the square's centre. When he looks again, it's gone.

'Shall we call an ambulance?' Anya asks.

'She's tougher than she looks,' opines a woman dressed similarly to Evelyn, who gestures at the moon, the stars, the candles in the concert hall, the raised and fallen lights, as though they will corroborate the claim. Wolf asks his mother what's wrong. Anya tells him she doesn't know.

Selda arrives at the concert hall. Janice, who is directing *Snow Trio*, is at the back row. She stands with her gaze to the stage in a long, dark coat that matches her hair, her solemnity undermined by wet snicking sounds as she masticates nicotine gum. Beyond the stage, they watch musicians waiting in the pit. The camera operators, the lights pointed at the swept-clean stage, the cave's open dark beyond it: everything is ready. Selda feels and suppresses the lurching conviction that this whole performance will be a disaster, not just artistically but morally, even medically. In rehearsals she and Janice have repeatedly clashed. Selda, to her surprise, has felt more attracted to maximalism, to spectacle: some latent desire to write a West End musical, to terrorize bourgeois restraint and distance herself from classical music. A broad genre, or collection of genres, she often disdains and which, to the extent she is associated with it, wants to distance herself from.

Janice, however, has protected Selda from herself. She has steered a more stripped-back path. And she has almost always been right. Reworking the opera's third section, the daring staging, the austere costumes – these were all her ideas, for which Selda will absorb much of the credit, if indeed there is credit. And now the moment is upon them, the low impulses to which she has felt attracted – desire to bicker, to pull rank, to prove wrong – drop away, though she has always known them to be cowardly, unimaginative. *You have been here before.*

'We can get started,' Selda said. 'We might even start on time.' When Janice doesn't react in the way that Selda expects, she says: 'What?'

Janice tells her something, an urgent look in her eyes. It takes a few repetitions for the words to settle in. It took a moment for the sound to make sense. Something was wrong. Someone was sick. Edgar, the conductor, had lapsed. Collapsed. Was attacked. Heart attack. The conductor had a heart attack.

It appears as a star at first, then a beetle, black and glossy against the dark. The air ambulance comes quicker than anyone expected; within minutes of Eugene putting in the call from a payphone. The blades' roar fills the square, reverberates off the white walls, the mountains' slope, amplified. Wolf watches it descend on the centre of the square, near the bronze plaque which his mother stops at and reads, and which informs her that it marks the spot where Agnes – the, or a? 'Where *an* Agnes was burned,' she says. The door opens, a man and a woman in boiler-suits step out.

There is some confusion. They haven't come for Evelyn, but for a man stretchered out from the main hall, suited, masked and oxygenated, seemingly alive. They load him in, take Evelyn too, close the door, start the engine, set the thrumming, roaring blades in blurry motion, and ascend, the crowd squinting and raising their arms against the wind. Once the helicopter is far enough above as to be mistakable for a wayward star, the square is restored to calm. Stones glow faintly in the lunar light as spindrifts chase themselves. Now the music can begin.

The crowd turns back to the venue. Word has got around. The conductor's cocained heart had stopped. (Evelyn's ailment has yet to be diagnosed.) Of all the parts to fail, perhaps his is the best, or least worst, from Selda's point of view, as she stands in the backstage and swallows. She can replace him, but badly – she has neither training nor choice – but who else is more familiar with the piece? She knocks back a glass of water she wishes was vodka and heads to the pit, aware of the television cameras, the jittery director, the snaking wires and buzzing boxes, the gubbins of the spectacle.

Why this venue, so remote and tumbledown, with its atrocious acoustics and weepy ceiling? Was it her idea, this holy place, where Agnes herself – or a version of her – was supposedly born and died, and where, after her burning, in full view of the crowd, she stood up from the smouldering pyre, alive as she had been before the first spark, her flesh unharmed, draped in ash and embers, and announced that she now lived in the land of the dead, a godless place, beyond all time, where all that remained of the soul was language, and that the entrance to this place, the heavenhell of the endless present, was a cave in the mountain behind her. Selda was standing in it now, a series of caverns worn into the rock by glacial melt. The place where Agnes – or a version of the prophet reborn, the latest iteration in an infinite chain – walked with her followers, and then vanished. That transition called for a sacrifice, apparently a human one: a practice that had seen the town condemned by Rome, sacked, abandoned, left to crumble and fray in the elements, only recently reclaimed by local authorities. She takes to the podium, announces the change of plan. The baton trembles as she raises it to practice. Selda holds her breath and listens. Soon the snow will fall.

The hall leads into the mountainside via a series of caves, the air cooler and damper the deeper they go. The third and final cave is by far the largest. To Anya, it brings to mind an immense but run-down concert hall in Budapest, in which city, this past winter, Selda's friend was laid out in an open casket: the first dead body Wolf had seen. He viewed it not with fear but the sanguine inquisitive air of a medical student. The ceiling in this cave is several stories distant, tan stone visible through a thin haze of humid air. A section of the roof has crumbled away, trimmed by hanging ferns, mosses and ivies. The drips of liquid light plummet down to a pool of water in the floor of the cave, beside the stage, a vivid mineral blue lit by arc-lamps that cast shifting nets of light against the sheer, rough-textured wall, which are stippled at points with carvings, many of them crude, or perhaps just time-worn, the features softened. The ground underfoot, by contrast, is dry and bare. Rows of seats are laid out on the bare stone as they would be in any concert hall, TV cameras either side. Why else all this fuss, performing opera on a rubbly slope in a cave that will make her mother's music sound terrible? She looks up. Two flying things, bats presumably, flit in the column of light. Others hang immobile. On the floor, the fine white dust under her shoe could either be snow or guano.

They locate their seats in the third row, to the left. It smells strange in here. Stony, wet, vegetal, and overlaid with smoke and spice: incense, maybe. People mill around in glinting jewellery and wafty dresses, tuxes and shiny shoes, everyone with the same hypnotized expression.

Wolf fidgets with the programme until his mother tells him to stop. Sulking, he turns away. A white bob is briefly visible in the darkness to one side of the stage, if stage is the word, pale and distinct in the dark. Wolf tugs his mother's arm, but by the time they glance back Selda, if indeed it was her, is gone.

Shortly afterwards, the musicians filter out from behind a curtain, a flautist whose eyes are swollen and red, a corpulent cellist with a stain on his jacket, and at last Selda herself. Brief applause. They gather at the rear of the stage, settle in their seats, which are arranged in a horseshoe. The cave falls silent with a ruffling sound like a flock of birds coming to land. For a moment, the musicians prepare, tuning their instruments to middle A.

Wolf loves this part of the music. The notes played at random intervals and durations, moving towards but never reaching a perfect frequency. He loves the sense of expectation and newness the sound expresses, as if the orchestra, like some hibernating creature, is slowly waking up. The music is accompanied by other sounds, from around his head. Water dropping from the roof, trickling down the stone channels worn to mother-of-pearl as spring water deposits minerals.

The stage is a bare patch of stone, swept and pale. Towards the back are dead trees painted white. Closer to, a brazier. To stage right, a lopsided wooden cart. Strategically placed around the edge are lamps which, as Wolf watches, now come on, illuminating the stark whitish square of the stage. The audience holds its breath. Apart from the man in the back who's been coughing since they arrived and who coughs again now: the dry bark echoes around the cave.

Three figures appear on the stage. Their plain grey clothes resemble pyjamas or prisoners' jumpsuits. The house lights dim. There is a pause as the room calms, throats are cleared, conversations are hissed at and buttocks clench, shimmy and relax into new positions. Stage lights rise. The orchestra starts up.

Two harps, harpsichord, piano, celesta, glockenspiel, percussion, tapes, pedals, and an FM synthesizer whose sound recalls bells or glass. The opening bars are repeating patterns, interlocked, modulating, conjuring the sinister quiet of falling snow. Four short high notes followed by three longer, lower ones, the sequence repeating and changing as Selda raises, lowers, flicks her arm. As the melody returns, evolves, mutates, Wolf begins to feel that he has heard it before. Maybe Selda sang it to him, or showed him how to play it.

He watches the music in a state between rapture and boredom. The melody fades from the music. For large sections, there appears to be no tune, just soaring, keening strings which remind him of the drone of aeroplanes passing overhead. From the choir come long-held chords which make him think of Agnesian chapels. The stage, the story, are lifeless to him. The singers' voices rise and fall, and he picks out words he can't be sure are right or wrong: light or ice, plague or play. Who is the woman, why is she singing, when will she stop? Why is the man swinging his arms about? There's a child on stage, clutching his chest, barefoot. They gather under the tree at the back, where a man is kneeling by a candle, pawing at the dirt. They sing. Other figures in white step onstage. Lit from the side, the bright lights bleach the colours. Wolf's gaze drifts over the heads of the singers, up; by the tree's leafless branches, beyond the chunks of the staging, which resemble a model of a glacier, and towards the back wall of the cave, where the web of blue light shifts and shimmers, he fidgets. Anya tells him to stop. His eye catches

431

a movement. A white flake spinning down from the roof of the cave – but when he turns his head, it's the trace of a waterdrop plummeting from the open roof. He turns to look at the seats behind him. Faces pointed to the front, the light on them changing. Some look bored. One older woman is asleep. Most are alert; two or three have tears in their eyes. Another movement up above – this time, he catches it. A small thing. A scratch. Almost weightless, dancing. He grips his mother's elbow, tries to force a turn. But she shrugs loose.

'Stop. Fidgeting.'

There is a swell in the string section, a looping, repeated sound, voices forming dense patterns mid-air. In the loudness and excitement that follow, Wolf slips off his seat. Anya is looking at the stage, sitting very upright. She's so transfixed that she hasn't noticed Wolf is missing. No one has. He is reminded of the time he hid from Selda and his mother in the South Wing.

The singer, a woman, steps forward. She sings of hunger that gnaws in the gut, a newborn mewling in bundled sacks, the bells at matins and evensong, of a plague that has swept the land, of her employment by the Minster of York. She delivers what will later become the most famous section of *Snow Trio*: a woman and her daughter alone in the cold. The instrumentation falls away. Only voice and piano. The lights dim, except for a spotlight that picks the singer out against the trees, the lyrics looping over simple, archetypal images, lone, moon, moan, moors, snow, sorrow, fire.

Wolf wanders in the shadows round the edge of the cave, where he realizes a superpower: he is invisible, like a ghost. He touches the smooth sheened surface of a stalagmite, moving closer towards the lights, where the adults' attention is focused.

Snow begins to fall. He watches it spiral and curve through the air, coming to land on the shoulder of a woman a few rows in front, where it settles like dandruff. Another, another, and yet more fall; now a handful of flakes are drifting. He looks up at the ceiling again, the bats and stalactites hanging.

Now it falls thickly, obscuring the stage, swirling from hidden machines or invisible clouds. Snow settles on the shoulders of the singers, dusts their heads. Soon the whole stage is adrift like a swarm of white butterflies coming into land, pouring through the air and settling on the stage. Wolf is standing closer to it. He steps forward, into the heat of the light, on the edge of the stage, in Selda's world. A flake drifts towards him. He tilts his head back, sticks his tongue out. Anya spots him. So does Selda. And for an instant, the cave falls silent.

VIII. 2015

Twice a week, on Tuesday evenings and Saturday afternoons, children arrive at Bell Hall. These music lessons, offered free to kids who could not otherwise afford them, are Selda's good deeds. They also serve a vainer purpose: to assuage her local reputation as a cranky recluse. Less comfortable to admit is the simple fact that she is lonely. How desperate she must be, how far she must have fallen, to barter for the company of children. But this is where she finds herself, deep in the woods, late in her life.

Compare these to the private lessons she taught early in her career, when Anya was a toddler and Garth was working late (or not) at the lab. Selda would ride the tube or take steamed-up buses in curdling traffic to rich people's houses, where she would teach clotted-cream kids, rich and thick, how to stumble their way through *Für Elise* so that Anya could visit the cinema or have a new pair of plimsolls, and she could spend an afternoon at her desk.

She calls her daughter. They talk about work and music, and what Anya has been watching, reading, thinking, eating, the latest from Todd and of course Wolf, who she has not seen since they spent two weeks together in Portugal after *Snow Trio*. She tells Anya about her new students and the weather and her neighbours' goings-on: who's died, who's having an affair. Her words reach towards her daughter, seeking something she possesses and represents. She has spent her life being independent, as far as possible. Only recently has she begun to understand this as a paradox of her character: that she, who hears antecedents in the gift and in music, who recognizes as a principle of belief that her existence is dependent on countless other beings and cannot therefore be thought of as separate, should believe herself to be so self-reliant as to not need others at all. And yet to reach towards them. To please her father, to move her mother, both long dead and silent and yet still present in her. Can opinions be inherited, along with everything else, passed down to our descendants as surely as eye colour, skin tone, high cholesterol, height? Love is a kind of harmony, except for when it isn't. She asks why Anya hasn't visited in a while, why the trips down are less frequent. A pause. Anya breathing. Then: 'There isn't a reason. You do live quite far away. It's harder to take the time off at the moment.'

'You like it down here. So does Wolf.'

'We do.'

'I expect you're just bored of me, then.'

'Stop that.'

'What else am I meant to think?'

Anya agrees to visit, but the commitment is vague, and hedged by the fact that she's busy at work, and Wolf has just started a job at the Everyman.

Time passes in fits and starts. It pools and quickens and pools again.

Selda drinks coffee and watches the driveway, waiting.

Her students arrive, Tuesdays and Saturdays. No sign of her daughter or grandson. Then again, why *would* they come?

Minutes move like treacle. Days drag. Months, however, pass in a flash.

Even as a child, mortality was never far from Selda's mind. It comes from the gift and from her father. How he spoke about the night she was born, how close she had come to not existing at all: the full moon and the burning city.

An old question sounds in her mind. It has a medieval ring to it, of mystery cycles and wandering players. What is a good death?

Her body is decaying, not yet dying. Or not imminently, as far as she knows. All the same, how can she ensure that she does it properly, when the time comes? Painlessly. A good meal with friends, then a sleep from which she doesn't wake up (and in which she does not dream).

Two paths present themselves: do good deeds; make good work. The former social and self-denying, the latter artistic, egotistical. Torn between them, or deciding the dichotomy is false, she pursues both. She will not feed the poor or tend the sick, but she will continue to teach children for free – this may have been part of the reason for taking them on in the first place: a preparation for death.

In the time remaining, she will finish her final work. Whatever that may be. Something cold, she thinks. Cold and clear as snowmelt. But she has done that already.

Perhaps a good death is outside her power. But to plan for it feels like preparing a piece of music, a kind of show, less danse macabre than grand finale. It does not feel morbid or depressing. Death doesn't scare her. Dying, however, does. The world to come will either be a nothingness deeper than sleep, or this world again, the heavenhell of the here and now, the same earth her grandmother walked and her grandson walks, her voice roaming free of the body.

How will it end? What chord will she resolve on?

She knows who she might turn to for advice. She commands them to speak.

Writing, writing, as she has done since she was a child. She has much less energy, but she knows how to direct it better. If only her rheumatic hands with their swollen joints wouldn't cramp up so easily.

Music, then. What is it? She must remind herself.

A life has a certain form. It begins and ends. It moves through stages.

What form might her last piece take? A grand and overarching composition that ties everything together, or a simple and pared-back song, a kind of ballad, that will linger long in the mind?

Perhaps she can write her own requiem, as Mozart did. That would be the closest thing to a state to which she has, at various points, aspired: to become her work, to dissolve into music. Getting rid of her body altogether. (Remember Wolf, who climbed into her piano as a tiny child: he wanted the same thing.)

For a month, work goes well. She cancels her students – so much for her good deeds. Then one morning she comes downstairs and reads over the pages and hates them.

She scraps the whole thing. That's it. Over. Finished. Done. She should never have bothered and will never try again. Her grand 'retirement', which she spoke about to the press, to the extent that they listened and cared, was an attempt to divert from her the attention in the wake of the Varèse, which endorsed and in doing so paralysed her.

For a time, it worked. People believed that she'd stopped writing. In fact, she continued, as Mendelssohn did, to write songs without lyrics for pop and rock acts, and jingles and occasional scores, and she contractually obliged her agent not to mention her name to anyone, but which work paid the bills, repairs, food, clothes, and so on: a habit that will not leave her; the restless need to work.

A final piece. Something to round it all off. What would the subject be?

She is walking through the woods when she hears it. A familiar chiming sound. And with it, the trace of a melody. She rushes home and jots it down. It sits there on the page like a cutting, waiting for soil in which to grow. She gives it time. Days pass. She resumes teaching her students, and together in the South Wing the broken scales rise, falter, rise again, memories moving with them. She sits at the piano and plays. The cutting begins to grow.

Two months later, she drives to Fischer's house and shows him a set of new pages. The old slow man plays them with grace. But the music is wrong. Too leisurely, ponderous. No urgency to it at all.

The original. The first theme. What was it?

For a time when she was younger she had wanted to locate where it all began, herself, her family. It was a kind of compulsion. A desire to heal, too. Like a dog licking a wound. To diagnose was too seek an origin, which quest assumed that her condition was in need of a cure. She wanted to understand a pattern that exceeded the limitations of her being, and having found that pattern, break it, set herself free. Does she still feel this way? How much closer is she, if so?

Snow Trio was one attempt. She had traced the lines back, drawing partly on the gift and partly on Anya's research. A journey north, a migration in winter. (Later the family moved the other way, south, from the mountains to the moors and from the moors to the towns; another branch came over the Irish Sea, their ancestors having migrated in the opposite direction in an earlier century.) The piece is loosely speaking a sonata, with three main parts or movements, although each contains sub-structures within it, and motifs that recur and are changed across them all, shifting like snow-crystals or genes. The piece is set in the deep past, somewhere in what we now call England. The deadly perfection of cold. Yes. That idea appealed to her. Something formal about it. Those death-destined figures were intensely alive. On fire with instinct as the first snows whirled, living at the ends of their nerves.

A family heading from place to place, fighting to survive in a cold which strips them bare, which reveals their essential life, which brings them close to the land of the dead, which summons spectres from the land until the isle fills with noises. But this sequence of events are the scaffold over which Selda hung, not a story exactly, but a series of emotional moments distributed through time. Her dark secret is this: it all came from the gift. From her listening exercises at Agnes's. From her days in the School of Silence. And they held a hypnotic power over her mind, which prompted her to wonder how experiences are passed down, not just from parent to child and grandchild but across larger gaps, centuries rather than decades: one form for this was music.

Anyway, it was an attempt. One of several.

Try again. Yes. The old adage. Keep going until you can't.

She holds rehearsals in an old pool hall on the edge of the harbour. Big dour sturdy Victorian building. The atmosphere reminds her of her earliest rehearsals, the ones held in Agnesian halls and pokey back rooms of old pubs, before she could command a proper orchestra. A kind of scratch choir, all amateurs. She pays them money that might otherwise have gone on a new car or roof repairs or a holiday or just to line the coffers and pass down to Anya and Wolf. Instead she organizes them once a month for three months at the end of which she has the shape of something new. A sonata only in the loosest sense. A cycle in three main moments. In length it approaches an epic but its real concern is the stuff of songs, of ballads even: what takes place when people meet, how it changes who they are. After each rehearsal, she returns to the South Wing and revises her pages. They aren't perfect. This frustrates her. But not as much as it used to. Dwelling on faults compounds their power. She holds rehearsals here from time to time, invites musicians and plies them with wine to lift morale (and to have some company). More than once, she comes downstairs the following morning to find a singer passed out on a sofa, bundled up in a blanket or old coat.

She walks along the coast and across the moors. She swims in the bay. Good for the ticker, the internet tells her. She could die in the water. It could all just stop. Her heart quickens when she stands too fast, shadows leaking inwards from the edges of the world. A good death? What a luxury that would be, to choose how we go. There would be worse ways than that.

She wants to live long enough to finish this thing. That may be what a good death means. It has a formal quality. C Major, after all that dissonance. Letting go. Peace and rest. Love eternal. All that. But more immediate concerns distract her. Fatigue, pain, dizziness, heart-flutters, palpitations, incontinence. Wine, sherry, vodka soda, Dunhills on the lawn, brown bread and cheddar, kitchen radio day and night. Memory. Old chestnut, yes.

She has begun to forget things which should come easily. Names of people, places. Is this it? The tape degrading. What she was up to yesterday, the day before. The days lack definition. Years passing in a flash.

440

Sometimes she will come to in a faraway town and be unable to explain how she got there. She attributes these wanderings to energy, to a restlessness within her. Even now, in this loneliness and boredom, forgetfulness and tiredness, satisfaction and regret that comprise old age, even now there is renewal. How many times is a person born?

Fischer visits one afternoon out of the blue. He was 'in the area', he says. His studied casualness doesn't fool her. Have rumours been spreading again? Selda hosts him in the South Wing, the only room she really uses these days. There are piles and piles of manuscript paper, arranged into songs and movements. He wanders from pile to pile.

'Are you backed up?'

'Not with all the prune juice,' she replies. She realizes, not after but during the crass joke, that she has not had a conversation with a living human being in a fortnight. She has been 'socially deprogrammed' and is now more comfortable conversing with shadows than real and living people. She clears her throat and composes herself. As it were.

'Do I keep backups?'

'In the cloud.'

She squints at him. How comforting to feel, if only for an instant, like the least insane person in the room.

He explains what kind of cloud he means, but it doesn't clarify things all that much.

'Nope. Pencil and paper hasn't failed me yet. I'm superstitious about all that data existing out there.'

'What if there's a fire?' He looks up at the iron balcony, which Selda lacks the knees to access, the shelves groaning with books.

'A flood's more likely.'

'Is it? You're on a hill, aren't you?'

'It feels that way. Damp everywhere.' She isn't able to articulate herself. Words wadding up in her mouth. She feels a jolt of simple love for her instrument, which is visible behind him; the same jolt she did when first she played it, which allowed her to bypass words altogether, arrive at the heart of things.

'You take my point, though. A lot of work, here. You've been busy.'

Just then a gust blows a small window wide open. Wind swirls into the room, blowing a few pages loose. Selda crosses to it.

'Damn latch. Keep meaning to fix it. But the weather, you see. It has designs.'

There are weeks of rain and thunder. Fogs roll in off the ocean, submerge the view. Outside, tending the garden and sweeping the paths, light drains down the levelled air. She removes her shoes, the cold bite of the pebbled of drive reminding her of Brighton Beach, the streams in the Forest of Dean. In recent days her thoughts have returned to Ellen and Garth so often that she can spend hours believing that she is living in the past, not the present. She reminds herself that Ellen isn't dead, last time she checked, and nor is her ex. But it is Ellen she misses most. She will call her again. One day. What's stopping her? The fact that it's easier not to? That she's afraid of what her fried might say? That doesn't sound like Selda. What about the last words Ellen said to her? Why do some ir-relevant moments keep returning, while others, which she'd wish to keep forever, crumble to nothing? For many years, the case was closed, the matter settled. They were friends, then former friends. It was awkward, but it was over. She rarely thought about it, she had work to do, she moved on, that was her mode, to keep going: to work, to please her father, to distract him from his disappointment and in so doing prevent his collapse. The memory was buried. And now, thinking back, it rises again to the surface, disturbed by a new current.

She still has the bell that Ellen made for her. She made it herself in the Agnes foundry. It was a symbol of connection between them. Bells from birth to death. She takes it out. She is reassured by its weight, by the sound it makes when struck, how the notes hang in the air a fraction longer than one might expect. The sound helps her to remember.

Winter arrives. Her heart feels sluggish, the house is cold, strange bruises have appeared on her forearms. She is no longer teaching or working and rarely sees friends, but for the most part, she is happy. There are stretches of forgetting. 'Coming to' in the woods or a library. But she keeps putting off the GP, because there is work to finish. And because she is no stranger to these maladies. Soon she will contact her daughter and her grandson and play them the new music. Though the idea inspires guilt. What if all she has done is curse them? Wolf is gifted. She did that to him. He will fall into maladies, just as she does. What if he lacks the strength to find his way back? She has seen it happen, how a mind can destroy itself. It happened at the hospice. She must warn him, but how? If it *does* happen, she knows who she'd want him to see. She'd tell him go there, walk to Ellen, listen to the ring of the bell. If necessary, she will walk him there herself.

She listens back to her own new pieces and hears in them something she has not achieved before. They feel almost like diary entries.

Sudden frosts grip the land and thaw just as quickly. These cold snaps are a shock after the summer's thick heat, with its high blue skies, its evaporated ponds, its dead frogs and alarming fires. Selda listens to the wind in the chimney. She talks with the gift. With them around her, she will not feel completely lonely. The nights grow shorter. She listens for a phone call that never comes.

A minor 9, sustain pedal down. The chord, long familiar, now puzzles her. It hangs in the air like a question mark. For the rest of the day she is unable to shake a sensation that something is wrong.

She walks into town to buy bread. The walk takes just over two hours; normally, it takes twenty minutes. By the time she arrives she is so exhausted she takes a window seat in a café and promptly falls asleep, woken a moment later by a ponytailed waitress who asks if Selda needs an ambulance. An ambulance? She laughs it off. Ridiculous. Almost says: *ambulance schmambulance, I gave birth to my daughter by candlelight, I myself emerged from the crucible of global WAR*. Instead she calls a taxi, falls asleep on the backseat, wakes in the driveway, flops onto the sofa where the room throbs, the dead wheel around her like bats.

Perhaps she should visit her GP. But there is work to do. She puts it off.

The phone rings. It is not the call she wishes would come. It is that journalist again. He sounds like a juvenile, eager to please. But Selda, mistrustful, sees the charm offensive for what it is. Her reputation precedes her. What is his image of her? How does he imagine she lives? A loner, a crank, a toad, a crone... Why does he want to talk to her at all?

'I'm not doing an interview.' She adds, impulsively: 'I'm a teacher now. I'm running a kind of school, like Agnes. It's not exactly secret but I'm telling you very much off the record. We're investigating death. Music and death. We're looking into it. That whole situation. We have some questions.'

'We could I mean ah, that sounds brilliant and – I mean, I'd really love to come down at a convenient um, time and ah –'

Why the sudden interest? Does he detect the opportunity to 'revive' a forgotten female composer, maligned by history, by patriarchy, and in doing so absolve his own discredited gender? *Has* she been maligned? She was able to work. Her music was performed and recorded, even celebrated. She is one of the lucky few.

'I won the Varèse. I've done nothing since. That's the story.'

He tries again the following week, says he'd like to do a profile. All of it, the works.

She declines again. Partly as the thought of being photographed, now, terrifies her. But she has been wondering about this very question. Or rather, it is a subset of the related question, the overarching one. Given that death cannot be bargained with, even if she wanted to, how to have a good one? Which leads her to wonder how the life that preceded it might be remembered.

She would like to become her work, she thinks. And the closest thing to achieving that end is to finish, in the final years, perhaps months, of one's life, a work rivalling the most significant of her career.

She knows it means nothing, ultimately. Yet she cannot help but pursue it. And the thought that anyone, let alone this upstart, who sounds fresh out of his teens from the voice on the line, would tell that story – *bleuargh*. She would rather not be forgotten, either. So, which? Tell the story or let it wither? If the former, who will tell it? Will she dissolve instead into so many anecdotes, like

Orpheus ripped to bits? The thought of someone putting down a version of her cradle-to-grave, and it could only ever be a version, what happened and how she felt and who she interacted with, at a distance, narrating her days, artful with the shape of it, lingering on instants, artful silences... arriving at the now, this moment, as she sits in the living room thinking...

Unless it is someone she knows... loves...

But even then...

Anya? Wolf?

Selda can't see it, wouldn't want it.

The future, then. Maybe Wolf will want to write a musical about her. Ha. Yes, a West End number with special effects and gut-wrenching love songs and a cast of a thousand voices, herself one of any number of spectral presences pacing in circles around the stage.

Such dark moods can come over her. Glooms that gather in the afternoons and linger for hours, depressions which do not focus on her own decline but that of a planet humans are burning and extraction has ravaged, as if the two mortalities have become confused. The oceans soaked in acid. That dull ache in her bowels. The horizons black with smoke. A weak feeling in her heart. She imagines a time when she herself is a ghost, and voice in someone's ear. Will anyone be left alive to listen?

Her appetite shrivels almost to nothing. She eats her favourite suppers on rotation, portions so small they might as well be canapés. Sliced ham with gherkins. Shredded kelp. Potato soup, like her grandmother made. With each dish she has brown bread and white wine. Afterwards a big cognac and a Mars bar ice cream. Some nights, she forgets to eat at all. Just the wine and the cognac. Perhaps a Dunhill on the porch, the stars and clouds above her.

She has too much and not enough memory. Events from fifty years ago have a liquor-like quality, unctuous, intoxicating, and somehow too strong. But how last Tuesday differs from last Wednesday, and the Thursday before that; what she did two weekends ago between dawn and dusk – these are anyone's guess. She should put it all in a diary, slap post-it notes on cupboards and jambs and turn Bell Hall into a bona-fide memory palace. Better to have begun in Clay Lane, recorded every thought as it formed. Then again, reading the document back would have made her sick: she would have been recording for posterity the very thoughts she would later repress. It chills her to think that somewhere – in the gift, the transcendent record – nothing that happened is ever lost.

Christmas looms. In recent years she has spent the day at her musician friends' houses, or they have spent the afternoon at the Boatman, and she has had a pleasant time, comatose on sofas after sherry and cheese, and perhaps a few songs at the piano. This year, after some lobbying on Selda's part, Anya and Todd invite her to London, to spend a full week at the house – the longest they have spent together in, how long? Wolf will be there too. Polite and moody, another link in the chain. He has taken two days off from the Everyman: no small ask in the panto season. Selda accepts. Of course she does. She thinks about the trip several giddy times a day.

Rehearsals in the hall across the bay. Local singers and musicians work with her on new music. Sometimes her young students come along. All these singers, all these ghosts. The moon waxes and grows full. It was full on the night she was born. The gift reminds her of this fact, as if it was born then, too. (Strange to find herself, at the end of her life, revisiting these moments, as if they did not belong to her, and finding pattern there. How her own birth mirrored her daughter's. The flames in the window, the smell of the wick.) Afterwards, she and her singers convene at the Boatman, where she buys them dinner.

A week or so into December, she begins to feel unwell. The previous night, after rehearsals, one of the singers started coughing in the hot, packed pub. They said it was nothing, just a tickle, they were fine. Selda should have gone home that moment. She did not. She stayed until close, ordered a cab, spend the journey babbling on the back seat.

It starts with an itch in the throat at lunchtime. Then the evening descent into aches and sweats. Next morning she wakes at dawn, her body ablaze with fever.

She lies in bed, delirious. She believes she is already dead. She has long conversations with Garth, communicates with Ellen by whispering into upturned bells. She talks with a girl overlooking the tin mines under the stars and calls out to her, Agnes! The girl turns and looks at Selda and opens her mouth as if to sing, but water pours out instead, pooling at Selda's feet. Cold water rises. Other voices fill the air, mixing with the clang of blacksmiths' hammers. The dead rise up, the stars ignite and drip white fire, and golden arcs repair the heavens.

Weightless, feeling no sensations, Selda passes into and out of her body as if it were a foyer in a museum. On one such journey, she lingers there, in her bed in Bell Hall. Believing herself cured, if peculiarly lacking in feet, she floats along the corridor to the top of the stairs, and looks down at the hallway, where her daughter and grandson step through the open front door. She withers to nothing: a snatch of sound, a broken echo. She organizes herself into the simplest melody, two short high notes followed by a long, low one. Night and day quicken and blur into a uniform grey, until at last the delirium lifts. Just like that, in a matter of minutes. She is in back in her aching body in her sweat-drenched bed in Bell Hall. Sheets and duvet in tortured knots, pale daylight at the window.

A few days later, she feels almost back to normal. She crosses to the bathroom and drinks from the tap, then slowly makes her way downstairs to the empty kitchen, holding on to the wall for support. The radio has been on all this time. Enough with these voices. She switches it off.

Next morning, she feels different. Better, she thinks, but strange. Weather warnings. There were floods this spring, then a summer of parched fields, and now the winter bringing storms. This is music, too. A disturbance in the harmony. The sky's cracked bell. She nourishes herself with lemon tea and chicken broth and works for an hour in the South Wing, under a blanket, determined to push through. Her magnum opus. Put it in order. Melody is pattern in time. Give it a good end. C Major. No. Give up. She needs rest. Heading back through the house the front door is wide open again. Her breath fills the air. She closes the door. Once she is back in her bed, she hears it blow open again.

Dreams about Garth over the next few days. The first notes of *Snow Trio* keep returning to her: they fall and fall again through her mind. Was that the first time, listening to the tape, in a basement in Agnes's? Or does the melody have a deeper origin? Perhaps Selda's mother sang it, a tune her own mother sang to her.

Another morning. Restored to her old self. Sprightly,

even, capable of anything. Looking forward to spring. To seeing Anya and Wolf. What year is it? She forgets. The door is open.

The radio brings news of a coming storm. Warning: no travel unless necessary. Insulate your pipes. Vulnerable people at risk. Don't use the roads. Snow litters the hallway. She must ask Fischer to fix the latch.

There's a smudge on the horizon. She watches it move towards her, over the fields. Its energy is violent, but it moves without sound. Isn't this how *Snow Trio* opens? In fact, it seems to smother noises, to subsume the sounds of wind and animal life into its massive commanding quiet, the snowfall whitening all it touches, brightening the earth below and darkening the sky, transforming everything. Soon it has the forest, and then the garden. The snow has a violence to it, but a gentle kind. It gathers on the statue, it fills its open mouth. Then it overcomes the house. Distances are erased. There are only flakes flying everywhere. All this muted and furious movement. The storm is total. Its howling sound calms her beyond measure, reaches down into a part of her being she hadn't realized needed cooling, soothing, the flakes against the window, beating, falling, accreting on the sill. How much longer until the house is buried?

She holes up in the South Wing. Flakes fall. Voices rise to meet them. Soon she is surrounded by movement and stillness and silence and noise.

She must make music. It must begin here. (Hasn't it already? Was *Snow Trio* a premonition? No, it came from the gift, her distant ancestral past.) But the piece, her final work – it isn't finished.

Then it hits her. It will never be finished, will never end.

Selda on the stool, picking out a tune on the piano.

This is the way to end it all – yes, this is it: the simplest cadence of chords, a melody rising and falling and finding its home.

Quick, then. Write it down, put a note there. Where has she heard it before? Is she plagiarizing herself? ('I have plagiarized you,' she tells the gift. 'I have drunk your life like ash in water.') No, no, the voices sang it to her. Did they? Or did it come from something else, the quiet, the snow, the delirium from which she has only recently recovered? The worst of it passes. A quietness falls. Through the snow-starred windows she looks out at blank fields. Darkness. The moon behind cloud. The faintest glitter on the surface of the snow.

She hears something, then. A clear high note. Hard to locate its origin. It could either be there, in the world, or there, in the gift. How unlike her to draw that distinction: the two, of course, inhabit the same earth. She knows what it tells her, though. It is a message. A reminder. Others are out there. She is not alone, she has been here before. She is six centuries in the past and a plague is abroad on the island. She is in her front hallway in the wake of a storm. She is in Clay Lane and her father has just come home with a stolen record player tucked under his arm.

That sound again. Memories overlapping like tones in a bell. Or more than that, perhaps. Temporalities themselves, layered like sound, occupying the same space, their proximity only now becoming apparent to her, in a newfound clarity.

Where did it come from, that sound?

Something heavy in her hands.

Looking down, she sees Ellen's bell. The rough dark metal, the figures walking circles round the rim. A bell to wake the living, a bell to raise the dead. She feels an urge to ring it. To hear it sound in the storm.

The cold feels different to how it normally does. It brings no pain, only a fresh, clean feeling. The storm fills her vision with movement, with life.

That sound. Who made it?

She follows the sound through the dark house, searching for its source. As she does, she grows more certain that he, her grandson, is making it. He is somewhere beyond these walls, in the storm and the silence it brought.

She must do something about that latch. The door is open. It frames the white driveway, the blue light. The clouds have thinned. A waning moon. The hard dark glitter of the night sky visible in places.

Stepping onto the threshold she sees a figure moving across the fields at some distance. Wolf. Could it be him?

Her heart quickens. She walks into the blizzard. She rings her bell. She has something to tell him.

Acknowledgements

Selda's surname honours the English tenor Heddle Nash. His niece Mary Nash, a pianist and répétiteur, was my grandmother.

Thank you to Jacques Testard, whose patience, creativity and foresight allowed this novel find its proper form; Ray O'Meara for typesetting, design and Spotify links; Joely Day, Clare Bogen, and everyone at Fitzcarraldo Editions; Ben Eastham and Sam Solnick, for helpful notes on early drafts; Francesca Wade, for perceptive and encouraging reads, and for pointing me to H.D.'s *The Gift*; Polly Graham, for sharing her musical expertise and drawing attention to my errors (those that remain are mine); and Kat Black, whose intelligence and generosity throughout the writing, including many conversations and insightful notes, enriched this book enormously. I am indebted to my family, particularly Caz, John and Georgia. I gratefully acknowledge the support of Arts Council England, Banff Centre and Cove Park.

Fitzcarraldo Editions
8-12 Creekside
London, SE8 3DX
Great Britain

ISBN 978-1-80427-050-9

Design by Ray O'Meara
Typeset in Fitzcarraldo
Printed and bound by TJ Books

fitzcarraldoeditions.com

Fitzcarraldo Editions